The Nineteenth Century Revis(it)ed

The New Historical Fiction

The Nineteenth Century Revis(it)ed: The New Historical Fiction explores the renaissance of the American historical novel at the turn of the twenty-first century. The study examines the revision of nineteenth-century historical events in cultural products against the background of recent theoretical trends in American studies. It combines insights of literary studies with scholarship on popular culture. The focus of representation is the long nineteenth century – a period from the early republic to World War I – as a key epoch of the nation-building project of the United States. The study explores the constructedness of historical tradition and the cultural resonance of historical events within the discourse on the contemporary novel and the theory formation surrounding it. At the center of the discussion are the unprecedented literary output and critical as well as popular success of historical fiction in the USA since 1995. An additional postcolonial and transatlantic perspective is provided by the incorporation of texts by British and Australian authors and especially by the inclusion of insights from neo-Victorian studies. The book provides a critical comment on current and topical developments in American literature, culture, and historiography.

Ina Bergmann is associate professor of American studies at the University of Würzburg, Germany. She is the author of one monograph, *And Then the Child Becomes a Woman: Weibliche Initiation in der amerikanischen Kurzgeschichte 1865–1970* (2003); the (co)editor of nine volumes of essays and special sections of journals, among them *Liminality and the Short Story: Boundary Crossings in American, Canadian, and British Writing* (2015), *Cultures of Solitude: Loneliness – Limitation – Liberation* (2017), and *Intermediality, Life Writing, and American Studies: Interdisciplinary Perspectives* (2018); and a frequent contributor to peer-reviewed journals and international book projects. She has held fellowships with the Rothermere American Institute at the University of Oxford, the Trinity Long Room Hub Arts & Humanities Research Institute at Trinity College Dublin, and the Huntington Library, Art Museum, and Botanical Gardens in San Marino, California, USA.

Routledge Studies in Nineteenth Century Literature

For more information about this series, please visit: https://www.routledge.com/Routledge-Studies-in-Nineteenth-Century-Literature/book-series/RSNCL

The Nineteenth Century Revis(it)ed

The New Historical Fiction

Ina Bergmann

Routledge
Taylor & Francis Group

NEW YORK AND LONDON

First published 2021
by Routledge
52 Vanderbilt Avenue, New York, NY 10017

and by Routledge
2 Park Square, Milton Park, Abingdon, Oxon, OX14 4RN

Routledge is an imprint of the Taylor & Francis Group, an informa business

© 2021 Taylor & Francis

Library of Congress Cataloging-in-Publication Data
A catalog record for this title has been requested

ISBN: 978-0-367-63466-7 (hbk)
ISBN: 978-0-367-65151-0 (pbk)
ISBN: 978-1-003-12807-6 (ebk)

Typeset in Sabon
by MPS Limited, Dehradun

Contents

Acknowledgments

This monograph is an abridged and updated version of my *Habilitationsschrift*, the German equivalent of a second book, which was accepted by the Faculty of Arts & Humanities of the University of Würzburg, Germany, in 2010. I am grateful for the professional guidance Jochen Achilles provided during the creation of the original version of the manuscript. I acknowledge the constructive criticism the two anonymous reviewers offered during the publisher's review process. I thank Michelle Salyga, senior editor at Routledge, for her ongoing support of this book project, and the whole production team for their valued service, especially Jeff Anderson for his eagle-eyed copyediting. Last but not least, I am thankful to Sophie Renninger for her assistance with proofreading and preparing the index.

1 History, Fiction, and the USA

1.1 The New American Historical Fiction

The turn of the twenty-first century not only marks the beginning of the new millennium but also signals what some historians mockingly call "a new golden age of historical popularization" (Wilentz). The "renaissance of the historical novel" (Byatt, *Histories* 9) is transnationally documented (Nünning, *Fiktion II*; Hutcheon, *Canadian*; Bölling; Meinig; Green; Friedrich). It is one segment of "a worldwide florescence of popular interest in the past" (Harlan 109), which also includes forms of visual and virtual history (Scheiding, "Introduction"; Groot, *Consuming, Remaking*; Hulbert/Inscoe). The comeback of historical fiction is embedded in the overall return of narration (*"Wiederkehr des Erzählens,"* Friedrich 7) and the general "renaissance of the book" (Ribbat 17). A popular revival of historical fiction (King 2) can be traced since the 1980s and 1990s (Kunow, "Making" 187). Especially the last twenty-five years have seen an unprecedented height in the genre, even surpassing its heyday in the nineteenth century (Harlan 109). At the turn of the twenty-first century, historical fiction "has finally come into its own" (Johnson, *Historical* xvii).

This revitalization of historical fiction in the USA is a phenomenon informed by a number of dichotomies. The most striking of these is that the contemporary historical novel has managed to please both readers and critics, a trend that is obvious for twenty-first-century fiction in general (Ribbat 11). The popular book in the US today – to borrow the title of James D. Hart's seminal study *The Popular Book: A History of America's Literary Taste* (1950) – is the historical novel. The literary market is flooded with historical fiction of all kinds, the publishing houses readily accommodating the demand. Relevant novels are recommended to a broad public by popular and very influential book clubs and TV shows. Bookstores increasingly feature separate sections for historical fiction (Friedrich 12). Historical fiction has always been a genre favored by the audience (Burt xi), but this level of success is new.

The acclaim the texts find not only with the reading public but with literary critics is probably the most significant aspect of the present-day success of the genre. Contemporary historical fiction bridges the gap between supposedly serious and popular literature, a demand raised as early as the 1970s by Leslie A. Fiedler with his catchphrase "cross the border – close the gap." "[L]iterary historical novels" (Johnson, *Historical* 465) top the best-seller lists while at the same time meeting the critics' approval. Established writers try their hand for the first time or time and again in the genre (e.g., Susan Sontag, *In America*, 2000; E. L. Doctorow, *The March*, 2005; Thomas Pynchon, *Against the Day*, 2006) (Johnson, "What"), and new writers successfully start their career in it (e.g., Charles Frazier, *Cold Mountain*, 1997; Jeffrey Lent, *In the Fall*, 2000; John May, *Poe & Fanny*, 2004). For a long time, the historical novel bore the stigma of genre literature (Sauerberg 12). Historical fiction was often a field of critical controversy (Johnston/Wiegandt 9; Burt xi; Engler/Müller; Kurt Müller 35; Johnson, *Historical* 2; Borgmeier/Reitz 8–11). Many of the contemporary books are enthusiastically reviewed in journals, newspapers, and magazines and satisfy the aesthetic requirements of a literarily trained, intellectual audience. The most blatant manifestation of the literariness of the new historical fiction is the success of the genre when it comes to prestigious prizes. If one applies the simplest, naturally contestable definition of the genre – "a novel in which the action takes place during a specific historic period well before the time of writing" (Baldick 114) – most of the winners of the Pulitzer Prize for Fiction and the National Book Award over the last twenty-five years can be identified as historical fiction (Harlan 109). But what is even more striking is that a majority of the novels are set in the nineteenth century.

Georges Letissier asserts that "[i]t is now a well-established fact that the Victorian age has become historically central to late postmodernism" (111). Along with the rise of the neo- (Shiller), retro- (Shuttleworth), or post-Victorian novel (Kucich/Sadoff xiii; Kirchknopf 64–66) in British and New English literatures (Moore 136; King 6), the nineteenth century has prominently come into focus in American historical fiction. In a modification of Eric Hobsbawm's designation of the long nineteenth century in Great Britain (1789 to 1914), Jürgen Osterhammel's global definition of the long nineteenth century in *Die Verwandlung der Welt: Eine Geschichte des 19. Jahrhunderts* (2010) spans the period from 1770 to 1918/19 (102–03). This periodization, if applied to literature, yields the result that the dominating number of new historical novels work with a nineteenth-century *sujet*. I suggest here that the long nineteenth century in the United States roughly straddles the years between 1776 and 1914/17, from the Declaration of Independence until the beginning of or the American entry into World War I, with an important caesura – the American Civil War of 1861–65 – dividing the time period near the middle (Schlereth xii; Joyce 3). The early starting point of the period ties in with the attempts of Americans to create a cultural identity for their nation soon after the colonial era came to a close. In this endeavor, historical fiction played a vital role. The late terminus emulates the well-known efforts by noteworthy modernists "to pinpoint a moment of transition – Virginia Woolf's 1910, D. H. Lawrence's 1915, Ezra Pound's 1922 – a historical caesura from which a new dispensation would begin" (Kunow, "Making" 178; see also Joyce 3).

Historical fiction has shifted its focus from "the movers and shakers of times past – great men and the countries they ran and conquered," to "people and themes that [had] previously remained in the back-ground ... neglected topics, such as common people's daily lives and how they were affected (or not) by major events" (Johnson, *Historical* 4). In contemporary historical fiction, the "maps and chaps version" (Carol Shields qtd. in Hollenberg 341) of history has given way to an interest in social history. The innovations in the historical-novel genre are related to transformations within historiography (Robinson 3–53). Authors aim at a rewriting of history when choosing their topics (King 3). The new historical fiction takes a revisionist stance toward established historio-graphy. Often this coincides with a return to the storytelling tradition, especially from the marginalized perspectives of women or racial and ethnic minorities (Rothaug 10; Heilmann/Llewellyn 5). The texts are influenced by postmodern discourses of feminism, multiculturalism, and postcolonialism (Elias, *Sublime* 219) and incorporate or reflect de-velopments in literary and historical theory, for example, post-structuralism, radical constructivism, and especially new historicism (Fluck, "Activist"). The categorizations of contemporary fiction vary from what has been labeled neo-realistic (Versluys; Claviez/Moss; Bradbury, "Neorealist"), prepost- (Bradbury, "Writing" 18), and post-postmodern (Hassan, "Beyond") literature. The forms the writers of new historical fiction use range from seemingly traditional historical novels to more inventive ones. The historical novel's revisionism today is twofold: it revises and reinterprets the historical record, often exposing it as the traditional version of the past, and it transforms the conventions and norms of historical fiction (McHale 90).

I am adopting and adapting the term 'new historical novel' from Martha Tuck Rozett's study *Constructing a World: Shakespeare's England and the New Historical Fiction* (2003) for the American texts discussed in this study. I find this term to be fitting for various reasons. First of all, the historical fiction discussed in this study is literally 'new,' as contemporary novels, published over the last twenty-five years, are the subject of scrutiny. The adjective 'new' further points to the current literary period or movement in the US, which has, for its recourse to or reinvention of realism, been labeled "new realism" (Fluck, "Surface" 65). Furthermore, 'new' evokes an intentional reference to the "New American Studies" (Rowe), which adopt a transnational critical focus since the 1990s, questioning the paradigm of American exceptionalism and viewing the US as a multicultural nation in a globalized world – likewise an objective in the texts I discuss. And finally, and perhaps most importantly, the phrase 'new historical' highlights the strong affinity of this literary trend to the theories of "new historicism" (Greenblatt, *Power* 5). The new historicists' trajectories of the non-hierarchical juxtaposition of literary and nonliterary texts, their focus on questions of ideology and power in historiography, and their assumption that the past is only available in textualized form strongly inform the new American historical fiction.

This study attempts to chart and structure the field of the new American historical novel by raising a number of questions: Why does American fiction at the turn of the twenty-first century concern itself with the past? Which notions of history and historical awareness predominate in these novels? Is the fascination with historical fiction a form of millennial escapism? Or do historical novels communicate a historical lesson by providing us with knowledge of the past? Why is it especially the nineteenth century that fuels the imagination of writers and stimulates the fantasy of readers? Do the texts possess the power to revise contemporary perceptions of American history? Do they thereby influence the perception of the American present and future? What are the political, ethical, and emotional functions that historical novels fulfill? What are the formal and stylistic changes in historical fiction? And, perhaps most importantly, do all of the findings signify an utterly new trend in American fiction after postmodernism? These are some of the questions that drove the research for this study. I would like to state that the explanations and answers offered here cannot be completely exhaustive, especially since the field is still evolving as I am writing this. The study in hand merely hopes to bring some light to these issues and thereby tries to broaden the canonical scope of American historical fiction at the turn of the twenty-first century.

And before I proceed with my analysis of the new historical fiction, I would like to issue another caveat. It is impossible to analyze or even list all historical fiction that has been published in the United States throughout the last two or three decades. This study will therefore sacrifice any attempt at a survey or a cataloging of this vast material. In order to reduce the subject to manageable proportions, the following choices have been made to narrow down the corpus and focus of this work: the first, obvious choice was to limit the focus to the genre of the historical novel. This study will only concentrate on longer prose narratives, not on shorter texts like novellas or short stories. In the following, the term 'historical fiction' will be used synonymously with the term 'historical novel.' Of course, this does not mean that historical fiction in the short(er) form does not deserve further scholarly scrutiny (Engler/Scheiding). The corpus has then been reduced to contemporary historical fiction set in the nineteenth century. The preoccupation with the nineteenth century seems to be preeminent within the genre of the historical novel in the USA today. Thus, the analysis of this phenomenon may yield representative results, as it may be presumed that within this corpus the most diverse, or even all possible, subgenres of historical fiction may be covered. The next choice has been to restrict the discussion to works that are set in the United States and concern American issues. Whether or not the author of the work is American was of no concern for the selection. Indeed, the texts discussed in more detail in this study include the work of one Australian and one British writer. These choices differ greatly from the ones underlying the few existing studies of the contemporary American historical novel in temporal, formal, geographical, and subject range, as shown by, for example, the titles of studies by Timothy Parrish, Michael Butter, and Philipp Löffler, namely *From the Civil War to the Apocalypse: Postmodern History and American Fiction* (2008), *The Epitome of Evil: Hitler in American Fiction, 1939–2002* (2009), and *Pluralist Desires: Contemporary Historical Fiction and the End of the Cold War* (2015).

This study aims at in-depth analyses of selected novels that are representative of larger themes as well as formal experiments within the genre. The degree of public recognition a text has already received was not a criterion for selection, although in some cases it coincided with the other requirements. The framework outlined by the questions listed earlier and approached in the following introductory section of this study – by touching upon relevant aspects of narratology, genre studies, memory studies, cultural studies, postcolonial theory, gender studies, transatlantic studies, and historiography, among other fields – will be applied to twelve novels which revisit and revise the nineteenth century in the United States. They are Valerie Martin's *The Great Divorce* (1994), Caleb Carr's *The Alienist* (1994), Christopher Bigsby's *Hester* (1994), Lauren Belfer's *City of Light* (1999), Alice Randall's *The Wind Done Gone* (2001), Diane Glancy's *Stone Heart* (2003), Matthew Pearl's *The Dante Club* (2003), Erik Larson's *The Devil in the White City* (2003), John May's *Poe & Fanny* (2004), Geraldine Brooks's *March* (2005), Michael Cunningham's *Specimen Days* (2005), and David Ebershoff's *The 19th Wife* (2008). Although the number of novels selected may not be large enough to give a universally valid diagnosis of the field, it nevertheless should allow for the identification of representative trends. Generally, I am interested in the significance of this body of writing as a literary and cultural phenomenon. This study should be understood as a first positioning of this vast trend. Finally, as fiction is both a cultural document and a form of criticism (Kirchknopf 75), I would like to claim, adapting a phrase by Peter Middleton and Tim Woods, that this study is a provisional contribution to a cultural poetics of contemporary American literature (13).

1.2 A Brief History of the Historical Novel

The beginnings of historical fiction or the recounting of long-ago events goes back very far, to the era of the oral tradition in literature. Sarah L. Johnson, drawing on one of the earliest commentaries on historical fiction, Alessandro Manzoni's essay "Del romanzo storico" (1850; published in English as "On the Historical Novel," 1984), claims that "[h]istorical fiction is one of the oldest forms of storytelling" (*Historical* 2). Richard Lee declares that "in all cultures, historical fiction is the most natural form of story-telling." This ties in with C. Vann Woodward's verdict that "[i]n a sense, all novels are historical novels. They all seek to understand, to describe, to recapture the past, however remote, however recent" (142). If historical fiction is the oldest form of narrative, this also makes historical fiction the most enduring literary genre. Yet when all novels are seen as historical novels, the explanatory power and informative value of the genre label is diluted.

In a more critical approach, Sir Walter Scott's *Waverley; or, 'Tis Sixty Years Since* (1814) is usually recognized as the first historical novel in English and regarded as the prototype of the whole genre. With his novels, Scott created an individual Scottish national identity for his country, distinct from the British, and thereby struck a strong chord with nationalists and patriots in the United States. Scott's success was soon to be followed by calls for a similar invention for American literature. At the beginning of the nineteenth century, when the United States experienced its newly gained independence from Britain, the "two key features" of the United States were "its novelty and its fragility" (Parish 9). American intellectuals were striving to establish a distinctive cultural identity for the new nation and felt a strong need for cultural products to complete the work of the previous generation, who had first established Americanness through the political work of revolution. Walter Channing claimed in his "Essay on American Language and Literature" (1815) in the *North American Review* that the nation's "colonial existence" was "opposed to literary originality" (307–08). A "[n]ational literature" needed to be rooted in the "native peculiarities of the country," among them the "various objects of history" (312). At the time, the American nation was generally deemed "an imitative one" (49) by Washington Irving in his essay "English Writers on America" (1819/20). It seemed self-evident that Americans, following in Scott's footsteps, needed to recover their own history in the New World and declare it the main field of "the exertion of their own intellectual powers" (Channing 314; see also Orians; Spiller; Fluck, *Imaginäre* 84–104; Glazener 40–43).

The genre of the historical novel soon found its way across the Atlantic, briskly promoted by American intellectuals, who campaigned for the development of a distinctly American national identity, culture, and literature. In the following decades, many American writers concentrated on the portrayal of America's antecedents. Creating fictional images of the nation's past became a part of the emancipation of American culture from British influence. The writers were drawing on the historical novels of Scott for the mold of the genre but creating something original by filling it with typically American ingredients, such as strongly religious Puritan settlers, Native Americans and their exotic cultures, and the challenges of the unique American landscape (Scheiding, *Geschichte*; Engler/Scheiding 12–13). Ernest E. Leisy generally asserts that "[t]he first experimenters with Colonial material ... tried in one way or another to adapt the technique of Sir Walter Scott to native subjects" (66).

James Fenimore Cooper's novel *The Spy* (1821) is regarded as the first American historical novel. His oeuvre, most prominently the so-called Leatherstocking Tales, comprising the novels *The Pioneers* (1823), *The Last of the Mohicans* (1826), *The Prairie* (1827), *The Pathfinder* (1840), and *The Deerslayer* (1841), was strongly formative for the evolution of the whole genre in the USA and earned Cooper the sobriquet "the American Scott" (Dekker, *James*), although he complained about the "poverty of materials" (Cooper, *Notions* 108) in American history. But Cooper was not simply a "transatlantic imitator" (*"Lionel"*). He differed from Scott, as he introduced a certain historical pessimism to the genre which became a distinctive quality in the American historical novel (Scheiding, "James"). With Charles Brockden Brown's and William Gilmore Simms's historical novels, "a strong sense of epistemological skepticism" was then added to the characteristics of "serious historical fiction in the United States" (Kurt Müller 37). Other early texts in the genre, such as Lydia Maria Child's *Hobomok* (1824) and Catharine Maria Sedgwick's *Hope Leslie* (1827), centered on women and Native Americans, and have only since the 1990s been added to the canon (Arch; Domhnall; Opfermann). The proliferation of historical romances in the early republic has been critically discussed with varying foci (Staehelin-Wackernagel; Bell; Dekker, *American*; Gould; Samuels; Breinig/Opfermann; McElwee; Ackermann; Fluck, "Romance"). It shall therefore suffice here to jump forward to the best-known American historical romance published in the nineteenth century: Nathaniel Hawthorne's *The Scarlet Letter* (1850). It marks the climax and at the same time a first terminus within the early development of the genre. Herman Melville's *Israel Potter* (1855) can already be read as a "radical deconstruction of traditional models of historical interpretation and meaning construction" (Kurt Müller 38).

"[H]istorical fiction of a literary kind" (Elias, *Sublime* 16) slipped into a phase of dormancy toward the middle of the nineteenth century, with the occasional exception. So-called costume novels, which use the historical setting only as a canvas and not as an integral part of the narrated story (Burt xiii) – and which may also, devoid of any literary claim, be regarded as light entertainment – dominated the field for a long time. Mark Twain's *A Connecticut Yankee in King Arthur's Court* (1889), a historical fantasy, and Stephen Crane's *The Red Badge of Courage* (1895), with its perspective on the insignificance of the individual, are border cases of historical fiction (Kurt Müller 39).

During the era of late modernism, literary interest in historical topics underwent a fundamental change (Engler/Müller 9). The modernist era, though marked by the notion of the end of history (Irving Howe 15), brought forth a few important examples of the historical novel. One of the "most impressive modernist examples of historical fiction" (Kurt Müller 41) is John Dos Passos's *U.S.A.* trilogy, consisting of *The 42nd Parallel* (1930), *1919* (1932), and *The Big Money* (1936). Its form of montage mirrors the modernist experience of fragmentation, while in terms of content an impetus toward revisionism of traditional historiography is apparent. But mostly, the modernist flowering of the genre was regional and tied in with, for example, the Southern Renaissance. Important Southern writers of historical fiction of the era are Ellen Glasgow, Robert Penn Warren, Allen Tate, and, most eminently, William Faulkner, especially with his groundbreaking novel *Absalom, Absalom!* (1936). This novel has often been labeled a book about storytelling (Kurt Müller 41), expressing the construction and constructedness of history. Early postmodernism, too, did not fully succeed in the literary regeneration of the historical *sujet*. Novels such as John Barth's *The Sot-Weed Factor* (1960) did find a lot of critical acclaim (Hoffmann 414), but not a broad general readership. Barth's text is typical of the acme of postmodernism, which was dominated by the "pervasive feeling of the absurdity of American history itself, and the unreality of its reality" (Bradbury, *American* 199). Other texts of the era that take a parodist stance toward the usability of the past are Ishmael Reed's *Mumbo Jumbo* (1972) and *Flight to Canada* (1976) and Robert Coover's *The Public Burning* (1977) (Kurt Müller 45). These texts "focus on the violent and destructive aspects of history and replace the traditional notion of history as a meaningful, teleological process with concepts such as discontinuity, absurdity, contingency, apocalypse, entropy, and paranoia" (Kurt Müller 43). Further examples of such an "unmaking of history" (Kunow, "Beginning" 81) are Joseph Heller's *Catch-22* (1961), Kurt Vonnegut's *Slaughterhouse-Five* (1969), Doctorow's *The Book of Daniel* (1971) and *Ragtime* (1975), John Berger's *G.* (1972), and Pynchon's *Gravity's Rainbow* (1973). It has been noted that "[t]his was historical fiction in its formalist phase – what the critic Linda Hutcheon so aptly termed 'historiographic metafiction': highly self-referential historical novels that simultaneously deployed and undermined not only their own sources but their own explanations of those sources" (Harlan 113). Norman Mailer's *The Armies of the Night* (1968) is an outstanding example of "non-fiction novels which come very close to historiographic metafiction in their form and content" (Hutcheon, *Poetics* 117).

The renewed triumph of historical fiction was not generally apparent until the late 1970s and the early 1980s, with the worldwide success of popular novels such as James Clavell's *Shōgun* (1975), Alex Haley's *Roots* (1976), Umberto Eco's *Il nome della rosa* (1980; published in English as *The Name of the Rose*, 1983), and Isabel Allende's *La casa de los espíritus* (1982; published in English as *The House of the Spirits*, 1985). The wide recognition these texts received was extremely furthered by their film and television adaptations, which followed the publication of each text in quick succession, proving that "film has been the salvation of fiction, not its downfall" (Shechner 36). In the 1980s, these worldwide popular successes were followed by both critically acclaimed and best-selling novels in the USA (Johnson, *Historical* 3), such as Larry McMurtry's *Lonesome Dove* (1986; Pulitzer Prize), Toni Morrison's *Beloved* (1987; Pulitzer Prize), and Charles Johnson's *Middle Passage* (1990; National Book Award), to name just new historical fiction focusing on the nineteenth century in the United States (Bergmann, "To", "New").

In the new historical fiction, extreme experiments are seldom practiced anymore, and contemporary texts differ from the products of the earlier phase of postmodernism. "[T]he highly parodic, self-mocking and sometimes bitter fiction" of the early postmodern era, "fiction in which the past [was] little more than a playful artifice," has given way to "intensely earnest novels," "fiction that is obsessed with the past" (Harlan 114). Thirty years ago, Rüdiger Kunow observed: "Whether it is really possible to differentiate between an earlier ebullient, experimental, anti-realistic and 'anti-social' postmodernism and a more cautious, rea-listic, 'engaging' one, is at this moment uncertain, but an undeniable resurfacing of the historical is to be found in different areas of post-modernism today" ("Making" 186). Today, we can be sure that such a change, a "second 'postmodernist turn'" (Tönnies 58), has taken place.

The new historical fiction, evident around the turn of the twenty-first century, is determined "to figure out how [America] works and what went wrong and how to fix it" (Elias, "Metahistorical" 165). It is thus engaged in a new form of what Jane Tompkins in *Sensational Designs* (1985), referring to nineteenth-century fiction, labels "cultural work." It is offering "powerful examples of the way a culture thinks about itself, ar-ticulating and proposing solutions for the problems that shape a particular historical moment" (Tompkins xi). The trend toward the revisionist re-writing of the past from the point of view of marginalized groups, "groups that have been excluded from the making and writing of history" (Kunow, "Beginning" 79), and a return to old literary virtues and deep human desires such as "[c]oherence and closure" (Byatt, *Possession* 422), while at the same time questioning the possibility of knowing the past – this "double task of historiographic de-construction and re-construction" (Kurt Müller 47;

see also Kunow, "Beginning" 91) – is a significant quality of the contemporary historical fiction.

1.3 Nineteenth-Century Historical Romance as National Literature

In his essay "Confidence and Anxiety in Victorian America" (1991),
Peter J. Parish credits America in the nineteenth century with an iden-
tifiable "sense of its national past." He claims that "[t]he notion that
American culture is characterised by a lack of interest in the national
history and a lack of awareness of the national past is surely one of the
most dangerous and widespread fallacies about the United States"
(Parish 15; see also Kunow, "Manifest" 60; Grabbe). Parish's observa-
tion seems accurate. Soon after the achievement of independence, the
American "historical consciousness" (Kurt Müller 35) awoke. Daniel
Webster's bicentennial oration on the landing of the first settlers at
Plymouth, "The First Settlement of New England" (1820), laid down a
basic outline for the treatment of the nation's early history:

> By ascending to an association with our ancestors; by contemplating
> their example and studying their character; by partaking their
> sentiments, and imbibing their spirit; by accompanying them in
> their toils, by sympathizing in their sufferings, and rejoicing in their
> successes and their triumphs, we seem to belong to their age, and to
> mingle our own existence with theirs. We become their contempo-
> raries, live the lives which they lived, endure what they endured, and
> partake in the rewards which they enjoyed.... Let us hope that the
> present may be an auspicious era of literature.
>
> (5–6, 48; see also Arch 116; Hebel)

James Wallis Eastburn and Robert Sands were the first to make fictional
use of the early era of settlement in their narrative poem *Yamoyden,
A Tale of the Wars of King Philip, in Six Cantos* (1820). Contemporaries
hailed this text as the starting point of a new, truly American mode
of writing: "We are glad that somebody has at last found out the un-
equaled fitness of our early history for the purposes of a work of fiction"
(Palfrey 480). In the following years, American authors were trying
to construct an American national identity by fictionalizing the past.
They were focusing on typically American topics such as Puritan settlers,
Native Americans, the War of Independence (Fluck, *Imaginäre* 95, 97),
and depictions of the unique American landscape. Many of them were
concentrating on the portrayal of the Puritan age in their historical
romances.

Some fifty romances set in the colonial era of the seventeenth
century and published during the first half of the nineteenth century

(Leisy; Staehelin-Wackernagel; VanMeter; Kunow, "Manifest" 60; Bell ix) take "a peep at the pilgrims," to use the title of Harriet Vaughan Cheney's novel (1824). Most of these historical romances have been forgotten. James McHenry's *The Spectre of the Forest; or, Annals of the Housatonic: A New-England Romance* (1823), the anonymously published *The Witch of New England: A Romance* (1824), Garrit Furman's *Redfield* (1825), the likewise anonymously published *Salem Witchcraft; or, the Adventures of Parson Handy from Punkapog Pond* (1825 or 1835), Cheney's *The Rivals of Acadia* (1827), and John Neal's *Rachel Dyer* (1828) are just some of them published in the 1820s. Child's *Hobomok* (1824), Sedgwick's *Hope Leslie* (1827), and Cooper's *The Wept of Wish-ton-Wish* (1829) are the historical romances of that decade with a Puritan *sujet* that have aroused new scholarly interest and been added to the canon.

The unchallenged status of Hawthorne's *The Scarlet Letter* (1850) as the paradigmatic American novel puts emphasis on the fact that the historical novel either equaled what we today label American literature or at least strongly furthered its parturition, a claim that has similarly been made with regard to Canadian literature (Wylie/Andrews/Viau). Historical fiction is not only the most enduring literary genre but also the one which has always had an important function in building a national identity. Susanne Opfermann affirms that for the United States, "[t]he historical novel as a genre contributed to the symbolic construction of America" (32).

In the following, I will support this thesis by taking a closer look at a text which, "like many others of [its] time, ... took part in the discursive construction of an American national identity that was foremost on the cultural agenda in the 1820s" (Opfermann 31). *Hobomok – A Tale of Early Times – By an American* is, although the title obviously does not reveal it, a novel about a young woman, Mary Conant, living in New England in 1629. She is in love with Charles Brown, an Episcopalian, very much to the distress of her Calvinist father. Mr. Conant, a strict Puritan, is possibly modeled after the historical Roger Conant, the founder of Salem, Massachusetts – then called Naumkeak – in 1626. Because marriage with Mary seems impossible, Charles goes on a journey back to England and is subsequently reported dead. Mary finds consolation with the eponymous Native American Hobomok, probably another fictionalization of a historical figure, a highly regarded translator for the settlers. Mary marries him according to Native American rites and gives birth to their son, significantly named Charles Hobomok. Hobomok is an even more unwelcome son-in-law to her father than Charles, and so Mary cuts all ties with him and lives with the Native Americans. When Charles surprisingly returns alive, the selfless Hobomok backs out of the marriage. He ritually divorces Mary and vanishes into the forest, never to be seen again. Hobomok, the noble savage, is clearing the way for the white man, Charles, and for a happy ending, including the reconciliation of Mary and her father.

On a metaphorical level, Child's text, when viewed as an instance of American national literature, is as revealing as it remains ambivalent. On the one hand, *Hobomok* depicts female rebellion against the patriarchal norms with an interracial as well as an interreligious marriage. Therefore, it strongly represents both the high individualization and the diversity of America during its early settlement. On the other hand, the failure of the interracial marriage and Hobomok's vanishing into the forest speak a different language. The reader's last glimpse of him clearly implies the coming forced relocation and genocide of his race: "He paused on a neighboring hill, looked toward his wigwam till his trained vision could hardly discern the object, with a bursting heart again murmured his farewell and blessing, and forever passed away from New England" (Child 139). This can also be seen in the depiction of little Charles Hobomok's assimilation to the predominating white culture, which significantly constitutes the final passage of the novel:

> Partly from consciousness of blame, and partly from a mixed feeling of compassion and affection, the little Hobomok was always a peculiar favorite with his grandfather. At his request, half the legacy of Earl Rivers was appropriated to his education. He was afterwards a distinguished graduate at Cambridge, and when he left that infant university, he departed to finish his studies in England. His father was seldom spoken of; and by degrees his Indian appellation was silently omitted.
>
> (Child 149–50)

Child, only twenty-two at the writing of the novel and not yet matured into the abolitionist and civil-rights activist she would become later in life, seems to assert that, though the beginnings of the United States are grounded in a diversity of race and religion, the prevailing culture – white Anglo-Saxon – equals the identity the nation has taken on in the nineteenth century through assimilation and extinction rather than amalgamation.

A categorical triad of race, gender, and religion clearly constitutes the foundation pillars of this novel. Religion, which Stanley Fish proclaimed "would succeed high theory and the triumvirate of race, gender, and class as the center of intellectual energy in the academy," is already a basic category in the early instances of national American literature. In fact, it can be proved that religion has always played a vital role in the mindset of the United States, probably much more so than the category of class. In *Hobomok*, the strict Puritan Conant in the end accepts his Episcopalian son-in-law Brown as the lesser evil compared to his first, Native American son-in-law, a "toleration of a quite limited sort:

Protestants talking to each other" (Arch 112–13). This is particularly significant since Brown is merely a mirror image of his father-in-law. As a young man, Conant, a Puritan separatist, had eloped from England to the New World with Mary's mother, the daughter of the British Earl Rivers, a member of the Church of England, who had refused his consent to their union. Hobomok's Native American spirituality and a subplot revolving around the Antinomian Crisis further add to the topic of religious diversity. Religious differences are at the basis of the father's disapproval and the daughter's and son-in-law's rebellion. As such, they echo not only the older generation's insurgence but also more generally the American settlers' religious rebellion against the Church of England, which preceded the political uprising against British colonialism: "While the text celebrates the achievements of the forefathers – who enable both the present prosperity of the United States and its glorious future – it simultaneously criticizes the authority of literal and symbolic fathers" (Opfermann 32). Mary's insurrection against her father, which is almost miraculously rewarded by her being reinstated as the wife of her allegedly dead lover, also anticipates the young nation's rebellion against the British in the pursuit of independence, which at the time of the writing of the novel was a mere half-century old – as notably also was the women's suffrage movement.

A closer look at, for example, Cheney's *A Peep at the Pilgrims in Sixteen Hundred Thirty-Six* (1824), Sedgwick's *Hope Leslie* (1827), or Cooper's *The Wept of Wish-ton-Wish* (1829) would ultimately yield comparable results. There is a similar central message in these novels, which are dominated by the ideological triad of race, gender, and religion. In *A Peep at the Pilgrims*, Major Edward Atherton falls in love with Miriam Grey, whose strict Puritan father looks unfavorably on a prospective marriage because Atherton is loyal to the Church of England. In the course of the events, Miriam becomes a captive of the Native Americans and Atherton takes part in brutal raids on the Pequods that virtually annihilate the tribe. Finally, Atherton becomes a liberal Puritan and marries Miriam. *The Wept of Wish-ton-Wish* thematizes the Heathcote family's religious emigration from England and their opposition to the Church of England as well as to the Puritans. Ruth Heathcote, the "wept" of the title, marries the Native American Conanchet during her captivity with them, but this intermarriage ends in the death of the two partners. The child of this marriage is expunged from the novel toward the end. *Hope Leslie* similarly depicts the "conflict between Native American and Euro-American culture" as well as "the power imbalance between men and women" (Quentin Miller 121). The "retreat to the authority of white patriarchy" (Arch 113) is here again expressed in two ways: first by the disappearance of the Native Americans Magawisca, Oneco, and Faith Leslie, the latter a former captive turned into an assimilated Native American through marriage;

and second by making the free-spirited title character, Alice Leslie – whose name is changed by her strongly religious stepparents into the telling Hope Leslie – understand that the repressive Puritan society demands a marriage from her (Fluck, *Imaginäre* 102–04).

These early historical romances are genuine American cultural products, signifying the uniqueness as well as the unity of the country by presenting its origins in the seventeenth century. But because the roots of the American nation do lie in an era of severe religious and racial differences as well as stern gender norms, the texts emphasize the diversity of the country's people and hint at their inconsistency and irreconcilability as well. As Tompkins has it, nineteenth-century American literature is cultural work, giving expression to the marginal-ized situation of the individual, promoting change and progress by offering solutions, while on the other hand holding on to and perpetuating traditions (xi–xix). As an authentic American art form, the genre of the historical romance emerged in the nineteenth century, giving apt expression to the competing functions of the literature of the time, the project of cultural self-definition and the concept of the condition of the individual. Often the same literary work can be read as a field of contestation between the striving for a common national identity for the many and the expression of an individuation of the one: "Calling a novel a 'historical romance' is ... to direct attention to its extraordinarily rich, mixed, and even contradictory or oxymoronic character" (Dekker, *American* 26). The motto of the American nation, *e pluribus unum*, can be found exemplified in the historical romance, but so can its counterpart, *e pluribus plura*.

Above that, Lion Feuchtwanger's observation that "[t]he portrayal of times past was never the point and purpose but always only a means or vehicle for expressing their own experience of their own time" (130; see also Schabert, *Roman* 14; Friedrich 1) – the assumption that historical fiction is a critique of the present, transferred into a past setting – is true for this form of historical fiction. In these texts, the seventeenth century is not only a "by-gone time" (2), to quote from Hawthorne's famous preface to his romance *The House of the Seven Gables* (1851), but also seems to mirror contemporary developments and changes of the nineteenth century. The historical romance's "public function ... [seems to be] not just to mourn lost cultures but to purvey a certain story of contemporary cultures" (Brodhead 121). After all, the long nineteenth century was an era of enormous political change (Declaration of Independence, 1776; ratification of the Constitution, 1788), in which feminist concerns (e.g., Seneca Falls Declaration, 1848; suffrage, 1920), racial issues (e.g., Indian Removal Act, 1830; Trail of Tears, 1838), and slavery and its abolition (e.g., Fugitive Slave Act, 1850; Emancipation Proclamation, 1863) would come to the forefront; the conflict with the British would culminate and be resolved (War of Independence, 1775–1783; War of 1812, 1812–15); and the deep-seated differences among Americans would find their all-time climax in the American Civil War (1861–65). The genre of the historical novel was "created specifically to forge a nationalist consciousness and cultural identity," yet it "exhibited the same central contradiction as American history itself ... between an ideology based on the premise that all men are created equal and a political structure based on the assumption that people of color and white women do not fall under the rubric 'men'" (Karcher xv). The urge to create a national consciousness and a cultural identity is inherent to the genre of historical fiction. The new American historical fiction at the turn of the twenty-first century, with its revisionist impetus, follows in the paths of the nineteenth-century historical romance, aiming at creating not one hegemonic history but multiple histories of the people.

1.4 The Fact/Fiction Dichotomy

The positivist view that there is an "objectively founded difference between fact and fiction," which makes it possible to distinguish between them, is still "a commonly accepted premise of our sense of history" (Sauerberg 58). The fact/fiction dichotomy is a controversy inherent to the discussion of the genre of the historical novel (Mitchell/Parsons 2–3). Scholarship on and popular reception of historical fiction often has been preoccupied with the attempt to discern which aspects of a novel are based on facts and which parts are products of the imagination of the writer. The label 'historical novel' is itself a contradiction in terms, since the first word points toward fact, the second toward fiction (Carnes 14). The term "combines history and fiction, fact and fancy, truth and fabrication, blended together" (Steuber 245). With the renewed rise of the genre of the historical novel in the last decades of the twentieth century, the "conventional dichotomy between 'fact' and 'fiction' has of late been called into question" (Nünning, "Fictional" 198). There is the claim that "there should be no simple alignment of fact with truth and fiction with invention, indeed that fact/fiction divide can be regarded as a false polarity" (Bird 23).

A brief glimpse at the development of the discipline of historiography seems worthwhile here. Reinhart Koselleck, in his influential definition of the terms *"Geschichte"* and *"Historie,"* specifies them as indicating the sequence of past events as well as their depiction (*"sowohl den Ereigniszusammenhang wie dessen Darstellung"*; 647). Sigrun Meinig, drawing on Koselleck's designation, defines the term as follows: "'History' refers to the events or sequences of events in the past (*res gestae*) and to the cultural representations of such events (*historiae rerum gestarum*)" (37). The double meaning derives from the German, where *Geschichte* means both 'history' and 'story.' This double connotation is even further confirmed by the etymology of the word:

Etymologically, the word *history* is related to the Old French *historie* (fourteenth century) and the Latin *historia*, both meaning "narrative, account, tale, story," the Greek *historia*, "a learning or knowing by inquiry, history, record, narrative," as well as *historein*, "inquire" and *histor*, "wise man, judge." Thus the meaning of *history* as "account of events" comes before *history* as "events," which suggests that what appears to be stable and objective is in fact a subjective representation of events constructed post-factum, the authenticity of which is highly arguable.

(Tofantšuk 60)

The "consolidation of history into a discipline" (Elias, *Sublime* 37) occurred in the nineteenth century. In its early decades, Leopold von Ranke formulated the programmatic postulation of historical objectivity, namely that historiography needs only to state how it really was (*"bloß sagen, wie es eigentlich gewesen ist"*; Ranke VI). But this "positivistic standard of the exact representation of historical facts" and "the concept of the teleological progression of history" (Engler/Müller 9) has been problematized since. R. G. Collingwood early on in the debate stressed that "all history is the re-enactment of past thought in the historian's own mind" (215), viewing the historian's imagination as the constitutive aspect of historiography (Rothaug 28). Michel de Certeau points to this oxymoronic element inherent to the term 'historiography,' which establishes a relation between "two antinomic terms," "'history' and 'writing,'" "the real and discourse." It is historiography's "task" to connect the two and, "where this link cannot be imagined, [to work] as if the two were being joined" (xxvii). This implicitly points to aspects important for the definition of historical fiction. Hayden White is probably the most prominent historian, though not the first, to question the difference between fiction and historiography:

Historians are concerned with events which can be assigned to specific time-space locations, events which are (or were) in principle observable or perceivable, whereas imaginative writers – poets, novelists, playwrights – are concerned with both these kinds of events and imagined, hypothetical, or invented ones .... What should interest us ... is the extent to which the discourse of the historian and that of the imaginative writer overlap, resemble, or correspond with each other.

(*Tropics* 121)

In *Metahistory: The Historical Imagination in Nineteenth-Century Europe* (1973), he claims that there is no essential distinction between art and science and that historiography is generally subject to narrative patterns. In Stephanie Bird's words "'[e]mplotment' is the process by which the facts are fashioned by the historian into a sequence or story of a particular kind" (23; see also Adamson, *Recreating* xix). Stephen Slemon concludes that "history is a mode of discourse that is culturally motivated and ideologically conditioned; it is a mirror of contemporary concerns and dominant, institutionalized practices. It consists not of things, but of words" (159).

The past cannot be represented without interpretation, selection, and humanization. This makes history "in fact a collection of narratives by historians" (Elias, *Sublime* 37; see also Stanzel 123; Nünning, *Fiktion I* 89). History is conceived as a mere "pattern which men weave out of the materials of the past, ... a set of ordered relationships which is the creation of the human mind and not otherwise present in nature" (Lévi-Strauss 110). Paul Ricoeur's and White's theories both stress the importance of the role of narrative for the understanding of history (Meinig 33) and the means for its representation of history: "[N]arrative is a basic human way of making sense of the temporality of human existence .... History is thus a construct, it is meaning found and organized in the form of narrative" (Kunow, "Making" 196; see also Doctorow 26; Mengel 50, trans. in Kurt Müller 36). The driving force behind emplotment in historiography, as in literature, is a desire for coherence (Sauerberg 61), a coherence which is not inherent to the data itself (Engler 14). Narrativization plays a crucial part in the process of sense-making. The use of language and the act of writing corrupt the historian's assumed neutrality. From this perspective, there is "very little, if indeed any, difference between the historical account and the work of fiction" (Sauerberg 59–60).

Ricoeur, investigating Aristotelian mimesis, distinguishes three levels, which represent its respective stages: prefiguration, configuration, and refiguration. Historiography and fiction share the first two levels, but differ on the third one (*Time I* 52–90). Historiography functions on the basis of a truth claim, something that does not generally exist in literature (Meinig 44). Historiographical narratives and fictional narratives differ in this respect: "[T]he *ambition of truth* by which history ... claims the title 'true' ..., displays its full meaning only when ... opposed to the deliberate suspension of the true/false alternative, characteristic of fictional narrative" (*Time I* 226). But "historical narratives contain at least in part a nomological component and engage in historical explanation, which is lacking in fictional narrative" (Meinig 366). Therefore, Ricoeur "reserve[s] the term 'fiction' for those literary creations that do not have historical narrative's ambition to constitute a true narrative" (*Time II* 3). To him, the achievement of that "past-like" (*Time III* 192) character of historical narrative is legitimate. Middleton and Woods call this the "quasi-past" (68) of historical fiction. Bird asserts that "there can never be a 'correct' version of the past: any narrative interpretation of facts, however much it conforms to criteria of objectivity, must always be a manifestation of the author's ideology. The fact/fiction dichotomy is a false one which obscures the ideological tenets of the dominant discourse" (23).

Kunow aptly remarks that "history is a factual horizon impossible to verify" ("Beginning" 80). Amy J. Elias reintroduces the "historical sublime" (*Sublime* xviii) to identify this "unknowability of the past" (143), drawing on White's usage of the term in *The Content of Form: Narrative Discourse and Historical Representation* (1987). To her, it denotes "a desired horizon that can never be reached" (Elias, *Sublime* xviii, see also 4; see also White, *Content* 81; Runia). In White's theory, "history is unnarrativized, alogical, unorganized, nonrational. History is sublime because it is both unknowable and unrepresentable in discourse" (Elias, *Sublime* 42). The new historical fiction, therefore, "is linked to the invocation of the historical sublime as both a gesture of interrogation and a gesture of assertion" (Elias, *Sublime* 48).

1.5 Master Narrative vs. Micro Narrative

Since the 1960s, the "mimetic connection between art and reality is no longer taken for granted" (Engler 14). Jean-François Lyotard called this the "postmodern condition," in his book of the same title (1979), and Fredric Jameson has, more generally, labeled it the "crisis of representation" (*Postmodernism* viii). What these notions have in common is "a deeply felt loss of faith in our ability to represent the real" (Bertens 11), which includes "new skepticism or suspicion about the writing of history" (Hutcheon, *Politics* 106).

Lyotard formulates a thesis of the deligitimization of or "incredulity towards metanarratives," narratives of historical meaning, knowledge, or experience (xxiv; see also Kurt Müller 36; Friedrich 8). Traditional historicism is replaced by "the abandonment of representations of the whole (master narratives), the relinquishment of a centre which allows us to comprehend the historical processes, the conscious limitation to the fragments of various historical processes, whose relation to one another is not finally determined" (Hohendahl 78, trans. in Meinig 31–32).

Meta-, master, or grand narratives are intended to legitimize "certain ways of seeing, and thus of shaping, the world" (Gamble 32). The "historical account given the greatest credence always belongs to the ruling culture." History is the "[m]aster narrative a dominant culture tells about itself" (McKible 223; see also Benjamin 2). In the postmodern era, these narratives' lack of a comprehensive explanation of historical experience or knowledge is exposed and therefore they are questioned or deconstructed (Kunow, "Beginning" 77). As narratives of continuity, *les grands récits* give an evolutionary explanation, ignoring the roads not taken and implying a totality which is based on exclusion. They neglect the histories of marginalized groups, "the voices of those who did not win" (Reichardt, "New" 70). Those "'Others' … tend to write 'narratives of emergence' or 'Bildungsromane' which search for a past to constitute an identity" (Reichardt, "New" 70–71). While in Scott's romances history still appeared "as the manifestation of a divine 'master plan'" (Kurt Müller 36), the new historical fiction can be seen as the stringent enhancement of the pretense of the postmodern era to delegitimize all metanarratives, "the abandonment of ... the 'grand narratives' of history in favour of 'local knowledges'" (Middleton/Woods 31). Global history is displaced by discontinuity and breach, to clarify the ideological and totalizing aspects of history:

> [T]he notion of discontinuity assumes a major role in the historical disciplines .... Discontinuity was the stigma of temporal dislocation that it was the historian's task to remove from history. It now has become one of the basic elements of historical analysis.
>
> (Foucault 9)

The new historical fiction "faces the chaos of the past ... yearning for form and meaning, sense and sequence, but knowing that such pleasing illusions have all the texture and substance of smoke" (Harlan 115). The main hinge is then the "idea that the postmodern, metahistorical imagination faces the chaos of history and yearns for something more, thus continually struggling to make sense of history but in its heart of hearts convinced that such surety is an impossible, rationalist dream" (Elias, "Metahistorical" 165).

History as micro or little narrative turns into a means of dissociation and of defining a group identity for minorities and women (Rothaug 50). Revisionism focuses on previously marginalized aspects of history writing: "[T]he eclipse of the master narratives that once dominated American culture, the poverty in our mythic lives has had to be filled by local myths and regional and ethnic stories that give consciousness to our group affinities and form our identities" (Shechner 32). *Les petits récits* draw an alternative image of history, without a claim to totality or universality (Rothaug 16, 47, 57, 59, 237). In this respect one may speak about a resuscitation of the historical as a sense-making entity, albeit under the supposition that it is always only groups which confront their own history to establish their place within hegemonic culture (Rothaug 50).

The question remains whether the silence concerning the grand narratives in these texts has to be interpreted as a shared "for-granted presence of background knowledge" or whether "silence is a form of resistance" (Middleton/Woods 31). Kunow diagnoses a reliance of the silenced groups on the hegemonic history, which for them is a history of domination, exploitation, and exclusion, as a frame of reference ("Return" 258; see also Rothaug 57). Ulfried Reichardt similarly claims that marginalized groups situate themselves within this history in order to develop a sense of identity. The resulting "narratives of emergence" are revisions of the dominant history ("New" 71). Furthermore, the "attempt to appropriate history for subordinate groups finds itself confronted with the possibility that its object as such is simply not 'there' any more" (Kunow, "Beginning" 87). The urge that "women, along with members of minority ethnicities and nonheterosexuals, need a narrative history" (Heilmann/Llewellyn 5) remains valid. Overall, revisionist historical fiction may be read as a supplement to official historiography, hegemonic history, or the dominant ideology.

1.6 Academic History vs. Pop History

There are two influential ways of thinking about the past in American contemporary culture, "contemporary notions of history as a construct and the ideology of the 'end of history'" (Kunow, "Beginning" 79). Postmodernism declared the end of history:

> If we are now at a point where we cannot imagine a world substantially different from our own, in which there is no apparent or obvious way in which the future will represent a fundamental improvement over our current order, then we must also take into consideration the possibility that History itself might be at an end.
> (Fukuyama 52)

This is one of several attitudes of dealing with the past in historical cultural studies – the postmodern position (Jay Clayton, *Charles* 27). Yet the *posthistoire* position reveals a cultural contradiction, in which the waning of historical consciousness and cultural amnesia is accompanied by a memory boom (Huyssen 5; see also Kunow, "Beginning" 89). Postmodernism has also been described as "a cultural mindset characterized by an obsession with history" (Elias, *Sublime* xvii). The vantage point after the end of history provides a perspective from which the past appears concluded, allows for contemplation from a distance, and therefore becomes narratable (Heise 74). Ultimately, "[m]uch of the 'end of history' rhetoric is, of course, just that: rhetoric" (Kunow, "Beginning" 87).

Among postmodern cultural critics, the notion that history in the postmodern American world of mass culture can only be experienced as a mere spectacle predominates. Historians view what they label "popular history – historical novels, Hollywood films, museums, historical comics, online websites, and so on" (Harlan 108; see also Middleton/Woods 22) – as opposed to professional academic history: "[A] new history is being produced, outside the academy, by novelists, memoirists, autobiographers and filmmakers" (Harlan 121). "Heritage industry" (Hewison) and "society of the spectacle" (Debord) are two buzzwords which describe the loss of historical awareness that critics diagnose in contemporary society. History is reduced to entertainment and becomes an object for theme parks (Rothaug 14). Popular history "reconstructs the past as a theatre of the present," it is "a neon epic of mind-numbing nostalgia .... It is a seductive and captivating history that opens the heart but castrates the intellect" (Harlan 120; see also Wilentz). Contemporary society is a "retro-chic culture," and the interest in the past is a "fascination with collectables" (Harlan 120; see also Lowenthal, *Possessed*).

Jameson diagnosed "a new and original historical situation in which we are condemned to seek history by way of our own pop images and simulacra of that history, which itself forever remains out of reach" (*Postmodernism* 25). The "reproduction of history in the entertainment format" by the mass media, "erodes ... any historical perspective, leaving only an empty historicism of yesteryear fashions and 'quaint' décor" (Kunow, "Beginning" 88). There is a "host of simulations of the past, based very much on the Disney model, which the heritage industry is spreading all over the North American continent today" (Kunow, "Simalcrum" 25). Jörn Rüsen ironically states that "ever since history has been declared to be at its end, 'historical matters' seem to have come back *with a vengeance*" ("Preface" vii; my emphasis).

This view has also especially been adopted for historical fiction, for example in the claim that historiographical metafiction reduced "real history ... the traditional object ... of what used to be the historical novel" (Jameson, *Postmodernism* 21) to "a proliferation of meaningless but marketable images" (Harlan 114), which have been immersed into "the cultural logic of late capitalism" (Jameson, *Postmodernism* 21). The literary occupation with history "is symptomatic of the economic sphere's penetration into the aesthetic that Jameson regards as a key feature of industrial capitalism's inaugural stage" (Kucich/Sadoff xv–xvi).

However, "[w]ithin the interstices of popular culture, a rich collective counter-memory carries on the tasks of historical thinking in new and significant ways" (Lipsitz 231). And "[i]t is not professional history that will shape historical consciousness in the future but the yet-to-be-defined relationship between its own highly specialized representational strategies and the unconstrained profusion of popular histories" (Harlan 108). Overall, "other cultural, but non-academic, practices of 'sense formation'" are "equally important forms of human orientation and self-understanding (in their general function not much different from the efforts of academic thought itself)" (Rüsen, "Preface" xii). The past is "very much alive," although it "has many mansions." (Rosenzweig/Thelen 180). One can draw from that that "[t]o live the past as part of the present in everyday life might be construed as a burden of unfinished suffering and grief or a rich experience of sustained meaning, emotion and connection with the achievements of one's predecessors, and with their contribution to the making of oneself and one's world"

(Middleton/Woods 32). And that "the desire to connect to history, the impulse to pose present problems in historical terms, and the assertion of a temporal and social reality beyond one's own immediate experience pervade popular culture in significant ways" (Lipsitz 36).

The authors of the new historical fiction implicitly present their findings as relevant and no threat to academic history; rather, they claim that academic history has ignored the changing role of history in contemporary culture (Middleton/Woods 32). There is "a need for the two forms of historicism to engage in a dialogue, rather than for the scholars to treat populist examples of historical cultural texts as symptoms of an ethical failure of historical awareness" (Middleton/Woods 30). The fact that David Lowenthal adopts the title of a historical novel for his study *The Past Is a Foreign Country* (1985) proves that "[h]istorical literature must be of some help if it can provide an image which a historian can take seriously" (Middleton/Woods 23). Or, as White has it, "history is no less a form of fiction than the novel is a form of historical representation" (*Tropics* 122; see also Carnes 15–16). Where do we draw the line, then, or is it really necessary to draw it? Jerome de Groot's *Consuming History: Historians and Heritage in Contemporary Popular Culture* (2009) explores exactly "the blurring of the lines between professional historians and others who 'access' the past" (1) by taking into focus historical presentations of new media as part of the "'virtual turn' in historiography" (2).

The new historical fiction as a phenomenon of popular history has a specific function. Undeniably, "[t]he idea that 'all history is fiction' led to a new interest in fiction as history" (Byatt, *Histories* 38). These "unconventional histories" (Brian Fay) have "the capacity both to deepen and enrich academic history" (Harlan 110). The best of them "can reveal new conceptual resources and novel forms of representation that might be useful in deepening the possibilities of history as a discipline" (Brian Fay 2–3). Historical fiction can "yield both a historical lesson and a worthwhile reading experience," it is "valuable both aesthetically and educationally," and when "[r]ead prior to or simultaneously with a history text, it can provide a base for historical study of an era" (Adamson, *Recreating* xi, xxi). More generally, "the sense of history is the result of a highly compounded input of perceptions and impressions, to which art should be added, since art plays a significant if often neglected role for the formation of the historical awareness" (Sauerberg 59).

There is "a considerable degree of functional overlapping between … historical and fictional texts" (Sauerberg 97). It is the task of the historical novelist "to fill the gaps in received knowledge with events and characters absent from but not incompatible with the known records" (Sauerberg 61). The claim that "[l]iterature becomes redundant when it tells us what can be gleaned from other documentary sources" (LaCapra, *History* 126) is challenged by the fact that "literary works make felt the world which they represent in ways that set them apart ... from 'ordinary,' non-literary texts" (Mathijsen, trans. in Pieters 4). Literary works provide an insight into "a society's basic conflicts and obsessions" (Mathijsen, trans. in Pieters 4). Historical novels not only "confirm, modify or deepen the knowledge derived from other, non-literary historical sources, they also 'translate' this knowledge into a shape that is often more appealing and even touching, in the sense that the feeling of authenticity surrounding the subject is heightened" (Mathijsen, trans. in Pieters 4). In short, literature and especially historical novels reveal the often conjured-up "truth of the human heart" (Hawthorne, *House* 1), or they give us a "touch of the real" (Greenblatt).

1.7 The Illusion of Veracity

The historical novel can certainly be deemed the popular book of the late twentieth and early twenty-first centuries. Readers propel the most interesting and entertaining texts of this kind to the best-seller lists. There is a host of publications aimed at readers who long for assistance in navigating the broad field of historical fiction. Some of these are Daniel S. Burt's *What Historical Novel Do I Read Next?* (1997), Vandelia VanMeter's *America in Historical Fiction: A Bibliographic Guide* (1997), Lynda G. Adamson's *American Historical Fiction* (1999), and Johnson's *Historical Fiction: A Guide to the Genre* (2005). But why are readers so strongly drawn to historical fiction? The example of a class on historical fiction and film yields some insights. In their responses to an online class summary, students at Central Oregon Community College were mainly concerned with the question of historical accuracy. One student wrote: "I enjoyed watching *Braveheart*, but am not sure that much of the movie is based upon actual history. I decided to write my paper about this movie because I wanted to see how much was truth and how much was make-believe" (Agatucci). And another student claimed:

> Much discussion was spent on whether *Huck Finn* is historical fiction or not. Some of the students in class felt very strongly that it is *not* historical fiction. I however think it is. It is a book set in the author's past with historical events. The places and the characters may not be true, but the general idea of what Jim and Huck went through are real. There were slaves back in that time and it is quite possible there could have been an abused little boy that lived at the same time. The idea of it is not so far fetched. Just because the story does not have to do with a war that took place or the rise of a nation, does not mean it is automatically disqualified as historical fiction.
>
> (Agatucci)

What both students articulate here is symptomatic of what the general audience might be looking for in the historical genre. Recipients are searching for truth. But truthfulness in creating and reflecting a historical era is something different from the truth, or the historical truth. Still, the promise of learning the truth seems to be the main motivation to peruse historical fiction. Readers of historical novels are on a quest for the truth of the past.

More often than not, historical novels are based on a true story. In a world void of any fixed handholds, readers feel they might at least learn the truth about the past from their vantage point in the present. The literary phenomenon of "the turn to history at the end of the twentieth century signals this desire to rediscover meaning, to make sense of the Void, in a way that potentially avoids the mistakes of the past" (Elias, *Sublime* 47–48). Historical accuracy is an important issue for readers. Burt, in his reader's guide, dedicates a separate category of each entry to the historical accuracy of the discussed novel. Johnson, in her guidebook, even commits a whole chapter to "Determining Historical Accuracy" (*Historical* 9). She lists bibliographies, author's notes, epilogues, genealogical tables, glossaries, photographs, diagrams, maps, and footnotes as indicators of how well-researched a novel is (9–10), and calls these elements "reader aids" (9) provided by the author to determine historical correctness. These are "paratexts," a term coined by Gérard Genette which labels "liminal devices and conventions both within the book (peritext) and outside it (epitext), that mediate the book to the reader: titles and subtitles, pseudonyms, forewords, dedications, epigraphs, prefaces, intertitles, notes, epilogues, and afterwords – all those framing elements" (Macksey xviii). Genette's own description of the function of paratexts is illuminating:

> [T]he paratext is what enables a text to become a book and to be offered as such to its readers and, more generally, to the public. More than a boundary or a sealed border, the paratext is, rather, a *threshold*, ... or, as Philippe Lejeune put it, "a fringe of the printed text which in reality controls one's whole reading of the text." Indeed, this fringe, always the conveyor of a commentary that is authorial or more or less legitimated by the author, constitutes a zone between text and off-text, a zone not only of transition but also of *transaction*: a privileged place of a pragmatics and a strategy, of an influence on the public, an influence that – whether well or poorly understood and achieved – is at the service of a better reception for the text and a more pertinent reading of it (more pertinent, of course, in the eyes of the author and his allies).
>
> (Paratexts 1–2)

Historical novels, no matter how true to fact, are, after all, novels – a genre identification which accounts for the inherent fictionalization.

Some novelists consciously deceive their audience by on the one hand making use of extensive prefaces and epilogues to document their research and on the other classifying the work as a novel, by on the one hand using narrative devices that should be reserved for fiction writing and on the other claiming authenticity by using historical documents and firsthand accounts. One cannot help but suspect that some of these writers wallow in their power to play with their audience in a deliberate, postmodern way. But readers crave reality references as "verification possibility" (Sauerberg 97). Johnson asserts apropos the reading experience that "historical novel readers ... believe that authors should make their best attempt to ensure their work is historically accurate .... Frequent historical novel readers tend to be quite unforgiving of obvious mistakes, because they can cast doubt on the author's overall research" ("What"). This is a statement that underlines the general impression that readers are drawn to historical novels because they are looking for truth and authenticity. But the historical novel should not be mistaken for history – first and foremost it is fiction.

Assuring the reader of the authenticity of the story is a topos as old as the genre of the novel itself. Most historical novels abound with implicit and explicit claims for authenticity, "to such a degree even, that for fear of libel lawsuits publishers of fiction will allow publication only if the narrative is preceded by the disclaimer formula which dissociates the characters and action of the novel from historical events and figures" (Sauerberg 97). Among the most common devices the early practitioners of the genre used to give their writing the touch of truthfulness was the reference to an old manuscript. For example, in *Hobomok* (1824), Child has her male narrator persona claim that his writing is only an update of an "old, worn-out manuscript" written by an "ancestor," which he "accidentally" came across but with which he takes "the liberty of substituting [his] own expressions for [the other's] antiquated and almost unintelligible style" (6–7). The best-known of these claims is Hawthorne's reference to an alleged manuscript in the introductory chapter to *The Scarlet Letter* (1850), "The Custom House," titled after the place of its supposed discovery. He points directly to the problematic truthfulness of historical fiction, and although inventing the legend of the old manuscript, nevertheless puts emphasis on his debt to fiction:

> [I]t should be borne carefully in mind, that the main facts of that story are authorized and authenticated by the document of Mr. Surveyor Pue. The original papers, together with the scarlet letter itself, – a most curious relic, – are still in my possession, and shall be freely exhibited to whomsoever, induced by the great interest of the narrative, may desire a sight of them. I must not be understood as affirming, that, in the dressing up of the tale, and imagining the motives and modes of passion that influenced the

characters who figure in it, I have invariably confined myself within the limits of the old Surveyor's half a dozen sheets of foolscap. On the contrary; I have allowed myself, as to such points, nearly or altogether as much license as if the facts had been entirely of my own invention. What I contend for is the authenticity of the outline. (26)

Melville's *Israel Potter* (1855), on the other hand, is spun off from an actually existing text, *Life and Remarkable Adventures of Israel R. Potter* (1824). Melville declares in his preface "To His Highness the Bunker-Hill Monument" that he has taken some liberties with this model and even with historical facts:

> [T]his performance ... with the change in the grammatical person, ... preserves, almost as in a reprint, Israel Potter's autobiographical story. Shortly after his return in infirm old age to his native land, a little narrative of his adventures, forlornly published on sleazy gray paper, appeared among the peddlers, written, probably, not by himself, but taken from his lips by another .... [T]his blurred record is now out of print. From a tattered copy, ... the present account has been drawn, ... with the exception of some expansions, and additions of historic and personal details, and one or two shiftings of scene, ... in its general fidelity to the main drift of the original narrative. (v–vi)

Melville consistently ends his preface by signing as "The Editor" (vi), not as the author of the novel. Other authors of historical fiction in the nineteenth century use different metafictional strategies of narration to persuade their readership of the authenticity of their tale. Cooper's *The Pioneers* (1823) does not really abound with self-reflexive passages, but in a few instances the author-narrator addresses the recipient directly:

> We have made our readers acquainted with some variety in character and nations, in introducing the most important personages of this legend to their notice: but in order to establish the fidelity of our narrative, we shall briefly attempt to explain the reason why we have been obliged to present so motley a dramatis personae. (96)

While often understood as an author's claim at authenticity, these and similar passages are rather markers for readers to notice the fictionalization of the material. This little excursus has shown that right from the beginning, the authors of the historical romance, though they knew that the genre was calling for authenticity, at the same time put emphasis on the fact that they were writing fiction. Surprisingly, readers tend to notice the hints at truth and authenticity more than the – often only slightly concealed – allusions to fictionalization.

Charles Brockden Brown, seemingly prompted by his fellow authors' claims to authenticity (Engler 29), composed a "concept of the fundamental fictionality of historical representation" (Engler 28), published in his essay "The Difference between History and Romance" (1800):

> History and romance are terms that have never been very clearly distinguished from each other. It should seem that one dealt in fiction, and the other in truth; that one is a picture of the *probable* and certain, and the other a tissue of untruths; that one describes what *might* have happened, and what has *actually* happened, and the other what never had existence.
>
> These distinctions seem to be just; but we shall find ourselves somewhat perplexed, when we attempt to reduce them to practice, and to ascertain, by their assistance, to what class this or that performance belongs.
>
> Narratives, whether fictitious or true, may relate to the processes of nature, or the actions of men. The former, if not impenetrable by human faculties, must be acknowledged to be, hitherto, very imperfectly known. Curiosity is not satisfied with viewing facts in their disconnected state and natural order, but is prone to arrange them anew, and to deviate from present and sensible objects, into speculations on the past or future: it is eager to infer from the present state of things, their former or future condition.
>
> The observer or experimentalist, therefore, who carefully watches, and faithfully enumerates the appearances which occur, may claim the appellation of historian. He who adorns these appearances with cause and effect, and traces resemblances between the past, distant, and future, with the present, performs a different part. He is a dealer, not in certainties, but probabilities, and is therefore a romancer.
>
> (Brown 251)

He argues that historiography is primarily based on speculation, and characterizes fiction as the only activity by which human beings can satisfy their longing for coherence and order (Engler 28). In other words, "truthiness" – "'the quality of preferring concepts or facts one wishes to be true, rather than concepts or facts known to be true'" (Grossman) – is what readers are (unconsciously) looking for, or at least it is what they get. Readers want to be deceived "as long as 'the emotional truth is still there,'" "'[t]he underlying message'" is not distorted. They crave 'true stories,' but there is "no corresponding willingness … to give up the quirky characters and vivid details and sexy twists and pleasing, rounded endings they're used to in fiction" (Grossman). David Shields describes twenty-first-century culture as both "desperate for authenticity and in love with artifice" (5). Contemporary "reality hunger" – also the title of Shields's book – is paired with the desire for 'good stories.' These expectations are met by the hybrid texts of the new historical fiction.

In his preface to *The House of the Seven Gables* (1851), Hawthorne states that the romance "sins unpardonably so far as it may swerve aside from the truth of the human heart," but "has fairly a right to present that truth under circumstances ... of the writer's own choosing or creation" (1). Roughly one and a quarter of a century later, John Barth claims that history in works by contemporary novelists is "a symbol of their real concern, which will be the passions of the human heart and the possibilities of the human language" (191). When reading a historical novel, the reader enters into a deal with the author that the book will convey the truth about a certain time period, but not necessarily accurate facts (Harlan 118). Or, as Middleton and Woods suppose, "[s]ome postmodern novelists and their readers clearly believe that a moral responsibility to the past need not entail uniform and unremitting accuracy" (65). Carol Shields finds this contradiction, inherent to her historical novel *The Stone Diaries* (1993), useful: "[Y]ou are asked this question, 'What is fiction, what's real and what isn't?' and I suppose that is useful to what I want to have happen in this book – the contradiction and correspondence" (qtd. in Joan Thomas 59). As a kind of summary, Peter Freese asserts that "the historical novel is no longer a freakish interloper between two disparate ontological realms, but just one of several possibilities to 're-invent' the past by means of language" ("Doctorow's" 346–47).

In a chapter titled "What Do Readers Look For?", Johnson gives the following ideas about the main appeal of historical fiction, and affirms what has been asserted here about the writer's need to change and amend facts in order to create good fiction:

> This historical frame must be presented as authentically as possible so as not to shatter the illusion, but accuracy in historical facts isn't nearly enough to satisfy readers .... [T]he 'fiction' part of historical fiction adds emotional intensity, something that straight history can't easily provide. The best historical novelists make the history an integral part of the story but weave it in gradually so that readers aren't overwhelmed.
>
> In reading historical novels, readers enjoy immersing themselves in the day-to-day lives and mindsets of people who lived in earlier eras. Readers want to learn firsthand about the hopes and dreams of people who lived long ago, marveling at how different their experiences are from those of people today. At the same time, historical fiction makes the unfamiliar seem familiar. Many novels express the same overarching theme: Despite changes in politics, culture, and religion over the years, human nature doesn't change.

Most important of all, historical novel readers want to be enter-
tained. *They want to be seduced into believing that the historical
world an author creates is real.*

(Historical 5; my emphasis)

The historical novel's potential for illusion is one of its most noteworthy
and distinctive qualities. With regard to contemporary historical fiction,
Meinig distinguishes two kinds of illusions:

> The first group includes the primary illusion which arises from the
> diegetic level and occurs in traditional historical novels. It has to be
> distinguished from the secondary and narrative illusion, which refers
> to illusion created on the extradiegetic level. The second group of
> illusion encompasses the referential illusion, which denotes the
> illusion resulting from the text's reference to elements in the real
> world (again dominant in the realist type of the historical novel), and
> the illusion of experience. The latter refers to a phenomenon readers
> probably enjoy most when reading: the semblance of "living" in the
> reality of the text, identifying with the experiences of the characters.
> In general, historical novels which eschew such strategies and
> destroy illusion, i.e. produce anti-illusion, are more likely to question
> their own rendering of history. (50)

Samuel Taylor Coleridge's dictum of the "willing suspension of disbelief,"
established in his *Biographia Literaria* (1817) – in other words, the
"attitude of mind, whereby the reader allows him- or herself to be
transported to an invented world in the full knowledge that the literary
text will supply no 'true' information about reality" (Nünning/Nünning) –
seems more than ever valid for readers of contemporary historical fiction.

1.8 Nostalgia, Escapism, or Historical Lesson?

The enormous popularity and broad spectrum of historical fiction has
contributed to its overall perception as a form of lowbrow or genre literature (Johnson, *Historical* 2, see also 3). Genre literature is often perceived as a tool for or form of escapism. The historical novel can easily
become a means "for escape into the past as an exotic locale for fantasy
and wish fulfillment" (Burt xiii; see also Rousselot 7). Historical novels
likewise participate in "postmodernism's 'nostalgia mode', creating the
past through the recreation of its surfaces" (King 5). Jean Baudrillard
asserts that "only nostalgia endlessly accumulates," "everything is
equivalent and is mixed indiscriminately in the same morose and funereal
exaltation, in the same retro fascination" (44). This nostalgia is giving
voice to a wish for the past as a time "safely fixed and transformed[,] ...
[t]he past ... turned into icon" (Bigsby, qtd. in Onega 439–40). The

historical novel offers the opportunity for sentimentality for the past and the possibility of avoiding the banality of daily life.

But there is a counter-perspective. A. S. Byatt opposes the notion of historical fiction as mere nostalgia or escapism:

> During my working life as a writer, the historical novel has been frowned on, and disapproved of, both by academic critics and by reviewers. In the 1950s the word "*escapism*" was enough to dismiss it, and the idea conjured up cloaks, daggers, crinolined ladies, ripped bodices, sailing ships in bloody battles.... My sister, Margaret Drabble, in an address to the American Academy of Arts and Letters, spoke out against the "*nostalgia*/heritage/fancy dress/costume drama industry." ... I want to ask, why has history become imaginable and important again? Why are these books *not* costume drama and nostalgia? The renaissance of the historical novel has coincided with a complex self-consciousness about the writing of history itself.
>
> (*Histories* 9; my emphasis)

As has been argued earlier, historical fiction can yield a historical lesson and be a source of knowledge about the past. The new historical fiction can be entertaining as well as educating.

Nostalgia, escapism, or historical lesson – which of its promises makes the historical novel such a durable and enduring genre? One clue to an answer might be the correlation between past and present. Ezra Pound saw the meaning of history as determined by its relevance for the present, when he asserted that the notion of history as synchronicity and a spatial sense of time displace history as chronology: "We do NOT know the past in chronological sequence. It may be convenient to lay it out anesthetized on the table with dates pasted on here and there, but what we know we know by ripples and spirals eddying out from us and from our own time" (Pound 60; see also Kunow, "Making" 181). Modernism's achievement hence was "the discovery of the perspective-quality inherent in history[,] ... the search for a significant past taken from very remote historical contexts that compared favorably with the contemporary reality that so obviously withheld meaning. Thus history was not so much material content as a perspective on contemporaneity" (Kunow, "Making" 182–83). This aligns with Dominick LaCapra's theory of the relationship to the past as dialogic, engaged with voices from the past, the present, and even the future. He labels this phenomenon by the psychoanalytic term "transference" (*History* 72) and formulates the problem as follows: "How should one negotiate transferential relations to the object of study whereby processes active in it are repeated with more or less significant variations in the account of the historians?" ("Representing" 110). The "concept of transference" allows us "to think

[of] the relation to the past as one not of 'objectivity,' not, as he says, as in the historicist's dream 'of recounting the past purely in its own terms and for its own sake' but neither as a total imposition of present concerns on the past – the pitfall of presentism" (Reichardt, "New" 72). Thus, LaCapra's concept "offers a means to thematize the subject position of the historian, to make graspable her or his point-of-view as it emerges as an affective investment in the reconstruction of the past" (Reichardt, "New" 72). It furthers an understanding of the fact that "a skeptical epistemological position *vis à vis* history as well as postmodern forms of narrative are themselves historically situated and imply dimensions of the subject position." (Reichardt, "New" 73). White asserts that "the contemporary historian has to establish the value of the study of the past, not as an end in itself, but as a way of providing perspectives on the present that contribute to the solution of problems peculiar to our own time" (*Tropics* 41). Roy Rosenzweig and David Thelen observe that "the most powerful meanings of the past come out of the dialogue between the past and the present, out of the ways the past can be used to answer pressing current-day questions about relationships, identity, immortality, and agency" (178). Elodie Rousselot argues that the contemporary historical fiction is aimed at "answering the needs and preoccupations of the present" (5).

From these theories, one may draw the conclusion that historical novels also gain their importance from the universality of the topic depicted. This conforms with Johnson's definition of the category of historical fiction she labels "literary": "fiction set in the past ... which emphasizes themes that pertain back to the present ("What"). Johnson here seems to lean on Avrom Fleishman's *The English Historical Novel* (1971), which claims that "[t]he historical novelist writes trans-temporally: he is rooted in the history of his own time and yet can conceive another" (4). Similarly, Middleton and Woods assert that "historical literature ... show[s] a concern with the relation of the past to the present, with where the past is and how it persists in our lives, and how it can be experienced or resisted" (22). The interaction between past and present, "this oscillation[,] is the foundation of the genre" (Meinig 49; see also Humphrey 88–89). In short, there exists "the truism that historical novels are always about the present, the time of writing, as well as the past" (Hodgkin 15). Of course, these statements echo Feuchtwanger, who argues that the historical novelist

> has no other intention than to give expression to his own (contemporary) attitudes and a subjective (but in no sense historical) view of the world, and to do so in a way that these could be perceived directly by the reader. Whenever he chose to use historical wrappings, it was for the purpose of elevating the subject out of the

personal and private realm in order to set it on a platform and achieve a degree of distance.

(qtd. in Burt xiv; see also Adamson, *Recreating* xxi–xxii)

How a culture represents time and space reveals much about its values, priorities, and politics (Elias, *Sublime* 103).

It seems that, in the new historical fiction, "a historical event is depicted and deployed both for its own rich literary and imaginative content and for the parallels and comparisons it evokes with more contemporary or topical concerns.... History can often be evoked ... for the purposes of comparison or contrast" (Sanders 139–40). There is "a critical discomfort with the idea of a static past" (Moore 136). Hutcheon argues: "Postmodern fiction suggests that to re-write or to re-present the past in fiction and in history is, in both cases, to open it up to the present, to prevent it from being conclusive and teleological" (*Poetics* 110). Compare also Lee's statement that "historical fiction, then, is the artistic form that springs from this impulse to give a shape to the past. But it's not JUST to give a shape to the past. It is to bring part of the past ALIVE into the present."

These theoretical considerations may suggest that historical fiction is pointing toward the recurring elements of history, thereby following the somewhat didactic aim of teaching its readers a historical lesson, instead of tending to a sense of escapism and nostalgia. But one must not forget that the topicality of historical fiction cannot simply be equated with the perception of the repetition of history: "While acts of individual and collective reminiscence offer the promise of bridging the hiatus between then and now, it can never be completely erased. Otherwise we would repeat the past" (Kunow/Raussert 11). If at all, it is merely a repetition with variations, a concept introduced by Giambattista Vico, one of the first modern thinkers in the field of philosophy of history, in his *Scienza Nuova* (1725).

1.9 The Appeal of the Nineteenth Century

The predominant amount of new historical fiction features a nineteenth-century *sujet*. A brief look at one guidebook shall justify this statement here. In *What Historical Novel do I Read Next?* (1997), Burt gives lists of the most popular time periods, settings, subjects, and historical figures, based on a corpus of almost 7000 novels, 3338 of which cover a story set in the United States. The United States takes first place among the top ten countries of settings. With 1070 texts, the nineteenth century takes the first place among the top ten centuries, and the top five decades depicted are, in order, the 1860s, 1810s, 1850s, 1910s, and 1870s. Given this general dominance of the nineteenth century, the specific subjects as well as the historical characters that appear in the texts are genuinely nineteenth-century as well. The top five subjects are the American West, followed by fictionalized biographies, Native American, mystery, and the

Civil War. Among the top fifteen historical characters, seven lived during the time period covered by the long nineteenth century: George Washington, Abraham Lincoln, Benjamin Franklin, Ulysses S. Grant, Robert E. Lee, George Armstrong Custer, and Franklin Delano Roosevelt (Burt xxxii–xxxiii). Further scrutiny of other guidebooks (Adamson, *American* 18–188; Adamson, *Recreating* 127–214; Lesher 183–253, 299–325, 371–88) and my own extended research support these findings. The nineteenth century is the dominant field of preoccupation when it comes to historical fiction in the US.

The nineteenth century has generally come into focus in fiction in the English language published around the turn of the twenty-first century. The criticism on British and New English counterparts of the American new historical fiction is drawn upon here to gain some insights. This is not to assert that the flowering of historical fiction portraying the nineteenth century in the United States is just a transplanted British phenomenon. Rather, this is to put emphasis on the convergence and interdependence which mark the development of literary historical fiction in both nations (Scheiding, "James" 189).

The reemergence of interest in the Victorian era in Britain is owed to Margaret Thatcher's and other revivalists' call for a return to Victorian values (Joyce 4–5), a neoconservative stance which will be explored in more detail below (Jay Clayton, *Charles* 23; see also Moore 137). The centennial of the death of Queen Victoria, the monarch whose name terms the age, in 2001 played a crucial part in the renewed attention to the nineteenth century, too. In 1998, Sally Shuttleworth diagnosed in "Natural History: The Retro-Victorian Novel" an "extraordinary popularity in England at the current time of the historical novel (in all its post-modern guises)" and identified that "the reading public has an insatiable appetite for high-brow historical novels" (254). In 2008, Grace Moore still asserted in "Twentieth-Century Re-Workings of the Victorian Novel" that "the reading public continues to devour reinventions of the Victorian" (142). But what is the source of the ongoing attraction of the Victorian period for authors and readers since the 1990s (Shuttleworth 253)?

Shuttleworth, concerned with what she calls the "natural history novel" – "a literary subset of the retro-Victorian novel" (253) – discerns some kind of scientific nostalgia as a reason for the readers' (and authors') interest in the era:

> [P]revalent fears no longer focus on the relationship between man and the animal kingdom, but on the relationship between man and the machine, the human brain and the micro-chip .... Faced with what appear to be frightening technological capabilities with regard to the control of human and animal reproduction, the random mutations of a Darwinian order start to seem quite benign .... While computer circuits flatten out history, transposing temporality into spatiality, a

concatenation of images and fragments of knowledge, the bomb and potential ecological disasters threaten to end all human measure of temporality. The Darwinian order, with its endless vistas of minute changes, and its base within a self-governing natural order, takes on a reassuring, almost sentimental appeal .... Perhaps this is the ultimate key to the current nostalgia for the Darwinian era. For the Victorians there was a decisive crisis of faith, a sense that the world was shaking under them, an ecstatic agony of indecision. For the postmodern era no such form of crisis seems possible, for there are no fixed boundaries of belief. It is an age of "ontological doubt" without any fixed point of faith against which to define itself. Many of the retro-Victorian texts are informed by a sense of loss, but it is a *second order* loss. It is not loss of a specific belief system, but rather the loss of that sense of immediacy and urgency which comes with true existential crisis .... We look back nostalgically not to an age of safe belief, for that holds few attractions for us now, but rather to a point of crisis. It is the intensity of emotion and authenticity of experience at that moment which we long to recapture. (259–60)

In his study *The Articulation of Science in the Neo-Victorian Novel* (2002), Daniel Candel Bormann agrees that the appeal of neo-Victorian fiction lies in the (seeming) accessibility of the science of the time:

[D]uring the Victorian period science was for the last time historical, narrative, easily understandable, part of a common culture, and not the current hocus-pocus of mathematical equations that none but the initiati can comprehend .... As readers of neo-Victorian fiction, this is the true but simplified picture we expect of Victorian science, and this is therefore one of the formulae which may guarantee the commercial success of neo-Victorian fiction.

(14; see also 65–66, 80)

Julie Sanders, in *Adaptation and Appropriation* (2006), similarly argues that

the Victorian era proves ... ripe for appropriation because it throws into sharp relief many of the overriding concerns of the postmodern era: questions of identity; of environmental and genetic conditioning; repressed and oppressed modes of sexuality; criminality and violence; the urban phenomenon; the operations of law and authority; science and religion; the postcolonial legacies of the empire. (129)

In *Inventing the Victorians* (2001), Matthew Sweet, in much the same way, identifies the basis of the possible attraction to the nineteenth century when he asserts that the Victorians "moulded our culture, defined our sensibilities, built a world for us to live in" (231). And most prominently: "Victorian culture was as rich and difficult and complex and pleasurable as our own" (xxiii). The similarity of the nineteenth century to our own century and the revelation that the Victorians "are more like us ... than is commonly supposed" (Kaplan 6) might be the most appealing aspects of historical novels: "Most of the pleasures we imagine to be our own, the Victorians enjoyed first" (Sweet x, see also xxiii). In "Parody as Revisionary Critique" (2004), J. Hillis Miller argues that the late postmodern preoccupation with the nineteenth century satisfies "conservative nostalgia" and "historical curiosity" (135). In their introduction to *Victorian Afterlife* (2000), John Kucich and Dianne F. Sadoff diagnose a "postmodern fixation on the nineteenth-century past ... in which the present imagines itself to have been born and history forever changed" (x) and observe a strong tendency of "postmodernism's privileging of the Victorian as its historical 'other'" (xi) and, more generally, of "the nineteenth century as the essence of the past" (xxviii). Postmodernism seems occupied with a "nostalgic retrospective look at its own origins" (xii). And "major critical texts that claim to have found in the nineteenth century the origins of contemporary consumerism (Baudrillard), sexual science (Foucault), gay culture (Sedgwick et al.), and gender identity (Gilbert and Gubar, Showalter, Armstrong)" abound (xiii–xiv). In *The Victorians in the Rearview Mirror* (2007), Simon Joyce argues that the nineteenth century may be "a period that no longer seems as distant as we might like to think, but instead forms the horizon for many of our pressing debates" (16). Marie-Luise Kohlke subsumes these theses in her assertion that the nineteenth century is today perceived as "a harbinger of our own culture" (7). The Victorian age is viewed as a parallel age to the late twentieth and early twenty-first centuries, or at least as the era in which the current age is rooted.

In the USA, the preoccupation with the nineteenth century is a mirror of the specific position this era holds within the cultural memory of Americans. The era is an age of cultural emergence and of twin characteristics with our own age. Daniel Walker Howe affirms that "[t]he period marked a crucial – probably *the* crucial – transformation of the United States; it was a time of industrialization, knowledge explosion, immigration and vast population growth, urbanization, geographical expansion, changing race relationships, and the greatest armed conflict on American soil" (3). Parish asserts that "Victorian American society was rapidly expanding and highly mobile – and potentially explosive. To live through several decades of its history was to experience an emotional roller-coaster ride. Hope and fear, optimism and pessimism, excitement and frustration, security and insecurity, lived precariously together" (23). The era was equally marked by unity and diversity, continuity and change. Parish summarizes that "Victorian America was widely perceived as the most astonishing success story in the modern world – and for many Americans it was just that. It was also beset by huge problems and challenges, stemming from economic aggrandizement, sectional division, ethnic diversity, racial injustice, sexual discrimination and social inequality" (25). And does not this précis sound all too familiar in the twenty-first century?

Belfer describes the timeliness, or even timelessness, of her historical novel *City of Light* (1999), set at the turn of the twentieth century, in the following way:

> The turn of the century was a time of incredible change and upheaval. The issues which riveted people then turned out to be the same ones which transfix us today: environmentalists battling with industrialists over the control of natural resources; controversies about the application of revolutionary new technologies; the fight of women and African Americans for equality; the question of the private vs. the public morality of presidents.
>
> ("On")

Kohlke adds important further explanations when she interprets the backward glance as part of the current cultural working on trauma:

> Increasingly, the period is configured as a temporal convergence of multiple historical traumas still awaiting appropriate commemoration and full working-through. These include both the pervasive traumas of social ills, such as disease, crime, and sexual exploitation, and the more spectacular traumas of violent civil unrest, international conflicts, and trade wars that punctuated the nineteenth century. With the extended military presence and continuing operations of US and allied forces in Iraq and Afghanistan, this has become a pressing current issue, as the recent strategic interventions resonate powerfully with nineteenth-century Western histories of empire-building, atrocities of colonialism, and the clash of opposing cultures .... Another traumatic legacy intimately linked to the age of industrialization is attracting growing interest, namely the trauma of human engineered ecological disaster, the commodification and destruction of the natural world and its biodiversity, and the resulting alienation of humankind from its environment.
>
> (7–8; see also Kohlke/Gutleben)

The neo-Victorian phenomenon can be seen as a field of trauma studies, which itself has strong links with the field of memory studies:

> For all its occasionally didactic overtones, neo-Victorian trauma writing – whether fiction, faction, or non-fiction – is actively

involved in consciousness-raising and witness-bearing. As such it directly counters and contests charges of de-politicisation, based on a decadent sentimentalism, nostalgia, or spurious liberalism some-times attributed to the neo-Victorian project.

(Kohlke 9)

The new American historical fiction is affected by the traumatic and traumatizing events of the last decades, especially, of course, the cataclysm of the terrorist attacks of 9/11 and its aftermaths.

1.10 Historical Fiction, Memory, and Genre

In 1918, Van Wyck Brooks famously claimed that "[t]he present is a void, and the American writer floats in that void because the past that survives in the common mind of the present is a past without living value. But is this the only possible past? If we need another past so badly, is it inconceivable that we might discover one, that we might even invent one?" He laments what he perceives as the lack of a cultural memory that could provide American writers with a sense of continuity, a sense of being part of a tradition (Virginia Tuttle Clayton 1). In 2005, Astrid Erll and Ansgar Nünning identify a *"mnemonic turn"* (4) as one division of the overall cultural turn in literary studies. The new historical fiction is a genre of specific significance within the field of memory studies. Julijana Nadj describes memory as a "result of retrospective sense-making strategies" (414), and Middleton and Woods call it the "super-highway to the past" (5). Today the past is "widely believed to depend upon memory, personal and social, traumatic and repressed, involuntary and planned" (Middleton/Woods 82). The contemporary historical novel is one of those sense-making strategies and is similarly perceived as a path to historical knowledge. A brief overview of the most significant aspects of the mnemonic turn with regard to historical fiction shall provide another theoretical basis for the analyses of the new American historical novels that will follow.

According to Erll and Nünning, three main branches of the occu-pation with memory can be identified within literary studies: the memory of literature (*"Gedächtnis der Literatur"*), memory in litera-ture (*"Gedächtnis in der Literatur"*), and literature as a medium of memory (*"Literatur als Medium des Gedächtnisses"*) (2). The defining term for the first branch of memory studies, memory of literature, draws on Renate Lachmann's study *Gedächtnis und Literatur: Intertextualität*
in der russischen Moderne (1990) and on her assertion that inter-textuality is the memory of literature (35). This theory paves the way for a study of the diachronic dimension of literature, that is, the rela-tions between works of art and the modes of repetition and updating of

aesthetic forms. Literature is understood either as a system of symbols ("*Symbolsystem*"), of which intertextuality, topoi, and genres are a result, or as a social system ("*Sozialsystem*") in which canon creation and literary historiography are the main forms of a memory of literature, going along with a self-reflexivity of the discipline (Erll/Nünning 2–3; see also Grabes/Sichert).

Intertextuality is one aspect that becomes especially prominent in the discussion of the new historical fiction. Today, the term is marked by a variety of uses and definitions, so that it may as well be seen as a "covering term for all the possible relationships which can be established between texts" (Miscall 44). The origins of the term lie with Mikhail Bakhtin, who insisted on the dialogic nature of language: "Every word is directed toward an *answer* and cannot escape the profound influence of the answering word it anticipates" ("Discourse" 280). Julia Kristeva "textualized" (Polaski 33) Bakhtin's theory: "What allows a dynamic dimension to structuralism is Bakhtin's conception of the 'literary word' as an *intersection of textual surfaces* rather than a *point* (a fixed meaning), as a dialogue among several writings: that of the writer, the addressee (or the character) and the contemporary or earlier context" ("Word" 36). She further coined the term 'intertextuality' and defined it: "Any text is constructed as a mosaic of quotations; any text is the absorption and transformation of another" ("Bounded" 60). Roland Barthes developed the concept of the "echo chamber" (74), which ties in with the notion of intertextuality. According to Barthes, "the text is conceived as an echo chamber in which the echoes of innumerable texts from the whole history of literature intermingle" (Broich 251). Contemporary memory studies has turned the term into one of its buzzwords and deduced from the concept that the present can be conceived as an intertextual echo chamber of cultural history (Nünning, "Moving" 411, see also 408).

The most comprehensive theory of intertextuality to date was developed by Genette in *Palimpsests: Literature in the Second Degree* (1982). He integrates various intertextual techniques in a poetics of "*transtextuality*" (1) and establishes five main categories: intertextuality, paratextuality, metatextuality, hypertextuality, and architextuality. Intertextuality means "a relationship of copresence between two texts or among several texts: ... the actual presence of one text within another" (1–2). Forms of intertextuality are "*quoting*," "*plagiarism*," and "*allusion*" (2). As mentioned previously, "a title, a subtitle, intertitles; prefaces, postfaces, notices, forewords, etc.; marginal, infrapaginal, terminal notes; epigraphs; illustrations; blurbs, book covers, dust jackets, and many other kinds of secondary signals" are "*paratext*[s]" (3). Metatextuality is the commentary within a text on other texts, "the *critical* relationship par excellence" (4). Hypertextuality is "any relationship uniting a text B (... the *hypertext*) to an earlier text A (... the hypotext), upon which it is grafted in a manner that is not that of commentary" (5). Architextuality labels inherent allusions to generic affiliations, while "determining the generic status of the text" (4) is the task of the recipient (1–7; see also Macksey xviii–xix; Scheiding, "Intertextualität," 56). Of the five types, intertextuality and paratextuality are the most significant categories with regard to the new historical fiction and its function as a reservoir of memory, while hypertextuality is an especially useful concept in considering one type of new historical fiction: reanimated classics.

Genre memory and memory genre, or the genre of memory ("'*Gattungsgedächtnis*' und '*Gedächtnisgattung*,'" Erll/Nünning 3; see also Humphrey), are also catchwords of this first branch of memory studies. In their introduction to *Genres as Repositories of Cultural Memory* (2000), Hendrik van Gorp and Ulla Musarra-Schroeder assert that

> literary history manifests itself largely as an echoing of former texts. Cultural memory, thus, often takes the form of specific or generic "intertextuality." … Since texts are themselves embedded in and referring, although indirectly, to a specific social cultural situation (*imitatio naturae/rerum*), new texts are recalling, in another context, the former situation (*imitatio veterum*). (iii)

Drawing on Elisabeth Wesseling's *Writing History as a Prophet* (1991) (18), they argue that genres "play an important role in activating cultural memory" (Gorp/Musarra-Schroeder i). Middleton and Woods maintain in *Literatures of Memory* (2000) that "literary genre is a technique of social memory – textual memory is at work in the invention of new genres and the transformation of old" (7).

The concept of cultural memory was formulated mainly by Aleida and Jan Assmann, building on Maurice Halbwachs's theories in *La mémoire collective* (1950; published in English as *On Collective Memory*, 1980). The concept is explained in Jan Assmann's *Das kulturelle Gedächtnis* (1997), where he defines most clearly what is to be understood by the term 'cultural memory,' namely an outer dimension of human memory (19–20; see also "Kollektives" 15). Gorp and Musarra-Schroeder define cultural memory as

> our capacity … to remember in a present situation "things" (human experiences, individual and collective attitudes, and discussions, reflected in any document) that in the past have been "relevant" to us as far as our cultural identity, our roots and our self-image are concerned and as far as their memory helps us to "solve" some problems we are confronted with. (ii)

Jon Thiem more specifically explains his understanding of cultural memory with regard to the past, historiography, and identity:

The origin of cultural memory (CM) lies in the painful recognition that we have lost the past, and that to know who we are we need to regain it. The loss of the past is cultural amnesia. Among the postmodern causes of this otherwise perennial condition are the mobility of populations and their loss of an organic sense of place; the destruction of inherited landscapes and historical settlements; the deconstruction of the belief that the past is knowable; and the reduction of the past to simulacra.

Born of the human longing for the past, CM is a response to the cultural amnesia of our time, and to the failure of historiography, traditionalism, or poststructuralism to deliver a usable past.

Cultural memory is a conscious process of retrieval, of pasts that are lost, forgotten or disappearing. CM differs from traditionalism by being critical and modern. It differs from historiography by being intensely personal. The term itself divides into "culture", which is collective, public, and "memory", which insinuates a personal, psychological factor. (422–23)

According to Gorp and Musarra-Schroeder, certain genres, especially historical fiction and (auto)biographical writing, are repositories for cultural memory (iii), or memory genres (Wodianka 184; see also Erll, "Gedächtniskonzepte" 219). The "postmodern historical novel … functions as a sort of 'library' or 'museum' in which culture is stocked for further use and reuse, with the awareness that our memory should also be concerned with the many possibilities in history which have not been realized" (Gorp/Musarra-Schroeder v). The new historical fiction, with its revisionist and identity-constructing impetus, must be understood as a genre of cultural memory.

The second branch of memory studies, memory in literature, is concerned with the depiction or representation of memory in literary works. Literature can be understood as a representation of remembering and memory (Wodianka 184). A differentiation exists here between the literary thematization and staging of individual and collective memory (Erll/Nünning 4). To Middleton and Woods, "collective memory, social memory and cultural memory" all define the same kind of memory, a memory that "is not just a passive or unconscious accumulation by a social group, or a kind of shared weather; it requires organized activity, conscious reflection and sustained social interaction" (85).

The aspects that influence the literary staging of individual memory include, for example, "the representation of time, the semantization of place, narrative mediation, aspects of focalization" (Basseler/Birke 123). What is especially interesting here with regard to the new historical fiction is the use of various forms of analepsis (Genette, *Narrative* 52, 62), of chronotope (Bakhtin, "Forms"), and of narrative perspective, especially metanarrative devices and the rhetoric of memory ("*Rhetorik der*

Erinnerung"; Löschnigg), or the "mimesis of memory" ("*Mimesis des Erinnerns*"; Basseler/Birke).

In contemporary fiction, the "interface between memory and identity has become a dominant thematic concern" (Neumann 149). Middleton and Woods claim that "memory is a ground of identity" (11); according to Rüsen, identity is shaped, even constructed by memory ("*Identität wird gestaltet, ja konstruiert durch Erinnerung*"; "Einleitung" 22); and Birgit Neumann asserts that remembering has a "fictionalizing nature" (149); while to Michel Foucault, "[c]ontinuous history is the indispensable correlative of the founding function of the subject" (13). Behind these theories is the "idea that personal identity depends upon the ability to tell a coherent narrative of one's history based on personal memory" (Middleton/ Woods 94). The "constructive aspects of memories and the essential role of narration in the construction of identities" (Neumann 149, see also 155: "*Identitätsarbeit ... ist ... stets Narrationsarbeit*") suggest a "role of literary narratives in forging individual as well as collective memories and identities" (Neumann 149). Although Nadj makes the assertion with regard to fictional metabiographies, I believe the point of view that these texts "highlight the assumption that memories are actively constructed" (414) can be adopted for the new historical fiction.

Literature can be viewed as part of the individual and collective endowment of meaning. Especially many contemporary novels become part of the memory culture by staging memory and identity in its individual and collective dimension, using their fictional freedom. This capacity has already earned them the label "*fictions of memory*" (Nünning, "Editorial"). This ambiguous term designates the fictionality of both the texts and the memories that are staged within them, as well as the fictions of the past that are generated by memory. It is a term that may also be applied to the new historical fiction discussed in this study, as especially the revisionism of the contemporary historical novel is concerned with the representation of previously neglected experiences (Neumann 164). Individual memory is often staged in homodiegetic narratives, in which a tension is created between the remembered and remembering I. The remembering I constitutes its identity in a dialogue with its past self. Collective memory is often explored in narratives that are told or focalized from various perspectives, that have multiple perspectives and are polyvocal. Thus, literary texts can contribute to the stabilization of collective identities and established value systems as well as question obsolete images of the past and perpetuate alternative versions of memory (Neumann 151, 163–64, 166–68, 171).

The new historical fiction also often depicts sites of memory, or, in Pierre Nora's term, *lieux de mémoire*. According to Nora, "a *lieu de mémoire* is any significant entity, whether material or non-material in nature, which by dint of human will or the work of time has become a symbolic element of the memorial heritage of any community" (xvii).

Lieux de mémoire can be geographical places, historical or mythical personages, buildings or historical monuments, or texts. The new historical fiction makes use of such sites of memory, as well as being itself able to create them. Or, as Kohlke asserts apropos the neo-Victorian novel,

> [i]n a sense, writers and critics and their works become alternative "sites of memory" ... ; that is, they enlarge "the scope of collective memory" by producing alternative "sources" and "traces," generating different kinds of conceptual archives, be they fictional or factual, to act as conduit of and to the nineteenth-century past for current and future generations. (13)

The third branch of memory studies understands literature as a medium of (collective) memory, displaying its "constructive, world- (and memory-)making nature" (Erll, "Literatur" 249; see also Goodman; Rozett). As such, it fulfills various functions in cultures of remembrance, such as (re-)creating versions of the past, circulating images of the past, and establishing collective identities (Erll/Nünning 5; Erll, "Literatur"). In literary memory studies, the historical novel is explicitly identified as a medium of collective memory or of cultural memory and historical signification (Nünning, *Fiktion I* 114; Erll, "Literatur" 249). Astrid Erll describes the twofold nature of literature as a medium of collective memory as follows: "First, it is an important *cadre médial* for individuals remembering in a socio-cultural context. Second, as far as the 'memory' of groups and societies is concerned, literature serves as a medium which stores ('cultural texts') and circulates ('collective texts') information to be culturally remembered" ("Literatur" 249).

Aleida Assmann developed the idea of cultural texts, a term with which she connotes all forms of texts of canonic and therefore cultural status. Of all literary works a culture produces and preserves, only some are received as cultural texts. They mediate concepts of cultural, national, or religious identity as well as collective values and norms. Overall, the reception of cultural texts is marked by enshrinement, repeated study, and rapture ("*Verehrung, wiederholtes Studium und Ergriffenheit*"; Aleida Assmann 242). The reception of such texts assures the recipient's belonging to a collective. An unreserved identification with the narrated story goes along with an acquisition of knowledge about provenience and identity, norms and values, and the search for truth. Cultural texts outlast trends because they mediate authoritative, irreducible, and timeless truth ("*verbindliche, unhintergehbare und zeitlose Wahrheit*"; Aleida Assmann 242). Therefore, the Bible is the paradigmatic cultural text (Erll, "Literatur" 260–62). In American studies, the nineteenth-century classics or originals that one type of new historical fiction, reanimated classics, builds upon are cultural texts, too.

Hawthorne's *The Scarlet Letter* (1850), Melville's *Moby-Dick* (1851), and Twain's *The Adventures of Huckleberry Finn* (1885) are texts that meet all the requirements mentioned, from enshrinement to the mediation of national identity and the conveyance of truth. Cora Kaplan, in her *Victoriana: Histories, Fictions, Criticism* (2007), in a somewhat similar stance draws on Sigmund Freud and adopts his concept of the "mnemic symbol" (7), defined as "a memorial or narrative that embodies and elicits a buried psychic conflict which cannot be resolved in the present" (7), for her discussion of Charlotte Brontë's *Jane Eyre* (1847) as a "popular icon" (7). This theory might as well be adopted for an identification of the corpus of texts Assmann labels cultural.

'Collective texts' is a category for literary texts that create, put into perspective, and circulate collective memory, that is, versions of the past, images of history, and concepts of identity. Literary texts that qualify as collective texts are, for example, historical novels such as Scott's *Waverley* (1814). Often, collective texts are part of the popular culture and not highbrow works of art. The defining aspect of a collective text is its reference to reality. This real-world reference must be bestowed upon such a text through its reception. Although literary theory points toward the difference between fictional and real worlds, the strategies of reception employed by empiric communities of interpretation transcend the theoretically postulated gap between fiction and reality. Literary texts thereby also shape versions of reality and of the past of a memory culture. But readers do not mistake historical fiction for historiography. For example, when it comes to autobiographies, readers tend to reject texts that too freely experiment with fictionalization. The literary text is received as literature, but at the same time an ascription of referentiality occurs. The reference is to the meaning-giving perimeter of the contemporary collective memory, a reality which already is symbolically condensed, narratively structured, and overwritten by genre paradigms. Collective texts convey truth in the sense of collective memory (Erll, "Literatur" 262–64). The American revisionist historical fiction discussed in this study meets all the requirements of collective texts.

Cultural artifacts can be models for and of reality, correlating with the functions of collective texts as memory formation and memory reflection ("*Gedächtnis*bildung *und Gedächtnis*reflexion"; Erll, "Literatur" 265). In terms of memory formation (models for memory, "Modelle *für* Gedächtnis"; Erll, "Literatur" 266), Erll differentiates between two functions: on the one hand, there is the affirmation or intensification of existing conceptions in a given memory culture; on the other hand, there is their deconstruction or revision. The role the teleological and progressive concept of history displayed in many nineteenth-century historical novels played in the creation of a national identity and a cultural memory in the United States is one example of the first possible function of collective texts in terms of memory formation. Such a "capacity for identity building" (Meinig 362) points toward such notions as Benedict Anderson's "imagined communities" and Hobsbawm's "invention of tradition," but also holds some problematic aspects, as Ricoeur remarks: "The problem is not unimportant in so far as the individual nationalisms, whose growths we deplore, actually set great store by common memories, which supposedly endow a collective identity with a profile, an ethnic, cultural or religious identity" (*Rätsel* 78, trans. in Meinig 362). The contemporary revisionist historical fiction is an example of the second possible function, as these texts create a counter-memory by depicting the memory of marginalized groups or by staging self-perceptions and moral values in opposition to those of the dominating memory culture. Collective texts can become media of memory reflection (models of memory, "*Modelle* von *Gedächtnis*"; Erll, "Literatur" 266) if they depict processes and problems of the memory culture. A large number of contemporary historical novels reflect upon history and memory. The spectrum ranges from the staging of an acquisition of an identity creating a past, in metahistorical novels, to the explicit thematization of the constructed nature and perspectivity of historiography, in historiographic metafiction. In the new historical fiction, memory formation and memory reflection do not preclude each other, although a specific novel will more often than not display a predominance of one or the other of those functions of collective texts (Erll, "Literatur" 265–67, see also 269).

Another aspect that is not addressed by other scholars with respect to the mnemonic turn, but to me seems to tie in with the discussion of literary memory studies, is that of the hybridity of the new historical fiction. The term 'hybridity' is today mainly used to refer to intercultural encounters, explicated in the critical cultural-studies theories of Homi K. Bhabha. When applied to literature, it may as well be understood as depicting how ideas are "repeated, relocated and translated in the name of tradition" (Bhabha, "Cultural" 207). Hybridity describes a "blend, fusion, or compound of influences at the level of both language and form" (Sanders 161). In American historiographic metafiction, "[a]s is characteristic of the postmodern condition in general, the blurring of the traditional border lines between fact and fiction, between historiography and literature, is accompanied by a blurring of genres as well as of the traditional hierarchies between 'high' and 'low' art" (Kurt Müller 49–50). Malcolm Bradbury's diagnosis of the British novel holds true for the new American historical fiction, too: one finds "generic crossovers, crossing of borders, easy passage between the high and the popular forms, or the literary and the media arts" (*British* 344). There is a "breakdown of the conventional borders of genre and narrative type" (407).

It can be claimed that "it is exactly this hybrid quality of the genre that has so occupied the fascination of both readers and authors since its rise in the 19th century" (Engler/Müller 9). Most of the contemporary novels discussed here are genre hybrids, as they merge or combine under the capacious umbrella of historical fiction several other genres. Jameson points toward this aspect, but sees "the randomness and confusion of generic messages today as one of the signs that the postmodern has forgotten how to think historically" (Jay Clayton, *Charles* 42). He puts forward that "the movement from one generic classification to another is radically discontinuous, like switching channels on a cable television set; and indeed it seems appropriate to characterize the strings of items and the compartments of genres ... as so many 'channels' into which the new reality is organized" (Jameson, *Postmodernism* 373). Accordingly, Hutcheon asserts that "[t]he borders between literary genres have become fluid" (*Poetics* 9). Wai Chee Dimock recognizes genre "less as a law, a rigid taxonomic landscape, and more as a self-obsoleting system" (73). She further states that "bending and pulling and stretching are unavoidable, for what genre is dealing with is a volatile body of material, still developing, still in transit, and always on the verge of taking flight in some unknown and unpredictable direction" (74). Lynda G. Adamson similarly claims that "[to] say that a book of historical fiction belongs in a specific genre can be constraining and misleading. War stories can be romances, and romances can be mysteries or adventures. Therefore, a book may have more than one genre that fits its content" (*American* viii). She names as many as twenty-nine genres (although some are debatable as proper genres) that are covered by American historical fiction (viii–ix).

This postmodern, playful use of genres is an important recourse to the nineteenth century. Many of the genres that the new historical fiction combines, as well as the historical novel itself, have their roots in or experienced a first apex in this era: "[T]he Victorian era offer[s] a diverse range of genres and methodologies to examine and appropriate" (Sanders 122). Andrea Kirchknopf therefore asserts for post-Victorian novels that

> [t]hey imitate prevalent genres of the nineteenth century, such as the Bildungsroman, or the social, industrial and sensation novels, creatively intermingled with conventions of the (auto)biographical and (pseudo)historical novels, thus creating a hybridity of genres abundant in parody and pastiche so characteristic of postmodern novelistic discourse. (54)

Elias, who is concerned with the American scene, likewise confirms the similarities between postmodern historical fiction and examples of the first flowering of the historical novel: "Postmodern historical fiction stands in the refracted light of nineteenth-century historical novels, and much that has been claimed as groundbreaking postmodernist historical experimentation was nascent in these works" (*Sublime* 6).

The phenomenon of the generic transgression of historical fiction is twofold: first, boundaries of factual and fictional writing are blurred in general. Then specific genre norms of various subgenres of the novel (and of fiction in general) are mixed to create a new genre hybrid.

A claim that was made with regard to the retro-Victorian novel can be adopted for the new historical novel: it "is not a new genre, it is the novel of all genres, the composite novel of its epoch, which highlights the cannibalizing, ever-broader, all-encompassing and all-assimilating nature of the novel" (Gutleben 223). In order to identify and tentatively label this function of the new historical fiction in the light of memory studies, I will call it multi- or poly-genre memory.

1.11 The Neoconservative, the Liberal, the Identitarian, and the Postmodern

In his study *Charles Dickens in Cyberspace: The Afterlife of the Nineteenth Century in Postmodern Culture* (2003), Jay Clayton raises a number of interesting questions concerning the future of cultural studies and the part the past might play in it. In an introductory chapter, "The Past in the Future of Cultural Studies: Crystal Palace to Millennium Dome," he outlines four general attitudes toward the past – or, more specifically, toward the nineteenth century – that today shape the cultural-studies arena (11–49): the neoconservative, the liberal, the identitarian, and the postmodern. Each of these attitudes reflects a larger position in present discourses and expresses an inherent cultural politics (23).

Victorian neoconservatism creates a linear narrative that is generally based on the premise of degeneration and regression: "Ethical in tone and intent, it holds up the nineteenth century as an admonishment to our wayward times and calls for a return to once-cherished ideals" (Jay Clayton, *Charles* 23). I believe such an uncritical or unbalanced stance toward the past might as well be called nostalgia, or amnesia, depending on which point of view one prefers. Neoconservatives certainly concentrate only on the values and virtues of the age, not on its drawbacks and downsides. They claim philosophical lineage from Edmund Burke. Clayton cites Gertrude Himmelfarb as the major exponent of the neoconservative cultural politics. Other seminal figures of the neoconservative position are Margaret Thatcher and Newt Gingrich.

The liberal branch of the current vogue for nineteenth-century culture "invokes a universal conception of culture as a repository of timeless truths that retain their importance regardless of the historical period. The liberal position uses culture as a touchstone with which to measure out praise or blame impartially to both yesterday and today" (Jay Clayton, *Charles* 23). Claiming Matthew Arnold as their "tutelary spirit" (23), contemporary representatives of this attitude are Martha Nussbaum and Eugene Goodheart. The liberals study nineteenth-century cultural products, drawing insights of universal significance from them, believing them to be equally valid in our age.

Both neoconservatives and liberals "end up relying on similar conceptions of the historian's task, which they see as that of producing a continuous unified account of how the present has emerged from the past" (Jay Clayton, *Charles* 23). Unified visions of the past, such as the neoconservative and the liberal, lack an "awareness of the contradictory legacies cultural objects can bestow" (24); they neglect historical difference. Identitarian and postmodern attitudes toward the nineteenth century, on the contrary, reject a unified vision of history.

Identitarianism views the past in terms of conflict and division. Areas of such dissection and partition in the nineteenth century are "race, nationality, class, gender, sexuality, age, disability, religious convictions, and more" (Jay Clayton, *Charles* 25). The identitarians favor a multicultural view and study alternative traditions and counter-histories. Clayton's own approach is similar to that of identitarian Victorianism.

Postmodern attitudes toward the past "challenge the very project of history itself" (Jay Clayton, *Charles* 25). What results is the already-mentioned adage about the end of history, drawn from theories by Foucault and Jacques Derrida, or from Francis Fukuyama and Baudrillard, who argued that the historical experience is no longer possible. Other exponents of this view, like Elizabeth Ermarth and Keith Jenkins, similarly diagnose a disappearance of history or question the usability of the past: "Given this position, it is no surprise that few postmodern approaches to nineteenth-century history exist" (25).

Identitarian and postmodern cultural-studies approaches to the past also have their pitfalls. The identitarian approach risks reliance on subjective experiences as general foundations of knowledge:

> Critics need to be wary of turning the personal into a foundation for monolithic counterhistory. Writing history from the perspective of formerly excluded subjects has done much to challenge received versions of the past. It has helped remedy one-sided, even discriminatory historical accounts. Ultimately, though, many alternative histories mirror, in their essentialism and their assumption of unproblematic referentiality, the very normative discourse that they aim to contest.
>
> (Jay Clayton, *Charles* 26)

The postmodern position toward the past is criticized because of its challenge to the disciplinary norms of historiography and its claim that there is no difference between fiction and historiography, thus blurring the status of genres.

I believe the four cultural-studies attitudes toward the past that Clayton outlines can be traced in the various approaches of the new historical fiction. The neoconservative stance emerges in historical novels that put emphasis on nostalgia and try to teach a historical lesson. The liberal view informs texts that portray events in the past as anthropological constants and the present as a repetition of the past. The identitarian position toward the nineteenth century coincides with the revisionist impetus of much of the new historical fiction. The postmodern attitude can be found in the metafictional level of the new historical fiction that questions the validity of historical representations in various ways. Overall, the new historical fiction never adheres to only one of these attitudes toward the past. More often than not, the historical novel at the turn of the twenty-first century is a display of or an exercise in two, three, or all of these positions. When Clayton declares that a "double commitment – to historical knowledge and to a self-reflexive perspective on that knowledge – is exactly the cognitive wager at stake in a historical cultural studies" (Jay Clayton, *Charles* 36), this is an apt estimation of the new historical fiction. The historical practice Clayton demands for the future of cultural studies – equally focusing on the anomalous and the analogous when tracing relationships between the past and the present, accounting for continuity and rupture as equally valid parts of historical experience, and adopting alternative modes of writing – seems to have been achieved by the new historical fiction. His call for "[m]ultiple perspectives, intertextuality, self-reflexivity, palimpsest structure, and recursive narratives" as responses "to the complexity of cultural history" (37) is answered by many turn-of-the-twenty-first-century American historical novelists. Indeed, Clayton asserts that often the most adequate response to the past lies in the methods of literature, which "can respond ... not only cognitively but also formally by embodying recurrence in a self-reflexive structure" (40). He calls for "[w]riting that enacts the cultural phenomenon it analyzes" (44) and constructs his own study accordingly. For example, when Clayton ends his introductory chapter, he refers first to the Victorian story of Joseph Paxton, the garden boy of humble origins, lacking formal schooling, who grew up to become the architect of the Crystal Palace of the Great Exhibition in London in 1851 and was knighted for his achievements. His second story is the interpretation of an illustration in *Punch* from 1851, which shows an Englishman in a winter garden. Clayton's interpretation of the illustration is that the cultivator of flowers embodies the national spirit. The third story is almost fully made up by Clayton and only sets out from a historical detail, the fact that shortly before his death, Paxton was taken once more to the flower show at the Crystal Palace. Clayton now imagines a wholly fictional tableau in which the dying old man, in a wheelchair, sits among the flowers and is soothed by their greenness and the fact that he remembers their names (47–49). What Clayton wants to express here is that all three stories, based on facts or texts to a varying degree, are equally valid, as they are equally factional and fictional at the same time. He concludes his theoretical musings with a statement that in a compelling way may be read not only as a call for new paths in cultural studies but also as a manifesto of the new historical fiction: "A historical cultural studies needs both narrative's power to create a world that can make critique persuasive and narrative's opposite power – its self-reflexive potential – to dramatize the limits of that world" (44).

1.12 Is All New Historical Fiction Historiographic Metafiction?

In *The English Historical Novel* (1971), Avrom Fleishman proclaims that "[e]veryone knows what a historical novel is; perhaps that is why few have volunteered to define it in print" (3). Indeed, most of the studies that discuss the historical novel significantly circumvent or evade defining the term or "abound in difficulty and vagueness" (Meinig 41; see also Nünning, *Fiktion I* 92). This is not too surprising, as it is indeed quite difficult to give an apt, all-encompassing definition of historical fiction (Borgmeier/Reitz 11–14). Nevertheless, I attempt to establish a working definition, or an approximation to one, that fits my corpus of texts. Also, I point toward the pitfalls of the definition, where I am not able to solve its problems within the framework of this study.

It is beyond the scope of this study – and above that an almost impossible task – to outline the results of all prior studies of the historical novel since Georg Lukács's groundbreaking work *The Historical Novel* (1937). This study will therefore give an overview of the scholarly work that has been done during the last couple of years in the field of late-twentieth-century historical fiction. To a large extent, this renders an ab ovo overview futile, as most of the more recent studies are strongly based on and heavily draw on earlier scholarship. I would like to claim also that there is no need to redo here what has already been done well by others. Nünning's seminal work on the historical novel, *Von historischer Fiktion zu historiographischer Metafiktion* (1995), gives a comprehensive overview of the existing definitions (*Fiktion I* 90–104) and a broad research report on the theories of the historical novel (*Fiktion I* 21–41). Further, geographically and temporally wide-ranging studies are Hans Vilmar Geppert's *Der Historische Roman: Geschichte umerzählt – von Walter Scott bis zur Gegenwart* (2009) and Jerome de Groot's *The Historical Novel* (2010).

It is therefore justifiable to be selective and start out directly with a look at Hutcheon's seminal theories. She coined the term 'historiographic metafiction' for "novels that are intensely self-reflexive but that also both re-introduce historical context into metafiction and problematize the entire question of historical knowledge" ("Pastime" 285–86), seeing it "as a descriptor of late-twentieth-century avant-gardist literature" (Elias, *Sublime* xix), the "dominant literary genre of postmodernism" (Nadj 411). The term, identifying the postmodern

enhancement of historical fiction, combines an allusion to historiography
with the definition of the texts as metafiction. In *Metafiction* (1984),
Patricia Waugh generally defines metafiction by the following statement:

> Metafictional novels tend to be constructed on the principle of
> fundamental and sustained opposition: the construction of a fictional
> illusion (as in traditional realism) and the laying bare of that
> illusion ... to create a fiction and to make a statement about the
> creation of that fiction. The two processes are held together in a formal
> tension which breaks down the distinctions between "creation" and
> "criticism" and merges them into the concepts of "interpretation" and
> "deconstruction." (6)

In the introduction to *Metafiction and Metahistory in Contemporary
Women's Writing* (2007), Ann Heilmann and Mark Llewellyn use the
term 'metahistory' to denote a combination of metafiction and historical
fiction. Following White's definition of the term in his seminal study
Metahistory (1973), which recognizes the "historical work as ... a verbal
structure in the form of a narrative prose discourse" (2), they provide the
following description: "By 'metahistorical' we mean those works of both
fiction and nonfiction in which one of the author's primary contentions is
the process of historical narrative itself" (Heilmann/Llewellyn 2).

Hutcheon's term "historiographic metafiction" provides such a
combination and suggests that such writing

> refutes the natural or common sense methods of distinguishing
> between historical fact and fiction. It refuses the view that only
> history has a truth claim, both by questioning the ground of that
> claim in historiography and by asserting that both history and fiction
> are discourses, human constructs, signifying systems, and both
> derive their major claim to truth from that identity.
>
> (*Poetics* 93)

In the preface to *Historiographic Metafiction in Modern American
and Canadian Literature* (1994), Bernd Engler und Kurt Müller define
historiographic metafiction similarly:

> The post-modern state of consciousness is reflected in the histor-
> ical novel in numerous and manifold forms of literary self-
> reflexivity. The use of metafictional narrative techniques that
> thematize the processuality of writing and the fabricatedness of
> our mental representations of reality is a prime example of literary
> self-reflexivity. Post-modern consciousness can also be found in
> playful, reciprocal superimposition of historiographic and literary
> discourse, which illustrates to what extent the construction of

historiographic plausibility and coherency depends on the use of archetypal narrative "models of world-making." (9)

It is Hutcheon's further claim "that postmodernists play with history and create a potentially subversive form of cultural critique" (Elias, *Sublime* xix; see also Kunow, "Making" 195). Historiographic metafiction is "the most prominent expression of the postmodern attack on the traditional view of art as a realistic or mimetic representation of reality" (Engler 13). Since the publication of Hutcheon's *The Poetics of Postmodernism* (1988), historiographic metafiction has become "a short-hand for the kinds of theorized approaches to the historical in literature which have become part of the mainstream culture" (Heilmann/Llewellyn 3).

In Hutcheon's argument, there is a "strong break between postmodernism and the historical novel tradition" (Elias, *Sublime* 88). Middleton and Woods, in *Literatures of Memory* (2000), also distinguish between the two modes of historical writing when they claim that

> [p]ostmodern historical fiction is unconvinced that there is a single unitary truth of the past waiting to be recovered, and is more interested in who has or had the power to compose "truths" about it, whereas historical realist fiction tends to assume that the literary narrative has a special power to present the past in a language of the present and give direct access to the thoughts, speech and events of that other time without distorting their significance. (21)

While Jameson "believes the postmodern historical novel to be a decadent form of the historical novel genre" (Elias, *Sublime* 89), Brian McHale sees the relationship between the classical historical romance and postmodern fiction as an evolutionary development (Elias, *Sublime* 89; see also Middleton/Woods 69). But it is obvious that seemingly older versions of the historical novel are still published today and exist alongside newer ones. I therefore agree with Shuttleworth, who uses the term 'historical novel' as an umbrella term for historiographic metafiction and for contemporary texts "which do not include any overt historiographic reflections" (254; see also Ickstadt 159; Kirchknopf 60).

In her introduction to the essay collection *Exoticizing the Past in Contemporary Neo-Historical Fiction* (2014), Rousselot suggests the label "'neo-historical' novel," which she identifies as a "coherent and recognisable sub-genre of contemporary historical fiction" in Great Britain and its former colonies (2; see also Johnston/Wiegandt 13–14). The characteristics of these novels are "creative and critical engagement with the cultural mores of the period" they revisit, a "mode of 'verisimilitude'" which distinguishes them "from the more explicitly self-reflexive mode of postmodern parody," and a "participation in, and response to, contemporary culture's continuing fascination with history" in the form of a problematization of "historical representation" and a striving for the exposure of "past wrongs and omissions of the historical record" (Rousselot 2–3, 4, 11–12).

I follow Bormann's argument, which maintains that nothing much is gained from establishing an opposition "between a classical historical novel, and a new kind of historical novel which has more often than not been seen as opposed to its classical precursor" (52). He therewith picks up on a trend, as

> more recent criticism of contemporary historical fiction ... prefers to just analyse historical fiction and dismiss definitions and classifications such as Hutcheon's, which turn out to be as problematic as they are enlightening.
>
> (17; see also Bölling 31; Johnston/Wiegandt 14; Butter, "Historiographic")

Given these developments in critical theory, it now seems mandatory, in order to define historical fiction or the historical novel, to find an all-encompassing characterization. In *History and the Contemporary Novel* (1989), David Cowart gives a definition which might seem "undemanding" (Middleton/Woods 59) at first glance, but ultimately furthers the view of all kinds of historical fiction as one cohesive genre: "I myself prefer to define historical fiction simply and broadly as fiction in which the past figures with some prominence" (Cowart 6). Nünning suggests that the term 'history' should solely be used to refer to events in the past, while 'historiography' should exclusively denote the cultural reproduction of those events (*Fiktion I* 110–15). He then further proposes that the definition of the genre of historical fiction should allow for an ambiguity of the concept of history ("*Mehrdeutigkeit des Geschichtsbegriffs*"; 111) which does not just reduce it to an equation with the past, since the definition of the genre needs to vanquish the criterion of post-narration ("*Kriterium des nachzeitigen Erzählens ... überwinden*"; 110). Thus, he has established a new unity in the genre (Meinig 44) which allows us to view the evolution of the historical novel as a continuum, by updating the definition of the historical novel so as to cover not only texts that are set in the past on the story level but also novels that discuss problems of historiography or question the possibilities of a representation of history:

> The replacement of the criterion of respective narration with the genre's central characteristic, the 'tension between the different levels of time' offers ... the great advantage that the theory of the genre of the historical novel re-joins the debates of the contemporary theory of history .... The insight that phenomena cannot simply be called historical because they are past, but that their historical nature

results from a specific quality of time ... accordingly provides a stable foundation for the modification and enhancement of the precision of our understanding of the genre of the historical novel.

(Nünning, *Fiktion I* 108, trans. in Meinig 44)

Sigrun Meinig, in her study of the Australian historical novel, *Witnessing the Past* (2004), is drawing on Nünning when she defines the historical novel as follows:

The only common denominator, as the very term 'historical' emphasizes, is the thematic orientation of the genre: historical novels are either characterized by the appearance of historical characters, by the portrayal of events of great political and historical significance, or, most frequently, by a certain time span that has elapsed between the (historical) time of the narrated and the (later, possibly contemporary) time of narrating. (42)

As far as I can assert from my research of the new historical fiction in the United States, it is exactly the mix of more traditional features of the historical novel, indebted to the nineteenth-century literary tradition and often labeled "realist" (Harlan 114), and innovative, postmodern elements that constitutes the defining aspects of the new historical fiction. One might adopt then for the American realm what Bormann diagnoses for the contemporary British historical novel:

Another problem of historically binary classifications is that certain features of the historical novel are allocated to the nineteenth century (especially techniques and views we would nowadays classify as realistic), and others to the twentieth (especially metafictional and metahistoriographic techniques and views), without there being a possibility of interchange. (54)

Elias defines historical fiction generally as follows:

[H]istorical fiction [is] a genre with a specific generic history. The historical novel is presented as a subgenre of the novel that exhibits three primary characteristics: (1) specific historical detail, featured prominently, is crucial to plot or character development or some experimental representation of these narrative attributes; (2) a *sense* of history informs all facets of the fictional construct (from authorial perspective to character development to selection of place); and (3) this sense of history emerges from and is constructed by the text itself and requires the text to participate in and differentiate itself from other discourses of various generic kinds that attempt to give a name to history.

(*Sublime* 4–5)

She labels the range of late-twentieth-century historical fiction from the United States, Great Britain, Australia, and Canada that she discusses in her study *Sublime Desire* (2001) "postmodernist metahistorical romance" (x, see also xiv). She claims that the "genre swings in pendulum motion from the 'realism' of Scott's historical novel form, through the abstraction of modernist spatial form and postmodern fabulation, back toward the 'realism' of postcolonial politics" (xviii). And though she differentiates between traditional historical fiction, modernist experimentation with historical fiction, and postmodernist metahistorical romance (89–91), she nevertheless stresses "that it is most useful to resituate postmodern historical fiction in literary history as an evolutionary form of the classic historical romance" (89). Her definition of post-1960s historical fiction then reads as follows:

Metahistorical Romance

1   assumes the cultural construction of history;
2   allows that the past may shape the present, but asserts that all we can know are its traces, and that all attempts to construct historical narrative are culturally contaminated. History is sublime, impossible to articulate, outside of representation, and as such leads to ethical action in the present;
3   radically questions the notion of cultural and personal value in any form, particularly those derived from Western capitalist economies;
4   conceptualizes History as planar, and replaces the notion of historical progress with the operation of deferral. (97)

Elias's choice of term marks on the one hand a return to the historical romance of the nineteenth century, implying recourse to realism as well as explaining the leeway some new historical fiction takes with exactly this realism when it comes to magical and supernatural, or – to use Tzvetan Todorov's terms, defined in his seminal study *The Fantastic* (1970) – fantastic, uncanny, and marvelous elements (41–42). On the other hand, the use of the prefix "meta-" implies that, different from the historical fiction of the nineteenth century, the new historical fiction displays a level of self-reflexivity about the writing of historical fiction and history writing itself. Self-reflexivity can be incorporated in the text in many ways:

> it can be consciously included in the subject matter of the book, indicated through irony, by emphasizing that language is a construct, or by provoking the reader to question the validity of the text as a transparent account of reality. Most fundamental, however, is the function of the narrator: the extent to which the narratorial voice can be identified with the authorial voice, whether the narrator is ironized or how far she or he is invested with omniscient powers.
> (Bird 22)

While Elias's definition generally outlines the conceptual aspects of what I label new historical fiction, Nünning's working definition of the historical novel will be used to further differentiate the varieties of the contemporary historical novel, as it is the most all-encompassing and useful:

> [A] historical novel is a fictional text which creates meaning from the background of an awareness of time as flowing and as poised uneasily between past and present; which secondly deals dominantly with topics which belong to the field of history, historiography and/ or the philosophy of history; and which thirdly can do so at all narrative levels and in any possible discursive form, be it through the narration of action, static description, argumentative exposition, or stream-of-consciousness techniques.
>
> (*Fiktion I* 120, trans. in Bormann 55)

Nünning also provides five subcategories of the coexisting forms of the historical novel, namely the "'documentary historical novel,' 'realistic historical novel,' 'revisionist historical novel,' 'metahistorical novel,' and 'historiographic metafiction'" (*Fiktion* I 257, trans. in Bormann 57). The first type, the documentary historical novel, is marked by a high level of reality references and evokes the impression of objectivity and authenticity, including a concealment of its fictionality. Documentary historical novels are dominantly oriented toward the past and narrate a specific historical event in a linear-chronological way (*Fiktion* I 259–62; see also Flis). As a representative example, Nünning mentions Thomas Keneally's *Schindler's Ark* (1982). The second type, the realistic historical novel is by comparison marked by a shift of the dominance of historical facts toward fictional elements. This type of historical novel comes closest to Scott's original model. The realistic historical novel conforms to the conventions of the traditional historical novel and equals literary realism. One of Nünning's examples is Andrew Sinclair's *The Far Corners of the Earth* (1991) (*Fiktion* I 262–67). Bormann describes the realistic historical novel as "a good read, fiction disguised as vivid reality, characterised by riveting plots full of action, and in line with the Victorian sense of history, chronological order, teleology, realism, congruence with historical reality and universal applicability" (72–73). The third type of historical fiction, the revisionist historical novel, can be defined as follows:

> The aim of the revisionist novel is to criticise standard histories and recover alternative histories. It will therefore, for example, typically oscillate between past- and present-oriented narratives to show the effects of the past in the present, and thus break the chronological

progression implicitly in the progressive continuity of standard history. It will often present more than one main character or narrator, some of them underdogs of society – like women, children, people from lower classes or different ethnic groups – to present both the traditional and the alternative historical accounts. Furthermore, while revisionist historical novels are packed with action, and in this resemble traditional historical novels, the coherence and meaningfulness of historical events is severely distorted because of both narrative mediation and a fragmentary, contingent concatenations [sic] of events. Last, not least, revisionist historical novels alternate between the creation and breaking of illusion, mainly because of the contradiction existing between official and alternative history.

> (Bormann 57–58, paraphrasing Nünning, *Fiktion I* 268–76)

Nünning subdivides the group of revisionist historical novels again into three subcategories: dominantly thematic revisions, dominantly formal revisions, and thematic and formal revisions (*Fiktion I* 275–76, my translation). Examples of these three types are, respectively, Rose Tremain's *Restoration* (1989), Lawrence Norfolk's *Lemprière's Dictionary* (1991), and Eva Figes's *The Seven Ages* (1986). The fourth type of historical novel, the metahistorical novel, can be described in the following way:

> Unlike the revisionist historical novel, metahistorical novels do not so much try to revise established historical fact as question historical method. This is a characteristic they share with historiographic metafictions; what they do not share is that this questioning takes place implicitly rather than explicitly. This can be observed in a number of features which are typical of metahistorical novels. Like revisionist historical novels, metahistorical novels propose two stories, one set in the past, the other in the present. Unlike revisionist novels, however, the orientation of these novels is clearly towards the present, via historical remembrance or research by characters located in the present. Events are therefore reflected on rather than presented. This internalisation of characters' experience often results in a semantic loading of spaces, objects, or characters, which can implicitly question historical method. The fact that, despite their two plots, these novels concentrate on the present recovery of the past and thus accord a decisive centrality to narrative mediation makes metahistorical novels similar to detective novels. The indirect questioning of historical method is also furthered by the presentation of events which generally lack action and chronological order, and appear as fragmentary and contingent.
>
> (Bormann 58, paraphrasing Nünning, *Fiktion I* 276–81)

As examples of this type of historical novel Nünning suggests Peter Ackroyd's *Chatterton* (1987) and Graham Swift's *Ever After* (1992) (*Fiktion I* 281). The fifth type of historical novel, Hutcheon's historiographic metafiction, is defined as follows:

> Historiographic metafiction, finally, is distinguished as a micro-genre because its questioning of history as an epistemological enterprise is an explicit one. This is clearly recognisable in the fact that the share of the "real world" that historiographic metafictions select is constituted by the academic field of philosophy of history rather than by historical events. In historiographic metafiction, the composition of space, time, character, and plot is marked by the non-narrative, argumentative exposition of history as against the more mixed approach of metahistorical novels to narrative and exposition. While making profuse use of "literary" strategies to load space, time, and characters with semantic connotations, historiographic metafiction relies less on this tactic than metahistorical fiction, since its questionings of history are so explicit as to be in little need of additional buttressing. As in metahistorical novels, the narrative mediation of historiographic metafictions is marked by its opacity or lack of transparency, but while the narrator of metahistorical novels focuses on the historiographic reconstruction of events, the narrator of historiographic metafictions explicitly focuses on issues relating to historiography and the philosophy of history. It is also this very explicitness which makes historiographic metafictions veritable invitations to a serious, cognitive, often academic appraisal of problematic issues surrounding historiography and the philosophy of history, thus often breaking the illusion the reader may have of reading what is, after all, classified as fiction.
>
> (Bormann 58–59, paraphrasing Nünning, *Fiktion I* 282–91)

Nünning's examples of historiographic metafiction include Salman Rushdie's *Midnight's Children* (1981) and Graham Swift's *Waterland* (1983) (*Fiktion I* 291). Nadj defines historiographic metafiction as

> broadly speaking, ... predominantly concerned with a postmodern critique of a positivistic approach towards historiography .... [H]istoriographic metafiction raise[s] questions about epistemological knowledge, the existence and problematic status of a clear cut fact-fiction boundary, and the possibilities and impossibilities of re-presentation .... [H]istoriographic metafiction explores the problems of the representation of the past and explicitly or implicitly discusses various postmodern crises. (411)

Overall, Nünning's five types or categories can be seen as stages on a continuum of historical fiction. Bormann summarizes as follows:

> [T]he group formed by the documentary and the realistic historical novel – the realistic type would roughly correspond with the classical historical novel – displays a basic belief in the aims, procedures and findings of history, whereas the group formed by the revisionist, metahistorical novel and the historiographic metafiction questions this belief. In this latter group both historiographic metafictions and metahistorical novels tend to question historical method rather than historical fact – the latter explicitly, the former implicitly – while revisionist novels, rather than question historical epistemology, only question the contents of standard historical accounts and try to revise them. (57)

Kurt Müller's observations concerning the spectrum of historiographic metafiction can also be understood along those lines:

> One can roughly distinguish two apparently opposed modes of meta-historiographic de-construction and re-construction. On one end of the spectrum, a novel may focus on the dramatization of a process of uncovering a hidden, forgotten, or suppressed history which the reader is supposed to take for the "real," authentic version…. On the other end, the meta-historiographic technique may convey the idea that all history, including the alternative version offered by the text, is an invention. Yet even if the alternative version is "nothing but" an invention, this does not necessarily mean that it is to be regarded as only an arbitrary fictional construct…. Between the two extreme positions outlined above, which one could conceptualize in the oppositional pair "modernist" versus "postmodernist," there can be intermediate positions or overlappings. (48–49)

As examples for the first type, Müller mentions Ernest Gaines's *The Autobiography of Miss Jane Pittman* (1971) and Leslie Marmon Silko's *Ceremony* (1977). He then sees the other end of the spectrum represented by Ishmael Reed's *Mumbo Jumbo* (1972) and *Flight to Canada* (1976) as well as Stephen Marlowe's *The Memoirs of Christopher Columbus* (1987) and Michael Dorris and Louise Erdrich's *The Crown of Columbus* (1991). The intermediate position is ascribed to Doctorow's historical fiction, such as *Welcome to Hard Times* (1960), *The Book of Daniel* (1971), *Ragtime* (1975), *Loon Lake* (1980), and *World's Fair* (1985) (48–49).

Whether a rigid differentiation such as Nünning's is helpful or necessary with regard to the new American historical fiction will be discussed later. Nevertheless, his categorization provides useful insights concerning the wide variety and complexity of existing forms of historical fiction today. At this point I conclude, with Jeannette King, that what generally characterizes historical fiction today is "its more direct engagement with the historical process itself, often blending historical documentation and events with its imagined narratives and characters" (3).

1.13 How Neo-Victorian Is It?

One remarkable aspect of the new historical fiction at the turn of the twenty-first century is its "multiplicity of forms" (Burt xiv). A survey, categorization, classification, or typology of the new historical fiction in the United States does not exist, and establishing one, or at least attempting it, is one aim of this study. Besides the already-mentioned categorizations of historical fiction by Nünning and others, there have been attempts at specifically classifying the phenomenon of the neo-Victorian novel. Again, viewing the renaissance of historical fiction as a transatlantic phenomenon and transcultural interplay will assist in charting or structuring the field of the new American historical fiction. As with the beginnings of historical fiction in the United States, when the "British and American cultures … were symbiotically intertwined" (Giles 11), there also seems to be an especially strong cross-fertilization between the national literature of the United Kingdom and the United States today.

As already mentioned, since the 1980s and 1990s there has been a "general resurgence of interest in the Victorians, an interest which reached a climax with the centenary of Victoria's death in 2001, but which has not gone away" (King 4). Embedded in this revival one can diagnose a "veritable deluge of Victorian-centered novels … published in the British Isles" (Shuttleworth 253). The prefix 'neo-,' etymologically originating with the Greek νέος, meaning "a: new: recent … b: … in a new and different form or manner" (*Merriam-Webster*), has turned out to be most commonly used when scholars are referring to the contemporary cultural preoccupation with the Victorian age, though there have been attempts to establish the terms 'retro-Victorian' (Shuttleworth) and 'post-Victorian' (Kirchknopf). The term 'neo-Victorian' to date has no entry in the dictionary. In analogy to terms like 'neo-gothic,' it might be defined as "of, relating to, or constituting a revival or adaptation of the [Victorian], especially in literature" (*Merriam-Webster*).

The question that seems to suggest itself here is whether American historical fiction portraying the nineteenth century may be labeled and regarded as neo-Victorian fiction, too. When Letissier argues that "[p]ost-Victorian fiction[,] … far from being merely confined to England, … concerns former British colonies, too, chiefly Australia … and Canada" (113), an inquiry into the exclusion of America obtrudes. In her introduction to the inaugural issue of the e-journal *Neo-Victorian Studies*, Kohlke argues that

> [n]eo-Victorian Studies is still in the process of crystallisation, or full *materialisation* so to speak; as yet its temporal and generic boundaries remain fluid and relatively open to experimentation by artists, writers, and theorists alike, a state of affairs that forms part of its strong attraction. What properly belongs *in* and *to* this emergent, popular, inter-disciplinary field of study remains to be seen. (1)

She further asserts, apropos the journal's scope, that it should be based on

> the widest possible interpretation of "neo-Victorian," so as to include the whole of the nineteenth century, its cultural discourses and products, and their abiding legacies, not just within Queen Victoria's realm; that is, to interpret neo-Victorianism outside of the limiting nationalistic and temporal identifications that "Victorian," in itself or in conjunction with "neo-," conjures up for some critics. (2)

Martin Hewitt argues that "historical boundaries are permeable, and questioning the nature and positioning of chronological [and, indeed, generic and national] markers helps to avoid closing off fruitful lines of inquiry" (395; see also Kohlke 2). All these arguments call at least for an examination of whether or not American cultural reflections on the nineteenth century might be subsumed under the heading neo-Victorian.

In all kinds of disciplines, the phrase 'Victorian America' has come into use, at least over the last decades of the twentieth century. There is a host of studies which uses the term, in the fields of architecture, the arts, biology, and medicine. And there are cultural and historical studies which adopt it, too. Daniel Walker Howe's seminal "Victorian Culture in America" – the introductory essay to a collection of articles by American historians called *Victorian America* (1976) – defends the use of the term:

> Using the name of a foreign monarch to describe an aspect of a country's history implies some relationship between the two countries, and indeed a close one existed between Britain and the United States in the nineteenth century. Although the United States had become politically independent, economic interdependence continued to characterize Anglo-American relations: ... The cultural connection was, if anything, even closer than the economic one. Victorianism was a transatlantic culture – though in the largest sense

it was only an English-speaking subculture of Western civilization. In fact, of course, there were a number of cultures and subcultures .... As they came into contact with each other they overlapped, and many a person came under the influence of several. But there was one of these cultures that exercised a kind of hegemony during the period of our focus, particularly over the printed word, and this was American Victorianism.

(3–6; see also Parish 6)

On the one hand, the United States in the nineteenth century was already in a postcolonial condition and independent from Queen Victoria's reign. So naturally, one would hesitate to label this era Victorian. As has been pointed out already, at the beginning of the nineteenth century there was a strong inclination to create an American culture separate from the British one. Particularly the genre of historical fiction was briskly promoted by American intellectuals, who campaigned for the development of a distinctly American national identity, culture, and literature, in opposition to Britain. Therefore, it seems problematic to call the literature and culture of this era Victorian.

On the other hand, the term "Victorian," defined as "1: of, relating to, or characteristic of the reign of Queen Victoria of England or the art, letters, or tastes of her time; 2: typical of the moral standards, attitudes, or conduct of the age of Victoria especially when considered stuffy, prudish, or hypocritical" (*Merriam-Webster*), allows for some geographical leeway, especially with respect to the phrase "of her time." Furthermore, scholars have argued that the term itself has changed its meaning over the decades (Kirchknopf 55–59), having become "both a useful shorthand and a barrier to understanding the complexities of a series of shifting cultural identities across a period of more than sixty years" (Moore 135). Some scholars argue that "it is precisely the instability of the term that has allowed it to be articulated to a broad range of political, social, and cultural interests" (Joyce 168). It shall suffice here to assume – consciously in a generalizing way – that the term today depicts the entirety of cultural specifics of an era significantly expanding the reign or lifetime of Queen Victoria. Terms like "Victoriography," "Victoriana," and "postmodern Victoriana" encompass the broader cultural occupation with the Victorian era, not limiting it to fictional output (Wolfreys; Kaplan 3; Kirchknopf 66). Stretching the term thus, many aspects of the overall culture of the American nineteenth century indeed emulate the Victorian (Himmelfarb 7).

Though Howe explicitly confirms Victorianism in "the printed word," when it comes to literary studies, most scholars shy away from adopting the adjective 'Victorian' for the American nineteenth century, as it is "a loaded term" (John/Jenkins 2; see also Kirchknopf 55–59). Dana Shiller, in her seminal essay "The Redemptive Past in the Neo-Victorian

Novel" (1997), was among the first scholars to define and label the literary preoccupation with the nineteenth century. According to her, "neo-Victorian novels" are "novels that adopt a postmodern approach to history and ... are set at least partly in the nineteenth century" (558). She then groups them into three classes: "This capacious umbrella includes texts that revise specific Victorian precursors, texts that imagine new adventures for familiar Victorian characters, and 'new' Victorian fictions that imitate nineteenth-century literary conventions" (558). As examples of these three types, respectively, she identifies Martin's *Mary Reilly* (1990); Ackroyd's *Chatterton* (1987) and Byatt's "The Conjugial Angel" (1992); and Byatt's *Possession* (1990) and Charles Palliser's *The Quincunx* (1989).

In her equally seminal essay "Natural History: The Retro-Victorian Novel" (1998), Sally Shuttleworth introduces the term "retro-Victorian novel" to define "Victorian-centered novels" (253). She asserts that "[s]uch novels generally display an informed postmodern self-consciousness in their interrogation of the relationship between fiction and history. They reveal, nonetheless, an absolute, non-ironic, fascination with the details of the period, and with our relations to it" (253). Shuttleworth extricates what she calls the "natural history novel" as "a literary subset of the retro-Victorian novel" (253). Her examples are Byatt's "Morpho Eugenia" (1992) and Swift's *Ever After* (1992), which "dramatise the Darwinian moment in Victorian history" (253). She further identifies three types of models or progenitors for the natural history novel. The first is John Fowles's *The French Lieutenant's Woman* (1969), which she mainly cites for its "self-reflexivity" (256). Jean Rhys's *Wide Sargasso Sea* (1966) is mentioned as "one of the first in a long line of texts which have sought to open up the silent spaces of history or classic literary texts" (256). Swift's *Waterland* and Byatt's *Possession* serve as examples of texts "where nineteenth- and twentieth-century stories intertwine" (256).

In his influential article "Using the Victorians: the Victorian Age in Contemporary Fiction" (2002), Robin Gilmour gives a list of "six uses to which Victorian history and Victorian fiction have been put" (190) in contemporary British novels, which might be considered forms of the American new historical fiction invoking the nineteenth century. He identifies the "historical novel written from a modern perspective and in a modern idiom, without much narratorial interference but implying a modern interpretation of the past" (190) as the first type, mentioning J. G. Farrell's *The Siege of Krishnapur* (1973) and *Possession* as examples. The second type consists of pastiche or parody, "whether in thoroughgoing form ... or in part" (190). His examples are Palliser's *The Quincunx*, and *Ever After*, as well as, again, *Possession*. He lists "the inversion of Victorian ideology" (190) as a third type, exemplified in George MacDonald Fraser's Flashman novels (1969–2005). A fourth use can be found in "the subversion of Victorian fictional norms" (190).

The classic example here is *The French Lieutenant's Woman*. "The modern reworking or completing of a classic Victorian novel" (190) constitutes Gilmour's fifth type. As typical texts he mentions *Wide Sargasso Sea*, Emma Tennant's *Tess* (1993), and *Waterland*. The sixth and last class of novels using the Victorians is, in Gilmour's words, "[t]he research novel" (190). By this he means "a work which, recognizing the prominence which the study of Victorian literature and culture plays in contemporary academic life, builds that into the structure of the novel, making it the subject or focus of the book" (190). He mentions David Lodge's *Nice Work* (1988) and, again, *Possession*, as examples.

Bormann creates the following definition of the neo-Victorian novel, on the basis of Nünning's definition:

> [A] neo-Victorian novel is a fictional text which creates meaning from the background of awareness of time as flowing and as poised uneasily between *the Victorian* past and the present; which secondly deals dominantly with topics which belong to the field of history, historiography and/or the philosophy of history in *dialogue with a Victorian past*; and which thirdly can do so at all narrative levels and in any possible discursive form, be it through the narration of action, through static description, argumentative exposition or stream-of-consciousness techniques.
>
> (62; see also Nünning, *Fiktion I* 120)

Kirchknopf, in her article "(Re)Workings of Nineteenth-Century Fiction: Definitions, Terminology, Contexts" (2008), offers the term "post-Victorian novel" (66, see also 64–66), drawing on Kucich and Sadoff's definition of it as a term that "conveys paradoxes of historical continuity and disruption" (xiii; see also Letissier 111), to identify *Wide Sargasso Sea*, *The French Lieutenant's Woman*, Peter Carey's *Oscar and Lucinda* (1988), Ackroyd's *Dickens* (1990), *Possession*, *Ever After*, Alasdair Gray's *Poor Things* (1992), Beryl Bainbridge's *Master Georgie* (1998), Matthew Kneale's *English Passengers* (2000), D. M. Thomas's *Charlotte* (2000), and Colm Tóibín's *The Master* (2004) (Kirchknopf 53). She also gives an extensive definition of what she initially calls "(re)workings of nineteenth-century fiction," "postmodern rewritings," and "postmodern rewrites of Victorian texts":

> [The] postmodern rewrites of Victorian texts keep the average length and structure of Victorian novels: The bulky 500 pages (ranging between 150 and 1000 pages) are usually divided into books or chapters, sometimes preceded by chapter summaries or epigraphs. They imitate prevalent genres of the nineteenth century, such as the Bildungsroman, or the social, industrial and sensation novels, creatively intermingled with conventions of the (auto)biographical

and (pseudo)historical novels, thus creating a hybridity of genres abundant in parody and pastiche so characteristic of postmodern novelistic discourse. The narrative design of these novels tends to be like that of their Victorian predecessors' and they typically employ narrative voices of the types dominant in nineteenth-century texts, i.e. the first person character narrator or the third person omniscient one.

The plots of these rewrites either take place in the nineteenth century or span both the nineteenth and the twentieth centuries. They are usually set at least partly in England, most often in London or in the countryside. Set in the age of the British Empire, the geographical locations may also vary between the centre and the colonies or territories of national interest, such as the West-Indies, Australia, or scenes of the Crimean War – and, in the case of twentieth-century plots, between England and its possible reverse colonizer, the United States. Thematically, the texts invoke typical Victorian controversies, such as the definition and status of science, religion, morals, nationhood and identity, and the (re)evaluations of the aims and scope of cultural discourses and products, especially constructions of literary, political, and social histories which also feature prominently in contemporary thought. Furthermore, by creating a dialogue between narratives of the present day and the nineteenth century, strongly based on the concept of intertextuality, contemporary rewrites manage to supply different perspectives from the canonized Victorian ones. (53–54)

Kirchknopf also diagnoses a revisionist impetus in post-Victorian fiction, "a drive to unearth – or invent – material not part of the official historiography of the nineteenth century, and utilise this to reinterpret the Victorians" (58). Heilmann and Llewellyn argue that the neo-Victorian novel is "more than historical fiction set in the nineteenth century," it "must in some respect be self-consciously engaged with the act of (re)interpretation, (re)discovery and (re)vision concerning the Victorians" (4).

Most of these scholars do not mention the American literary scene, but their findings can be probed for their adaptability to the new historical fiction in the United States. Shiller's very flexible definition, though restricted to British neo-Victorian novels, can easily be applied to the American texts discussed in this study. I will return to her type-one texts later, as Martin's novel, which retells Robert Louis Stevenson's *The Strange Case of Dr. Jekyll and Mr. Hyde* (1886) from the point of view of the housemaid, is what I call a 'reanimated classic.' Her type-three texts, Byatt's and Palliser's novels, invent new Victorian stories, but this is common in most new historical fiction and thus the term is not precise enough to suffice as a definition of a subset. Additionally, I find Shiller's phrasing for her second class of texts somewhat unprecise, as it does not aptly express what readers encounter among the pages of Ackroyd's novel and Byatt's novella. Rather, these texts must be seen as instances of what I term 'historical biofiction' in its broadest sense. Ackroyd's novel is preoccupied with the mystery of the life and especially death of the poet Thomas Chatterton. Byatt's novella focuses on the later life of Emily Tennyson, in the aftermath of her fiancé Arthur Henry Hallam's untimely death, her brother Alfred, Lord Tennyson's publication of the famous elegy "In Memoriam A. H. H." (1850), and her later marriage to another man. The texts have variously been discussed as biofiction (Franken; Nünning, "Intertextual"). With regard to Shuttleworth's explanations, I do not agree that the fixation on a scientific topic constitutes a subgenre of the new historical fiction, nor adequately covers the wide range of issues Byatt and Swift engage with in their books. As I will show in the discussion of several new American historical novels, science and technological progress, major themes of the nineteenth century, are pervasive in most of the texts, although to varying degrees. In my opinion, not much is gained by defining this group of texts as natural history novels.

Nevertheless, Shuttleworth's attempts at a classification can partly be made fruitful. While Fowles's text is a prime example of historiographic metafiction, the term may equally be applied to the entirety of new historical fiction, because be it overt or covert, all of them reflect upon the writing of historical fiction in one way or another. I will discuss Rhys's novel as a progenitor of reanimated classics. Her text may also be seen as an instance of 'herstory,' bringing to the fore the neglected history of women, although here it is the neglected history of a fictional character, the first Mrs. Rochester from Brontë's *Jane Eyre*. The novel is also a postcolonial response to Victorian fiction, giving a voice to ethnically and racially marginalized groups (Renk). "The Conjugial Angel" is also an instance of herstory, as it reclaims Emily Tennyson's place as Hallam's widow, a place usually acknowledged to her brother, as well as an example of biofiction. Still, contra Shuttleworth, I would differentiate between novels that "open up the silent spaces of history" (256), as Byatt's text does, and those that fill voids in "classic texts" (256), which is the impetus of Rhys's novel. Swift's and Byatt's novels then are of a group that I label the 'multi-time-level historical novel,' because of their peculiarity of combining multiple time levels or storylines from different eras in the narrative. Kirchknopf, throughout her article, uses the terms 'reworkings' or 'rewrites' interchangeably to denote post-Victorian novels. Such a practice confuses the differences between the overall genre – what she labels post-Victorian novels – and its various subgenres, which I would claim rewrites, rewritings, and reworkings are only one of, referring especially, within Kirchknopf's selection, to novels such as *Wide Sargasso Sea* and *Charlotte*. Though Kirchknopf also fleetingly mentions other subsets of the post-Victorian novel, such as "literary biographies"

(58) (*Dickens* and *The Master*), or "novels with a double plot" (68) (*Possession* and *Ever After*), she never really starts to engage in a discussion of possible classifications or even a typology within the field of post-Victorian novels – a fact that, in an article bearing the subtitle "Definitions, Terminology, Contexts" and explicitly stating "that contemporary rewritings require classification and characterization" (72), is somewhat surprising. But this lack of clarity notwithstanding, most of the aspects of the post-Victorian novel she mentions in her definition can, with merely a few modifications, be applied to the novels this study discusses. It is especially interesting that Kirchknopf observes an impetus of revision in the post-Victorian novel, which links it to the American new historical fiction. Another remarkable aspect of Kirchknopf's definition is the fact that she includes the United States.

Many aspects of these theories, though they are sometimes somewhat fuzzy, can be applied to the new historical fiction in the United States. But most scholars of the neo-Victorian phenomenon do not subsume the revisiting of the American nineteenth century in contemporary literature under the heading neo-Victorian. There are a few exceptions: Kucich and Sadoff at least mention American historical novels in their introduction, namely Carr's *The Alienist* (1994) and Doctorow's *The Waterworks* (1994). Unfortunately, they do so judgmentally, calling such texts popular mainstream examples (xi). Consequently, none of the articles included in their collection refers to American literature. Moore goes further when she observes that "owing to the expanse of Victorian cultural imperialism and its legacy in the era of decolonization, revisionism has ... become a much more global phenomenon" (137). She lists a wide variety of writers from Australia, Canada, and India "engaged in updating and rewriting the 'classic' Victorian novel" (137). She also mentions three novels from the North American region: Susanne Alleyn's *A Far Better Rest* (2000), Bruce Bueno de Mesquita's *The Trial of Ebenezer Scrooge* (2001), and John Irving's *The Cider House Rules* (1985) (137). But while some books Moore lists – for example, Carey's *Oscar and Lucinda* and *True History of the Kelly Gang* (2000) – are actually set outside of Britain, the novels mentioned for the United States seem to be odd selections in this respect. Bueno de Mesquita's novel is a revisionist sequel to Dickens's *A Christmas Carol* (1843), and Alleyn's is a rewriting of Dickens's *A Tale of Two Cities* (1859). Irving's, the only text set in the United States, may be read as a variation of "Dickens's orphan stories" (Joyce 15). It mainly covers the first half of the twentieth century and therefore should really not be considered a neo-Victorian novel. None of the three texts really engages with the American past during the nineteenth century. Moore seems to allow only for an expansion of the writer's origin, not for a globalization of the context.

The case is different with Jeannette King's *The Victorian Woman Question in Contemporary Feminist Fiction* (2005). She does not distinguish between European and North American literature, and analyzes British (Angela Carter's *Nights at the Circus*, 1984; Byatt's *Angels and Insects*, 1992; Victoria Glendinning's *Electricity*, 1995; Sarah Waters's *Tipping the Velvet*, 1998, and *Affinity*, 1999; Michèle Roberts's *In the Red Kitchen*, 1990), Canadian (Margaret Atwood's *Alias Grace*, 1996), and American novels (Morrison's *Beloved*, 1987; Andrea Barrett's *The Voyage of the Narwhal*, 1998) side by side. She puts emphasis on the fact that the prevalent gender roles of the nineteenth century were "'universal'" and "generally transatlantic in currency" (13). Similarly, Heilmann and Llewellyn include discussions of historical fiction by contemporary women authors from the United Kingdom, Australia, and North America, that is, Canada and the United States. Ultimately, though, the only text in their collection by an American and set in the United States is Sena Jeter Naslund's *Ahab's Wife: or, The Star-Gazer* (1999). This might be seen as a confirmation that the lives of women in the United States in the nineteenth century were determined by Victorian gender roles and that neo-Victorian women's writing is generally marked by the dominance of Victorian culture.

Besides the woman question, many of the other issues of new American historical and neo-Victorian novels are comparable as well. The advantages and drawbacks of technological progress and industrialization are at stake in both neo-Victorian and contemporary American historical fiction on the era. The problems that come with urbanization are likewise a focal area in both branches of historical fiction. Yet the American realm also includes the contrastive challenges of the vast country and the specific landscape the people were faced with in the New World. Other topics, such as the practices of slavery and the displacement of Native Americans, are discussed from a different viewpoint.

Contemporary American historical fiction relates back to the American literature of the nineteenth century, similar to the stance neo-Victorian fiction takes toward Victorian literature. It is typical of neo-Victorian and the corresponding American historical fiction that they take a critical position toward the norms and rules of the Victorian era, expressed by their giving marginalized groups a voice, in the vein of postcolonial literature. Bill Ashcroft, Gareth Griffiths, and Helen Tiffin's seminal study *The Empire Writes Back: Theory and Practice in Post-Colonial Literatures* (1989), which borrows its title from Rushdie's now-classic adage "The empire writes back to the centre" (Thieme 3), allows for a wide geographical range of postcolonial literature, significantly including the USA:

The literature of the USA should also be placed in this category. Perhaps because of its current position of power, and the neo-colonizing role it has played, its post-colonial nature has not been generally recognized. But its relationship with the metropolitan centre as it evolved over the last two centuries has been paradigmatic for post-colonial literatures everywhere.

(Ashcroft/Griffiths/Tiffin, *Empire* 2)

The United States declared its independence from Britain in 1776, and arguably after the War of 1812 had finally gained it. It became a postcolonial nation earlier than most of the other postcolonial cultures, and even before Queen Victoria's reign. Yet something of the general impetus of postcolonial literatures might still be recognizable in American literature today. American novels depicting the nineteenth century are writing back to the center as they also give voice to groups and issues that were marginalized in the nineteenth century and by hegemonic history. The overall approach the new American historical novel takes toward the era and its cultural products is similar to, and sometimes overlaps greatly with, the impetus of neo-Victorian fiction.

Concluding these theoretical remarks, the caveat needs to be issued that the complex problem of whether or not American historical fiction portraying the nineteenth century should be subsumed under the heading neo-Victorian is obviously hard to resolve. The foregoing considerations can only attempt to outline the pitfalls of either line of argumentation, and I can only hope that my findings initiate further discussion of this issue.

1.14 Revis(it)ing the Past

As mentioned at the outset of this study, historical fiction has more generally shifted its focus to social history. In *Chronoschisms: Time, Narrative, and Postmodernism* (1997), Ursula Heise diagnoses an increasing interest in "stories that had been repressed, or had seemed too marginal or too deviant to find an audience before" (16). Middleton and Woods observe that

> [r]ealist fictions by writers outside the dominant social formations are celebrated for their bold attempts to provide new histories of peoples whose religion, nationality, gender, sexuality, ethnicity, class and poverty denied them the opportunity to present their stories in the publicly accessible forms of literature (2).

Among these neglected stories are the histories of women, ethnic, racial, and sexual so-called minorities and it is the merit of the new historical fiction that it makes "available at last to a public culture" the "pasts which were suppressed, repressed or never given access to the basic means of publicity" (Middleton/Woods 22). The former minority perspective is brought to the forefront, and neglected or utterly forgotten aspects of history come into focus. Central historical events and their main consequences, as well as the great personalities, are not important anymore (Humphrey 89). The focus shifts to everyday life, especially of marginalized groups (Meinig 32). What happened on the fringes, special events, events of exceptional value, and the little histories on the side take center stage. For writers, the "lure of the … past" is partly the "lure of the unmentionable – the mysterious, the buried, the forgotten, the discarded, the taboo" (Atwood 19). With Middleton and Woods one may conclude that "[c]ontemporary historical literature has become an extremely active sphere of argument about history and the rediscovery of its elided potentialities, as well as an often highly conflicted struggle over what should be remembered and what forgotten" (1).

Critical perspectives on or revisions of the bequeathed reception of certain well-attended historical events challenge traditional, stereotypical conceptions of the past of the United States. A common feature and major aim of the new historical novels is their revisionist orientation. In this respect, historical fiction, often shunned by historians as a phenomenon of popular history, can function as an important addition to academic or professional historiography: "[H]istorical novelists typically recreate a portion of the past by (among other things) recovering the details of everyday life – details that are often so minute, so finely grained, that academic historians usually overlook them" (Harlan 121).

Tim A. Ryan, in his study *Calls and Responses* (2008), convincingly argues that "[t]he artistic self-assertion of traditionally marginalized groups and individuals in the face of repressive forces and tyrannical discourses comprises one of the most important and salutary cultural developments since World War II" (3). These texts may be read as a "critique of dominant ideologies" and bring to the fore "alternative voices and visions in historical fiction" (3). But he also criticizes scholarly inactivity or incompetence in dealing with this significant cultural trend:

> In order to highlight this development, however, critics often rely upon a problematic rhetoric that is organized around excessively general and overly simplistic binary oppositions. Existing studies frequently imply – and sometimes even overtly assert – a rigid dichotomy between dissenting fiction and conservative historiography, between the enlightened politics of contemporary culture and the benighted ideologies of traditional literature, between the subversive discourse of the margins and the oppressive discourse of the mainstream. (3, see also 10)

Historical discourse indeed is not singular, but defined by plurality, and therefore contemporary historical novels do not simply "reject and transcend established discourses of the past," but engage "with existing historiographical debates" (Ryan 4). Reichardt claims that "History, then, dissolves into different particular histories. We have to think of history in the plural" ("New" 73). Hutcheon similarly observes that the "unitary, closed, evolutionary narratives" of traditional historiography have given way to the "histories (in the plural) of the losers as well as the winners, of the regional (and colonial) as well as the centrist, of the unsung many as well as the much sung few, and ... of women as well as men" (*Politics* 66). Memory, as an "archive of the repressed" (Kunow/ Raussert 10), makes possible "a real challenge to hegemonic construc- tions of nation, culture, and history" (Singh/Skerrett/Hogan 6).

One may ask, though, "does the critique of the character of history as being constructed to legitimate a specific political position concern re-construction as well?" (Reichardt, "New" 71). The decisive aspect is the subject position, which means how the author is implicated in the history (s)he is writing. Minorities have to rely on the notion of history as linear development, as their impetus is to reappropriate what made them into what they are now. Only through counter-narratives can those groups work toward a cultural identity of their own. Therefore, one often does not find the same skeptical attitude toward history in texts by the previously neglected as one may find in postmodern writing (Reichardt, "New" 71). Overall,

> [n]ew histories of emergent groups serve two different functions – relative to the perspective from which we look at them. For so far marginalized people, the reconstruction of "their" histories works towards a sense of identity and is a way of entering history. Seen from the perspective of the "mainstream" culture, these "other" histories work to revitalize, to "de-naturalize" linear monological history, revealing its inherent prespectivism, its social constructed- ness. They participate in the critique of history as linear progress.
>
> (Reichardt, "New" 74)

By not solely focusing on the literature of marginalized groups and the "fictional 'historiography of the subaltern'" (Kunow, "Beginning" 79), but also including texts by American authors from the historical center who are nevertheless also engaged in a revision of historical subject matter, my study tries to emphasize the plurality of the new historical fiction and its diverse responses to historiography. I aim at expanding the lens to include the whole field of new historical fiction depicting the nineteenth century:

> It is true that, very broadly speaking, there has been a discursive hegemony of sorts in America .... It is also the case that the last quarter-century has witnessed a massive outpouring of narratives

that voice resistance to repressive ideologies. When, however, it comes to nuanced literary criticism, we require a more sophisticated theoretical basis than a series of simplistically generalizing binary oppositions between dissenting post-1960s texts and complicit pre-1960s texts, between subversive fictional and hegemonic historical narratives.

(Ryan 15)

As mentioned earlier, I will approach new historical novels in this study whose revisionism is twofold, in the sense of McHale's dictum about postmodern fiction: "First, it revises the content of the historical record, reinterpreting the historical record, often demystifying or debunking the orthodox version of the past. Secondly, it revises, indeed transforms, the conventions and norms of historical fiction itself" (90).

The nineteenth century offers manifold possibilities to revisit and revise the historical record. As shown before, the era was equally marked by unity and diversity, continuity and change. The major developments and historical events of the nineteenth century were the feminist movements, racial issues concerning Native Americans and African Americans, political conflict with the British, and, first and foremost, the American Civil War.

The traumatic events of the Civil War have since its day fueled the imagination of American writers of historical fiction (e.g., Stephen Crane, *The Red Badge of Courage*, 1895; Margaret Mitchell, *Gone With the Wind*, 1936; MacKinlay Kantor, *Andersonville*, 1955; Michael Shaara, *The Killer Angels*, 1974) (Johnson, *Historical* 16). The after-effects of this crucial event in American history even today constitute a main aspect of the nation's cultural memory (Kurt Müller 39; see also Borgmeier/Reitz 32). In the new historical fiction, goings-on away from the battlefield, such as the draft riots (e.g., Kevin Baker, *Paradise Alley*, 2002) and the impact of the war on civilians and soldiers (e.g. *Cold Mountain*; *In the Fall*; *The March*; Joseph O'Connor, *Redemption Falls*, 2007), receive more attention than the actual warfare.

Apart from this still-prevailing topic, other, often previously disregarded aspects of nineteenth-century life in the United States seem to occupy writers' minds. The topics of the new historical fiction invoking the nineteenth century are very diverse and range from the depiction of scientific explorations (e.g., William T. Vollmann, *The Rifles*, 1994; *The Voyage of the Narwhal*), especially the Lewis and Clark Expedition (e.g., *Stone Heart*; Brian Hall, *I Should Be Extremely Happy in Your Company: A Novel of Lewis and Clark*, 2003), to new versions of the sea story (e.g., Anca Vlasopolos, *The New Bedford Samurai*, 2007) and the Western and frontier novel (e.g., Annie Dillard, *The Living*, 1992; Jane Smiley, *The All-True Travels and Adventures of Lidie Newton*, 1998; Tom Franklin, *Hell at the Breech*, 2003). They range from the depiction of technological progress (e.g., *City of Light*; John Griesemer, *Signal and Noise*, 2003) or the development of psychoanalysis (e.g., Jed Rubenfeld, *The Interpretation of Murder*, 2006) to the striving for the realization of the American Dream (e.g., Steven Millhauser, *Martin Dressler: The Tale of an American Dreamer*, 1996; Kevin Baker, *Dreamland*, 1999) and the portrayal of crime as an effect of urbanization (e.g., *The Alienist*). Further topics include African American (e.g., *The Wind Done Gone*; Jacqueline Sheehan, *Truth*, 2003; Martin, *Property*, 2003; Edward P. Jones, *The Known World*, 2003) and Native American issues (e.g., Glancy, *Pushing the Bear*, 1996; Frazier, *Thirteen Moons*, 2006; Brian Schofield, *Selling Your Father's Bones: The Epic Fate of the American West*, 2008) as well as feminist (e.g., Peter Rushforth, *Pinkerton's Sister*, 2004; Lee Smith, *On Agate Hill*, 2006) and queer issues (e.g., Christopher Bram, *The Notorious Dr. August: His Real Life and Crimes*, 2000).

The field of the new historical novel in the United States is vast, so vast and diverse that it has been declared that "it may be a mistake to consider historical fiction as a distinct genre, given the range of writing it encompasses" (King 2). Further, it has been diagnosed that

> the intense preoccupation with history … is not limited to texts falling in the familiar category of historical fiction. This preoccupation not only extends to neighboring genres such as the nonfiction novel, to forms of individual historiography as biography, memoir, autobiography, and slave narrative, but also to popular genres such as science fiction, the western, or the comic strip.
>
> (Engler/Müller 49)

Contrary to Engler and Müller, I argue that the so-called "neighboring genres" are actually subgenres of historical fiction, which is why I will discuss them under the umbrella term of historical fiction. I believe it is possible to discuss historical fiction as a genre on the whole. It has been noted that "techniques such as metafictionality, achronology, use of popular culture genres, and carnivalization are used consistently to defamiliarize history and the process of historical writing" (Elias, *Sublime* 46). It is exactly the diversity of form of the new historical fiction, its inclusivity – repeatedly noted throughout this study so far – that makes this field of writing so interesting for scholarly investigation.

Johnson identifies many subgenres of the historical novel to organize the immense material. She classifies texts according to the following thirteen categories: traditional historical novels, multi-period epics, romancing the past, sagas, Western historical novels, historical mysteries, adventures in history, historical thrillers, literary historical novels, Christian historical fiction, time-slip novels, alternate history, and historical fantasy (*Historical* v–xiii). Under these headings she then provides "subcategories of themes, which are based mostly around eras/locales" (*Historical* xxiii). Though this approach makes the variants of historical fiction more visible, it nevertheless has its shortcomings. The categories comprise novels, judging them either by form, content, or geographical setting rather than by one consistent sorting category. Many novels fit more than one class, or, more unfavorable, the labels are too narrow to allow for some diversity within a category. Johnson herself admits to this, though somewhat half-heartedly: "Although most titles clearly fit within a single subgenre, a selected number will fit into more than one" (*Historical* xix). Additionally, she does not include the hybrid genre of nonfiction novels, which proves an interesting subgenre of the new historical fiction. I am concerned here mainly with what Johnson labels "literary historical novels":

> Literary historical novels use historical settings, eloquent language, and multi-layered plotlines to convey contemporary themes.... The use of language is important to readers of literary historicals, and the writing style used in these novels can be described as elegant, poetic, or lyrical. While some literary novelists choose to tell their story in a straightforward fashion, others use a more experimental style, making use of flashbacks, stories-within-stories, and multiple narrative viewpoints .... In addition to providing a detailed portrait of life during earlier times, authors of literary historical fiction use the past as a vehicle to express a universal or modern theme.... [L]iterary historicals are thought-provoking works whose ideas can be explored on many levels.
>
> (*Historical* 465–66)

I believe that literary historical novels can be found in all types of subgenres of historical fiction. The forms the writers of new historical fiction use range from seemingly traditional to more inventive. The main categories that I have found and created for turn-of-the-century new historical fiction are the following: historical crime fiction (including the historical nonfiction novel), multi-time-level historical novels, historical biofiction, reanimated classics, historical novels with a magic twist, and alternat(iv)e history. These categorizations are a mix of form- and content-based aspects, and I believe they provide enough leeway to fit in all the material while still being gripping enough to be useful.

Historical crime fiction is either based on true crime or invents crimes against the background of a consistent rendering of the social circumstances of the times, increasingly as historical serial-killer fiction (e.g., *The Alienist*; *The Dante Club*; *The Interpretation of Murder*). Historical nonfiction, often a subgenre of historical crime fiction, prominently raises the question of the dichotomy between fact and fiction when creating fictional narratives of real crimes under the pretense of complete authenticity (e.g., Larson, *The Devil in the White City*; and *Thunderstruck*, 2006). Multi-time-level historical novels use two or more parallel plots from different timelines, unfolding their themes on multiple levels, affirming Vico's historical-philosophical theory of the repetition of history (e.g., *The Great Divorce*; *Specimen Days*; *The 19th Wife*). Historical biofiction about more or less famous historical characters (e.g., Russell Banks, *Cloudsplitter*, 1998; *Poe & Fanny*), often in its manifestations as herstorical biofiction (*In America*; *Stone Heart*) or neo-slave narrative (*The Wind Done Gone*; *Truth*) has become as fashionable as – and almost indistinguishable from – real (auto)biographies or memoirs, and features largely as a subgenre of life writing. Reanimated classics mimic and re-create a past that does not even have its roots in historical reality itself, but in a work of fiction (Bergmann, "Reanimated"). These novels are sequels, prequels, parodies, retellings or -writings, variations, and updates to/of/on American classics (e.g., *Hester*; *Ahab's Wife: or, The Star-Gazer*; *The Wind Done Gone*; *March*). Historical novels with a magic twist weave into the tale elements of the fantastic, the uncanny, and the marvelous, to use Todorov's categories, sometimes stepping into the tradition of magic (al) realism (Bergmann, "I"), gothic fiction, and science or speculative fiction, overthrowing the logical and empirical framework of reality and therewith distinctly turning their backs on comprehensible authenticity (e.g., *The Notorious Dr. August: His Real Life and Crimes*; Andrew Sean Greer, *The Confessions of Max Tivoli*, 2004). Last but not least, alternat(iv)e histories are even more nonchalant when it comes to veracity, as they are presenting the reader with a what-if scenario, their counterfactual reality references not even pretending a claim to truth anymore (e.g., Steven Barnes, *Lion's Blood: A Novel of Slavery and Freedom in an Alternate America*, 2002; Newt Gingrich and William Forstchen, *Gettysburg: A Novel of the Civil War*, 2003; Robert Conroy, *1862*, 2006).

Two of these six classifications will not be discussed in detail in this study. First, the category of historical novels with a magic twist will not be considered separately. Though many new historical novels display a "magical view of the past" (Middleton/Woods 44), they always fit one of the other categories of historical fiction, too, and therefore may as well be subsumed under one of the other headings. As will be shown in the following chapters, various elements of the fantastic, the uncanny, and the marvelous can be found in historical biofiction, for example in *Stone Heart*, where the protagonist sees and feels ghost horses, which might be read as supernatural elements or at least as symbols of Native American spirituality. Concerning historical crime fiction, the serial killer in *The Alienist* at first seems to have supernatural powers, owning to the neo-gothic elements of the novel. In multi-time-level historical fiction, elements of science fiction intrude in the third part of

Specimen Days, while the first part can be read as a ghost story in which the protagonist is guided by a ghost in the machine. In *The Great Divorce*, voodoo magic is introduced when the nineteenth-century heroine's mind enters a leopard. Although these instances can be explained within the logic of the novels, they nevertheless constitute what I would define as a magic twist. It shall therefore suffice here to include this aspect of the new historical fiction within the discussion of other main subgenres, although this is not to say that there do not exist historical novels in which the magical twist is the dominant aspect. The decision not to present this type of new historical fiction more fully here is not meant to imply a futility of this classification, nor does it mean that further research should not be added to the existing studies (Bergmann, "I"; Saldívar; Spaulding). Alternat(iv)e histories are the other class of texts that will not be discussed in-depth in this study. Although there are innovative and extremely successful novels in this category, such as Philip Roth's *The Plot Against America* (2004) and Michael Chabon's *The Yiddish Policemen's Union* (2007), alternat(iv)e histories that depict the nineteenth century tend to be hardly fruitful for scholarly interest. Mimicking MacKinley Kantor's archetypal model of *If the South Had Won the Civil War* (1961), most of these texts are unfortunately concerned with or limited to exactly this one question. Furthermore, much of the scholarly occupation with the historical novel then and now has in general been preoccupied with depictions of the American Civil War (Schabert, *Roman* 180–88). As it is the aim of this analysis to add new perspectives to the study of historical fiction generally and bring to the fore so-far neglected aspects of the new historical fiction, it seems acceptable to disregard this topic here. Besides, a host of studies have already covered a lot of ground regarding counterfactual histories (Butter, *Epitome*; Dannenberg; Hellekson; Rosenfeld; Widmann). It seems justified to concentrate here on four of the most prolific manifestations of historical fiction depicting the nineteenth century in the United States – namely, once again, historical crime fiction, multi-time-level historical fiction, historical biofiction, and reanimated classics.

Before I proceed with the discussion of these four subgenres, I would like to issue a last caveat. As hinted at before, although I am creating a typology of contemporary historical fiction here, I am not assuming that it is impermeable, nor that it is complete. Contemporary literature is subject to a "tendency towards permeable boundaries" (Wägenbaur 373, trans. in Meinig 47), especially concerning genres: "While basic definitions of genres are useful markers for certain textual strategies and concerns, which help to create a productive interpretative path through the many forms that literature assumes, the clear-cut 'headings' of a typology abstract too strongly from the highly individual complexity of specific works of literature" (Meinig 47).

In the following, I will give an impression of publications in the four categories, without restricting this stocktaking to just the United States but also including British and New English examples where useful. Then I will give a detailed case study of three novels in each chapter, selected for their representativeness. I will try to do justice to the wide range of historical topics depicted. Furthermore, I will pay tribute to well-established writers and their recent works, but I will also include works by lesser-known and promising newcomers. As historical fiction at the turn of the twenty-first century is "a female-author-dominated genre" (Heilmann/Llewellyn 5; see also King 3), my selection reflects this. It additionally includes representations of African American and Native American history as well as a nod toward queer issues.

2 Historical Crime Fiction

2.1 Theoretical Conceptions

In Josephine Tey's classic detective novel *The Daughter of Time* (1951), Inspector Alan Grant, the protagonist of a whole series of her fictions, is hospitalized and bedridden due to an injury sustained in pursuit of a criminal. Both physically ill and mentally depressed because of being condemned to idleness, the Inspector whiles away the days in the ward. A concerned friend, who knows of his interest in faces and of his notoriety at Scotland Yard for being able to "pick [criminals] at sight" (Tey 26), brings him pictures of historical personages whose life stories include a mystery to pass his time. Although most of the images fail to grasp Grant's attention, there is one portrait which especially arouses his professional instincts. It is the well-known portrait of Richard III, the king remembered in history books mainly for the monstrosity of having killed or at least commissioned the killings of his two young nephews, the Princes in the Tower, to confirm his entitlement to the throne. Grant is struck by the fact that Richard's face does not seem to fit that of the "monster of nursery stories"; rather, it seems to him the face of "[a] judge? A soldier? A prince?" (28). Subsequently, the Inspector spends much of his convalescence on the case of the "most revolting crime in history," though, due to his condition, he is restricted to "academic investigating" (95), as he calls it.

Unable to go to a bookshop or a library himself, he first inspects the history schoolbooks a nurse lets him have, then asks colleagues and friends to find him more literature. Two of the texts he reads are Thomas More's *History of King Richard III* (1543) and a historical novel on Richard's mother, *The Rose of Raby*, invented by Tey, authored by the fictitious Evelyn Payne-Ellis. The schoolbooks reduce the story to the murder of the Princes in the Tower, which the nurse believes to be an instance of "just giving facts" (Tey 41). Grant finds More's piece of historiography, which is the source of all subsequent reworkings of the story, much fictionalized and greatly biased:

Everything in that history had been hearsay …. Grant had dealt too long with the human intelligence to accept as truth someone's report of someone's report of what that someone remembered to have seen or been told. (83–84)

The Rose of Raby, on the other hand, is to him "the almost-respectable form of historical fiction which is merely history-with-conversation, so to speak. An imaginative biography rather than an imagined story" (Tey 59). Unable to extract the truth by comparing the various books at hand, further including Joseph Robson Tanner's *Tudor Constitutional Documents* (1922) and an invented textbook, Sir Cuthbert Oliphant's *History*, Grant acquires a research assistant, the young American Brent Carradine, and puts him on another track: "After all, the truth of anything at all doesn't lie in someone's account of it. It lies in all the small facts of the time. An advertisement in a paper. The sale of a house. The price of a ring.… Truth isn't in accounts but in account books …. The real history is written in forms not meant as history" (Tey 111–12). Using this approach, Grant and Carradine, over the course of the novel, are able to rouse reasonable doubt against the historical accounts that portray Richard III as the murderer of his two nephews.

The attempt at "rewriting of history" (Tey 164) that Grant and Carradine are undertaking is an early version of the revisionist approaches to history one finds at the basis of many of the new historical novels. The inclusion of non-historiographical and nonliterary texts and artifacts and the alignment of historiography and fiction is in line with new historicist methods. Grant's résumé of historiography is very revealing:

> "I'll never again believe anything I read in a history book, as long as I live, so help me …. A man who is interested in what makes people tick doesn't write history. He writes novels, or becomes an alienist, or a magistrate …. Or a confidence man. Or a fortune teller. A man who understands about people hasn't any yen to write history." (208, 217)

Ultimately, Grant and his sidekick Carradine cannot arrive at a conclusion about who was the murderer of the Princes in the Tower, or whether they were murdered at all. With Henry Ford, they have to conclude that "*History Is The Bunk*" (Tey 159), which is meant to become the title of a book Carradine, after all their biases, plans to write about their investigations. Tey's book is a forerunner of a trend in British fiction in which scholarly and amateur characters research archives and libraries (Keen). The new American historical fiction also has a certain fondness for scholars, researchers, and historians.

With the "renaissance of the historical novel" (Byatt, *Histories* 9) in general, the subgenre of historical crime fiction has also gained momentum.

Since the late twentieth century the literary market has seen what has been called a "veritable explosion of crime fiction placed in a historical setting" (Bertens/D'haen 147). The benchmark text, whose year of publication is commonly accepted to mark the "take-off year for historical crime fiction on a large scale" (Bertens/D'haen 147), is Eco's *Il nome della rosa* (1980). Franciscan monk and amateur detective William of Baskerville and his sidekick Adso of Melk solve serial murders in an abbey in Italy in 1327. Despite the novel's being laden with complex philosophical questions and whole paragraphs in Latin, it became a major best seller. A movie adaptation in 1986, which reduced the action mainly to the whodunit plot, turned out to be a major success as well. Patrick Süskind's *Das Parfum* (1985; published in English as *Perfume*, 1986) is another noteworthy early best seller in the field of historical crime fiction. The novel narrates the life story of apprentice perfumer Jean-Baptiste Grenouille, a serial killer in eighteenth-century France, who murders women in order to create the perfect scent. The novel was adapted for the big screen in 2006.

Historical crime fiction is usually defined as "[a] sub-genre of crime fiction" (Scaggs 145; see also Burgess/Vassilakos ix). Johnson calls this variant "historical literary thrillers," and her definition reads as follows:

> Historical literary thrillers don't necessarily deal with literature and books, although many do .... The quality of the writing is important, and the language used by the authors is erudite, complex, and appropriate to the period. Literary thrillers have great appeal outside the thriller genre: the labyrinthine, intelligent plots will appeal to readers of literary fiction, and the suspense and detection will please mystery fans as well.
>
> (*Historical* 435–36)

What I label historical crime fiction can be either "set in some distinct historical period" or feature "a detective in the present [who is] investigating a crime in the remote, rather than recent, past" (Scaggs 145–46). Agatha Christie's *Death Comes as the End* (1944) is one of the earliest fictions to deal with historical multiple murder. With its action set in ancient Egypt in 2000 BC, it also looks at the remote past. In the novel, the young Egyptian widow Renisenb turns into an amateur detective, trying to solve a series of murders in her family with the help of the family scribe and the family matriarch. *The Daughter of Time* fits the second type, which is identified as "trans-historical crime fiction" (Scaggs 125), because of its characteristic transition between the present and the past. Transhistorical crime fiction becomes a type of multi-time-level historical fiction when the events of the past are presented firsthand. This chapter will be concerned with the first type of historical crime fiction as a manifestation of historical fiction, or rather, with its "various permutations" (Scaggs 125).

Along with the rise of the neo-Victorian novel in Britain, a preoccupation with nineteenth-century crime in literature can also be detected (Ashley 13; Johnson, *Historical* 339–46, 363–73, 436–63; Bertens/D'haen 148). Examples are Margaret Atwood's *Alias Grace* (1996), the fictionalized life story of the supposed murderer Grace Marks, who was sentenced to thirty years in prison for killing two people in Ontario, Canada, in 1843; Andrew Motion's fictional autobiography *Wainewright, the Poisoner* (2000), an imagined confession of London writer, painter, and murderer Thomas Griffiths Wainewright; and – though set in Edwardian London and not exactly a tale of murder – Julian Barnes's *Arthur & George* (2005), a narrative about the historical Great Wyrley Outrages of 1903, Arthur Conan Doyle's involvement in the case, and the story of the man falsely accused, George Edalji.

Some of the notable American fiction and nonfiction publications in this field are Amy Gilman Srebnick's *The Mysterious Death of Mary Rogers* (1995), a historical study of the death of a young woman in New York City in 1841 that inspired Edgar Allan Poe's short story "The Mystery of Marie Rogêt" (1842) and is also the subject of Daniel Stashower's *The Beautiful Cigar Girl* (2006); Patricia Cline Cohen's *The Murder of Helen Jewett* (1998), a narrative about the murder of a young prostitute in New York City in 1836; Karen Haltunnen's *Murder Most Foul: The Killer and the American Gothic Imagination* (1998), a study which traces the changing view of murder in public and literary accounts throughout the nineteenth century; Lauren Belfer's *City of Light* (1999), a murder mystery developing around the building of the hydroelectric plant at Niagara Falls in 1901; and Jennifer Donnelly's young-adult novel *A Northern Light* (2003), a fictional approach to the Gillette/ Brown murder case of 1906 in New York, which had also inspired Theodore Dreiser's *An American Tragedy* (1925). In terms of genre, the texts mentioned here do not simply constitute crime fiction proper but range from scholarly studies to narrative histories and from detective fiction to fictional (auto)biographies (Srebnick).

The increasing interest in nineteenth-century homicide may be rooted in the fact that the origins of detective fiction date back to that very era. Poe is commonly accepted to be the inventor of the detective story. His tales of ratiocination – "The Murders in the Rue Morgue" (1841), "The Mystery of Marie Rogêt" (1842), and "The Purloined Letter" (1844) – were genre-defining and set the standard for all crime fiction to follow, especially Arthur Conan Doyle's creation of the archetypal nineteenth-century detective, Sherlock Holmes (first novel: *A Study in Scarlet*, 1887). Others of Poe's tales, among them "The Tell-Tale Heart" (1843) and "The Cask of Amontillado" (1846) – psychograms and confessional narratives of murderers – have heavily influenced other strands of crime fiction, from Patricia Highsmith's Ripley novels (first novel: *The Talented Mr. Ripley*, 1955) to Bret Easton Ellis's *American Psycho* (1991),

Joyce Carol Oates's *Zombie* (1995), and Stewart O'Nan's *The Speed Queen* (1997).

Beyond that, probably the most popular and evocative true crime of all time – the serial killings of Jack the Ripper in London in 1888 – also fall into this period. Public interest in this case has never ceased, and it still reverberates in popular cultural memory (Burstein; Clerc; Lonsdale). Around the millennium, the ongoing fascination with the unsolved mystery of the Whitechapel murders reached a new peak with *The Complete History of Jack the Ripper* (1994), a comprehensive study by historian Philip Sugden; the launch of a major website called *Casebook: Jack the Ripper* (1996); the publication of Alan Moore and Eddie Campbell's graphic novel *From Hell* (1999) and its adaptation for the big screen (2001); and Patricia Cornwell's *Portrait of a Killer: Jack the Ripper – Case Closed* (2002), a documentary attempt at solving the historical crimes (Schmid 31–65).

Today, the serial killer is mainly perceived as a truly American, twentieth-century phenomenon, inextricably connected to the problems of urbanization, the anonymity of mass societies, the dissolutions of community bonds, and the sexual objectification of women in media (Dyer 14). But serial murder is not such a comparably recent phenomenon. The gunslinger of the Western genre has been identified as an early prototype of the American serial murderer (Seltzer 1; Blake; Schmid 49–51), a fact that ignited a "debate whether a murderer was an archetypal or aberrational American" (Schmid 49). The emergence of the urban serial killer as we know him (Schmid 199) – it is still an undeniable fact that the majority of them are (white) men – coincides with the closing of the frontier proclaimed by Frederick Jackson Turner in "The Significance of the Frontier in American History" (1893). The "traits of the frontier," especially "that dominant individualism, working for good and for evil" (Turner 57), seem to have found another vent in serial killers.

Since the 1960s, media attention on real serial killers has dramatically increased (Blake 200). Ted Bundy, Jeffrey Dahmer, John Wayne Gacy, and others have become "pop culture heroes" (Caputi 8), "superstars of our wound culture" (Seltzer 2), cultural icons of our age (Conrath; Philip L. Simpson 2; Schmid). Their fame has been kindled as well as equaled by FBI profilers such as Robert Ressler and John Douglas and their memoirs, most notably *Whoever Fights Monsters* (1992) and *Mindhunter* (1995) (Kich). The idolization of both the perpetrators and investigators of these crimes has probably triggered the enormous cultural preoccupation with the phenomenon of the serial killer in fiction and film (Conrath 149; D'Cruz 328). Though the beginnings in visual media lie with Alfred Hitchcock's *Psycho* (1960), the "public explosion of interest in serial murder" (Philip L. Simpson ix) has become distinctly recognizable since the 1980s, with the filmic adaptations (1986/2002, 1991, 2001, 2007) of Thomas Harris's best-selling Hannibal Lecter series (*Red Dragon*, 1981; *The Silence of the Lambs*, 1988; *Hannibal*, 1999; *Hannibal Rising*, 2006). Other best sellers in the field have followed, among them Val McDermid's Tony Hill series (first novel: *The Mermaids Singing*, 1995), which was turned into a successful TV series titled *Wire in the Blood* (2002–08). A myriad of motion pictures about serial killers has been released during the last two and a half decades. Most noteworthy or controversial among those are probably *Kalifornia* (1993), *Natural Born Killers* (1994), *Seven* (1995), *Copycat* (1995), *Summer of Sam* (1999), *Monster* (2003), and *Zodiac* (2007).

Taking into account all of these diverse cultural, literary, and popular traditions and developments, it is not surprising that historical serial-killer fiction looms large at the turn of the twenty-first century. Crime fiction set in the nineteenth century and featuring a serial killer has become one of the major trends in the subgenre, and certainly one of the most popular. Jack the Ripper's American cousins are "all the rage" (McDowell) with contemporary readers, to adopt the title of an early-1990s *New York Times* article on the enormous demand for serial-killer fiction. Despite their lurid topic, many of these texts possess noteworthy literary merit. The three American historical novels that will be discussed in more detail are Caleb Carr's *The Alienist* (1994), Matthew Pearl's *The Dante Club* (2003), and Erik Larson's *The Devil in the White City* (2003). Other texts that are beyond the scope of this study, but are equally remarkable examples of this trend, are Carr's *The Angel of Darkness* (1997), a sequel to *The Alienist*; David Fulmer's *Chasing the Devil's Tail* (2001), a story about a Creole detective solving serial murders of prostitutes in New Orleans in 1907, with jazz pioneer Buddy Bolden as a prime suspect; Jeffrey Ford's *The Portrait of Mrs. Charbuque* (2002), in which a portrait artist becomes entangled in a series of mysterious deaths of women in New York City in 1893; and Jed Rubenfeld's *The Interpretation of Murder* (2006), which constructs a plot of serial killing around Sigmund Freud's visit to New York City in 1909.

2.2 Caleb Carr's *The Alienist* (1994)

Caleb Carr's *The Alienist* (1994) is one of the best-known instances of historical serial-killer fiction. It was adapted into a TV series starring Daniel Brühl, Luke Evans, and Dakota Fanning in 2018. The novel was followed by a sequel, *The Angel of Darkness* (1997), featuring the same investigation team solving the case of a female serial killer, Libby Hatch, who abducts and murders children in New York City in 1897. With *The Alienist*, Carr creates a genre hybrid made up of the basic ingredients of a detective story, a police procedural, serial-killer fiction, a historical novel, social history, and psychological study. He is "blending the modern thriller genre with historical reconstruction and then adding a healthy dollop of psychological theory to the mix" (Macintyre). The novel is set mainly in New York City in 1896 and is told from the point of view of John Schuyler Moore, a journalist, who is the Watson to an American Holmes. Moore tells the tale from his own perspective, but an analepsis is created by an introductory chapter, which is set in 1919. The death of Theodore Roosevelt provides the narrator with the occasion to tell his nineteenth-century tale, thereby implying that 1896 and 1919 belong to two wholly different eras. Yet the past time bears significance for the present, and maybe even the future – the present time of the reader.

The alienist of the title is Dr. Laszlo Kreizler, "a pioneer in the nascent field of forensic psychology" (Katzenbach). Carr's description of the psychologist's method is lauded by present-day practitioners and described as not dissimilar to today's techniques in the field (Packer-Fletcher/Fletcher 312). The psychological profiler is unofficially called upon in a case of serial killings by his old Harvard friend, police commissioner Theodore Roosevelt, one of a few historical characters in the novel. Kreizler assembles an investigating team which comprises two forensic analysts, the brothers Lucius and Marcus Isaacson; the first female police detective, Sara Howard; and two former patients of Kreizler's, street urchin Stevie Taggert and convicted murderer Cyrus Montrose. In the background is Mary Palmer, Kreizler's former patient turned maid turned bride turned victim. This character lineup obviously deviates from the classic two-man detective team familiar from Poe and Doyle. The team tellingly consists of a cross-section of New York society at the time, from its upper echelons to the marginalized and disenfranchised. The character constellation apparently owes a debt to Bram Stoker's *Dracula* (1897). In his hunt for the count, Professor Abraham Van Helsing is aided by Jonathan Harker, Arthur Holmwood (later Lord Godalming), Quincey Morris, Dr. John Seward, and Mina Harker née Murray, while Lucy Westenra, the object of almost all of these men's desires and Holmwood's bride, becomes the most prominent victim.

The crimes Kreizler's team investigates are ghastly murders of young boys from the social margins, forced by social circumstances to eke out a living as "transvestite prostitutes" (Bertens/D'haen 157). One of Carr's models for the murders is the crimes of Jack the Ripper. While the detailed description of the settings generally allows for a categorization of the novel as "urban historical fiction" (Katz 831), the crime scenes are horridly violent and evoke the typical settings of the gothic novel. *The Alienist*'s first crime scene is a tower of the newly constructed Williamsburg Bridge and the last is even more reminiscent of the venerable castle of gothic fiction: the Croton Reservoir, which looked like an ancient Egyptian pyramid – a tomb (Carr 553). The team's headquarters, the Renwick at 808 Broadway, situated next to the

"Gothic edifice of Grace Church" (Carr 157) and overlooking a grave-yard, is a case in point too, as is the killer's seemingly supernatural ability to scale high structures on his "labyrinthine cross-city routes on the roofs of buildings" (Tallack 261). His victims, boy prostitutes disguised as virginal maidens, complete the classic gothic character constellation of villain, damsel in distress, and knight in shining armor.

The dialectical tension between villain and savior, the Manichean struggle between good and evil, is reinforced and at the same time blurred into an ambiguous analogy in *The Alienist*. Its origins can be traced back to the beginnings of crime fiction in the nineteenth century, though it also bears reference to postmodern theories such as Derrida's 'double,' or Foucault's 'other.' Starting with the parallels between Auguste Dupin and Minister D – in Poe's "The Purloined Letter" and Doyle's juxtaposition of Sherlock Holmes and Professor James Moriarty, the doubling of protagonist and antagonist, of detective and perpetrator, has become a classic topos in crime fiction (Rollason 19).

The antagonist in *The Alienist* is a fictitious character. Japheth Dury grew up as the son of immigrant Huguenot missionaries who relocated from Switzerland to upstate New York. Harassed by an unloving mother and disciplined by a hard father, because he is a living reminder of marital rape, he develops violent spasms of the face, which make him the focus of cruel harassment by other children. The boy becomes an outsider. On top of that, he is raped by George Beecham when he is eleven years old. As a result of all this exposure to cruelty during his childhood, Dury starts torturing animals and moves on to kill his parents. Finally, he transforms himself into John Beecham, trying to erase the traumatized child by metamorphosing from victim into per-petrator (Gonshak). As a serial killer, he is "symbolically reenacting the sexual mutilation he had suffered" (Gonshak 13), seeing the "dead children ... only [as] a representation of what he felt had been done to him" (Carr 193).

Kreizler, the investigator, is the son of immigrants of Hungarian and German ancestry. Although his parents belong to the intellectual elite of New York City, the boy suffers childhood violence. A severe beating by his father leaves him with a disabled left arm at the age of six. The young Kreizler channels his own suffering into an interest for the emerging dis-cipline of psychology and becomes a physician. On top of his physical challenge, his avant-garde methods of psychology make the adult Kreizler an outsider to society. It is obvious that he is a double as well as a foil to Beecham. He proves that it is possible to draw different lessons from a childhood trauma (Purdy). A binary opposition of country vs. city is in-voked here as well. And while Dury serves as "threatening villain," Kreizler functions as a figure of "audience identification" (Philip L. Simpson 47). However, Kreizler feels akin to Beecham when his fiancée Mary is killed during the investigation, for which he blames himself: "'We've been hunting a killer, John, but the killer isn't the real danger – *I* am!'" (Carr 450). This is supported by the thesis that both characters which make up the double "are excluded from a dominant social order. The monstrous killer is ... brought in to illustrate the possible consequences of that exclusion," but "the killer acts out desires that the more sympathetic double has repressed" (Philip L. Simpson 47–48).

Another important dichotomy that the novel as psychological study plays out, which ties in with the parallel and antithetical life courses of murderer and detective, is introduced by the conflict between two opposing schools of theory within psychology, the theories of determinism and free will. Kreizler, who like Roosevelt is said to have studied with William James, believes in psychological causation, while James and Roosevelt believe in free will. This conflict is further emphasized when another historical character, Anthony Comstock, the United States postal inspector known for his rigid moral stance, is introduced. Comstock has variously been labeled an "antiobscenity crusader" (Joyce 168) and interpreted as an eminent American Victorian (Morone 240). In the novel, his character speaks out against the theory of psychological causation: "'The idea that every man's behavior is decisively patterned in infancy and youth – it speaks against freedom, against responsibility! Yes, I say it is un-American!'" (Carr 368). Since Kreizler is of European ancestry, a much more venerable conflict – that between the Old and the New World – manifests itself here. It is an unnerving analogy to the twenty-first century, when Philip Jenkins ascribes a similar mindset to the New Right movement in his *Using Murder: The Social Construction of Serial Homicide* (1994): "[W]rong-doing and deviancy [are viewed] as issues of personal sin and evil rather than social or economic dysfunction" (9).

It has been remarked that "*The Alienist* ... explores the causes of insanity and criminality, and ultimately the nature of evil" (Lehmann-Haupt, "Erudite"). While the narrator of the story, Kreizler's confidante Moore, perceives New York City as the "absolute pandemonium" (Carr 32) and believes the murderer to be "the devil himself" (216), Kreizler's profiling takes a different stance. He tries to understand the killer's motivation and to put himself in the murderer's position:

> Kreizler emphasized that no good would come from conceiving of this person as a *monster*, because he was most assuredly a man (or a woman); and that man or woman had once been a child. First and foremost, we must get to know that child, and to know his parents, his siblings, and his complete world. It was pointless to talk about *evil* and *barbarity* and *madness*; none of these concepts would lead us any closer to him. But if we could capture the human child in our imagination – then we could capture the man in fact.
>
> (160, my emphasis)

The novel suggests that the murderer is "a figure of considerable psychological complexity" (Gonshak 12) and must be understood as such.

Yet another dichotomy, between affluence and poverty, is employed in the novel and has been read as "psychogeography" (Tallack 260–61). Some members of the investigating team frequent the fashionable restaurant Delmonico's for their briefings and live in elegant mansions equipped with the latest technical gadgets, such as the telephone. The investigation leads them to Sing Sing prison, Five Points, and Hell's Kitchen. The description of the slums of New York, the abode of the poor and the immigrants, highlights the disastrous living conditions in New York's tenement districts (Carr 11, 13; Burgess/Vassilakos 25; Katzenbach; Bertens/D'haen 157). This is a realm which especially the narrator, who is a stand-in for the upper class, has not taken much notice of before. The story is different for Kreizler, who has previously worked with the downtrodden and disregarded – children, women, gays, criminals, and African Americans – in his institute, which is suitably situated on the outskirts of Manhattan. It is therefore hardly surprising that until Roosevelt calls Kreizler in on the case, the serial killer's murders of immigrant children have largely gone unnoticed (Katzenbach). When the team finally tracks down the murderer, he proves to belong to the same sphere as his victims. The primary doubling of serial killer and alienist is here further played out on the character level, as Beecham's victims, neglected and abused immigrant children, "criminals in embryo" (Link 34), can be read as versions of both his and Kreizler's childhood selves. Additionally, Kreizler's protégés Stevie Taggert, Cyrus Montrose, and Mary Palmer, as well as the historical Jesse Harding Pomeroy, the youngest murderer ever convicted in Massachusetts, are mirror figures for Beecham. They are "representative of society's ills" (Athanasourelis 42), namely "sexual exploitation, racism, poverty, and war," but also "xenophobia, abjection, and dehumanization" (Stelzriede 86). They experienced childhood abuse, enabled by the social inequality of the time, and have become juvenile murderers (Philip L. Simpson 129–30). All this ties in with a general loss of Manichean simplicity.

In *The Alienist*, Carr evokes the turn of the twentieth century, a time during which big cities such as New York were marked by "unrest among the masses of cheap immigrant labor" (Lehmann-Haupt, "Erudite"). Some nonfictional characters who appear in Carr's novel give additional emphasis to the topic of social inequality and the problems of urbanization. On the one hand, Jacob Riis, author of the accusatory *How the Other Half Lives* (1890), and Lincoln Steffens, a muckraking journalist, clearly function as icons of social reform. On the other hand, J. P. Morgan, one of the financial tycoons of the era, functions as a symbol of its unbridled competitiveness. The message of the novel boils down to criticism of the social condition. Inequality of women, immigrants, gays, and Native and African Americans is caused by "white bourgeois heteronormative patriarchal power" (Link 32; see also Stelzriede), issues that still have validity in the twenty-first century. Beecham's choice to present his victims at New York City's landmarks is an act of protest (Link 37). Carr seems to emulate George Bernard Shaw's interpretation of the Whitechapel murders: "Whilst we conventional Social Democrats were wasting our time on education, agitation, and organisation, some independent genius has taken the matter in hand, … by simply murdering and disembowelling four women." This ties in with the notion that "the word *monster* is linked to the word *demonstrate*: to show, to reveal. This link reminds us that monsters signify, that they function as meaningful signs…. Their function was, and still is, critical" (Gelder 81). The causes for the multiple murders are to be found in the social condition:

> "He was – perversely, perhaps, but utterly – tied to that society. He was its offspring, its sick conscience – a living reminder of all the hidden crimes we commit when we close ranks to live among each other. He craved human society, craved the chance to show people what their 'society' had done to him. And the odd thing is, society craved him, too." … "[W]e revel in men like Beecham, Moore – they are the easy repositories of all that is dark in our very *social* world. But the things that helped make Beecham what he was? Those, we tolerate. Those, we even enjoy."
>
> (Carr 592)

The serial killer is depicted as "the product of negative conditioning" (Lehmann-Haupt, "Erudite"), "of his entrapment in a particular social and historical environment" (Waltje 113), a victim of the social inequality at the turn of the twentieth century. Yet the claim that childhood trauma and the failure of society to integrate are the main factors in the creation of a serial killer explains away the existence of evil, and is, after all, a rather simplistic psychological formula (Gonshak 13; Lehmann-Haupt, "Erudite").

The topicality of the novel and its references to the present social situation in the United States are more than obvious. Carr himself stresses this when he declares that "historical novels are always about the time they're written in" (Garner). In *The Alienist*, "the crime plot becomes an ideal frame to touch upon past as well as present injustices, their backgrounds and explanations" (Bertens/D'haen 147).

2.3 Matthew Pearl's *The Dante Club* (2003)

Around the turn of the millennium, there was an increase in the intermedial reception of Dante in the USA (Bergmann, "Eine"). In popular media, diverse adaptations and appropriations of the *Divina commedia* (1303–21) appeared, for example, David Fincher's movie *Seven* (1995) (Scheidweiler 228); Vincent Ward's movie *What Dreams May Come* (1998), which is based on Richard Matheson's novel of the same title (1978); and the novels *A Rich Full Death* (1986) by Michael Dibdin, *Hannibal* (1999) by Thomas Harris, and *In the Hand of Dante* (2002) by Nick Tosches (Ó Cuilleanáin; "Critics"; Gaudenzi; Phillips; Scheidweiler; Kretschmann).

Matthew Pearl's *The Dante Club* (2003) is a case in point. It was his debut novel, and the first in a series of literary historical mysteries. It was followed by *The Poe Shadow* (2006) and *The Last Dickens* (2009). *The Poe Shadow* is concerned with the mysterious circumstances of Edgar Allan Poe's death in 1849 and a fictive story of its investigation. *The Last Dickens* describes a fictive hunt for the ending of Charles Dickens's unfinished novel *The Mystery of Edwin Drood* (1870), supposedly lost after his death. All three of Pearl's historical novels were best sellers and were favorably received by the critics.

The Dante Club is a productive transatlantic reception of the *Divinia commedia* by Dante Alighieri. Pearl's novel is set in Cambridge, Massachusetts, in the year 1865, immediately after the end of the American Civil War. Significantly, 1865 is the year of Dante's 600th birthday. *The Dante Club* is first of all the only slightly fictionalized story of the beginnings of the reception of Dante in the USA in the nineteenth century. More specifically, it focuses on the genesis of the first comprehensive American translation of the *Divina commedia* by poet Henry Wadsworth Longfellow and the origins of the Dante Society of America, which began as regular meetings of some Boston Brahmins, the eponymous Dante Club.

The historical background and facts can be summed up as follows: with the publication of "Paul Revere's Ride" (1861), a patriotic poem about an episode of the American Revolution, Longfellow had become one of the nation's most popular poets. As early as 1828, he had begun to read the *Inferno* in Italian. He had intensified his Dante studies on a trip to Europe, where he fled when his first wife died in childbirth in 1835. Upon his return to Cambridge he became a professor of modern languages at Harvard; starting in 1838, he taught a class on Dante for the next sixteen years (Gaudenzi 13; Mathews, 13–14, 19). After the death of his second wife, Fanny, in 1861, he drifted into severe depression and a crisis of creativity (Pearl, "Preface" xiii.) The poet retreated from society and again turned to Dante: "*The Divine Comedy* ... somehow held out a promise to Longfellow .... 'I have taken refuge in this translation of the Divine Comedy,' he informed a friend. 'I have done this work,' he told another, 'when I could do nothing else'" (Pearl, "Preface" xiii, xv; Pertile xviii). Friends called Longfellow's occupation with Dante his "'restorative labor'" (Pearl, "Preface" xv). The translation of Dante's poem became "a way of keeping himself alive as a poet"

(Pertile xviii). Longfellow invited his friends and colleagues, all of whom belonged to Cambridge's intellectual elite, to weekly meetings at his house to discuss his progress with and the pitfalls of his translation. Apart from himself, two other members of this Dante Club were part of a group of poets known as the Fireside poets. Oliver Wendell Holmes was a professor of medicine at Harvard, but due to his literary successes, he was likewise part of the literary elite. He had studied Italian in college and had, like Longfellow, already read the *Inferno* in 1828. In 1881 he composed a poem with the title "Boston to Florence" on the occasion of a Dante meeting (Matthews 18). James Russell Lowell began reading Dante as a student of law at Harvard in 1836/37. From 1840 on, he made a name for himself as a poet. After Longfellow's 'retirement' from the professorship of modern languages at Harvard at the age of 47 in 1854, Lowell succeeded him and taught the already-mentioned Dante class for the next twenty years. During the last nine years of his life, Lowell served as president of the Dante Society of America, which had been founded in 1881 (Matthews 20). Further attendees of the meetings of the Dante Club were James T. Fields, an influential Boston publisher; George Washington Greene, a historian and professor of modern languages at Brown University; and Charles Eliot Norton, the editor of the *North American Review* (although Norton was not turned into a character in Pearl's novel). Beginning in 1867, Longfellow published the first comprehensive American translation of the *Divina commedia* and thereby furthered Dante's entry into the American mindset, which had languished until the middle of the nineteenth century (Pearl, "Preface" xii; La Piana; Straub).

So far Pearl's fiction, with the mentioned small omissions, follows the historical facts of the lives of the authors and might therefore be labeled "author fiction" (Savu 9). The novel belongs to the category of historical biofiction. But Pearl adds a criminal case which is wholly invented and revolves around a Dante-inspired serial killer. Because of the addition of this completely fictional story, which dominates the plot, *The Dante Club* is a "historical detective story" (Gaudenzi 85) or "historical crime fiction" (Bergmann, "Jack," "From").

The novel is also a "bibliomystery," *per definitionem* a crime story which is rooted in the world of literature, a detective story with a decisive literary hinge, or a mystery story "set in the world of books" (Penzler). Eco's *Il nome della rosa* (1980) can be seen as an early instance, and further examples are John Dunning's *Booked To Die* (1992), Julie Kaewert's *Unsolicited* (1994), and Dan Brown's *The Da Vinci Code* (2003). A typology of this subgenre of crime fiction identifies three types: the crime plot can be inscribed into an existing literary plotline of a canonical work, it can be embedded into the biographical world of authors and their works, or a literary work can take on a prime function in the crime novel (Föcking 14–15). Pearl's novel belongs to the third category. Another subgenre which seems to be very closely related to the bibliomystery is the "academic mystery," "academic detective story" (Gaudenzi 92), or "college mystery novel" (Nover), a subgenre of the campus novel (Showalter, *Faculty*; Moseley; Fuchs/Klepuszewski). For simplicity's sake, I label this subgenre "campus crime fiction." Prominent examples are Amanda Cross's *Death in a Tenured Position* (1981), Alfred Alcorn's *Murder in the Museum of Man* (1997), and Joanne Dobson's Karen Pelletier series (first novel: *Quieter Than Sleep*, 1997). Of course, *The Dante Club* – with its setting, plot, and characters rooted in the Harvard environment – qualifies.

In Pearl's novel, the members of the Dante Club, consisting of professors, poets, and publishers, join the first black policeman in Boston, the fictional Nicholas Rey, to investigate the crimes and track down the murderer once they realize that the *Divine Comedy* is the key to the murders: "'Dante! It's Dante!'" (Pearl, *Dante* 85). A thorough knowledge of the *Divina commedia* is needed in order to solve the case. The literary methods and processes of reception, translation, and interpretation become detecting methods. The literary detection self-reflexively points toward the process of reading and writing (Gaudenzi 9), and in this respect *The Dante Club* can be identified as "historiographic metafiction" (Hutcheon, "Pastime"). The author himself wants the fictional plotline to be read as a reimagination of the first part of Dante's *Divine Comedy*: "[P]utting poets into a journey of confronting evil ... That is what the *Inferno* is: two poets, Dante and Virgil, travel through hell and confront violence and evil" (Pearl, qtd. in Mehegan). The amateur detectives and poets take on the roles of Dante and Virgil and go on a quest. They follow the serial killer into his hell, which is a metaphorical one, a hell of the soul (Bergmann, "*From*"). They do this in order to free themselves from suspicion, since only very few people at this particular time and place know Dante's text well enough to be the culprit. And they try to solve the crimes in order to not endanger Dante's reputation in the USA (Gaudenzi 6, 12; Maslin, "All").

The murders in *The Dante Club* are "copycat killings" (Gaudenzi 8), as they minutely imitate the *contrapasso*, the symbolic counterpart of crime and punishment Dante describes in the *Inferno* as punishment for the sinners in hell. A Massachusetts Supreme Court justice, Artemus Healey, is found with gash wounds, which are covered over and over with flies and maggots. The knowledgeable reader identifies this punishment as the one for neutrals. The minister Elisha Talbot is punished as a simonist by being buried alive, headfirst, while his feet are set on fire. Phineas Jennison, a rich businessman, is punished as a schismatic, his body severed in the middle. And Harvard's treasurer, Augustus Manning, is left to die in Cambridge's frozen Fresh Pond in punishment for being a traitor, but he is saved. All the murders are in line with the system of punishments in Dante's epos.

In analogy to Dante, the detectives first perceive the serial killer as the incarnation of evil, "their Lucifer" (Pearl, *Dante* 350). The gruesome murders indeed seem to point to supernatural elements, and *The Dante Club* makes use of the tradition of the gothic novel (Gaudenzi 7). The gloomy settings of the crimes – for example, subterranean passageways which aid the murderer in seemingly vanishing into thin air after the murders – and a scene in which Longfellow believes he is observed by a ghost add to the neo-gothic atmosphere of the novel (Bergmann, "Jack," "From"). But when the detectives finally uncover their foe's identity, he is only "a mere boy" (Pearl, *Dante* 350).

Benjamin Galvin is a veteran of the Civil War, who also has a past as a conductor of the Underground Railroad, an initiative which helped fugitive slaves safely reach the North of the US. The young man idealistically joins the army to further the abolition of slavery. But soon he realizes that the hypocrisy of the Northerners denigrates the cause. Galvin's distinct sense of justice (Pearl, *Dante* 338) is further shaken when he is ordered to execute fellow soldiers, enemies as well as deserters. His only tie to home during the war is symbolized by an edition of Longfellow's poems, reminding him of his wife's admiration for the poet. Ironically, he himself is illiterate. After the war that turned him into a multiple murderer, the traumatized and disillusioned Galvin (Gaudenzi 91) experiences a lecture series on Dante for veterans, given by George Washington Greene at the soldiers'-aid home, as a silver lining (Pearl, *Dante* 344). Subsequently, the twenty-four-year-old man closely identifies with Dante, "a man who understood," "a former soldier, too, who had fallen victim to a great divide between the parties of his sullied city and had been commanded to journey through the afterlife so that he might put all mankind right" (344). This affinity and his emotional attachment to Longfellow trigger him to act, or react, when he incidentally overhears that the translation of Dante is endangered. Many officials at Harvard see the attempt of the first American translation of Dante critically. They disapprove of Dante's works as "immoral and irreligious" (288) and of Dante himself as a literary charlatan, and favor a traditional focus on Latin and Greek classics (Pearl, "Preface" xi, xii). Religious conflicts and xenophobia, which find vent in accusations against the Catholic Italian immigrants of Boston, strongly add to this controversy (Gaudenzi 89; Champagne; Pearl, "Preface" xii). Some even see Dante as a threat to national stability and American identity (Gaudenzi 89).

Galvin transforms himself into Dan Teal, an appellation which is the result of his failed attempt to sign a work contract as 'Dante Alighieri.' He becomes a clerk at the publishing house of Ticknor & Fields by day and a worker at Harvard University by night. He makes it his "mission" (Pearl, *Dante* 338) to save the translation, in an analogy to his futile attempt to free black people as a soldier in the Civil War. Galvin's character is an exaggeration of actual fervent admirers of Dante in nineteenth-century America, who, led by Longfellow, worshipped the poet as their hero and sacralized the translation of his work (Redling 65–70). By murdering the opponents of the translation one by one in accordance with Dante's *contrapasso*, Teal creates an interpretation of the *commedia* which is in line with the English reception of Dante as the "poet of Hell" (Gaudenzi 90). The victims are tortured and killed because of their opposition to Dante. Healey is eaten by insects because he did not defend Dante against the members of the Harvard Corporation; Talbot is turned into a human torch because he has taken money from Manning as remuneration for discrediting Dante and his translator Longfellow; and Jennison is punished because he tells Longfellow's publishers Ticknor & Fields, as well as the Harvard Corporation, whatever they want to hear. Teal's strong identification with Dante is obvious. While the historical Dante took revenge with words and punished some of his enemies by turning them into characters in his *Inferno*, Teal punishes Dante's American enemies with actual violence (Gaudenzi 91–92). He is a textbook protagonist of a historical novel, the subject of differing loyalties within a greater historical conflict (Baldick 114): the American Civil War and its aftermath.

As in Carr's *The Alienist*, the opposition between the detectives and the perpetrator is constructed as well as deconstructed. While there is an obvious opposition between the analphabet Teal and the literati Longfellow, Holmes, and Lowell, there are also striking parallels and analogies. These exist among Longfellow, Teal, Oliver Wendell Holmes, Jr., Pietro Bachi, and Dante. That criminal and detective function as doppelgänger is a topos of the detective story. But here, further doubling excels the genre topos and leads directly to Dante.

Longfellow, who mourns the death of his wife, is heavily traumatized. His motivation to occupy himself with the translation of Dante is born from his fear that he might never be able to write poetry again. For him, Dante's work is the place of last resort. The same holds true for the serial killer Teal. He also identifies with the poet Dante and his situation in life. Pearl calls this a "gripping emotional partnership between poet and translator" (Pearl, "Preface" xv). In his *Divine Comedy*, Dante is granted a glimpse of his beloved, deceased Beatrice in the highest spheres of heaven. It is this scene which, among other moments of identification, certainly appealed to the mourning widower Longfellow. He reads the *Divine Comedy* also as a chronicle of his own life. This becomes evident when he opens the Dante Club meetings with an only slightly modified version of the first lines of the *Inferno*: "Midway through the journey of *our* life, I found myself within a dark wood, for the right way had been lost" (Pearl, *Dante 55*, my emphasis). Longfellow's translation of Dante must be read as "a rebirth of sorts for two poets" (Pearl "Preface" xv), himself and Dante. Lowell's interpretation of Dante further confirms the identification with the poet and his work: "*We* read ... Dante's *Comedy* as a chronicle of our inner lives .... From the very first line of Dante's poem, *we* are involved in the journey, *we* are taking the pilgrimage as much as he is, and *we* must face our Hell as squarely as Dante faces his" (Pearl, *Dante* 67, my emphasis). Longfellow, Holmes, and Lowell are on a Dantean quest (Scheidweiler 231–35). The personal crisis of the popular and patriotic poet Longfellow also points to the crisis of the nation, a nation which must find itself or build itself once again in the era of Reconstruction.

A further parallel is established between Teal and Oliver Wendell Holmes, Jr., Holmes's son. Holmes, Jr., like Teal "not yet twenty-five" (Pearl, *Dante* 84), has returned to Harvard to complete his studies after being released from the army as a thrice-wounded war hero. He, who in real life would later become an eminent US Supreme Court justice, is introduced as the serial killer's doppelgänger. Due to his strong sense of justice, he had refused his father's offer to buy him out of conscription. Like Galvin, he is heavily traumatized by his war experiences. "Wendy" (254), who had been the class poet at his Harvard commencement, has now lost all his sense for poetry: "Dante was a soldier .... He wondered whether it had made Dante a better poet to see his friends die beside him for the soul of Florence.... In battle, Junior had seen something that Dante had not, and it had kicked the poetry – and the poet – right out of him" (253). Different from Teal, who feels a spiritual kinship with Dante and is inspired to his gruesome deeds by his poetry, Holmes, Jr., has left behind the literary realm and henceforth strives for justice in a nonviolent way. In a lecture, notably not attended by his eldest son, Holmes, Sr., draws the following conclusions:

> Healing is a living process, ... greatly under the influence of mental conditions. He told them how it was often found that the same wound received in battle would heal well in the soldiers that have prevailed but would prove fatal in those who were defeated.... "There were a good many hearts pierced in this war, too, that have no bullet mark to show." (181–82)

His thoughts about physical war wounds and psychological traumata seem to directly refer to the doubling of his son and the killer.

Holmes, Sr., is himself a noteworthy character among the group of amateur detectives, as the namesake of Sherlock Holmes (Maslin, "All"). And since he is both a physician – or rather, a professor of medicine at Harvard University – and a poet, he is a mirror image of both the seminal literary detective and his chronicler, Dr. John H. Watson. Furthermore, he echoes Holmes's creator, Doyle, who practiced as a general physician before he became a writer, and the model for his literary creation, Dr. Joseph Bell, one of Doyle's medical-school professors.

Pietro Bachi – Italian immigrant and former lecturer of Italian at Harvard University – is a fictionalization of a historical figure and a further character with Dantean traits (Gaudenzi 98). In the novel, the young Pietro Batalo, a graduate of the University of Padua, falls in love with a young woman in Sicily. But her family belongs to an opposing political camp to his family's. The Batalos fought tirelessly against papal control of the state, so when the young woman felt betrayed by Pietro, her family immediately plotted for him to be excommunicated and banned. After serving as a soldier in various armies, Batalo changed his name to Bachi and came to the US, where he secured a post as lecturer of Italian at Harvard University in 1843, when Boston was still a more cosmopolitan city. But after yet another unhappy romance and his subsequent decline into alcoholism, he was fired. He felt let down by Longfellow and Holmes, who did not object to his dismissal and therefore proved disloyal. After the Civil War, Bachi leads a meager existence as a private tutor. He lives in poor circumstances, lonely and bitter. He is exiled twice – first driven out of Italy and later dismissed from Cambridge. The parallels to Dante and the *Divine Comedy* are more than obvious. And the similarities to Longfellow are apparent, too. Like the American poet, Bachi works on a translation of the *Divina commedia* with a group of old friends, his own Dante Club, but with only moderate success. These friends likewise connect their own fate with Dante and the translation: "*We* thought, I suppose, that if *we* can show ourselves that Dante could be as alive in English as in Italian, *we* too could thrive in America" (Pearl, *Dante* 316, my emphasis). Like Longfellow and Teal, Bachi identifies with Dante: "The greatest bard had no home but exile. One day to come, perhaps, I shall walk on my own shores again, once more with true friends, before I leave this earth" (162).

It is in passages such as this one that Pearl's historical novel seems to refer directly to contemporary issues, such as the wars in the Middle East, terrorism, immigration, religious and racial conflicts, and xenophobia (Scheidweiler 227). War is presented as the source of all evil. It distorts human beings and turns some of them into killing machines. This holds true for the civil war in Florence in the Middle Ages, the American Civil War of the nineteenth century, and the war in Iraq in the twenty-first century. The general suspicion toward people with a migrant background or a different religious affiliation can be read as a critique of the present social intolerance. The novel is an instance of the cultural processing of past and present traumata in American culture. It might be an interesting aside here that one of the functions of Longfellow's previously mentioned poem "Paul Revere's Ride" is, similar to Pearl's novel, to establish a relationship between the past and the present.

The symbolic personification of good and evil is paralleled in the novel by the topography of the setting, the spatial dichotomy between Cambridge and Boston. *The Dante Club* is "a detailed appreciation of the interaction of various social classes in the Boston/Cambridge vicinity" (Champagne 98). Boston is depicted as "the low world," "where slums and public houses and brothels and cheap hotels had driven out those residents who could afford being driven out, where chalky steam gushed from pipes bending outward from glass- and ironworks" (Pearl, *Dante* 119). Boston is the underworld, an image of hell itself. Cambridge, with Harvard University, is presented as the realm of the intellectual and affluent elite, the "Yankee Athens" (Maslin, "All"). By a perverse impetus, Teal wants "to make Boston good" (Pearl, *Dante* 349), and in an act of hubris, he transforms himself into an angel of revenge who reinstates divine justice (Scheidweiler 226). Teal, the crusader for what he believes is good, is a representation of a warrior in a holy war or a terrorist for a good cause, in an analogy to David S. Reynolds's argument in *John Brown, Abolitionist: The Man Who Killed Slavery, Sparked the Civil War, and Seeded Civil Rights* (2005). Indeed, Teal manages to direct the attention of the intellectual caste, the Boston Brahmins, to the plights of war veterans, the black population, and European immigrants. As in Carr's *The Alienist*, social injustice is the cause of all evil. It turns a young idealist into a traumatized serial killer.

Pearl takes the reader "on the same kind of allegorical journey into the darkest places imaginable, both spiritual and psychological, as Virgil brought the pilgrim Dante, in order to raise questions about the nature of sin and divine justice and to seek order in a dark world" (Phillips 210–11). The journey through hell is therefore not only Dante's and Virgil's, it is metaphorically also Teal's, Longfellow's, and the Dante Club's. The reader, too, has been to hell and back after reading Pearl's novel. The author takes on Virgil's role of the guide on this trip.

The Dante references lend a certain literary authority to Pearl's novel, even if the text can be categorized as popular or genre fiction. But Dante is a model for Pearl in this respect as well. The decision to write in Italian instead of Latin shows that Dante wanted to be read and understood by a broad or even the widest possible audience, an aim that the author of the *Divine Comedy* shares with creators of popular literature. The various levels of meaning, which make the *Divina commedia* attractive to such a wide variety of readers (Gaudenzi 93), are mimicked by *The Dante Club*'s genre hybridity and, through it, the ability to serve a wide variety of reader expectations or *Erwartungshorizonte*. The boundary between high and popular culture is closed (Gaudenzi 93), along the lines of Leslie A. Fiedler's dictum "cross the border – close the gap."

Moreover, the narrative structure of the novel follows the model text. *The Dante Club* is divided up into three canticles, each of which consists of seven chapters. The *Divine Comedy* is similarly divided into three parts, *Inferno, Purgatorio,* and *Paradiso,* which themselves are divided into cantos. Furthermore, the numbers three and seven are very important in medieval numerology and can be found in various contexts in Dante's epic work as well as Pearl's novel (Gaudenzi 3;

Scheidweiler 228). By way of marked and unmarked intertextuality – such as quotes from and references to Dante's epos, murders which minutely follow the *contrapasso* in the *Inferno*, the Dantean quest of the members of the Dante Club, the structure borrowed from the *Divina commedia*, and much more (Gaudenzi 2–3) – *The Dante Club* is a rewrite. The canonical status of the *Divine Comedy* makes it possible for Pearl to create a reanimated classic with *The Dante Club*.

The novel, which is set immediately after the American Civil War in 1865, was written after the terror attacks of September 11, 2001, and published in 2003, during the second war in Iraq, refers to issues outside the book and to anthropological constants by this parallelism of events and their impact. Instrumental to this juxtaposition of the historical past and the present is the preface to the novel. In this pretext, Pearl creates a false or fictive authority (Morgan 69–72), "Professor C. Lewis Watkins," the "Baker-Valerio Professor of the Civilization and Literature of Italy and Rhetorical Oration," who introduces himself as a "recognized authority on the subject of the American reception of Dante's *The Divine Comedy*" (Pearl, *Dante* vii–viii). It is interesting that many readers were not able to identify this obvious literary hoax for what it is, but believed the preface and the professor to be genuine (Morgan 71; Gaudenzi 88). In this respect, another link between Dante and Pearl has been noted: "While Dante's *commedia* apparently presents the reader with a truth veiled in beautiful poetry, Pearl's preface to *The Dante Club* introduces an elaborate fiction to suggest that the work is based on historical facts" (Gaudenzi 87–88). The pretext functions as an affirmation of the supposed authenticity of what follows and as a blurring of the lines between history and fiction (Morgan 71). One may agree with the interpretation that "[f]or Pearl, the whole hoax was an attempt to force readers to understand the relativity of Truth and consequently to question it" (Morgan 71). The preface establishes a reference between past and present with a fictional newspaper article of 1989, which reports the renewed appearance of a species of insects which for a long time has been believed extinct. These insects do not kill immediately; rather, they infest their victim and feed on it from the inside, until it dies excruciatingly days later. According to the newspaper article, a boy, Kenneth Stanton, was attacked by the insects during a school trip. Scientists immediately began to breed the insect in laboratories for research purposes, allegedly under safe conditions. Since then, the insects have appeared in the Middle East, seemingly introduced to the area by freight ships from the US. Currently, the insects are said to be decimating livestock in northern Iran. And lately scientists have brought up the idea that the divergent development of the insects originates from the Northeast of the US, around the year 1865 (Pearl, *Dante* vii–ix).

The preface, with its reference to the Middle East and the raging plague of insects in the area, points toward a critique of the present, inherent to the genre of the historical novel. The depiction of conflicts between liberal and conservative positions in the nineteenth century refers to the USA in the twenty-first century (Gaudenzi 94). The death of the schoolboy described in the preface refers to the agonizing death of Justice Healey which opens the novel. And both scenes refer to the corresponding *contrapasso* in the *Divine Comedy*. The "renewal" (Pearl, *Dante* vii) of the insects is paralleled by a renewal of the *Divina commedia*. The title of the preface is "Caution to the Reader" (vii), and it ends with a portentous passage:

> I have waived any recompensation, for this was no longer a preface I set out to write but a warning. Kenneth Stanton's death throws wide open the closed portal of Dante's arrival to our world, of the secrets still lying dormant in our own age. Of these I only wish to caution you, reader. Please, if you continue, remember first that words can bleed. (ix)

The last sentence refers to the ability of Dante's words to prompt bloodshed (Gaudenzi 88) and therefore to the Dante-inspired serial killings. In addition, this passage mimics the most popular passage from the *Divine Comedy*, the warning which Dante beholds at the gates of Hell: "All hope abandon, ye who enter in!" (Alighieri 13).

Pearl achieves the creation of a *Divine Comedy* for the twenty-first century. This observation is based upon much more than the mere analogy of the initial letters of the titles of both works (Gaudenzi 86). The author, a Harvard and Yale graduate and awardee of the Dante Society of America, is hailed for his "genuinely scholarly interest" (Gaudenzi 86):

> [*The Dante Club*] provides a fascinating illustration of Dante's continuing appeal, intellectual as well as emotional…. *The Dante Club* effectively sums up the range of cultural interest, from high to low, that Dante's epic work has exerted since its first appearance…. [T]he novel explores … the social and political relevance that Dante's work may still have in the modern world.
> (Gaudenzi 85–86)

The topics that the *Divine Comedy* debates are timeless and deeply rooted in human nature (Phillips 202). Pearl presents and approaches these themes or anthropological constants in *The Dante Club*: war, violence, death, morality, treason, exile, justice, friendship, love, faithfulness, and loyalty. In the light of the theory of literary anthropology (Iser), *The Dante Club* can be read as a historical update of the *Divina commedia*.

2.4 Erik Larson's *The Devil in the White City* (2003)

The case of the supposed first American serial killer – Herman Webster Mudgett, a.k.a. H. H. Holmes, who in his Castle of Horrors murdered between twenty-seven and 200 visitors to the World Columbian Exposition in Chicago in 1893 – has induced a considerable amount of cultural resonance. Some noteworthy publications are Allan W. Eckert's novel *The Scarlet Mansion* (1985); a popular history by Harold Schechter, *Depraved* (1994); a graphic novel, *The Beast of Chicago* (2003), by Rick Geary; Alec Michod's novel *The White City* (2004); a documentary film titled *H. H. Holmes: America's First Serial Killer* (2004); and a republication of three contemporary nineteenth-century documents, including Holmes's autobiography as *The Strange Case of Dr. H. H. Holmes* (2005) (Schmid 31–65).

Erik Larson's *The Devil in the White City* (2003) is a nonfiction or "documentary novel" (Flis 1). As Sauerberg explains, "[n]onfiction 'fiction' supposedly turns into narrative a segment of documentable reality without interfering with it" (2). The genre, a mix of fact and fiction, was popularized by Truman Capote. His novel *In Cold Blood* (1966), the account of a "true crime" (Tüllmann 18) – the holdup murder of a family for a haul of only a few dollars – and the conviction of the murderers, is identified as "faction" (Flis 1). Other examples of this genre range from Norman Mailer's *The Armies of the Night* (1968), a report about anti-war demonstrations in 1967 with the significant subtitle *History as a Novel, the Novel as History*, and *The Executioner's Song* (1979), the story of murderer Gary Gilmore – who in 1976 sued for his right to the consummation of the death penalty – to John Berendt's *Midnight in the Garden of Good and Evil* (1994), a story about a murder in Savannah, Georgia, in the 1980s and a genre picture of the society, and *The City of Falling Angels* (2005), which approaches Venice, Italy, after the destruction of the La Fenice opera house in a fire in 1996. Larson, like other authors (Cuddon 302; Abrams 202), turns the form into a variety of the new historical novel. His books *Isaac's Storm* (1999), a narrative about the destruction of Galveston, Texas, by a storm in 1900, and *Thunderstruck* (2006), an interweaving of the stories of Hawley Crippen, an American doctor who is supposed to have killed his wife in London in 1910, and the inventor of wireless communication, Guglielmo Marconi, are examples of this new variant. The historical nonfiction novel *The Devil in the White City* is historical serial-killer fiction, since "the serial killer narrative spans both fictional and non-fictional genres" (Newitz 38).

Larson's novel is set in Chicago at the time of the World's Columbian Exposition of 1893, held to commemorate the 400th anniversary of Christopher Columbus's arrival in the New World. It contrasts the story of the chief architect of the exposition, Daniel H. Burnham, with that of the first serial killer recognized by the media in the United States, H. H. Holmes. The typical doubling in crime fiction is used even more prominently in this text. While Burnham makes use of architectural and technological innovations to present the world with an idealized version of the United States, a "magical dreamscape" (Böger 271), Holmes implements technological progress to build a "Castle of Horrors" (Larson 441) at the fringes of the exhibition grounds. His hotel becomes the perfect trap for visitors to the fairground, and the scene of his ghastly crimes. While Burnham tries "to 'out-Eiffel Eiffel'" (29) and thereby surpass the success of the 1889 Exposition Universelle in Paris, France, Holmes, the devil of the title, seems to be eager to outdo his infamous British predecessor Jack the Ripper (Achilles). Larson not only highlights an oedipal rivalry with European paragons but also evokes a melodramatic dichotomy between the White and the Black Cities. The White City originally identified the Court of Honor, the neoclassical center of the World's Fair, but soon became a synonym for the entire exposition. The Black City was the moniker for the metropolis of Chicago, where the problems of urbanization and mass society were surfacing more and more prominently toward the *fin de siècle* (Böger 265–68).

The juxtaposition of Burnham and Holmes, and of, respectively, the White and the Black City, is stylized as another episode in the Manichean struggle between absolute moral forces. It is an affirmation of a typically Victorian outlook: "In the end it is a story of the ineluctable conflict between good and evil, daylight and darkness, the White City and the Black" (Larson 10). Subplots, paralleling and varying the two main plots, are introduced to further the black-and-white dichotomy of the overall concept of the narrative. At the fair itself, the White City, the simulacrum of civilization, is contrasted with Buffalo Bill's Wild West Show, the representation of a vanished way of life, and Holmes's killings are flanked by the assassination of Chicago's mayor, Carter Harrison, Sr., by Patrick Prendergast (Achilles). Yet the focus on the obsessions of both Holmes and Burnham unravels their similarity (Cayton 334).

The constant alternation between the two stories of Burnham and Holmes exposes the text's fictionalization. The narrative "whips back and forth from character to character, anecdote to anecdote, building plenty of momentum in the process" (Homans; see also Fierman). The end of each chapter is additionally used for rich foreshadowing, which creates suspense and "the dramatic effect of a novel" (Maslin, "Add"). The cliff-hanger is a device familiar from crime fiction, an analogy Larson himself evokes when he describes his research method as detective's work (442). Contrary to the conventions of the detective story, the investigation plays only a minor part in the narrative. The parallel stories are inserted into a frame tale which involves the sinking of the Titanic, to further dramatize the plot. Finally, the climax of the story, the detailed description of a murder of a young woman in Holmes's torture chamber, is fully imagined by Larson, who claims to have "used threads of known detail to weave a plausible account, as would a prosecutor in his closing arguments to a jury" (441–42; see also Cayton 334). Larson further suggests a high level of veracity and creates the semblance of a textbook by including a contents page (7), authentic visual elements such as contemporary photographs (13, 21, 131, 263, 437), and a historical map of Chicago (6), which are also properly credited (483). He gives a bibliography of his copious research materials (475–80), making use of extensive footnotes (442–74), and providing a subject index (485–96). These paratexts serve as "an authenticating presence" (Sanders 141; see also Tüllmann 102–07). In a peritext preceding the novel, with the lurid title "Evils Imminent," Larson puts emphasis on the fact that his is "*not a work of fiction*" (9). But this attempt to trick the readership notwithstanding, *The Devil in the White City* is of course a work of fiction.

The plot revolving around the impostor and murderer Holmes combines all the typical elements of the gothic novel (Schmid 53). The villain lures mainly female victims, the damsels in distress, into his World's Fair Hotel, the gothic castle, complete with torture chambers and secret passageways. The hotel is Holmes's "own human slaughterhouse" (Homans), as one might label it in analogy to the meat industry, for which Chicago, named "Hog Butcher for the World" in Carl Sandburg's poem "Chicago" (1916), was infamous at the time. The young, innocent women succumb to Holmes because of his charm, his good looks, and especially his "striking blue eyes" (Larson 50). Larson presents Holmes as the personification of evil, the devil himself, by taking an excerpt of his confession and making it one of the epigraphs of his text: "I was born with the devil in me. I could not help the fact that I was a murderer, no more than the poet can help the inspiration to sing" (11). As the devil, Holmes revels in Chicago, stylized as the netherworld, "a world of clamor, smoke, and steam" (24). The serial killer's devilishness is further heightened by Larson's reticence to give a comprehensible motivation for Holmes's deeds. The references to a perverted entrepreneurial motive, childhood episodes involving Holmes's fear of a skeleton and a prosthetic leg, and a hint at the possibility that he suffered childhood violence from his overly strict and exceedingly religious parents (53–55) are not really elaborated.

The depiction of Holmes is almost minutely paralleled by the description of Burnham. Holmes's opening epigraph is significantly combined with the following dictum by Burnham: "Make no little plans; they have no magic to stir men's blood" (Larson 11). The architect is presented as a man who, against all odds, will complete his mission to build the ultimate architectural showcase, using his "blue gaze" (69) and his persuasive charm as his weapons. Clearly, "Burnham and Holmes are two sides of the coin, creatures of the new metropolis, using American energies and know-how to radically different purposes" (Homans). Both are versions of the "self-made man" (Larson 81), their striving being the "genius and flaw of the modern city" (Homans). They appear as icons of the American Dream or of American hubris: "both handsome, both blue-eyed, and both unusually adept at their chosen skills. Each embodied an element of the great dynamic that characterized the rush of America toward the twentieth century" (Larson 9).

The combination of the fair and the serial killings, "their temporal coincidence," implies "more profound thematic similarities" (Schmid 52). The mystery of the source of evil and its inexplicability remain mostly intact, although the final predication of the text culminates in the assertion that technological progress is the catalyst of evil: "The rational explanation laid blame on the forces of change that during this time had convulsed Chicago" (Larson 18). In this respect, Larson's book is reminiscent of a Dickensian connection between urbanization and evil, while at the same time taking a position toward contemporary controversies such as stem-cell research, genetic modification, or nuclear phaseout.

The Devil in the White City furthermore bears references to events of more explicit topicality. In addition to the overall apocalyptic sentiment of the novel, one scene becomes especially significant considering the terrorist attacks on the World Trade Center in New York City on September 11, 2001. The description of a devastating fire in the Cold Storage Building of the World's Fair reveals striking analogies with the televised images of the cataclysm of the Twin Towers, the firefighters' futile attempts at saving the workers as well as the buildings, and the catastrophe's aftermath and reverberations:

> Suddenly flames erupted from the tower at a point about fifty feet *below* Fitzpatrick and his men. Fresh air rushed into the tower. An explosion followed. To the firemen, … it appeared 'as though the gaseous contents of the air-shaft surrounding the smokestack had become ignited, and the entire interior of the tower at once became a seething furnace.' … Captain Fitzpatrick grabbed a rope and swung down through the fire to the main roof below, where he lay with a fractured leg and internal injuries, half his huge mustache burned away. Other men jumped to their deaths, in some cases penetrating the main roof…. In all, the blaze killed twelve firemen and three workers…. The next day attendance exceeded 100,000. The still-smoking rubble of the Cold Storage Building had proved irresistible.
> (Larson 339–40)

This scene functions as what Marita Sturken has labeled a "cultural reenactment" (17) of the terrorist attacks. It is exactly this topicality that allows for the conclusion that historical crime fiction is not simply a "simulacrum of the past" (Lehmann-Haupt, "Erudite"), but equally a simulacrum of the present: "Historical novels often say as much about the present as about the past. The same thing is true for their counter-parts in crime writing" (Bertens/D'haen 147).

Historical serial-killer fiction is "not an escape, but an attack" (Santaulària 63); it "disclose[s] the endemic problems in the social fabric" (56). It is an "effective instrument of socio-political critique," "address[ing] issues of class, race and gender" (Horsley 158). To call these novels "no more than escapist entertainments" (James), whose readership seeks "sedation in nostalgia" (Anne Simpson), is to disregard the enormous social critique as well as the applicability to the present situation. The serial killers are not manifestations of absolute evil, but symptoms of the ills of their society:

> [T]he serial killer [is presented] as the ultimate alien outsider or enemy of society, [but] simultaneously reflect[s] back upon society its own perversions, fears, and murderous desires. Thus, the serial killer is 'psycho' – aberrant and depraved – while still remaining a recognizable product of American culture.
>
> (Philip L. Simpson 1–2)

H. H. Holmes seems to be driven by a Faustian greed for knowledge, money, and power; John Beecham suffers from the aftermath of child-hood neglect and abuse; and Dan Teal endures post-traumatic stress disorder. All three reinvent themselves and create another identity, a fact that is most obvious from their self-/renaming. As different as the reasons for their respective pathologies may be, in the end they are children of the society of their age, which creates the real crime: social inequality.

3 Multi-Time-Level Historical Fiction

3.1 Theoretical Groundwork

A. S. Byatt begins her novel *Possession: A Romance* (1990) with a very significant scene. Her character Roland Michell discovers love letters in an old book in the London Library which a poet addressed to an unknown lady in 1858. This incident launches a plot that wavers between detective fiction, campus novel, and historical romance and between two time periods, the late twentieth and the mid-nineteenth century. The novel revolves around two university scholars, Michell and Maud Bailey, in the 1980s, whose story is mirrored by and interwoven with a secret love story between a famous poet and a lesser-known one in Victorian times, Randolph Henry Ash and Christabel LaMotte. What is especially intriguing is the fact that Michell does not discover the letters in just any old book:

> The book was thick and black and covered with dust. Its boards were bowed and creaking; it had been maltreated in its own time. Its spine was missing, or rather protruded from amongst the leaves like a bulky marker. It was bandaged about and about with dirty white tape, tied in a neat bow .... It had been exhumed from Locked Safe no. 5 .... Roland had only recently discovered that the London Library possessed Ash's own copy of Vico's *Principj di Scienza Nuova* .... It was immediately clear that the book had been undisturbed for a long time, perhaps even since it had been laid to rest.
>
> (Byatt, *Possession* 1–2)

Giambattista Vico (1668–1744) is one of the first modern thinkers in the field of the philosophy of history, and the *Scienza Nuova* (1725) is his major work. In Byatt's novel, the book Michell finds has been treated badly in its time. So was its author, since Vico's theories were not received with much enthusiasm by his eighteenth-century contemporaries. Fame and recognition came much later, after his death

(Verene). Further, the narrator's remarks about the bad physical condition of the book are probably an allusion to the highly selective translations and almost distorting interpretations Vico's theories became subject to during the nineteenth century (Verene). A few lines down, the narrator – or is it the author herself? – gives us her own brief interpretation of what she believes to be the essence of Vico's studies: "Vico had looked for historical fact in the poetic metaphors of myth and legend; this piecing together was his 'new science'" (Byatt, *Possession* 3). One of Vico's main aims was to "formulate a philosophy of mythology and to base both philosophical and historical knowledge on a conception of narration" (Verene). The title of one of Ash's collections of poems, *Gods, Men and Heroes* (allegedly published in 1856), hints at the fact that Vico's principle of history is based on a cycle of ages, the ages of gods, heroes, and humans. He believes that these stages repeat itself in *corsi* and *ricorsi*. History is perceived as a series of cyclical – or rather, spiraling – repetitions of the three ages (Emerson 180–81). Ash's cycle of poems appears to be heavily indebted to Vico.

This close scrutiny of the first chapter of *Possession* leads to two basic assumptions. Byatt is not acting on a whim when she starts her book with the description of a copy of the *Scienza Nuova*, sprinkles her first chapter with many allusions to Vico, and, throughout the novel, returns and refers ever so often to the Italian's historical philosophy. Vico's new science is a key to understanding *Possession*. The theory of *corsi* and *ricorsi* finds its equivalent in the manifold parallels between the nineteenth- and twentieth-century storylines, the most obvious intersection between the two narrative levels being the interest in Vico itself. Ash's possession of a copy of the *Scienza Nuova* and his references to Vico in his poems indicate the historical fact that the Italian philosopher's teachings were rediscovered by English writers and scholars in the nineteenth century. When Michell exhumes the book in 1986, this is an illustration of the real twentieth-century resurrection of a theory that had been laid to rest in the nineteenth century (Verene).

Possession represents what one may, in an admittedly trivial comparison, with the Propellerheads and Shirley Bassey call a case of "History Repeating" (1997). Byatt is neither the first nor the last British author to use the device of more or less parallel storylines in different time periods to put emphasis on the fact that history is merely a repetition, with variations, of the same events. But she is the first to point to this fact with determination, by literally starting her book with a clear reference to Vico.

This manifestation of the contemporary historical novel has since flourished, and not only on British soil. The novels construct "a virtual relationship between past and present" (Kaplan 9). It is typical of this type of the new historical fiction to narrate at least two (Hodgkin 16), but usually three or even more stories from different eras separately or interweavingly. Often, a plot in a historical period is paralleled by a story in the present time, and occasionally there even is a story set in the future. My label for this category of the new American historical novel is 'multi-time-level historical fiction.'

Vico's concept of cyclical time is not the only meaningful theory with regard to a discussion of the American multi-time-level historical novel. The novels seem likewise indebted to Foucault's notion of the spatiality of history, expressed in *The Archeology of Knowledge* (1972). Elias summarizes Foucault's theory as follows:

> History is layered because it is made up of many different kinds of history: social history, material history, philosophical history, etc.... Foucault's metaphor of archeology is particularly apt for this kind of historical analysis, since the earth is geologically stratified, and these strata layers are both asymmetrical (running at different speeds) and directly reflective of material history (the earth's conditions at any given moment in geological time).... Not only is history layered in this way; because they are the output of human activity, these historical layers also backtrack, intersect, and repeat themselves.
>
> (Elias, *Sublime* 110–11)

Foucault's concept goes further than Vico's, although "[c]onstructing history this way allows for history paradoxically to repeat itself with a difference" (Elias, *Sublime* 111) as well. A novel that seems to directly express Foucault's archeological theory of history is N. Scott Momaday's *House Made of Dawn* (1968). Momaday divides up the pages of his novel in units, representing Foucauldian layers, in order to spatialize history by simultaneously telling a story from Kiowa Apache mythology, Kiowa ethnographical history, and personal memories from his life (Elias, *Sublime* 142), thereby giving visual expression to the belief that history is multilayered and simultaneous, a planar alternative to the notion of linear history. Nünning calls this the narrative staging of the synchronism of the unsynchronized ("*Inszenierung der 'Gleichzeitigkeit des Ungleichzeitigen'*"; "Moving" 396). These structural features, quite common in more recent British fiction (407), put emphasis on the return of the same in the historical process ("*Wiederkehr des Gleichen im historischen Prozess*"; "Moving" 407, see also 408–09). Kirchknopf discusses "novels with a double plot" (68) – *Possession* and Graham Swift's *Ever After* (1992) – as a type of post-Victorian fiction that "indicate[s] both generic and thematic repetitions in fiction" (68). Further, those "repetitions [in double-plot novels] ... display critical perspectives, particularly in postcolonial and feminist revisions of canonical texts" (68).

The multilayered new historical fiction is equally indebted to Vichian and Foucauldian thought concerning narrative techniques and historiographical hypotheses. In contemporary historical novels, the "[*h*]*istorical periods themselves* are subject to quick cutting, montage, and juxtaposition in a postmodernist attempt to signal the layered indeterminacy of History and its lack of order and comprehensibility" (Elias, *Sublime* 119). Drawing on Ihab Hassan's statement in *The Postmodern Turn* (1987) that "postmodernism strikes us ... as playful, paratactical, and deconstructionist" (91), Elias introduces the term "*paratactic history*" (*Sublime* 123) as a notion of history created by the narrative structure of the novels. In the texts, "parataxis ... can be both formal and conceptual" (Elias, *Sublime* 125). The new historical fiction, in its manifestation as multi-time-level historical fiction, constructs paratactic and simultaneous history.

"[U]sing a divided time frame" (Maslin, "Dead") has become almost a commonplace in British literature, with many noteworthy cases such as Peter Ackroyd's *Hawksmoor* (1985) and *Chatterton* (1987), and David Mitchell's *Cloud Atlas* (2004). Some notable American examples are T. C. Boyle's *World's End* (1987), Michael Cunningham's *The Hours* (1998), and Elizabeth Kostova's *The Historian* (2005). Boyle's *World's End*, which won the PEN/Faulkner Award, illustrates how the past haunts and determines the present and the future by interdigitating the stories of three families, the yeomen Van Brunts, the aristocratic Van Warts, and the Native American Mohonks in the Hudson River Valley in the seventeenth century, the 1940s, and the 1960s. In his "Author's Note," Boyle stresses that the novel is "an historical fugue" (vi). The musical fugue is "a strictly controlled form in which a musical subject is announced in one voice and then is echoed, varied, and developed in other voices; the composition leads to a resolution of these voices" (Elias, *Sublime* 128; see also Bergmann, "I"). Cunningham follows suit in his Pulitzer Prize-winning novel *The Hours*, alternatingly telling the stories of three women, one historical and the others fictional: the stories of the last days of the suicidal Virginia Woolf in 1941; of the despairing housewife and mother Laura Brown in the 1950s; and of the lesbian New York intellectual Clarissa in the 1990s, inspired by Woolf's *Mrs. Dalloway* (1925). Kostova's *The Historian* is advertised as "[a] spirited update" of Bram Stoker's *Dracula* (1897). While the text is inspired by Stoker's classic, an equal or even larger share is based on thorough research about the historical Vlad Țepeș. Despite inventing letters, manuscripts, chronicles, and other documents from various times, and thereby paralleling the multiple perspectives of *Dracula*, the plot mainly unfolds in three parallel narratives. Bartholomew Rossi, a history professor, is searching for Dracula's grave in the early 1930s; his protégé Paul and daughter Helen, university scholars too, trace his tracks in the 1960s; and their unnamed daughter, the narrator, tries, with the help of a college student, to lift a curse from her family in the 1970s. The frame tale, at the time of the novel's publication, even anticipated the future, the year 2008, and reaches as far back as 1476. *The Historian* is inspired by *Possession*, blending the genres of campus novel, detective fiction, romance, and gothic novel. *The Hours*, with its tracing of a crucial time in the life of a writer and juxtaposing it with the lives of other people in similar situations, is indebted to *Chatterton*. *World's End* is indebted to the magic realist tradition, most obviously Gabriel García Márquez's *One Hundred Years of Solitude* (1967).

Octavia Butler's *Kindred* (1979) is an early example of American multi-time-level historical novels that use a nineteenth-century storyline, although the two time levels, the antebellum period and the year 1976, are not simply juxtaposed. The protagonist Dana time-travels back and forth between the two eras. More recent examples that fit my corpus criteria are William T. Vollmann's *The Rifles* (1994) and Marianne Wiggins's *The Shadow Catcher* (2007). *The Rifles* follows Sir John Franklin on his fourth and fatal Arctic voyage in the mid-1800s. One hundred fifty years later, in 1990, a white man who has seduced, impregnated, and left an Inuit woman, reenacts Franklin's journey and meets the same fate. *The Shadow Catcher* interweaves the life story of photographer Edward S. Curtis, who became famous for his pictures of Native Americans in the late nineteenth and early twentieth centuries, and of a writer in the present day, named Marianne Wiggins, who is writing a novel about him. The three multi-time-level historical novels *The Great Divorce* (1994) by Valerie Martin, *Specimen Days* (2005) by Michael Cunningham, and *The 19th Wife* (2008) by David Ebershoff will be discussed in this chapter.

3.2 Valerie Martin's *The Great Divorce* (1994)

The Great Divorce (1994) is a historical novel by upstate New York writer Valerie Martin. Among her novels, *Mary Reilly* (1990) and *Property* (2003) have received the widest recognition. *Mary Reilly*, a rewriting of Robert Louis Stevenson's *The Strange Case of Dr. Jekyll and Mr. Hyde* (1886) from the point of view of the housemaid, was turned into a film in 1996, starring Julia Roberts and John Malkovich. *Property*, the story of the daily hardships on an antebellum plantation and the even harsher realities of slavery from the perspective of a young unhappy wife, won the Orange Prize. *The Great Divorce* has not received a lot of attention. It consists of three storylines, which are told in irregular alternation, "cutting back and forth cinematically" (Kakutani, "Captive"), in altogether fifty chapters. The first story focuses on zoo veterinarian Ellen Clayton and her husband Paul, who are going through a divorce. At the center of the second story is Camille, the keeper of the big cats at the same zoo, who has a personality disorder and is not able to build functioning relationships with men. Both stories are set in New Orleans at the time of publication of the novel. The third story takes place mainly at a plantation near Saint Francisville, upriver from New Orleans, between 1842 and 1845. The focus of this third plotline is Elisabeth Boyer's rebellion against her brutal husband Hermann Schlaeger.

Martin "[ties] her plot lines together through shared motifs and themes" (Kakutani, "Captive"), most prominent among them the wild, animals, and (human) nature on the one hand and, on the other, the supernatural, mental disorder, and madness (Makowsky). Although the stories are told from various perspectives, alternating between a range of third-person limited-point-of-view narrations and omniscient narrators, the focus lies on the three female characters and their struggle to come to terms with patriarchal society. Ellen and Paul have been married for twenty years and have two teenage daughters. Although Paul has been unfaithful to Ellen again and again over the years, she has become used to the fact. But this time, Paul falls in love with the young Donna and wants a divorce. When he moves out, Ellen has to come to terms with the new situation. The second story centers on eighteen-year-old Camille, who lives with her alcoholic mother and has a history of abuse and neglect. In the past, she tried to kill herself, and now she is afflicted by the sensation of transforming into a feline when she feels rage and anger. Her relationships with men are purely physical and abusive. When her favorite cat at the zoo, the leopard Magda, dies of a mysterious disease, Camille enters into a final spiral of parental cruelty, sexual exploitation, and alcohol abuse, culminating in her suicide (Martin 25–26). The third story, set in 1842, concentrates on Elisabeth Boyer, a beautiful and strong-willed Southern belle, who marries the older widower Hermann Schlaeger. He is of German descent, a newcomer to New Orleans society, and has recently acquired Montague Plantation. While Elisabeth imagines her life as "mistress of a truly grand house" (95) as a dream come true, Hermann sees her as a new chance for reproduction. His last name is telling, pointing to his violent behavior (Makowsky). When the roles of husband and wife literally have become those of keeper and inmate, Elisabeth resorts to voodoo practices to rid herself of her oppressor. In the end, she transforms into a leopard and kills Hermann, which leads to her execution as a murderer. The three stories of *The Great Divorce* not only intersect in the women's crises, they are also literally connected (Haven). When the leopard Magda at the New Orleans Zoo falls ill, vet Ellen and keeper Camille work together. Elisabeth's story is the research object of Ellen's husband Paul, a historian. The chapters of the novel that straightforwardly narrate Elisabeth's story supposedly are chapters of the book he is writing.

The title hints at one overall theme of the novel. In the initial chapter, Ellen reads an article titled "The Great Divorce." Significant excerpts from this magazine piece constitute the very opening passages of the novel:

The contemporary zoo, the "Zoo Eden," is the final irony: a false paradise in which the last representatives of soon to be extinct species are displayed to a public eager to be absolved for their extinction. The expensive exhibits conjure up a world that never did, never will, exist, in which predator and prey gaze stupidly at one another across visible but effective barriers, while plant life flourishes, water supplies are stable, and all of nature is benign.

(Martin 1)

The paradoxical situation of the zoo (Malamud 398) serves as a simulacrum of nature, while it is in fact the opposite. The central thesis of the article culminates in the statement that *"[i]n nature, as in our society, ... we will not rest until we have eliminated all possibility of 'the wild'"* (Martin 1). Ellen wonders, "[W]hat exactly did this journalist mean by 'the wild?'" (2), a question that will implicitly resurface throughout the novel. The title provides a "controlling metaphor" (Houston) that befits both major topics of the text. First, it depicts the divide between nature and human beings (Martin 2). It points toward the fact that human beings have lost touch with their wild side, their animal drives, and their instincts, their sense of belonging to and being part of the natural world. The human world is "closed off" from nature and "controlled" (4), like the zoo. An additional meaning of the title refers to Ellen's separation from Paul (119–20). Ellen adopts the term to describe the falling apart of her marriage, but it may as well be used to generally describe the rift between men and women in general. Moreover, the expression addresses Camille's problems creating functioning relationships with men, as well as Elisabeth's abusive marriage.

Animals play an important role in the novel. Many characters are described as or compared to animals (Martin 92, 217, 242). All three female protagonists form strong relationships with animals, see the world through the eyes of a predator, or identify with a creature as their mirror image. The women's destinies are paralleled by the fates of captive animals (Makowsky). Elisabeth is "a willful young woman" (Martin 67), "a high-spirited society girl, accustomed to a lively, carefree life" (Kakutani, "Captive"), who faces disinheritance in order to marry the much older widower Hermann. But after the wedding, Hermann cruelly exercises his power as master over all creatures on his land, including not only the slaves but also his wife. Following Elisabeth's futile attempt to run away, Hermann restricts her freedom more and more, and finally she literally becomes his prisoner. He locks her up in her room for good and rapes her regularly. One hot summer night, a black leopard appears on the lawn in front of the house (Martin 310–12). Because of a rite she has previously performed with the voodoo priestess Mambo Pitou, Elisabeth recognizes in the animal "her deliverer" (312), the embodiment of "the spirit of rage against imprisonment" (254). Despite her physical confinement, Elisabeth's spirit enters the leopard, she magically becomes the animal, and she takes revenge:

> She opened her eyes again. She was outside on the lawn, looking up at the figure of a woman she did not recognize, looking away at the world around her through the leopard's golden eyes ....
>
> A man appeared, carrying a lamp .... She knew him; he was the man who took everything away .... A hard, smoldering coal of rage flamed up in her head .... In a delirium of purpose, her claws, her teeth found their marks, and she held on to him as he let out one startled cry and fell sideways onto the landing. He fought her, kicked her, his fists pounded her head, but she hung on, her eyes closed, steadily tightening her jaws while the blood filled her mouth and poured down her throat. The beating of her own heart filled her ears, growing stronger, louder, faster, even as the man's heart flagged beneath her paws. His struggles diminished, became only the unfocused twitches and reflexes of defeat. Gradually she loosened her grip on him, opened jaws, lifted her head, and pressed into the dark, still air of the house.
>
> (Martin 312–14)

When her spirit is almost broken and she seems to drown in madness, the leopard enables Elisabeth to free herself from her tormentor. After the attack, Elisabeth's "mind and soul" are "at peace, entirely and perfectly free" (Martin 315). But Elisabeth's liberty is short-lived. She is imprisoned again and hanged for murder. Her claim that she killed her husband while transformed into a leopard earns her the sobriquet "'catwoman of Saint Francisville'" (5).

   Camille's identification with Magda, the leopard at the zoo whose keeper she is, is so strong that in situations of powerlessness she believes she is transforming into a big cat herself (Martin 38). In one of her feline frenzies, she attacks the painter Jack, who is sexually assaulting her:

> The man was over her, oblivious of her, pounding at her relentlessly, making sounds now that were almost words .... She made a sound too, a low groan. Now she opened her eyes and looked out into a sea of red. She gasped, closed her eyes, tried again, but to no avail. Everything was red, a wall of blood. She tried to speak but could not frame a word. Her tongue was like a wad of damp leather; she thrust it out of her mouth. Still the man did not sense that anything was wrong .... With one hand she reached across her shoulder and caught him by his hair. Then he saw her face, and his offensive fell apart. "What the fuck," he said, pulling back from her. She released his hair, though reluctantly, so that some of it

came away in her hand.... She dug her nails into his shoulders, tried to sink her teeth into his neck, but he turned his head to protect himself, and she caught him at the side of the face.

(Martin 76–77)

Because of this incident, Shelbourne, an art dealer who is also her pimp, calls her a "little hellcat" (Martin 97). To Camille, as to Elisabeth, the transformations are exceptional moments of empowerment: "I am vengeance" (78).

Ellen is repeatedly depicted as an animal too. In a picture she looks like a hawk (Martin 326–27). At another instance, she is portrayed as "a tired old lioness" (121). Ellen has a brief fantasy of letting her animal drive get the better of her: "She imagined shooting her husband" (121). The scenario of letting one's wild nature get the upper hand parallels Elisabeth's and Camille's transformations. Another identification with an animal is added toward the end of the novel. When the jaguar Minx contracts a mysterious illness, but despite all bad prognoses recovers and lives, Ellen experiences an epiphanic moment:

He gave her a long, steady look, his yellow eyes betraying nothing of his sentiments, if he could be said to have any. In fact, Ellen thought, his look was the opposite of sentiment. This was the look that sees no moment beyond the present, that contemplates the world in an eternal *now*, the natural, healthy, straightforward, and increasingly rare regard of the wild and predatory cat.

(Martin 340)

This miraculous recovery, in an allusion to Elisabeth's invocation of a voodoo sorceress, is preceded by Ellen's listening to voodoo chants on a tape on her ride to the zoo. Ellen takes the animal's recovery as a sign that she will likewise recover from "the other, more metaphysical death, the death of her marriage" (Martin 123). The fact that Minx lives is "a small, a pitiful triumph" (340) considering the human-caused extinction of animals. The "divorce, from nature and from our own natures, is a central, irreversible attribute of civilization" (Houston). Minx's survival is a silver lining for Ellen and for the natural world, especially since this scene concludes not only Ellen's story but the whole novel.

The strongest motif in all three stories is the recurring image of a black leopard, a wild creature who cannot be subdued, despite its captivity (Kakutani, "Captive"; Martin 135). The leopard becomes an overall emblem of female liberty. It turns into "a symbol of the vanishing world of nature" for Ellen, for Camille "a symbol of her own spiritual imprisonment," and for Elisabeth a "symbol of the freedom she has lost to a domineering husband" (Kakutani, "Captive"). The whole novel is a meditation on imprisonment and freedom. Even Paul does not want to end up a "domesticated academic" (Martin 327), and breaks free from the confining strains of his marriage.

The Great Divorce is a genre hybrid, mixing historical fiction with elements of crime fiction, fantastic fiction, and the gothic novel. Elisabeth's transformation is reminiscent of Edgar Allan Poe's "*The Murders in the Rue Morgue*" (1841), a locked-room mystery in which the murders are committed by an animal. The conversion of young women into evil predators is also reminiscent of the doubling in Stevenson's *Dr. Jekyll and Mr. Hyde*, a novel Martin knows well (Martin 322). Different from Stevenson's texts, where the fantastic remains impenetrable, but similar to Poe's, where a rational explanation is offered, Martin, in addition to descriptions of the marvelous metamorphoses, delivers realistic explanations for the animalistic transformations. Camille's transformation is explained as a symptom of her personality disorder. The novel minutely presents her description of the sensation (14–16) as well as her psychiatrist's sober reaction to it: "You could probably find some people today who think it's possible, but I'm not one of them. People can't turn into animals and animals can't turn into people" (138).

Elisabeth's murder of her husband in the shape of a leopard is also rationally explained. Paul believes it was the result of a house slave's making use of a unique opportunity, when a runaway animal from a menagerie roamed the grounds of Montague Plantation (Martin 205, 316, 323). In Paul's book, Charles lured the leopard into the house with a dead rabbit and the hungry animal attacked and killed Hermann. Elisabeth found her dead husband after the door to her room was unlocked by Charles. In her deranged state of mind, she wallowed in his blood and subsequently believed that she had killed him (323–26). The only mysterious element of the novel for which no alternative explanation is offered is the miraculous revitalization of the jaguar Minx, which, of course, is the mildest of these elements. The marvelous or magical scenes are all proceeded by hints of voodoo practices.

The Great Divorce includes manifold intertextual and intermedial allusions (Makowsky). Most notably, there is the recurring reference to the painting *The Peaceable Kingdom* (c. 1820–1846) by Edward Hicks. He developed his signature *sujet* in a series of paintings, which he combined with a quote from the Bible: "The wolf also shall dwell with the lamb, and the leopard shall lie down with the kid; and the calf and the young lion and the fatling together; and a little child shall lead them" (Isaiah 11:6, see also 11:7–9). The painting shows predator and prey, wild and domesticated animals, and humans in peaceful community. This naïve portrayal of the natural world is negligent of the great divorce between humanity and the natural world (Martin 56–57, see also 110). Hicks's painting reappears several times in the novel. Most remarkably, "an update on the Peaceable Kingdom" is the cover painting of a book, "a collection of essays about zoos, about their function as arks, trying to carry endangered species over the flood to a time when it would be safe to return them to the world. A hopeless mission" (336).

Another intertextual reference occurs when Camille, during the final hours of her life, comes to the river. When she finds herself alone and desolate, she recalls a poem "about a man, the poet himself, watching birds, or perhaps it was bees" (296). This is a hint at Samuel Taylor Coleridge's sonnet "Work without Hope" (1828), which is supposed to have inspired the idiomatic expression 'the birds and the bees.' As Hicks's painting, the poem bridges the gap between the nineteenth and twentieth centuries. It draws a parallel between the emotions of Coleridge and Camille, the Romantic British poet and the young American girl. The verse Camille remembers – "And I the while, the sole unbusy thing" (Martin 296) – reveals her sense of isolation and her rupture from the natural world after Magda's death. The poem, with its melancholic tone and juxtaposition of nature and the unbelonging human, hints at Camille's devastation. Coleridge points toward the great divorce between nature and humanity, the great divide between humankind and the animal kingdom (384) – the overall issue of Martin's novel.

The fact that Paul is a historian, a stock character of historical novels (Humphrey 89; Carnes 20–21), who works on a book about a nineteenth-century murder case provides the opportunity for general reflections about history writing. Paul comes across Elisabeth's case in an old newspaper, dating from April 30, 1846. The notice mentions the public execution of a white woman, giving her name and that of her husband, whom she is said to have murdered, although "[t]o his knowledge – and not many people knew more about such matters than he did – no white woman had ever been executed in the state of Louisiana" (Martin 5). Paul's impetus is revisionist, although he is interested not solely in recovering the facts of Elisabeth's story but also in the possibly sensational story behind it. He aims more at popular history with his book than at serious scholarly historiography to satisfy his readers. They crave "stories of grand passions, of beautiful women and wealthy, cultivated men, of power, greed, treachery, great successes, greater failures" (7, 206). This desire for true but good stories is reminiscent of Grossman's and Shields's theses, mentioned in the first chapter of this study. Paul is writing historical crime fiction, true crime in particular. He is creating a documentary or nonfiction novel.

Paul's fictive book bears a lot of similarities to Martin's actual novel. Elisabeth's story is at the center of both texts, while other stories, connected to hers, are told as well (Martin 206). Both the actual novel and Paul's book are genre hybrids, wavering between gothic novel, crime fiction, and historical novel. But whereas Paul's book remains within its mid-nineteenth-century time frame, Martin connects the nineteenth-century tale with stories set in the present and even points toward the future with her superimposed topic of the coming extinction of all species (59). The novel manages to effectively point toward the theoretical problematic of the narrative aspects of history writing, reflects on public demand and how it dominates the literary market, and most obviously points toward what is recognizable as Vichian or Foucauldian thought: "[Paul's] subject was a doomed world; everyone knew it and read accordingly, with little sense that their daily newspaper offered them a vision into a similar decline" (7).

3.3 Michael Cunningham's *Specimen Days* (2005)

Michael Cunningham's *Specimen Days* (2005) is a "literary triptych" (Duggan 381), as is its predecessor *The Hours*, significantly explicating "the inextricable interrelation of the three extases of time – past, present, and future" – inherent in all "stories of the past" (Meinig 349). Three stories are told in chronologically arranged chapters. The first part, "In the Machine," is set in New York City in the nineteenth century, at the beginning of the Industrial Revolution. The physically disabled thirteen-year-old Lucas has lost his older brother Simon in an industrial accident and is taking over the job at the machine that killed his brother. Lucas is repeating again and again verses by Walt Whitman in a mad frenzy, probably a symptom of post-traumatic stress disorder (Mousoutzanis 134; Banita 259). After a meeting with the great American poet, which is either factual or a "hallucinatory twist" (Banita 259), and an epiphanic experience of nature in Central Park, Lucas realizes that his late brother's pregnant fiancée Catherine is in danger. In an act of self-sacrifice to the machine, he succeeds in saving her and her unborn child from a fatal fire. The second story, "The Children's Crusade," is also set in New York City, but in the twenty-first century, after the terrorist attacks of 9/11. Cat, a psychologist with a PhD, is working for a police hotline for potential felons. She gets a call from a boy whom she classifies as innocuous. But soon after there is a suicide bombing close to Ground Zero. The attack seems to have been carried out by a child terrorist, and further assaults follow. An old woman who calls herself Walt Whitman proves to be the mastermind behind the terror campaign, acting on behalf of a globally operating terrorist group. When Cat finds a potential suicide bomber, a physically disabled boy, on her doorstep, on impulse she flees with him, but realizes that she has made herself part of the conspiracy. Part three, "Like Beauty," takes place in the future. New York City has become a theme park, in which one can venture from district to district in touristy time travels. Simon, a so-called simulo, an artificial human being, and Catareen, a saurian alien from the planet Nadia, try to flee the oppression of the postapocalyptic surveillance state, reminiscent of George Orwell's *1984* (1949). Their journey through the USA, degenerated into a wasteland after nuclear fallout, is modeled after a road movie. Luke, a physically disabled boy, joins them and together they meet with Simon's creator in Denver. He, another Whitman figure, is preparing for a journey to the New World, a new planet, with his sect.

Because of the three formally separate parts of the text, the stories have been called and even discussed as novellas (Banita; Borges; Munteán 39), though *de facto* the text is one novel (Duggan 382; Mousoutzanis 129–30) – more specifically, a historical novel. This is clearly obvious because of the interweaving of the three parts and their many striking similarities. They are connected by the principal setting of the action, New York City, with its recurring locales such as Broadway and Bethesda Fountain in Central Park, marked as a place of grace by its allusion to the healing fountain of the New Testament. These sites become palimpsests, carrying an overlay of different time zones and thereby spatializing time (Nünning, "Moving" 410). Bakhtin labeled this phenomenon a 'chronotope' ("Forms"), which is created by the memory a character connects with a place. Here the chronotope is created by the reader (Basseler/Birke 142–43). But most importantly, the three parts are knit together by the character constellation. The same group can be found in each part: a physically disabled boy, a young man, an older woman, and a creator figure. In the first part, the physically disabled Lucas is at the center, and the other main characters are his dead brother Simon, Simon's fiancée Catherine, and the poet Walt Whitman. The second part is told from the point of view of Cat, who has an affair with the younger Simon. The young, physically disabled assassin, raised by an old woman who calls herself Walt Whitman, becomes a surrogate for Cat's dead son Luke. In the third part, the humanoid Simon is attracted by the older extraterrestrial Catareen, who has lost her entire family. Together with the physically disabled boy Luke, they search for Simon's constructor Emory Lowell. This basic configuration is supplemented in each part by the appearance of a woman named Gaya, earth mother, who outlasts all ages. Further, there are reappearing symbols such as a precious china bowl, which symbolizes the continuity of civilization; horses, which are emblematic of the persistence of nature; and a music box or radio, representing technological progress.

The entirety of the novel is pervaded with references to the Bible. Catherine, Cat, and Catareen are Mary figures, marked by a blue dress or cape and their role as mother figures. Lucas and Luke, namesakes of one of the Evangelists, are Jesus figures due to their supernatural or prophetic abilities, bringing hope or final destruction as redeemer or messiah. Simon is the namesake of the Apostle Peter, the founder of the Christian church in Rome. He is romantically involved with Catherine, Cat, and Catareen and thus completes this group of three into an image of the Holy Family. The Whitman characters can be understood as godlike figures or perverted creators. The historical Whitman is creating poetry and his own, alternative worldview; the instigator of the attacks is bringing up terrorists and thereby bringing on the end of the world; and Lowell is creating artificial human beings and searching for a new world. Lucas of the first part consequently dubs Whitman's *Leaves of Grass* (1855–92) "the book" (Cunningham 6). The text is his Bible, and Whitman functions as a god for him, especially during his death delirium (91–93). In keeping with the image of the Holy Family, Lucas and Catherine, during this death scene, form a pietà, an image of Mother Mary with the dead Jesus. The pregnant Catherine, who calls herself a whore, can moreover be read as a Magdalen figure. In the second part, the pseudo-religious children's crusade brings on Judgment Day. And Lowell's spaceship with its passengers of all human and humanlike races in the third part is a futuristic Noah's ark and a parodic repetition of the Pilgrim Fathers' journey. Additionally, the last scene is an evocation of another American myth, when the humanoid Simon, instead of entering the spaceship, opts for a trek west on horseback.

The most obvious device holding the three narrations together is the reference to Whitman. The title *Specimen Days* is adapted from his autobiography (1882). Lucas of the first part, the child terrorists of the second, and Simon of the third obsessively recite verses from *Leaves of Grass* in erratic forms of "literary Tourette" (Landon 68; see also Mousoutzanis 139). And transcending race and gender, Whitman appears as himself in the first, historical part, as an old woman in the second, and as an African American scientist in the third. Tying in with the revisionist impetus of the new historical fiction, Cunningham portrays immigrants and workers, the trailblazers as well as the victims of the Industrial Revolution in the historical part of the novel, "In the Machine." It seems even too politically correct that the protagonists of the other parts of the text similarly belong to an oppressed social or racial stratum. Cat, the protagonist of "The Children's Crusade," is subject to a double bind as an African American woman in the police force. Although she has reached a good professional position through education and outward rigidity, her private situation is not fulfilling. The third part, "Like Beauty," focuses on a humanoid and an alien, whose social position is evocative of the practices of chattel slavery in the nineteenth century (Cunningham 245). Furthermore, a central character in all parts of the novel is a boy who is physically disabled but possesses above-average or even supernatural powers of perception. With their physical or mental deviations, the Lucas/Luke figures can be read as "a social and cultural self-portrait of mankind" (Gorp/Musarra-Schroeder ix). Fully in keeping with Whitman's "Song of Myself" (1855–1892) – "I am large, I contain multitudes" – Cunningham presents the melting pot of the USA, as originally articulated by J. Hector St. John de Crèvecoeur and Israel Zangwill, with all its drawbacks. An *e pluribus unum*, and this seems to be Cunningham's conclusion, was, is, and will always be a utopia.

The three parts of the novel are grounded in at least three different genres (Mousoutzanis 129). The first part, which is a historical fiction, is labeled a ghost story on the book's cover. But this seems too clipped an understanding, as the ghosts in the machines, or their voices, are projections of Lucas's consciousness, a sign of his growing mania, or even a mark of his (pseudo-)religious enlightenment. The second part, set in the present time, is crime fiction, with the terrorist attacks and the search for the perpetrators. The third part, whose action takes place in the future, is dystopian, speculative, "slipstream" (Landon 67), or science fiction. The latter is a form of historical fiction, as in it "novelists address themselves to those broader events in the human aggregate that constitute history.... [I]n fictions of this type, the future recapitulates the past or satirically mirrors the present" (Cowart 76–77). Jameson even claims that "the historical novel of the future (which is to say of our present) will necessarily be Science-Fictional inasmuch as it will have to include questions about the fate of our social system" ("Historical" 298). The presentation of New York City as a theme park is an illustration of the theoretical debate over the loss of historical awareness in contemporary society and the popularization of the past. History is reduced to entertainment (Hewison; Debord; Rothaug 14). Lowenthal's *The Past is a Foreign Country* "compares the temporal distance of the past from the late twentieth century, to the spatial distance of some foreign nation from the centre of contemporary civilization, and this gives the past a place-like ontology" (Middleton/Woods 24). Such a view is mimicked by the Disneyfication of the past in Cunningham's text. In the descriptions of the theme park, the distorting nature of the "heritage industry" (Hewison) is in focus, when players who impersonate birds of paradise receive more attention than those who imitate regular twentieth-century New Yorkers (Cunningham 210).

Specimen Days is likewise a 9/11 or post-9/11 novel and has been discussed as risk or trauma narrative (Borges; Banita; Duggan; Rickli 141; Däwes 76). Apart from the obvious allusions of the second part to the terrorist attacks, the first part features a significant scene that functions as a "cultural reenactment" (Sturken 17) of the well-known, globally televised images of the collapsing Twin Towers of the World Trade Center in New York City. At the end of the historical "In the Machine," seamstresses caught in a burning sweat shop jump out of the windows of the building in desperation and become human torches:

> Above, another woman stood in a window. Her dress had caught fire. She stood like fire itself, in the shape of a woman. Lucas watched

as the others did. Her dress blazed, but her head was still a
woman's head…. The fire woman spread her wings and flew….
The fire woman shrieked toward the earth, trailing ribbons of flame.

(Cunningham 88–92)

The wasteland of the third part of the book must be understood as an
image of the nation after the terrorist onslaught, of which 9/11 has to
be understood as only the beginning. Overall, the intergeneric quality of
Specimen Days marks the novel as a genre hybrid.

The heavy use of intertextual devices, particularly quotations from
Whitman's poetry, turns the novel into a collage. It is a homage to
Whitman and his transcendental philosophy of universalism (Däwes 76).
The book emphasizes the natural philosophy of the circle of life as
expressed in his poetry: "The smallest sprout shows there is really
no death…. All goes onward and outward, nothing collapses," and
"Nobody really dies. We go on in the grass. We go on in the trees" (qtd.
in Cunningham 73, 122). In our present time of global terror, climate
crisis, and nuclear threat, Cunningham is propagating the new-age
wisdom of a return to nature and to basic values such as love and
care. This message may sound trite, but *Specimen Days* is a linguistic
masterpiece, which effortlessly merges with Whitman's lines.

Cunningham dedicates an "Author's Note" to the issue of truthfulness.
In his opinion, a writer has more leeway in handling historical facts than,
for example, a biographer or a historian. A writer uses it to make stories
more lively (Cunningham ix). Cunningham calls his method "semiaccurate"
but "true to historic particulars" (ix). While the fact that New York City
has become a theme park parodies theories of history as entertainment and
diagnoses a loss of historical awareness, where 'heritage industry' and 'society of the spectacle' are the buzzwords indicating a Disneyfication of
history (Kunow, "Simulacrum" 25), the reenactment of the great American
trauma of 9/11 and of the American myths of the early settlement and
westward expansion present a decisive return to meaningful history.

Against the background of Vico's *Scienza Nuova*, the trichotomy of
Cunningham's novel and its many recurrent elements allows for the
assumption that history is always repeating itself. The narrative stresses
"connections between past and present" (Hodgkin 16) as well as with
the future. This is especially evident in the motto preceding the novel, of
course a quote from Whitman:

Fear not O Muse! Truly new ways and days receive, surround you,
I candidly confess a queer, queer race, of novel fashion,
And yet the same old human race, the same within, without,
Faces and hearts the same, feelings the same, yearnings the same,
The same old love, beauty and use the same.

(qtd. in Cunningham vii)

3.4 David Ebershoff's *The 19th Wife* (2008)

The 19th Wife (2008) is David Ebershoff's third historical novel. It was adapted by Lifetime television in 2010, starring Chyler Leigh and Matt Czuchry. *The Danish Girl* (2000), Ebershoff's first novel, is a fictionalized account of the life of Danish artist Lili Elbe, presumably the first person to undergo sex reassignment surgery (in 1930/31). It was turned into a movie starring Alicia Vikander and Eddie Redmayne in 2015. Ebershoff's second novel, *Pasadena* (2001), deals with the transformations of his native city, and of the novel's protagonist, Linda Stamp, during the years following World War I. Both of these novels are instances of herstorical biofiction, queer historical fiction, and novels of development. These labels, among others, can similarly be applied to *The 19th Wife*, although it will mainly be discussed here as a multi-time-level historical novel.

The 19th Wife primarily covers two stories, one set in the present time and the other in the nineteenth century. The historical part tells the life story of Ann Eliza Young, the nineteenth wife of Brigham Young, leader of the Mormons, also known as the Church of Jesus Christ of Latter-Day Saints. Her tale starts with her parents' being drawn into the sect and into plural marriage. It then covers her own life story until her scandalous divorce from Young and her subsequent public crusade to end polygamy in the United States. The contemporary story, set in the twenty-first century, revolves around a gay young man, Jordan Scott, who was expelled from a Mormon renegade sect at the age of fourteen. Six years later he returns and attempts to solve the mystery of his father's murder, of which his mother, a 19th wife, is accused.

The 19th Wife begins, as so many historical fictions, with a paratext, which in this case consists of three mottos:

> Faith is to believe what you do not see; the reward of this faith is to see what you believe.
> SAINT AUGUSTINE

> Like all the other arts, the Science of Deduction and Analysis is one which can only be acquired by long and patient study, nor is life long enough to allow any mortal to attain the highest perfection in it.
> ARTHUR CONAN DOYLE

> And now, if there are faults they are the mistakes of men.
> The Book of Mormon, translated by JOSEPH SMITH, JR.
>   (Eberhoff ix)

The first and third epigraphs refer to the novel's overt issue of religion, more specifically to Christianity and to the Church of Jesus Christ of Latter-Day Saints. The second dictum acknowledges the genre of detective fiction, particularly *A Study in Scarlet* (1887), Doyle's first

Sherlock Holmes tale, as a model. In it, Holmes solves a crime whose origins reach far back into the history of the Church of Jesus Christ of Latter-Day Saints (LDS). With the second part of the novel set in the Mormon past, the structure resembles that of multi-time-level historical fiction. Ebershoff points not only to his postmodern epigonism but also to the bipartite structure of his own book. Doyle's novel does not cast a very favorable light on the sect, and the same holds true for Ebershoff's novel, which is a critique of the practices of the Mormons in the past, and of other, similar sects, in the present.

The 19th Wife has twenty-one chapters, in which two stories and time levels entwine alternatingly. The text mainly consists of an "autobiofic-tion" (Middeke 14) of Ann Eliza Young, titled *The 19th Wife* – a fictional refashioning of the original nineteenth-century document (Charles), Ann Eliza's actual memoir *Wife No. 19* (1875) – and another piece of life writing in Jordan Scott's voice, titled *Wife # 19: A Desert Mystery*. Additionally, the novel includes an enormous variety of texts, all authored by Ebershoff. The "documents (or 'documents')" (Ebershoff 510) are all based on the author's extensive research and are sometimes very closely modeled on original sources. Ebershoff's wide-ranging ventriloquism in-cludes alternative female views on the issue of polygamy. He incorporates, for example, a poem by Lydia Taft Webb, Ann Eliza's father's second wife, titled "In Our House," which expresses its author's belief in plural marriage (155), and a letter by Ann Eliza's mother Elizabeth Webb, written after the daughter's apostasy and renouncing Ann Eliza's daugh-tership because of her separation from Brigham Young (353–54). A sermon (140–41); a letter to Gilbert Webb, Ann Eliza's half-brother (149–50); and a prison diary (434–50) give Brigham Young, then the leader of the Mormons, a voice. Other male views on polygamy are provided by an open letter by Ann Eliza's brother Aaron (464–65); by a written deposition by Ann Eliza's brother Gilbert (269–87); and by her father's autobiography (56–64, 188–213). While Aaron Webb proves a strong supporter of the custom of plural or 'celestial marriage,' as this practice was called among the Mormons, his half-brother Gilbert's de-position and his father Chauncey's autobiography reveal the eventual drawbacks the practice held even for men. These and further faux-nineteenth-century documents create a polyphonic narrative on the issue of celestial marriage.

The novel is a collage or bricolage and also provides simulated twenty-first-century documents, for example, a Wikipedia entry on the Haun's Mill Massacre of 1838, a decisive event in LDS history (Ebershoff 74–76); a reproduction of an online community homepage, "19thwi-fe.com" (298–99); chat-room and e-mail conversations (7, 143, 460–63); and a seminar paper titled "The First Wife" by Kelly Dee, prepared for a course in women's studies with Professor Mary P. Sprague at Brigham Young University (111–31). Jordan's twenty-first-century, ghostwritten autobiographical narrative *Wife # 19: A Desert Mystery* in the end turns out to be Kelly's somewhat unorthodox master's thesis.

All the various kinds of texts and documents Ebershoff creates within the novel are combined to produce a multi-perspective on polygamy and the practices of the LDS in general: "[T]he multiplicity of perspectives serves to broaden Ebershoff's depiction not only of polygamy, but also of the people whose lives it informs. And this gives his novel a rare sense of moral urgency" (Louisa Thomas; see also Maslin, "Dead"). But the multi-perspective narrative does not combine to form a coherent picture of the practices of celestial marriage, then or now.

It is significant that the texts mostly feature first-person narrators and are highly subjective or personalized forms of writing. Memoirs, auto-biographies, diaries, letters, and poems repeatedly, on a meta-level, address the reader directly. It is Ebershoff's aim to simulate for his readers his own effort to make sense of the story of polygamy (Ebershoff 510–11). On the plot level, this is best illustrated by Kelly's endeavors to write her thesis: "[S]he was researching, reading, learning, talking, understanding" (399).

Ann Eliza's autobiofiction is an instance of herstory, as it recovers the personal female perspective that had been "completely left off. Edited out of [LDS] history" (Ebershoff 397), by giving her a voice. Ebershoff covers her life, her writings, and her legacy: the first two are addressed by the fictionalized historical story of Ann Eliza, and the third is approached in the modern-day fictional tale revolving around Jordan. Kelly, by writing up Jordan's story, makes his voice heard: "After many attempts I abandoned my voice for his .... [T]he words are Jordan's" (501). The novel highlights a feminist and queer perspective on history: "Ebershoff demonstrates abundant virtuosity, as he convincingly inhabits the voices of both a nineteenth-century Mormon wife and a contemporary gay youth excommunicated from the church" ("Books").

The symbolism of numbers further highlights the feminist approach. Within Mormonism, the numbering of women marks their victimization. They are reduced to countable objects and mere possessions of their husbands or fathers. Ann Eliza and Jordan's mother BeckyLyn Scott are both 19th wives. Jordan's stepsister Sarah, a runaway from the sect, is known as "Sarah 5" or simply "5" (Ebershoff 83), as, given the large families of the Firsts, many daughters often share the same name. In jail, BeckyLyn is allotted another, official number – "Booking No. 066001825 Inmate ID 207334 Last Name Scott First Name BeckyLyn" (15) – and the other inmates simply call her "Nineteen" (467). The women's numbers, it becomes clear, hold their identity. Despite their directness, these numbers are anything but lucid, as, notably, BeckyLyn's uncertainty about her position in the family chronology reveals:

"How many wives did he have?" "Total? Between twenty and twenty-five, but I can't be sure. He never said .... We each had our number, and we had a rough idea of where we fell on the list, but if you tried to add them up, it never made sense. There were gaps, and sometimes a wife would come and stay a year and then leave, and sometimes you'd get this feeling you were no longer the number you thought you were."

(Ebershoff 469)

When Jordan can finally make sense of the numbers, "polygamy's wacky math" (Ebershoff 469), they are the clue to solving the murder case. Jordan finds out that his father, when referring to "# 19" (7), actually meant not Jordan's mother but his next wife-to-be, Queenie, another of Jordan's stepsisters. The numbers in the end reveal the murderer, Queenie's (ex-)husband, whose marriage with her was dissolved on the grounds that he refused to take another wife and become a polygamist. Early on, this is hinted at in the novel: "The numbers are part of the mystery" (34). In a footnote of her thesis, Kelly concludes:

A final note on numbers: My research shows Ann Eliza was most likely Brigham's 52nd of 55 wives. As far as I can tell, she was called the 19th because removed from the total tally were the wives who had died, who were barren, or whom Brigham no longer had sexual relations with. This discrepancy in marital accounting speaks volumes about Brigham's complicated relations with his spouses and polygamy's moral corrosion. If anyone still wonders why Ann Eliza was so ticked off, they need only consider this footnote.

(Ebershoff 498)

Kelly asserts that "it must've had a huge psychological impact on these women to not know their number" (Ebershoff 398). The importance and humiliation of the numbers is also repeatedly emphasized in Ann Eliza's narrative. First, it is an issue in a conversation with her new husband on her wedding day:

"May I ask a question?"
"Of course, anything."
"What number am I?" ...
"Number?"
"Which wife?"
"It's distasteful to me to put a number next to you, or any woman."
"I appreciate that. But I'd like to know."
"In that case, you are number nineteen."
"Nineteen? What about the others?"
"Others?"
"At the Lion House?"
"They're friends, but not wives."

"But I've heard –"
"Ann Eliza, you'll hear many things now that you're my wife."
"Nineteen, really? That's all?"
"Nineteen. Really. That's all."

(Ebershoff 324)

Later, Ann Eliza uses the number for her self-punishment: "I took a great disliking to myself during this time, and in my thoughts referred to myself as simply No. 19" (Ebershoff 328). The feminist position *The 19th Wife* takes toward polygamy is expressed in the novel in manifold ways, but it is probably best illustrated by the significance and symbolism of numbers.

It is a general claim that "[b]iography and autobiography personalize history. They restore identity" (Cullick 4), and here the problem of identity construction becomes a coequal theme along with historical representation. Ann Eliza's tale is not only a feminist revision of historiography, it is also a novel of development. Her memoir covers her "full journey from daughter of polygamy to emancipator" (Ebershoff 491). Having experienced the detrimental effects polygamy had on her parents as a child, she is strong, rebellious, and self-reliant from the beginning. But nevertheless, as she was raised according to those religious principles, it takes a while until she can finally free herself from the norms and rules of Mormon society. Her first significant moment of doubt occurs, fittingly, during her endowment ceremony at the temple, a religious initiation central to every Mormon's spiritual life. Later, when she is forced to marry Brigham and very soon has to succumb to his obvious neglect of her, this is only the final straw that completes her transformation into a rebel. It is no coincidence that the crucial chapter of Ann Eliza's memoir bears the title "My Awakening," deliberately pointing toward Kate Chopin's *The Awakening* (1899).

Ironically, it is Young's suggestion that she needs to earn her own living, which she does by opening a boarding house, that provides her with contacts to the outside world. It is Ann Eliza's interaction with so-called Gentiles, especially non-Mormon women, which ultimately helps her to realize the possibilities for women outside Mormon patriarchy. Different from a typical male novel of development, where the initiate makes his experiences far away from home, the young nineteenth-century woman glimpses an alternative life, "a foreign land [she] had never visited before" (Ebershoff 343), while confined to the domestic sphere by social and religious norms. In the novel, Ann Eliza's own tale ends with a new beginning, her preface to her second edition of *The 19th Wife*, written in 1908. The text discloses a changed, worldly-wise, less biased Ann Eliza, whose rage against Brigham Young and the Mormons has cooled since polygamy was officially banned in 1890, though she is aware of the practice's thriving elsewhere.

The continuation of Ann Eliza's tale can be found in Jordan Scott's rite of passage. The protagonist has a history of abuse and emotional neglect, having grown up in a Mormon renegade sect called the First and True Latter-Day Saints, which is still practicing polygamy in the twenty-first century. He was excommunicated and forced to leave his home when he was fourteen years old. At the age of twenty he returns to Mesadale, because his mother is accused of the murder of her husband, his father. Jordan is on a twofold quest: he is searching for his father's real murderer and for his own identity. Only when he once again confronts his past can his development come full circle.

The same holds true for runaway Johnny Drury, whom Jordan picks up from the street. Johnny is Jordan's younger *alter ego*. At the age of twelve or thirteen, he too has become one of the so-called "lost boys" (Ebershoff 136; see also Connelly), excommunicated from the Mesadale community. A third young man, Tom, approximately twenty-five years old, joins the two. Though he is not a former member of the Firsts, he mirrors Jordan and Johnny, as he is a Mormon excluded from his community, in his case because of his homosexuality. Different from Jordan and Johnny, though, Tom has already made his peace with his faith and has found an alternative way to worship and a sanctuary in a gay-friendly religious community in Las Vegas: "Jordan, Johnny and Tom make a wounded trio, all estranged from the religions that formed them, cut off from and yet immutably trapped in their pasts" (Freeman). The function of Tom as a mentor for Jordan and Johnny and the typical stages of exit, transition, and (re-)entrance mark the text as a story of initiation (Freese, *American* 52). Jordan and Johnny are on a physical and psychological journey. The novel, for the most part a literary rendering of a road movie, gives expression to this. But the boys are not on a linear journey; rather, they go back and forth between First and non-First territory, between St. George, Kanab, Salt Lake City, and Mesadale. This zigzag course aptly conveys their being interrupted or arrested in their development, referred to in one chapter heading as "The Hardly Boys" (Ebershoff 151). Only at the very end of the novel, when Jordan has accepted that his mother, released from jail, nevertheless wants to return to Mesadale, does he achieve satisfactory closure. He set out to find the murderer of his father, and along the way he found himself. While Jordan has to irrevocably part with his original family in Mesadale, he can now start his own, alternative family with Tom and Johnny: "Endings are beginnings" (507). In many ways, Jordan's story can be understood as a continuation of Ann Eliza's story. Kelly and Jordan's *Wife # 19: A Desert Mystery* is the logical sequel to Ann Eliza Young's *The 19th Wife*. Ebershoff's novel mimics the Möbius-strip-like texts of postmodernism's apex, but with the solution of the crime it also delivers the closure and coherence characteristic of neo-realism.

Telling Kelly the story of his life and thus making sense of it for himself is an important step in Jordan's maturation process: "And so I told her. Everything. It just came out, and it took a long time, but I told her like I've just told you" (Ebershoff 398). His story is modeled after classic coming-of-age novels such as Mark Twain's *The Adventures of Huckleberry Finn* (1885), J. D. Salinger's *The Catcher in the Rye* (1951), and Nick McDonell's *Twelve* (2002).

Some critics have argued that Ebershoff does not do enough to bring together his two storylines (Freeman; Louisa Thomas). This is a grave misconception. First of all, the life stories of the two protagonists, Ann Eliza and Jordan, are consistently parallel. Though she is a woman living in the nineteenth century and he a gay young man of the twenty-first, both go through similar ordeals. First, they suffer from polygamy as children growing up in a plural-marriage household; then later, this practice (directly and indirectly) drives them away from their families and religious communities. Both of their mothers play a crucial role in their rift with their history, as both of them place their prophets' word over the well-being of their children. Furthermore, Ann Eliza and Jordan, in varying ways, fight polygamy. Their tales in many respects are "parallel stories of polygamy" ("Books").

One crucial scene from each storyline, when the protagonists finally confront their prophets face-to-face, can emphasize this further, and also illustrate the suffusion of the novel by magical elements that can be found occasionally in both tales. When Ann Eliza starts to rebel against Brigham's polygyny by quitting attending the family dinner with her husband and her numerous sister wives at the Lion House, an almost magical incident occurs:

> He rose from the bed and began to assemble himself, buttoning up and refastening his cuffs. He said nothing more, grunting incomprehensibly as he bent to pull on his boots. He left my room without another word, as if wounded and retreating to his lair. Yet the space where he had stood did not empty. It was as if he had left the spirit of himself behind, a black ghost, large and shaped to his form. This apparition watched me as I dressed. It penetrated my thoughts as I worried if I had somehow destroyed my soul's redemption, and that of my boys. I do not believe in phantasmagorical events, but this presence was so formidable, and real, I must describe it as it seemed to me.
>
> (Ebershoff 332)

It takes a while before Ann Eliza is eventually able to free herself from Young's black ghost (Ebershoff 405). Similarly, when Jordan returns to Mesadale for the last time, he has an almost supernatural encounter with the prophet of the Firsts:

It was the Prophet. And he was shocked to see me like this. Really shocked, not fake shocked. This wasn't part of his plan .... There we were. Two faces shaped by the same set of emotions at the same moment in time .... I don't know how long we stared at each other like that .... The way the Prophet was peering around the door, I could see only his head and a hand. A dried spotted hand, knuckles yellow and white. And that sunken, tired face. An old man. Almost any old man. The Prophet left, the door closing. The ghost of his face remained, hanging in the space where he had been, an afterimage, or maybe even a dream. Then it too was gone.

(Ebershoff 482)

Given these and further intersections of the two stories on the level of character and setting, one may, contrary to some reviewers' positions, very well assert that "[t]hese two personal tales are interwoven with each other" (McGuire). Many of the nineteenth-century settings of the novel persist over time and are revisited in the twenty-first-century storyline. For example, Jordan visits the Ann Eliza Young House, her last home before she broke away from Young and polygamy, which has become an active center in the struggle against polygamy and houses an organization that provides shelter for runaways, thus continuing Ann Eliza's legacy. In the novel, the place serves as a chronotope of polygamy. It is also the place where Jordan hears about Ann Eliza and her struggle for the first time. Further, it is revealed that Kelly is "the great-great-great-granddaughter" (Ebershoff 130) of Ann Eliza, a descendant of her first son, James Edward Dee, with her first husband, James Dee.

Another motif in both time levels of the novel is the recurring comparison of the system of polygamy with that of slavery. A fictional introductory essay by Harriet Beecher Stowe (Ebershoff 24–25) talks about the "enslaved state of the women of Utah" (24). Ann Eliza pointedly claims that she is "fighting for the abolition of marital bondage" (490). The secret resistance against polygamy in the twenty-first century is organized in the same way as the clandestine opposition to slavery in the nineteenth century, the Underground Railroad (385). And Kelly's ghostwriting of ex-First Jordan's story is reminiscent of the creation of slave narratives in the nineteenth century, when illiterate former slaves' life stories were recorded by white authors.

Mystery is a key concept that is applied variously in the novel. Most obviously, Jordan's narrative is a murder mystery. He and his "sidekick" (Ebershoff 143) Johnny try to solve the murder of Jordan's father. The typical amateur detective team of two appears as a variation of Doyle's Holmes and Watson. The solution to the murder case, which lies in Jordan's father's practice of unorthodoxly numbering his wives, in the end comes in textual documents too. A note from Queenie to Jordan

(484) and a letter by her husband Hiram Alton, the murderer, to the sheriff (485) reveal the perpetrator as well as his motive. Lorenzo Dee, in one of his mid-twentieth-century letters, seems to be commenting on this fact: "Any reader of mysteries will tell you the key to solving a crime is understanding the motive" (496). Furthermore, the most remarkable mystery is probably the vanishing of Ann Eliza after the publication of her second book in 1908. After this date, no trace of her can be found in any historical source. This mystery is a real-life, historical mystery, too. Concerning Ann Eliza's disappearance, the novel can only offer speculations (495–96, 498). As Kelly wraps it up: "I have come to the conclusion, alas, that the mystery of her final outcome cannot be solved. Indeed, there are some mysteries that must exist without answer" (500).

Truth or truthfulness is another issue the novel is concerned with. On the one hand, Ebershoff's decision to present his history of polygamy through multiple perspectives is grounded in the notion that (historical) truth can never be achieved, but can at best only be aimed at: "[T]here are at least two, and typically more, combative opinions on what each side sincerely calls 'the truth'" (Ebershoff 509). Ann Eliza, for example, wonders: "How to reconcile our competing truths? By obliterating one? Is it the only way?" (417). And even Young reflects upon the possibility of varying perspectives: "There is, and, to my mind, always will be, the problem of balancing the Truth, as I know it, with the rights of man, in which I believe. How to reconcile this problem?" (446). The characters of the twenty-first-century tale are similarly challenged by that question. Jordan, at one point, even states, "I don't know if this has sides anymore" (477). Nevertheless, *The 19th Wife* aims at a truthful rendering of the everyday reality of polygamy. The novel's function may equal what Kelly discerns as the merit of Ann Eliza's memoir: "[S]he said lots of nasty things about the church in her book, some of which were misleading and completely biased, but she also made us see the truth about something very important" (396).

The 19th Wife is based on a prodigious amount of factual research, both in archives and in the field, visiting sites and interviewing plural wives in Hildale/Colorado City. Ebershoff includes elements one would more specifically expect in a history textbook than in a novel, such as a detailed table of contents (xi–xii) and a bibliography (512–13). But otherwise, he declares:

> This is a work of fiction. It is not meant to be read as a stand-in for a biography of Ann Eliza Young, Brigham Young, or any of the other historical figures who appear in it. Even so, it's human nature to wonder if a historical novel is inspired by real people and real events, and if so to what degree .... [I]s *The 19th Wife* based on real people and real events? Yes. Have I invented much of it? Yes, for that is what novelists do.
>
> (Ebershoff 509–11)

The multi-perspective of the novel is an expression of Ebershoff's search for truth, "the difficult task of accuracy" (Ebershoff 509).

One of the main purposes of the novel is to revisit and revise history. Some of Ebershoff's characters seem to be created mainly for the reason of mouthing his opinions about memory, history, fiction, and truth. One such character is Lorenzo Dee, who, in a letter to the historian Professor Charles Green, points beyond his own narrative:

> I must say a few words about memory. It is full of holes. If you were to lay it out upon a table, it would resemble a scrap of lace. I am a lover of history.... Even so, history has one flaw. It is a subjective art, no less so than poetry and music. The true historian has two sources: the written record and the witness's testimony. This is as it should be. Yet one is memory and the other is written, quite often, from memory. There is nothing to be done about this defect except acknowledge it for what it is. Yet this is your field's Achilles' heel. You say in your letter the historian writes the truth. Forgive me, I must disagree. The historian writes a truth. And so on. My mother, we both know, wrote a truth in *The 19th Wife* – a truth that corresponded to her memory and desires. It is not *the* truth, certainly not. But *a* truth, yes .... Her book is a fact. It remains so, even if it is snowflaked with holes.
>
> (Ebershoff 362–63)

Professor Green's and Kelly's endeavors to research Ann Eliza's story exemplify the work of historians. Kelly describes her historical research as not so different from the task of the detective:

> I felt, you know, almost like a detective. It was very exciting because usually historians, we only meet people through documents, never in person .... That's when it hit me: This isn't a research project, these are people's lives, people's lives ruined by this doctrine that is a by-product of *my* church. Of course, I knew that before, but it's one thing to know something intellectually, it's another to meet it face-to-face.
>
> (Ebershoff 395)

Kelly forms her own point of view concerning the differences between historiography and fiction, which results in her resolution to hand in her ghostwritten autobiofiction of Jordan's life as a master's thesis in women's studies.

Ebershoff's novel is also a history of the LDS church, from its beginnings until today. The historical part covers most of the crucial aspects of the church's evolution in the nineteenth century. The story starts out in Kirtland, Ohio, where founder Joseph Smith is converting people, publicizing the story of his calling and revelation, his visitations by the angel Moroni, and the prophecy of the gold plates. The novel recounts the massacre of Haun's Mill, where many Mormons were killed by their raging neighbors. It gives an account of the subsequent thriving of the sect after their relocation to Nauvoo, Illinois, and relates Smith's so-called martyrdom and death. Further, it recounts the events of the era of Smith's successor as prophet, Brigham Young. This includes the exodus from Nauvoo to Utah, the founding of Great Salt Lake City, and the Handcart Tragedy, the trek of thousands of converted people across the Rocky Mountains to Utah during which many of them found their death. Finally, it hints at the Mountain Meadows Massacre, in which Mormons killed almost an entire trek of over 100 emigrants.

At a first glance, this story of polygamy and the history of the LDS church seems to be a very particular tale about a very specific aspect of American history in the nineteenth century. But in a way, Mormon history might equally be read as a metaphor for American history in general. The early Mormons parallel the Puritan settlers in their desire for religious freedom: they leave their allocated area or land, and they even have to do it twice. First, they found "Nauvoo, the shining city on the hill" (Ebershoff 116), reminiscent of John Winthrop's "city upon a hill" (41), and then, in an "exodus from Nauvoo" (Ebershoff 113) to find their "new Zion" (123), their "promised land" (128), they establish Great Salt Lake City in Utah, their endeavor into the desert recalling the Puritan byword of the "errand into the wilderness" (Danforth). To them, Salt Lake City is a "Camp of Israel" (Ebershoff 123), their "Mormon Canaan" (128), and Young is their "American Moses" (114). They view themselves as the "Saints of Deseret" (128), just as the Puritans saw themselves as saints. The history of the Mormons depicted in Ebershoff's novel is a paradigmatic story of the American frontier spirit and the struggle for religious freedom.

The topicality of *The 19th Wife* is astounding. There is the huge success of HBO's *Big Love*, a television drama series about a fictional fundamentalist Mormon family in Utah practicing polygamy, which began airing in 2006 ("Big"; see also Connelly). In spring 2008, the American public was captured by the legal removal of all children from the Yearning for Zion Ranch in Texas, a community of the Fundamentalist Church of Jesus Christ of Latter-Day Saints, on the grounds of child protection (Freeman/Bufferd; Decker 201). Ebershoff's book reveals the everyday reality of polygamy as one of systematic emotional neglect, sexual abuse, and exploitation. What seems to be a historical novel that transports its readers back to a remote 'site' of American nineteenth-century history turns out to be a historical lesson. The novel does not give any ready-made answers, but raises central questions which touch upon issues such as the right to privacy, freedom of religion, personal liberty, and physical and mental integrity.

The Great Divorce, Specimen Days, and *The 19th Wife* are inspired by Vichian or Foucauldian theories of history. They create parallel versions of the past, the present, and even the future, with a revisionist focus on the stories of the disenfranchised and oppressed, such as slaves, women, children, workers, and others. Multi-time-level historical fiction is thus the type of the genre which most obviously emphasizes a historical lesson.

4   Historical Biofiction

4.1 Theoretical Foundations

Immediately upon its release, James Frey's book *A Million Little Pieces* (2003) received mixed reviews. But when it was made an Oprah's Book Club selection in September 2005, it instantly became a nationwide best seller, topping the *New York Times* best-seller list in the nonfiction category for almost four months. Frey's text about alcohol and drug addiction and the resulting complications, including conflicts with the law, resonated with a large number of readers. In January 2006 the book garnered international attention, but not in a positive way. It was revealed that what readers had understood to be a piece of autobiographical writing was actually fiction. In February 2006, *Time* magazine published the following item:

> O.K., NOW HE'S IN A MILLION LITTLE PIECES. Thou shalt not lie to OPRAH WINFREY. In a tone reserved for condemning genocidal dictators, the talk-show host drove home that commandment of publishing by shredding author JAMES FREY on live TV for fabricating parts of his 2003 book *A Million Little Pieces* (published in paperback in 2005). "I really feel duped," said Winfrey, who chose the memoir for her book club, boosting it to last year's second-best-selling title in the U.S. After thesmokinggun.com revealed that details in the book – like Frey's claim of a three-month prison stay – never happened, Winfrey stood by him, calling in to CNN's *Larry King Live* to offer support. But after two weeks, Winfrey changed her mind. She made Frey squirm and squirm and then brought on guests to make him squirm some more. "You betrayed millions of readers," she said. Head down, Frey admitted to the lies. "This hasn't been a great day for me," he said at the end of the show. Actually, *that* we believe.
>
> (Keegan)

An earlier issue of the magazine featured an article titled "The Trouble with Memoirs," which had, besides dealing with the scandal surrounding Frey's book, also focused on the fact/fiction dichotomy inherent to literature in general. Frey was still holding his ground then: "A memoir is a subjective retelling of events.... It's an individual's perception of what happened in their own life. This is my recollection of my life" (qtd. in Grossman). He claimed that, despite some fabrication and rendering of facts, most important of all, "the emotional truth is still there." Winfrey similarly stated during her appearance on *Larry King Live*: "The underlying message of redemption still resonates with me.... And I know it resonates with millions of other people who have read this book" (qtd. in Grossman). The article concludes apropos Frey: "[W]hatever the bookkeepers and muckrakers turn up, his story has a psychological power that makes its factual status more or less moot.... Are you really going to make a federal case out of where you shelve him in the bookstore?"

In this vein of thought, leaving aside "the basic weirdness of a man's reputation being damaged by the fact that he didn't do jail time" (Grossman), the article follows up on the cultural implications of the case. It emphasizes that readers crave 'true stories,' but that there is no "corresponding willingness ... to give up the quirky characters and vivid details and sexy twists and pleasing, rounded endings they're used to in fiction." Therefore, it is "[n]o wonder that a panel of linguists chose *truthiness* – ... 'the quality of preferring concepts or facts one wishes to be true, rather than concepts or facts known to be true' – as 2005's word of the year." In *Reality Hunger: A Manifesto* (2011), David Shields describes twenty-first-century culture as both "desperate for authenticity and in love with artifice" (5). Contemporary "reality hunger" (Shields) is paired with the desire for 'good stories.'

In 2006, nonfiction outsold fiction by about 100 million books a year. The revelation that Frey had originally shopped the book to publishers as a work of fiction but it was declined under that label really does not come as a surprise (Grossman). Labeling the work nonfiction furthered its financial success. Yet the witch hunt regarding the fabrication of facts completely eclipsed the artistic achievements of the work. The most important question in this respect is already hinted at in the subtitle of Grossman's article: "Does truth really matter?"

In American literary history, *The Autobiography of Benjamin Franklin* (written 1771–1790; published 1793/1818/1868) and Henry Adams's *The Education of Henry Adams* (written before 1907; published posthumously 1918) are probably the best-known pieces of life writing. Over the last decades, life writing generally has had a veritable renaissance, which has been hailed as the "biographical turn" (Renders/Haan/Harmsma 3). The renewed popularity of life writing can be explained along the lines of a need for life to have value, even in a world of increased disharmony and conflict (Nadel 136). Another, similar explanation might be that 'true stories' seem to offer holding points in a chaotic and confusing world. But the question of truthfulness remains. Ralph Waldo Emerson claimed that "[a]ll history becomes subjective; in other words there is properly no history, only biography" (II 6). Sigmund Freud stressed that the author of a biography is committed to "lies, concealments, hypocrisy, flattery ... for biographical truth does not exist" (127). In the twenty-first century, postmodernist and post-structuralist critiques have intensified an epistemological challenge: "If language cannot transparently convey reality, if the self is a fictive construct or mere multiplicity of subject positions, if narrative itself imposes a false coherence on events, then no biographical account of someone's life can be in any sense 'true'" (Hoberman 111).

Life writing is not only evident in multiple types of auto/biographies and memoirs, it also includes certain types of fiction, which further complicates the issue. Various scholars attest a general generic closeness between biography and novel (Rose 111; Schabert, *Quest* 58; Keener 5). The fact/fiction dichotomy, blurred within the texts, is paradoxically stabilized by recent criticism, which establishes a boundary between fictional and factual narratives by continuing to conceptualize that boundary in generic terms (Keener 1; Perloff 4). While most of the relevant texts – see Frey's book – seem to blur generic boundaries between auto/biography, memoir, and fiction, there seems to be a demand to stick to old generic traditions when trying to define life writing in scholarly metalanguage. This current development is part of the "generic turn" (Nadj 411) in literary theory.

John F. Keener suggests that the field of life writing should be viewed as "a continuum of biographical narratives, from factual to fictional" (ii), which includes "a wide range of texts, connoting any narrative in any discipline or genre – novels, drama, film, history, biography, autobiography or journalism – whose subject is the life of an historical (or 'real') individual" (1). There have been numerous attempts to define the new hybrid genres (Nünning, "Fictional" 194–95, 209). A wide variety of terms are in use to label the fictional biographical narrative: invented biography (Grabes, my translation), "new fiction biography" (Jacobs), "fictional biography" (Schabert, *Quest*), fictive biography (Maack, "Charakter," my translation), "memographiction" (Maack, "Leben"), "metafictional biography" (Hochbruck), "biographical fiction" (Bird), "novel of biographical quest, or bioquest novel" (Thiem), "autobiografiction" (Saunders), and many more (Novak 2). The most handy and widely accepted umbrella term is probably "biofiction" (Buisine; see also Middeke). Julia Novak provides a basic definition of biofiction as "a narrative based on the life of a historical person, weaving biographical fact into what must otherwise be considered a novel" (9). Accordingly, Michael Lackey emphasizes that the genre of biofiction should be analyzed "through the lens of fiction rather than biography" (8).

Ansgar Nünning provides a categorization of what he labels "postmodern biofiction." He proposes a "typology of biofictions," consisting of five types: "'documentary fictional biographies,' 'realist fictional biographies,' 'revisionist fictional biographies,' 'fictional metabiographies,' and ... 'biographic metafiction'" ("Fictional" 200–01). The documentary fictional biography features a large number and wide variety of reality references, and foregrounds the commonly backgrounded factual world. The realist fictional biography, alternatively labeled "traditional fictional biography" (201), represents the life of a historical individual in conventional fictional form and foregrounds the plot against the backdrop of an identifiable historical context. The revisionist fictional biography revises the biographical record and renews the formal conventions of biographical fiction. The fictional metabiography and "fictional metaautobiography" (199) convert the conventions of traditional biography and autobiography by using the literary device of different time levels, thereby highlighting the continuity of the past with the present. Biographic metafiction destabilizes the conventional boundaries between biography and fiction (201–02).

Despite these efforts of defining biofiction, there is still some need for clarity regarding the actual subject of biofictional texts, as well as their relationship with the historical past. First, contrary to Ina Schabert's definition that the "fictional biography is engaged in the comprehension of real historical individuals" (*Quest* 4; see also Novak 9, 14–15), biofiction sometimes focuses on completely fictional characters. Herbert Grabes, in his study *Erfundene Biographien: Vladimir Nabokovs englische Romane* (1975) emphasizes this aspect when he reads Nabokov's novels *The Real Life of Sebastian Knight* (1941) and *Lolita* (1955) as invented biographies. Second, Nünning's use of Dave Eggers's *A Heartbreaking Work of Staggering Genius* (2000) as an example of a fictional metaautobiography shows that for him, biofiction does not necessarily also qualify as historical fiction. However, Martin Middeke's use of the term "biofiction" (3) must be understood as being implicitly accompanied by the adjective 'historical' when he applies it to novels about Romantic poets. Schabert's assertion that a fictional biography focuses on "a figure of the past of whom the author could not have direct, personal experience" (Schabert *Quest* 3; see also 23) appears germane here. I will adopt the term 'biofiction' for my discussion of this category of fictional life writing. However, in order to emphasize the connection between historical fiction and biographical narrative – that is, the twofold generic bases of the respective texts – I have modified the term by adding the adjective 'historical.' I also claim that a text constitutes historical biofiction even if it only features wholly fictional characters.

In the history of biofiction as a genre, the close relationship between biographical narrative and historical subjects has been central, but with a male focus. Schabert indicates the tradition of the fictional biography in the United States in the twentieth century by the following texts: Robert Penn Warren's *All the King's Men* (1946), Thornton Wilder's *The Ides of March* (1948), William Styron's *The Confessions of Nat Turner* (1967), Gore Vidal's *Julian* (1964), *Burr* (1973), and *Lincoln* (1984), George Garrett's *Death of the Fox* (1971), Steven Millhauser's *Edwin Mullhouse* (1972), and Louis Auchincloss's *The Cat and the King* (1981) (*Quest* 43, 51). A large chunk of these biofictions concentrate on rewriting or revising the nineteenth century, and they all focus on male biographical subjects. Though all of these texts are written by American authors, not all of them focus on American individuals.

Historical biofictions of eminent American men are quite numerous. Fictional biographies of American presidents, for example, abound: Vidal's Narratives of Empire series (also known as American Chronicles, 1967–2000) are a case in point, but so are Don DeLillo's *Libra* (1988) and Adam Braver's *Mr. Lincoln's Wars* (2003). Interestingly, Edmund Morris, within his own oeuvre, has moved from Pulitzer Prize-winning biography with *The Rise of Theodore Roosevelt* (1979) to biofiction with *Dutch* (1999), his book about Ronald Reagan. Two of the more recent and daring biofictions about American presidents are Seth Grahame-Smith's *Abraham Lincoln: Vampire Hunter* (2010) and George Saunders's *Lincoln in the Bardo* (2017). Many renowned American men of the nineteenth century have likewise become the focus of biofiction: Louis Rose, legendary survivor of the Alamo, is the title character of William Rainbolt's *Moses Rose* (1996); radical abolitionist John Brown is portrayed in Russell Banks's *Cloudsplitter* (1998); and famed photographer Edward S. Curtis is at the center of one of the storylines in Marianne Wiggins's *The Shadow Catcher* (2007).

The predominance of male subjects does not come as a surprise, if we take into account that the "maps and chaps version of history" (Carol Shields, qtd. in Hollenberg 341) for a long time equaled official historiography. Only recently have women begun to step out of the shadows of those eminent men and into their own biofictions. Many of these texts are "feminist interventions into traditional historical discourses" (Cooper/Short 13), but often it is still "the relation of the woman to the male subject" that is "of central concern" (Bird 5). Examples of such novels are Ellen Feldman's *Lucy* (2003), the story of President Franklin Delano Roosevelt's longtime lover Lucy Mercer; Nancy Horan's *Loving Frank* (2007), about architect Frank Lloyd Wright's affair with Martha Borthwick Cheney; and T. C. Boyle's *The Women* (2009), also about Wright's lover, as well as his three wives.

As early as 1928, Virginia Woolf, in *A Room of One's Own*, called for a rewriting of history from a gendered perspective. She lamented the fact that women too often featured only in the background in "the lives of the great" (*Room* 45). She postulated a history that focused on women's domestic experiences. Woolf's claims mirror the aims of social history, starting in the 1960s and 1970s, which furthered the establishment of a feminist revision of historiography by challenging "the narrative line of political history ('white men make history')" (Scott 21). 'Herstory' is a trend that, since roughly the 1970s, has compensated for the absence of women in historiography (Öhlschläger 241; Schabert, "Gender" 181). The term defines a reformulation of history from a gender perspective (Bird 16; Tofantšuk 59). Herstory shifts the focus toward recovery and revision. The history of the private sphere of family and home is added to the narrative of public events (Linda Anderson 130). Necessarily, such a perspective needs to question the traditional concepts, or rather, the conceptual limits, of history (Linda Anderson 130; Gordon 28). It also seems necessary to produce an imbalance toward herstory for a time (Lerner 101), to put the record straight.

Herstory emerged following the resurrection of previously neglected and almost forgotten women writers (with an emphasis on the nineteenth century) and the feminist attempts at reshaping or redefining the literary canon during the second phase or wave of feminism (Ashcroft/Griffiths/Tiffin, "Introduction" 249; Rothaug 39–40; Heilmann/Llewellyn 3; Nicholson). In literary studies, interest grew not only in the writings but also in the lives of the women writers of the past. In literature, as in history, women had until then played at best minor roles in a male-dominated discourse. The traditional definition of history as "[g]reat deeds of great men; chronological accounts of battles and borders, treaties and territories" (Warhol/Herndl 855) had degraded women to mere bystanders in the historical process (Rothaug 40). Hegemonic history excluded women as well as the female sphere.

Contemporary writers take up the concept of herstory, aiming, like historians and literary historians, at a feminist revision of history, but doing so by writing historical biofiction centering on women. Jeannette King, in her study *The Victorian Woman Question in Contemporary Fiction* (2005), asserts that "[b]y making female experience central to their narratives such novels gave women back their place in history, not just as victims but as agents" (3; see also Heilmann/Llewellyn 2). Indeed, "[w]omen writers' impulse to reassess not only their own position in history but also the nature of that history's right to represent the 'truth' has coincided with a wider cultural challenge to what constitutes 'History'" (Heilmann/Llewellyn 3). Diana Wallace observes in *The Woman's Historical Novel: British Women Writers, 1900–2000* (2005) that these texts are

> less like a nostalgic retreat into the past than a complex engage-
> ment with the ways in which representations of history change over
> time.... The novels ... contest the idea of a single unitary and linear

history. They emphasise the subjective, fragmentary nature of historical knowledge through rewritings of canonical texts, through multiple or divided narrators, fragmentary or contradictory narratives, and disruptions of linear chronology. (204)

Feminist discourse as a whole has "led to the re-valuation of personal or life narratives – journals, letters, confessions, biographies, auto-biographies, self-portraits" (Hutcheon, *Politics* 160). Personalized genres such as these have often been viewed as specifically female (Rothaug 141). Generally, it can be argued that "[b]iography and autobiography personalize history. They restore identity" (Cullick 4) – or, as Jörn Rüsen broadly asserts, historical narratives are a medium of the human quest for identity (*Grundzüge* 57, my translation; see also Harlan 126). Especially in texts by female authors, the issue of identity construction becomes an equally important theme along with historical representation (Rothaug 16), yet "[w]hat is emerging in feminist writings is ... the concept of a multiple, shifting, and often self-contradictory identity, ... an identity made up of heterogeneous and heteronomous representations of gender, race, and class, and often ... across languages and cultures" (Lauretis 8–9).

Texts that depict the identity construction of women and approach herstory through personalized history can be seen as "gendered memories" (Öhlschläger 227). This notion implies that gender-specific modes of remembrance exist and that concepts of gender and their conjunction with the social power (im-)balance and societal values perform cultural memory (Erll/Seidel 184–85; Öhlschläger 228). These texts are media "for the personal or individual transmission of cultural memory" (Gorp/Musarra-Schroeder v). As Sigrun Meinig observes, "[c]haracter focalisation promotes a subjective view of history, while narrator-focalisation has a tendency towards an overview of historical events and conditions" (50). Homodiegetic narration, often found in historical biofiction, is typically used to stage individual memory (Neumann 165–67), while multiple perspectives are often applied to represent a collective past.

What I label 'herstorical biofiction' makes "an attempt to rehabilitate historical women," trying to rectify "the injustice of women who, for whatever reason, have not been accorded a historical voice" (Bird 1). These specific instances of historical biofiction criticize the "silenced discourse" (Rothaug 34, 72) of women and may well be described as "project[s] of giving historical figures a voice" (Bird 1). Finding one's voice must always be read as an instance of emancipation and empowerment. It is an expression of the potential to articulate oneself: "Narrative power, then, may be the only strategy left for the weak and dispossessed: without narrative power, they may not be heard" (Bennett/Royle 47).

What Middeke asserts apropos the rewriting of Romantic lives in contemporary British fiction is true for American herstorical biofiction as well: the texts "are concerned with the hermeneutical problem of jux-taposing, correlating, and, after all, understanding our own experience in relation to the received experience of the past" (18–19). Or, as King states more specifically with regard to contemporary feminist historical fiction:

> Revisiting Victorian women's lives provides an opportunity to challenge the answers which nineteenth-century society produced in response to 'the Woman Question'. But the novelists ... are not merely carrying out a historical exercise. Their interest is ... in what the Victorian period can add to the modern reader's understanding of gender.
>
> (6; see also Glover/Kaplan 18)

There is a large number of new historical novels that tell herstory of the nineteenth-century past. Two novels that qualify for this label have already been discussed, in the chapter on multi-time-level historical fiction: Valerie Martin's *The Great Divorce* (1994) and David Ebershoff's *The 19th Wife* (2008). Other relevant texts also better fit another category of the new historical fiction. 'Reanimated classics' rewrite seminal works of American literature from a female perspective. Christopher Bigsby's *Hester* (1994), Alice Randall's *The Wind Done Gone* (2001), and Geraldine Brooks's *March* (2005) will therefore be discussed in the following chapter. Jacqueline Sheehan's *Truth* (2003) and Valerie Martin's *Property* (2003), together with Randall's novel, constitute yet another category of historical biofiction, the neo-slave narrative. Further note-worthy texts are Jane Smiley's *The All-True Travels and Adventures of Lidie Newton* (1998), a frontier tale of the headstrong title heroine settling in what was then the Kansas Territory; Andrea Barrett's *The Voyage of the Narwhal* (1998), which focuses on an Arctic expedition as well as on the women whom the explorers left ashore; Susan Sontag's *In America* (2000), the fictionalized biography of a Polish actor who makes a living for herself and her family in America; Peter Rushforth's *Pinkerton's Sister* (2004), the story of a 'madwoman in the attic,' who creates an alternative world crowded by her literary companions; Michael Cunningham's *The Hours* (1999), a rewriting of *Mrs. Dalloway* (1925) which juxtaposes a storyline centering on Virginia Woolf's sui-cide with two twentieth-century storylines; Joyce Carol Oates's *Blonde* (1999), a biofiction of Marilyn Monroe; and David Ebershoff's *The Danish Girl* (2000), about Lili Elbe. In this chapter, three instances of herstorical biofiction will be discussed in more detail: Lauren Belfer's *City of Light* (1999), Diane Glancy's *Stone Heart: A Novel of Sacajawea* (2003), and John May's *Poe & Fanny* (2004).

4.2 Lauren Belfer's *City of Light* (1999)

Lauren Belfer's debut novel *City of Light* (1999) is set in the city of Buffalo, New York, during its heyday, when it was the eighth-largest (Pierce) and probably second most important city in the nation. The narrative covers "a watershed time in that city's history" (Crittenden), the period of one year from March 1901 to February 1902, from a time when "the city [was] aglow with optimism, excitement, and civic pride" (Welsh 264) just before the Pan-American Exposition until all high hopes found an abrupt end with the financial disaster of the World's Fair and the assassination of President William McKinley. Belfer's two further novels to date, *A Fierce Radiance* (2010) and *And After the Fire* (2016) are also historical novels, but they are set neither in the nineteenth century nor in Buffalo.

The protagonist of *City of Light* is Louisa Barrett, the thirty-six-year-old headmistress of Buffalo's Macaulay School for Girls. Over the course of the depicted year, all the loose threads in Louisa's life combine and bring about a climactic period for her. She is caught up in the public and private battles that convulse the city of Buffalo behind its façade of glory. The brand-new possibilities of producing electricity at Niagara Falls divide the city and ignite a power struggle between mercenary industrialists and fanatic conservationists. Two murders and one abduction occur. The revelation that Louisa's goddaughter Grace is actually her biological daughter from a rape by former president Grover Cleveland, adopted by the Sinclairs, brings on the climax of the novel. While Louisa nurtures the dream of becoming her daughter's legitimate mother by marrying the widower Tom Sinclair, she unwittingly threatens the secret motivations of Buffalo's powerful men and their financial interests in the power station at Niagara Falls. Louisa's dreams shatter when she realizes that all along, she has only been a "pawn" (Croft 40) in the magnates' "power plays" (Pierce; see also Brady; Hanrahan). With the sudden death of her daughter Grace, Louisa returns to her old existence as headmistress and spinster, slowly falling into a stupor, like the city of Buffalo itself.

City of Light is a realist or traditional fictional biography and, with a female character at its center, an instance of herstorical biofiction. The protagonist "becomes embroiled in ... the struggle for women to break out of their Victorian restraints" (Crittenden). There were only two scripts for life available for women at the time. One was the traditional role of submissive wife and devoted mother, identical with the Victorian ideal of the 'angel in the house' (Patmore; Woolf, "Professions" 238) or the 'cult of true womanhood,' founded on the four cardinal virtues of piety, purity, submissiveness, and domesticity (Welter 152). The antipodal concept was that of the 'new woman,' who strove for self-realization outside the domestic sphere (Köhler; Bergmann, "Working").

Provided with a higher education, these women joined the workforce, entered the male sphere, and remained single (Wittke 9). The new woman is a frequent character type in late-nineteenth-century women's writing such as Elizabeth Stuart Phelps's *The Story of Avis* (1877) and *Doctor Zay* (1882), Sarah Orne Jewett's *A Country Doctor* (1884), and Mary E. Wilkins Freeman's *The Portion of Labor* (1901) (Masteller; Ward). In these texts, the topic of female education and professionalism is closely connected with that of spinsterhood (Bergmann, "Liberty"). Most of the nineteenth-century texts leave a remarkable asymmetry between emancipation in the professional and the erotic sphere. The women in these texts seem to live in sublimation in Freud's sense, a redirection of the sex drive toward intellectual and psychological aims. Some of the new women writers of the era were living in same-sex relationships. Such "a monogamous union based upon female values, in which one's life was spent primarily with another woman, each giving to the other the bulk of her energy and attention" (Fryer 615) was called 'Boston marriage' (Matthiessen 69–70; Smith-Rosenberg; Faderman; Donovan, *New* 38–49, and "Unpublished"; Roman; Sherman 80; Fetterley/Pryse; Fetterley, "Reading"; Schachinger; McCullough 15–92; Wilson 52, 92).

Belfer has taken her cue from nineteenth-century texts about new women and the lives of their female authors. With Louisa, she presents a new woman par excellence: ambitious, successful, independent, and self-reliant. As the headmistress of a prestigious school, she seems to hold a privileged position in the upper echelons of Buffalo society, with access to the male sphere of power (Belfer, *City* 57). And apparently she is even entangled in a Boston marriage with another new woman, architect and socialite Francesca Coatsworth. Louisa is the first-person narrator of her own tale, recounting "the year's experiences from the wisdom and distance of nine [sic] years later" (Woodcock). Her narration creates a tension between the remembering and the experiencing I, which is typical of a complete analepsis and turns into a staging of individual memory, which, on a more general level, gains universal relevance and validity as a collective memory of all women's past. Because *City of Light* was published in 1999, and not written in 1909 as pretended, the reader is allowed to take a glimpse behind the façade. Louisa only feigns the relationship with her friend Francesca and longs for heterosexual love, emotionally and physically. While she is regarded as a "bluestocking" and an "old maid," seemingly content with her life, only she herself knows that she is really "a woman of feeling, desire, even beauty," and that she is under "the constant effort of self-restraint" (Belfer, *City* 1, 202). But as most of the available men seem unsuitable to her, she opts for a sublimation of her sexual desires: "My chastity was much the better fate" (63). Her profession, too, is not so much wish fulfillment as it is an inescapable exigency for her: alone in the world after her father's death, she has no financial support (67). Ultimately, it is revealed that Louisa's life as a new woman seems substantially lacking in the emotional and sexual area, just as the lives of women confined to the traditional role of angel in the house might be short of independence and self-fulfillment.

At her school, Louisa aims to educate girls in a way that enables them to escape the confined circles of married women. But she also does not intend to turn them into "wise virgin[s]" (Belfer, *City* 6) like her. Rather, she hopes for them to be one day able to resolve the two seemingly disparate lifelines for women (6).

The life of Louisa's deceased friend Margaret Sinclair is presented as the model of a progressive life script for women. Margaret graduated from Vassar College and married Thomas Sinclair. The two of them forged a "marriage of rebellion," shunning "formal society" and allowing her to commit herself "to settlement house work, teaching English to immigrant children and marketable skills like sewing to their impoverished mothers" (Belfer, *City* 28). This reconciliation of the alternative cultural stereotypes appears as a real option available to Louisa herself during the course of the pivotal year depicted in the novel: "Modestia and the Winged Victory: two far different views of woman-hood, and how were we to steer between them?" (43). It is significant to note that Margaret is already dead when the novel sets in, so the ideal is after all a short-lived one.

Other female characters in the novel similarly suffer from the grid-locked life scripts for women and further emphasize the feminist and revisionist impetus of the novel. The character of Maria M. Love is modeled on the real Buffalo socialite and charity lady, who most notably set up a crèche for underprivileged children. She is the embodiment of the archetypal old maid, drawn as a caricature, for instance, when acting quite condescendingly toward the poor families she intends to help, and ridiculed, when dressing up like a young girl for a ball. Although Miss Love, different from the protagonist of the novel, comes from a wealthy family background, she seems to be caught in the same net and feels the same confinement in her position as does Louisa (Belfer, *City* 113). By contrast, an epitome of the angel in the house is introduced with the character of Frances, Grover Cleveland's young wife, who is likewise modeled on a historical person. At twenty-two she married the forty-nine-year-old president, becoming the "girl-First Lady" (411). In quick succession, she bore her husband four children, all the while, ostensibly impassively, enduring his extramarital affairs and his notoriety as a "profligate philanderer" (174). She even comes to her husband's defense, openly declaring that she was not abused by him (412), which recalls Hillary Clinton's position in the Clinton-Lewinsky scandal, which hap-pened around the time of the publication of the novel. When Louisa, fearing for her daughter's safety, resolves to approach her rapist, Mrs. Cleveland tries to shelter her husband from any unpleasant entanglements. She was once on the path toward becoming a new woman as "a college girl, a graduate of Wells" (410), but then she adopted the traditional role of devoted mother and submissive wife (410). But Mrs. Cleveland too seems to hide the drawbacks of her position behind an immaculate façade, one even she sometimes has trouble putting on (410–11). The necessity for women to play one of the two roles assigned to their gender, exemplified by Miss Love and Mrs. Cleveland, and the impossibility of merging the two is one of the dominating themes of the novel. In this way, the novel underlines what has been observed as the "simultaneous consolidation and subversion of patriarchal gender discourse during the Victorian period" (King 5).

Most prominently, this is illustrated by Louisa, who has to hide the disgrace of her rape and the subsequent pregnancy, as well as her dreams of a marriage and a family, behind the mask of the respectable head-mistress. This is already hinted at in the first pages of the novel, when Louisa addresses the reader:

> Yes, people misjudge me.... And when I rise in the gray shadow of dawn, a cooling breeze coming through the open window, my hair flowing around me, my nightdress loose, my body warm beneath it, I gaze in the mirror and see myself for what I am: a woman of feeling, desire, even beauty. Then step by step I create the person I must be: The warm, free body becomes corseted and covered with a high-collared navy-blue dress; the flowing hair is twisted into a tight bun; sturdy shoes take the place of bare feet. What do I hide?
>
> (Belfer, *City* 1)

Louisa May Alcott's *Behind a Mask, or a Woman's Power* (1866), in which governess Jean Muir famously declares, "Come, the curtain is down, so I may be myself for a few hours, if actresses ever are themselves" (123), is certainly the literary model for this scene. The necessities of acting and disguising are repeatedly stressed throughout the text (Belfer, *City* 311, 446).

The novel, published in time for the centennial anniversary of Buffalo's Pan-American Exposition of 1901, follows a twofold revisionist impetus. In addition to the dominant feminist issues revolving around Louisa, giving her and other women a voice, another main character of the novel is the city of Buffalo itself (Whitcomb 29; Kwiatowski). The story of the city parallels Louisa's story. At the beginning of the book, all ambitions for Buffalo seem to be attainable, but in the end, the financial disaster of the World's Fair and its entanglement in cultural memory with the assassination of President McKinley shatter all the dreams Buffalo's powerful men had for the city (William Gray). The decay and decline of the city, which persists today, coincides with the fading of Louisa's dream. The Pan-American Exposition, a temporary structure to begin with, is pulled down at the end of the fair, functioning as a symbol of the pivotal period in the life of Louisa that *City of Light* depicts. Active motherhood and romance are only fleeting experiences for her. When the fair is demolished, Louisa's short period of awakening from her school-marm existence comes to an end too. The hope that she could still choose an alternative lifeline for herself is exposed as a pipe dream. This element of the novel is reminiscent of a nineteenth-century classic, Kate Chopin's *The Awakening* (1899). For Louisa, the end of her dreams comes with the death of her daughter and brings about death-in-life: "[I]mpassivity was now the mask I wore each day" (Belfer, *City* 490). Stupor is the natural disposition of all women at the turn of the century and of the city of Buffalo after its apex of fame in the nineteenth century.

That Belfer's novel is a novel about the city of Buffalo may not come as a surprise, as the book goes by the title *City of Light*. As one review has it, "[t]he city is Buffalo in 1901, and the light comes from the electricity generated by the new power station at Niagara Falls" (Hoffert/Burns 49). The author, who grew up in Buffalo, aims at (re)claiming for her hometown the importance she believes the city is due in the story of the past. The text is driven by nostalgia for a time when Buffalo was not the sad epitome of the massive decline of the once-thriving economy of the United States, when the city was not perceived as a "downtrodden and depressed" place (Belfer, "Writing"). Buffalo is presented as "the Silicon Valley of its day" (Belfer, "Writing"), a symbol of the hopes and dreams Americans had for the twentieth century (Simon), a century that would indeed be known as the 'American Century.' Belfer's book became a nationwide best seller, and its impressive reception history since, including a "Lauren Belfer Day" and a "City of Light Bus Tour" (Kwiatowski; Free; Clarke/Clarke; Eaton; O'Gorman; Sommer, "City," "Light"), proves that the author succeeded in saving "the city's rich past from obscurity" (Sommer, "Paperback").

Belfer may portray her hometown with a lot of nostalgia, but she does not spare the reader the downsides of Buffalo in 1901/02 either. Even at the turn of the twentieth century, when "Buffalo was seen as a microcosm of an American society on the brink of a glittering, limitless future" (Patterson), the 'city of light' had its shadowy sides and was not a hopeful and magical place for all who lived there. The plot of Belfer's novel "is set against a background of severe poverty and degradation, trade union strife, violent ecological battles, snobbery and racism" (Patterson). Union workers, immigrants, women, and African Americans, due to their marginal standing and lack of power within Buffalo's society, experience the city not as the shining light at the dawn of the twentieth century but as "a city of darkness" (Lehmann-Haupt, "Illuminating").

Belfer understands that the individual is the "factor in which and through which historical process opens itself to human understanding" (Kunow, "Nineteenth-Century" 216; see also Belfer, "Writing"). With an abundance of characters worthy of a Dickens novel, her presentation of the social history of the time is always closely connected with characters whose function it is to direct attention to specific social problems. The Fronczyk siblings introduce the immigrant issue, for example, when it becomes obvious that Maddie Fronczyk, who is one of Louisa's students, significantly differs from her fellow students in her behavior because of her cultural background (Belfer, *City* 78–79), or when Peter Fronczyk, who is a worker at the power station, actively struggles for poor and immigrant workers' rights and denounces social inequality. Tom Sinclair, an Irish immigrant who has achieved the American Dream, is nevertheless snubbed by Buffalo's xenophobic high society. Franklin Fiske, a muckraking journalist, is secretly investigating corruption and bribery and thereby accusing the business titans of greed (William Gray). Daniel Henry Bates, the leader of a militant group of conservationists, and his follower, Louisa's fellow teacher Susannah Riley, put emphasis on the ecological issues of the exploitation of Niagara as well as on the social implications of the production of electricity. Mary Talbert, the only nonfictional character in this set, draws attention to racial issues. In real life, Talbert was a civil-rights activist who tried to further African American issues in many ways. In the novel, she is fighting for an adequate representation of her race at the Pan-American Exposition and openly demonstrates against the exhibit of "happy darkies" (Belfer, *City* 152) in an "Old Plantation" (269) scene at the fair.

All of these topics emphasize that *City of Light* is "an intensely modern novel" (Jeanne Fay; see also Hanrahan; Jefferson). The topicality of Belfer's text is manifold, as it addresses nineteenth-century problems that are still of concern today, such as feminist and environmental issues; the advantages and perils of technological progress; corruption in politics: labor, class, and race issues; and human rights (Clarke/Clarke; Sesto; Sandweiss). *City of Light* is a novel about all the "problems that still plague us 100 years later" (Pierce; see also Steele; Lehmann-Haupt, "Illuminating").

Especially the topic of the environmental controversy surrounding the exploitation of Niagara Falls strikes one as very up-to-date in the twenty-first century, when the advantages and disadvantages of technological progress are questioned. In the novel, the battle between the conservationists and the industrialists is presented as a battle between good and evil. Riley, who turns out to be a murderer, paints enchanting images of the power station as an aesthetic sublime, whereas her real belief is that it is the devil's territory. The environmentalists' leader, Bates, is stylized as a new Jeremiah, "cultivating the Old Testament prophet look," complete with "white beard," "long hair … uncombed and wild" (Belfer, *City* 232), flaming eyes, and apparent physical pain and suffering. He controls a group of people who follow him "in a religious ecstasy" (237) that makes them appear as an extremist sect, fanatically fighting a holy war. Their crusade does not stop at involving innocent children in their schemes, and finally involves bombing the power station. For them, the struggle is a Manichean battle in which all weapons are allowed. All this is, of course, reminiscent of the terrorist attacks of the late twentieth and early twenty-first centuries committed by religious fanatics, and also of the Western response to this so-called 'axis of evil.'

Formal and structural aspects of the book are noteworthy as well. The novel is divided into four parts, "Power," "Possession," "Prosperity," and "Passion." The alliteration of the chapter titles, as well as the allusion to power in all four of them, points toward an overall topic of the book, the various forms of use and abuse of power. Each part of the novel is pre-ceded by excerpts from nineteenth-century writings. These epigraphs function as mottoes for the covered events and evoke a manner "re-miniscent of much nineteenth-century fiction ... [with] copious literary quotations providing the shaping epigraphs to individual chapters" (Sanders 123). The frame tale, set in 1909, starts with an address or overall statement from the narrator and ends with an epilogue. Belfer also adds a historical note, in which she gives some of her sources and reveals the enormous amount of research that went into the novel. In this paratext, she explicitly points out the fiction she mixed with the facts (Sandweiss). Her "unapologetic appropriation of historic figures as some of her main characters" (Jeanne Fay; see also Dening) is countered by her claim that she maintained "the basic historical truth" (Belfer, "On"). In a metafictional note in the novel, Belfer significantly has her protagonist assert that "on some basic level history itself [is] forever unknowable" (*City* 454). Two intermedial elements in the novel – two maps of the rendered, partly fic-tional Buffalo – recall other fictional microcosms that are based on reality, such as William Faulkner's Yoknapatawpha County. In a stance similar to Faulkner's invention of a regional saga, Belfer ties her text firmly to the real Buffalo, all the while making use of her poetic license.

In an act of literary ventriloquism that fits the label "autobiofiction" (Middeke 14), Belfer lets Louisa recount her own story. The story is told in retrospect in chronological order, a technique prone to putting emphasis on the development of a character (Basseler/Birke 126). Within this analepsis, flashbacks are frequent. Sometimes Louisa relates events of only a few days or hours ago, and at other times the flashbacks return to her in her twenties or to her childhood. These flashbacks, or com-pleting analepses, fill in ellipses in Louisa's narrative. The function of these memories is to create suspense and, by and by, give more com-plexity to the main character. Two of the most prominent and far-reaching events in the novel are told in such a fashion: Louisa's childhood experience of visiting Niagara Falls with her father and her encounter with Grover Cleveland. Shifts in tense, especially from past to present as are employed here, point toward the significance of a scene in literature of memory (Basseler/Birke 128, 131).

The chapter depicting Louisa's rape has been described as "a small gem, almost a separate short story" (Feldman). It addresses an issue "surrounding sexuality and the body," "unspeakable [topics] for women of the past" (King 4). An authentic nineteenth-century text could not have been as outspoken about the rape. Louisa does not accuse Cleveland publicly; she hides her pregnancy and the fact that she has become a 'fallen woman' (Belfer, *City* 185). Many years later, she finds out that she was used as beautiful bait, laid out for Cleveland by the powerful men of Buffalo to make him support some of their business endeavors (449). This fact drives home the overall realization that women are living in a men's world. Louisa, the victim of powerful men in many respects, is given a voice in Belfer's *City of Light*. The subject gains renewed topicality in the twenty-first century with the Harvey Weinstein sexual-assault cases and the #MeToo movement.

Aspects of the murder-mystery genre are also prominent in *City of Light*. The fictional murders of two men – Karl Speyer and James Fitzhugh, chief engineers of the power station at Niagara – and the abduction of Talbert's fictional niece Millicent lend the novel the suspenseful drive of a detective story. Louisa and her accomplice Fiske emulate Holmes and Dr. Watson. Louisa's figure constantly wavers between her two incarnations as "schoolmarm or gumshoe" (Lange). Elements of gothic fiction abound in this text, too. Cleveland is the villain of the book, a date rapist and a misogynist. He is faintly mirrored in a marginal character, Dr. Hoyt, the director of the sanatorium (a gothic edifice), who appears to be (sexually) threatening the damsel in distress, Louisa. The power station, described like a cathedral but really a damp grave for exploited "power-station workers who risk life and limb" ("Forecasts"), bears a resemblance to the vaults, torture chambers, and subterranean passageways of the venerable gothic castle. And Niagara Falls itself, feared by Louisa and finally the cause of death of her daughter Grace, looms large not only as a powerful natural, but even a seemingly supernatural force in this novel about power in all its forms.

Belfer's *City of Light*, like so many other new historical novels, is a genre hybrid. It is "a quintessential crossover book" (Mantell 39). Among other labels it can be identified as a historical novel, a detective story, and a love story, all rolled into one (Brady; Belfer, "On"; Croft 40; Prose). Most prominently though, it is biofiction, reclaiming herstory of the nineteenth-century past.

4.3 Diane Glancy's *Stone Heart* (2003)

Stone Heart: A Novel of Sacajawea (2003) is the second historical novel by the Native American author Diane Glancy to cover a piece of Native American history in the nineteenth century. *Pushing the Bear* (1996) is, as the subtitle reveals, *A Novel of the Trail of Tears*. In this novel,

Glancy brings to life the trauma of her own nation, the Cherokee, and their forced relocation to Oklahoma in 1838. As a historical novelist, she gives a voice to Native Americans whose stories have been neglected or distorted by official history (Alberts 114). *Stone Heart* continues the tradition of Native American historical fiction that can be traced back to N. Scott Momaday's *House Made of Dawn* (1968) and was continued by James Welch's *Winter in the Blood* (1974), Leslie Marmon Silko's *Ceremony* (1977), Louise Erdrich's *Love Medicine* (1984), Michael Dorris's *A Yellow Raft in Blue Water* (1987), Stephen Marlowe's *The Memoirs of Christopher Columbus* (1987), and Michael Dorris and Louise Erdrich's *The Crown of Columbus* (1991), among others (Georgi-Findlay).

Stone Heart is a narrative of the Lewis and Clark Expedition (1804–1806) and a revisionist fictional biography. When Meriwether Lewis and William Clark were commissioned to find an overland track to the Pacific Coast, they employed the French-Canadian Toussaint Charbonneau as interpreter. When they learned that his wife, Sacajawea, was Shoshoni, they took her on as an interpreter and guide as well. At the time, she was approximately sixteen years old and had just given birth to her first child, her son Jean Baptiste. Not many more facts about her life are documented (Stephanie Gray 18–24). Around the bicentennial of the expedition, it became the topic of "a cascade of new books" (Habich). An appeal of this material seems to lie in the 'Americanness' of the expedition team, given that it reflects American society in its diversification of race, class, age, and gender. Almost each member of the expedition, from Clark's African American body servant York to Lewis's Newfoundland dog Seaman, has been given credit in various publications, seemingly along the lines of "[r]adical historians [who] now tell the story of Thanksgiving from the point of view of the turkey" (Cooley 35).

Moreover, the story of the expedition has repeatedly been fictionalized from the point of view of the young Native American woman. Sacajawea is the second-most famous Native American woman in American history after Pocahontas, who has fueled the American imagination ever since her lifetime, but she has only more recently come into focus. Among these texts are Anna L. Waldo's *Sacajawea* (1978), Della Rowland's *The Story of Sacajawea: Guide to Lewis and Clark* (1989), and Joseph Bruchac's *Sacajawea* (2000). In fictional retellings of her life, Sacajawea is often presented as the most important member of the expedition, without whom Lewis and Clark's mission would have failed. The recognition of her contribution to the expedition climaxed in the year 2000, when the United States created a new dollar coin in her honor.

It is Glancy's self-declared aim to draw an authentic picture of Sacajawea, to free her figure from all false perception, be it belittling or aggrandizing (152; Stephanie Gray 24–29). However, her novel continues the romantic ideal of the Native American (Evans; Leckie), aspiring to the image of the 'noble savage,' as it was formulated in Michel de Montaigne's essay "Des Cannibales" (1580) and perpetuated in American nineteenth-century fiction, most prominently in Cooper's Leatherstocking Tales.

The revisionist intention of *Stone Heart* is reflected in its textual structure, especially its multimodal composition. In Glancy's text "genres, forms, and voices constantly merge and diverge" (Justice 196). *Stone Heart* starts out with a double page that reveals what has been called the "fracturing" (Mackay 248) of the whole novel. The left page gives a map showing the route of the Lewis and Clark Expedition from Fort Mandan to Fort Clatsop in the upper half and an excerpt of a letter by President Thomas Jefferson, detailing Lewis and Clark's orders, in the lower half (Glancy 10). Intermediality is a common device in life writing (Balestrini/Bergmann), and here the visual element of the map and the text of the official order reveal that it was Lewis and Clark's mission to explore the waterways of the area. The text on the right page is similarly concerned with water and its mastering, but different than the matter-of-fact documents of map and letter, it has the appearance of a Native American chant or of nature poetry (Glancy 11). These two initial pages disclose a twofold approach toward a recovery of the past. Throughout the novel, Glancy juxtaposes original excerpts from Lewis and Clark's journals with Sacajawea's fictional interior monologue about the same events (Downing; Christopher Smith 132–34). In this respect, *Stone Heart* seems to be modeled after Momaday's *House Made of Dawn*. Momaday divides up the pages of his heteroglossic narrative into three units, using this technique to spatialize history by simultaneously telling a story from Kiowa Apache mythology, Kiowa ethnographical history, and a personal memory from his life (Elias, *Sublime* 142). Glancy uses her split pages to create a simultaneity of two different perspectives on one and the same event. Each voice serves as commentary on the other (Mackay 249). This "polyvocalism" gives expression to a "distrust of historical 'truth' (that is, metanarratives)" (Mackay 250). In "overt fashion ... Glancy frames the official version of United States history with her own story in order to fill some ... 'blank spaces'" (Alberts 129). By putting Sacajawea's tale next to Lewis and Clark's account, Glancy gives a character a voice who has been marginalized in traditional historiography (qtd. in Habich).

Glancy's sources are "the archive and the land" (Alberts 114). She bases her fictional account of the expedition on the historical journals of Lewis and Clark and on her own experiences traveling parts of the expedition's route (Glancy 151), believing that the land carries memories (Glancy, qtd. in Luckenbill 117–19). Therefore, the passages that are told from Sacajawea's perspective can be read as "literary ventriloquy"

(Neil Berry, qtd. in Maack, "Life" 145). With this technique the biographer seeks to obliterate the distance between herself and her subject by taking on the subject's voice (Peters 45). The method is often applied to cover insufficient or questionable evidence (Rubenstein 74). Anticipating such accusations, Glancy not only explains her working technique in two paratexts, she also lists the sources she researched for her novel (Glancy 7–8, 151–54).

There is a stark contrast between the fictional account from the young woman's point of view and the white male expeditioners' reports. While Lewis and Clark's journals are prosaic accounts of the daily events of the journey, Sacajawea's lyrical tale contrasts and complements these with emotions and sensual impressions (Downing). Sacajawea's narration abounds with "animistic images" (Habich), especially "ghost horses" (Glancy 20, 26, 30) in the sky, the river, and the ocean, most probably symbolizing fate. According to the animistic worldview of many Native American traditions, plants, animals, and even rocks are animate. This ghost world supports human beings and unites everything (Mauch 42). The diction of Sacajawea's narrative may be read as a clichéd transcription of Native American language (Leckie). But almost all indigenous languages include ecological metaphors, as trite as this way of expression might sound to an audience spoiled by too many Western movies (Mauch 41). And the contrast in style conveys perfectly the obvious cultural differences between the mature white men's point of view and the young Native American woman's.

The interior monologue gives the impression of orality. Native American cultures and hence Native American literatures are strongly rooted in a tradition of storytelling. The impression of orality in Sacajawea's tale furthermore hints at the fact that Native American history was long neglected by official historiography due to an absence of textual sources. The dominant culture depended on the written text, and due to the lack of presentation of Native Americans' "stories in the publicly accessible forms of literature" (Middleton/Woods 2), their past did not enter "textual memory" (6). Lewis and Clark's journal entries represent the Western tradition of written literature/textual memory. The way in which the texts are set is revelatory. Literally, Sacajawea's point of view is presented as equal to the expedition leaders', as the texts are printed facing each other. Sacajawea's lyrical verses are allowed to flow freely from page to page, the river obviously serving as metaphor for Sacajawea's voice (Habich). Glancy's style has been dubbed "staccato prose-poetry" ("Diane"), because her text sometimes gives the impression of a continuous prose text, sometimes of poetry. Lewis and Clark's texts are enclosed by frames which limit and restrict any possible dispersion. While Sacajawea's narrative leaves a lot of leeway for fluidity, transformation, and interpretation, Lewis and Clark's writing fixes fact and meaning. Interestingly, this seemingly clear categorization is simultaneously deconstructed. Lewis and Clark's texts are printed true to the original, with no consistent spelling, which in itself creates a certain fluidity (of orthography): "Lewis and Clark, phonetic spellers, could spell a word a dozen ways. Their language was fluid as the river. Their expedition took place before Noah Webster standardized the English language with his dictionary" (Glancy 152). Sacajawea's account of the expedition is presented in perfect, orthographically correct English: "Sacajawea did not speak English, but the story had to be written in English" (152).

Glancy additionally uses a peculiar narrative technique: Sacajawea is telling her story in a second-person narrative, equally constructing her individual story and her individual memory (Neumann). While the narrative may at first give the impression that she is in dialogue with the reader (Mackay 250), it soon becomes clear that she might equally, or even more convincingly, be addressing herself. As her tale progresses, it becomes obvious that she is more often than not her own and only listener. With her interior monologue, she tries to assure herself of who she is. Sacajawea always only sees herself through the eyes of others; she is 'you,' not 'I.' This specific narrative situation may also symbolize Glancy's, as well as the reader's, communion with the protagonist, or the narrative might be addressing Sacajawea, as indicated by the capitalized "YOU" (Glancy 12) at the beginning of the novel. In this way, her narration might be seen as a means of helping Sacajawea make sense of her own experiences, encouraging her to find herself. In the process of telling her tale, Sacajawea is creating her identity through an act of narration.

Throughout the novel, Sacajawea's life is presented as a constant valediction. The young woman's story is part of a "discourse of trauma and displacement" that "recurs repeatedly in the recent literature of history" (Middleton/Woods 2). As a young girl, Sacajawea loses her family when Hidatsa people abduct her from her Shoshoni community. Then, after she has lived with them for a while, they sell her to the man who becomes her husband. With him she lives for a while at Mandan Village in North Dakota, but when he is recruited as translator for the expedition, Sacajawea again has to leave her familiar surroundings (Glancy 14). As a consequence of all this disruption, her sense of self is shattered, she occupies a liminal position between cultures: "It is another parting from what you know. Another tearing away from yourself" (28–29). In the novel, she is presented as a victim of the patriarchal culture she lives in and of the double bind of race and gender: "By yourself you are nothing" (17). Glancy combines "the historical turn in women's fiction" with "the concerns of multicultural literature," thus adding to "a literature of the contact zone" which explores "identity in the racial and cultural borderlands of early American life" (Myles 53).

The spatial journey of Sacajawea in the novel is conflated with the process of identity formation, in which she learns to understand her role and place in the world. At the outset of the expedition, Sacajawea perceives of her position as insignificant. But throughout the journey, she feels a change. When she interprets, the expeditioners listen to her (Glancy 16). This must be understood not only in its literal but also in its metaphorical sense. Sacajawea realizes that her ability to translate Shoshoni for Lewis and Clark gives her a certain amount of power. Like Edward Waverley of Scott's archetypal historical novel, Sacajawea soon seems to waver between loyalty to the Native Americans and the white explorers: "You feel you belong to the explorers more than you do to [Native American of other tribes]" (90). As a so-called "token of peace" (82), a young woman with a baby, Sacajawea is the guarantor for the safety of the expedition team.

At one point, she finally speaks out and demands something for herself. When the Corps of Discovery spends the winter at Fort Clatsop on the coast of Oregon, Sacajawea asks to be taken on an expedition to see a whale. Lewis notes that

> the Indian woman was very impo[r]tunate to be permitted to go, and was therefore indulged; she observed she had traveled a long way with us to see the great waters, and that now that monstrous fish was also to be seen, she thought it very hard she could not be permitted to see either (she had never yet been to the ocean).
>
> (Glancy 101)

Lewis's matter-of-fact account is juxtaposed with Sacajawea's emotional reaction:

> You do not like the ocean, but you want to go see the large fish. The men prepare to go. Clark calls his men. He looks past you without seeing. He knows you want to go. But he does not consider you. You are nothing he wants.
> You walk from the fort. You leave Jean Baptiste sleeping. Your eyes fill with anger.
> You have walked as one of them. You have told the Indians the explorers were not a war party. They just want to pass through the land. Do Lewis and Clark know what the Indians could do to them? Do they know how feeble and few the explorers are?
> You hit the tree. You bang it with your weight.
> Your legs fall to the ground.
> You found roots and berries for them. You showed them what they did not see.
> You spoke to the Shoshoni for them.
> You left the Shoshoni for them.
> They do not know the weight you carry.
> You become a ghost horse. You feel the waves rise.

> You could pound them like a storm.
> What should you do? You know the way Lewis holds his anger. His feelings. You know Clark does not have them like Lewis does. You will give Clark yours.
> You return to the fort. Your voice is shaking. You speak to Clark. You *insist* you go with them. (100–01)

Sacajawea makes Clark see her and she makes her voice heard. By this active insurrection, she creates an identity for herself. This is her moment of crisis, her moment of recognition, and ultimately her initiation. On the return path, she becomes the leader of her group of the expedition, when she points out a pass through the mountains (152):

> You see Clark looking at the mountains. You see the pass you used to cross with the Shoshoni. You point it out to Clark. *He listens to what you say.*
>
> (Glancy 128; my emphasis)

And Clark's journal entry here exactly matches Sacajawea's account:

> [I]n every direction around which I could see high points of Mountains covered with snow.... The Squar pointed to the gap through which she said we must pass.... [S]he said we would pass the river before we reached the gap.... The indian woman who has been of great service to me as pilot through this country recommends a gap in the mountain more south which I shall cross. (128–29)

At the end of the journey, Sacajawea has found her voice and she has found her identity (Stephanie Gray 35).

Sacajawea's identity formation is also traced through the various spellings and meanings of her name(s). The identity of a person manifests itself in the name, as naming means being and possessing (Miyashita 192). Sacajawea's confusion about her identity is mirrored by the farrago about her name. Her old Shoshoni name was "*Boat Pusher*"; her Hidatsa name is "*Bird Woman*"; Lewis spells her name "Se car ja we au" and "Sah-Sah-gar-we-ah"; and Clark spells her name "Sah-kah-gar we a" and "Sahcahgagwea" (Glancy 82, 32, 151–52). A white stone shaped like a beaver reminds Sacajawea of her grandmother's prophecy in which a "small, white beaver without a tail" and "with short dull teeth" (40, 145) is the manifestation of her true self: "If you had another name, it would be woman-with-the-stone-beaver's-heart" (55). Her own dream of a transformed stone beaver, who now has "long teeth" and a "tail" (146), signifies the change that has come upon her and concludes the novel. *Stone Heart*, the title of the novel, refers to this dream and to her new name, which hints at Sacajawea's ability to hide as well as overcome her feelings. This becomes especially clear in an episode in which the expedition comes upon the place where she was abducted from her family. Lewis describes the event in the following way: "I cannot discover that she shews any emotion of sorrow in recollecting this event, or of joy in being again restored to her native country; if she had enough to eat and a few trinkets to wear I believe she would be perfectly content anywhere" (66). But Sacajawea's tale tells a different story, one of relived memory and trauma:

> The present camp is on the place where the Hidatsa took you.
> You are one-who-was-taken.
> You have returned.
> You dream your legs are oars.
> You are rowing, running from the Hidatsa.
> It's the ghost horses you see again.
> They take you from the Shoshoni.
> The horses are cutting you in half.
> You cry in a place the men cannot see.
> You see Otter Woman's hand stretched out to you....
> You leave part of yourself wherever you go; wherever-something-happens-that-takes-something-from-you.
> You see Beaverhead, the place you are from.
> There is a storm inside you. (66–68)

Toward the end of the journey, Sacajawea's concern is for her son. Through Sacajawea and Charbonneau's mixed parentage as well as through his exposure to the expedition team, Jean Baptiste's cultural identity is hybrid. When Clark offers to raise her son, Sacajawea pleads with Charbonneau to accept it, and succeeds (Glancy 142–45). The fate of Jean Baptiste completes the narrative's penetrations of past, present, and future (Adams 94). It brings to mind the destiny of other offspring of interracial marriages in literature about Native Americans, for example, Charles of Lydia Maria Child's *Hobomok* (1824), who ends up a fully assimilated Harvard student. In analogy to this text, Sacajawea may, by parting with her son, symbolically sacrifice the survival of her culture.

Apart from being an account of the Lewis and Clark Expedition, *Stone Heart* traces Sacajawea's rite of passage. While she is literally on a journey with Lewis and Clark, she is metaphorically on a quest for herself. By putting Sacajawea's tale next to Lewis and Clark's account, Glancy gives a character a voice that has been marginalized in traditional historiography. Her novel aims at a revision of Sacajawea's place in history, yet her rendering of her protagonist is often overly positive and pathetic.

4.4 John May's *Poe & Fanny* (2004)

John May's debut and, to date, only novel, *Poe & Fanny* (2004) is a realist or traditional fictional biography. It is one of many contemporary novels that find their subject in the lives of nineteenth-century writers. In general, literary productions of this kind have been labeled "author fictions" (Savu 9), identifying fiction at the "crossroads between the historical novel, biography, and the *Künstlerroman*" (Franssen/Hoenselaars 18). This kind of novel has become so ubiquitous in contemporary literature in English that the author or writer has even been dubbed "postmodernism's stock character" (Fokkema 41). Further examples that fit the category of historical biofictions of nineteenth-century American literati are Matthew Pearl's *The Dante Club* (2003), about the Fireside poets Longfellow, Holmes, and Lowell; Edmund White's *Hotel de Dream* (2007), about Stephen Crane; Colm Tóibín's *The Master* (2004) and David Lodge's *Author, Author* (2004), both about Henry James; and Jay Parini's *The Passages of H. M.: A Novel of Herman Melville* (2010).

Biofictions of Edgar Allan Poe's life are particularly numerous. The attraction for fictionalization can be explained by the appeal of his enduring works, his fascinating character, and the fact that Poe's life, with its well-known excesses, scandals, and feuds, simply is 'the stuff of fiction' (Hockensmith 17; Pate). Literary portraits of nineteenth-century writers may in general be inspired by the original, nineteenth-century portraits of authors that were so very fashionable at the time, for example, Poe's biographical sketches of American writers, which appeared in various magazines (1846–48) and which he had planned to compile in a collection called either *The Living Writers of America* or *Literary America*. Similar publications are Ralph Waldo Emerson's *Representative Men* (1850) and Lytton Strachey's *Eminent Victorians* (1918).

Furthermore, most of the novels which feature Poe as a character draw on his relevance to the genre of detective fiction. Over the last twenty-five years, a large number of such novels have been published (Stableford 383; Maack, "Leben" 170, 187). It will suffice here to name just a few examples: Andrew Taylor's *The American Boy* (2003; also titled *An Unpardonable Crime*) features Poe as a schoolboy in London in 1819/20, when one of his teachers becomes involved in murder and intrigue. Taylor's novel is inspired by Poe's tale "William Wilson" (1839), which in turn was inspired by Poe's own school days in Britain. In Louis Bayard's *The Pale Blue Eye* (2006), Poe is confronted with a mystery during his days as a West Point cadet. Matthew Pearl's *The Poe Shadow* (2006) is concerned with Poe's mysterious death and attempts to recruit the model for Poe's fictional detective Auguste Dupin to solve the mystery. And Joel Rose's *The Blackest Bird* (2007) turns Poe into a suspect in the true case that inspired his detective story "The Mystery of Marie Rogêt" (1842).

There are numerous texts that focus on the lives of eminent men, and especially on famous authors such as Poe. But there are fewer texts that focus on the lives of female historical characters, let alone female writers. Bird's assertion that "historical women are generally known to us through their association with great men" (5) seems to hold true for American historical fiction about writers as well. Some examples are Judy R. Smith's *Yellowbird* (2007), which intertwines the tales of three women – the two authors' wives Sophia Peabody Hawthorne and Lizzie Shaw Melville and a Native American woman/ghost, Yellowbird – and Paula McLain's *The Paris Wife* (2011) and Naomi Wood's *Mrs. Hemingway* (2014), about Ernest Hemingway's four wives. Lynn Cullen's *Mrs. Poe* (2013), like *Poe & Fanny*, fictionally explores the relationship between Poe and Frances Sargent Osgood (Bergmann, "Poe's").

The assertion that historical women are only interesting as subjects of biofiction because of their connection to important men seems to fit *Poe & Fanny*. The novel focuses not only on Poe but also on Osgood, a fellow poet, and their "little-known romantic interlude" (Ron Miller; see also Pollin). Though today fallen into oblivion, the Fanny of the novel's title was a celebrated poet at the apex of her fame when she first met Poe in 1845 (May 297). Poe, who had just published his most famous poem, "The Raven" (1845), was equally at the height of his literary career (Ron Miller). Both poets had long admired each other's work. Following their first encounter in New York City, Poe and Osgood published flirtatious poems to each other in magazines until this created a scandal, because both of them were married. Elizabeth Ellet, a fellow admirer of Poe's, threatened to ruin Osgood's reputation by making public that their relationship was not platonic. Osgood sent her friends Anne Charlotte Lynch and Margaret Fuller to make Poe return her letters to her. She eventually reconciled with her husband and gave birth to a child (Walsh). Whether Osgood and Poe were only playfully admiring one another or whether theirs was a consummated love affair will never be known. It is thinkable that their poetic dialogue was a publicity stunt, a possibility which does not appear too far-fetched in light of Poe's fondness for literary hoaxes (Jong 56). *Poe & Fanny* portrays the period in both authors' lives from the time they first met until the ending of their relationship. A paratext to the novel, an afterword based on historical facts (May 293–98), wraps up the remaining years of both poets' lives until their respective deaths in 1849 and 1850.

May is most interested in the details of Poe and Osgood's entanglement where there are no facts available (297), and he uses their poems as well as their other works as evidence of the alleged love affair. Excerpts of Osgood and Poe's flirtatious poems to each other are keystones of the storyline as the romance unfolds. An appendix to the novel (299–321) contains some of these poems. Poe's masterpiece "The Raven," most important for this period and for Osgood's initial attraction to him, is a recurring intertextual device throughout the novel. For example, at the beginning of one of two climactic scenes in hotel rooms, which feed readerly voyeurism (167–69, 211–14), Poe knocks at the door and Fanny is reminded of the effects of the tapping sound in the poem. She even identifies the poet himself with the bird of his creation (167). Similarly, Osgood's "Ida Grey" (1845) – an autobiographical short story in which the protagonist is in love with a married poet and, because she cannot marry him, ultimately retreats to a convent – not only serves as a model for Fanny's retreat to Providence, its publication is additionally presented as one of the causes of that retreat (May 201). In an allusion to Poe's "The Purloined Letter" (1845), Poe's aunt hides Fanny's last, revealing letter in his bureau, on top of the bundle of her letters, and he cannot find it until he realizes that it was in the most obvious place (May 273).

The novel is bursting with intertextuality and features further allusions to nineteenth-century literature. The premiere of *Fashion* (1845), a comedy by Osgood's friend Anna Cora Mowatt, is mentioned in the novel, as it is a known fact that Poe was present at the opening night (May 80–89). Another literary reference is the introduction of Harriet Jacobs as a character. The author of the slave narrative *Incidents in the Life of a Slave Girl* (1861) is escorted home by Poe one evening, in order to protect her from slave catchers (May 89–102). While this episode is completely invented, Jacobs, an escaped slave in a perilous position, was at the time indeed working as a nursemaid for Nathaniel Parker Willis, a friend of Poe's. The introduction of her character picks up on race as a social issue of the time.

The climax of May's fictional account of the poets' relationship is the suggestion that Osgood's third daughter Fanny Fay was Poe's child. This proposition feeds readerly sensationalism, yet there are certain aspects which make a relationship between Poe and Osgood plausible. Poe's young wife Virginia was already gravely ill at the time, and Osgood's husband, the painter Samuel Stillman Osgood, had temporarily separated from her. Poe and Osgood had a lot in common. Both were natives of Boston now living in New York, cities rivaling for hegemony in intellectual matters in the nineteenth century, and, more importantly, both were passionate poets and headstrong characters. Moreover, Osgood's appearance seems to match what has often been described as Poe's type. Portraits of her show a delicate dark beauty with large eyes. When she met Poe, she may also have been in an early stage of tuberculosis, to which she succumbed in 1850. Her childlike appearance and frailty bear a strong resemblance to all the women Poe loved throughout his life (Jong 32).

Most of the chapters in the novel are told alternatingly from either Poe's or Osgood's perspective. But there are also chapters that are narrated from the perspective of Maria Poe Clemm, Poe's aunt and the mother of his young and dying wife Virginia, and from the point of view of Willis, a famous journalist of the time. The juxtaposition of the four accounts creates a narrative of multiple perspectives on the relationship between Poe and Osgood. May uses the nicknames of all four of his main characters as recurring chapter headings: Poe, the distant literary genius of the title page, becomes "Eddy"; Osgood is "Fanny"; Clemm becomes "Muddy," derived from her daughter's "baby way of saying 'Mother'"; and Willis stays "Willis" (May 24, 36, 13, 14, 1). By this familiarizing device, the characters become more accessible to the reader. The nicknames additionally reflect how the characters are viewed and how they define each other. This effect is furthered by the use of a figural narrative situation, with the various characters serving as reflector figures or focalizers for different chapters. Though different viewpoints in fiction are often used to create a diversity of perspectives on or different versions of a tale, here the device is used to create a consistent picture and to affirm the credibility of the fictionalized story. Additive and episodic narration, montage, and parallelism are usually employed in revisionist historical fiction to question the existence of a usable past. The four perspectives here are utilized instead to render one of many possible perspectives convincing.

All four perspectives give a positive impression of Poe. May only chooses viewpoints of people who have an affinity for him: himself, Fanny, and Muddy, who love him, and Willis, who has a weak spot for him and pities him for his bad luck. More challenging views of Poe's behavior, such as those of his friend Thomas Dunn English, are not given a lot of space. In the novel, Poe is presented as a troubled man with problems, not as the eminent writer. May draws a likeable and pitiable picture of Poe, often rendering the depiction of the character into a cliché. In *Poe & Fanny*, it is not Poe himself, with his alcoholism and his temper, who is his worst enemy but the hypocritical society of New York City and its social rules, which are too constraining for a genius of his caliber.

In the chapters dedicated to her, we encounter Fanny wavering between the two alternative roles available for women at her time. When she meets Poe, she is a celebrated, renowned 'poetess,' but also a mother of two young daughters, who has only recently separated from her husband. She yearns to conform to the rules of society to be a good wife and mother, a 'true woman,' but she longs to be independent and fulfill her calling as a poet too. Though fascinated by the man, she first wants to win him as her mentor, and then gradually becomes entangled in a love affair with him. When the liaison has ended and she realizes that she is pregnant, Fanny must find a way to conceal this shame. As a 'fallen woman', she has no other choice than to try to save her reputation by returning to her husband and placing her fate in his hands. Social and financial constraints make her choose this path (Wells). The incompatibility of the traditional female role with the emerging image of the 'new woman' lends the passages about Fanny topicality.

The chapters told from Willis's perspective have a slightly different function in the novel, as they quite explicitly draw on the public background of New York society, the literary circles, the details of the literary marketplace, and the publishing and editing business of the time (Steelman; DeJong 60), thus contextualizing *Poe & Fanny* in its cultural-historical setting. His point of view is somewhat less emotionally involved, yet sympathetic to Poe. May offers a glimpse of the nascent American literature industry and its discontents at a time when Emerson labeled Poe a "jingle poet" and Poe called the Transcendentalists "Frogpondians" (May 221, 228). Clippings from New York periodicals, which often open the chapters, further illustrate the literary historical background. Their function is to give the novel a tinge of authenticity and veracity. In this respect, *Poe & Fanny* is a portrait of the pre–Civil War literary class and the intellectual feud between New York and Boston.

The fourth point of view provides Poe's personal context and relates the family background, past and present. Muddy, Poe's aunt, interestingly also reflects the point of view of his wife Virginia, whom she calls "Sissy" (May 13). Poe's wife does not have chapters that relate events from her own perspective. She is given no voice, and for most of the novel she is actually speechless, too. Whenever she is mad at Eddy because he has been drinking again – which is often – she decides to remain silent and retreats to her bedroom, leaving it to Muddy to straighten Eddy out. She acts like a child, and due to her grave illness and her young age she is treated as one as well. Sissy's outward appearance is described as otherworldly: she has pale skin, hollow cheeks, black hair, and black eyes. She seems to have stepped straight out of one of Poe's tales or poems, such as "Ligeia" (1838) or "Lenore" (1843). Because Sissy is seldom heard or seen in the book, she becomes, as the title characters in those texts, more of a ghost that haunts Eddy than a real person and wife who would stand in his and Fanny's way. It is as if she were dead already. Writing Poe's wife out of the book helps May draw sympathy for two romantically entangled characters who in fact are adulterers.

Poe & Fanny is a good example of the large number of historical biofictions that focus on eminent men, but with a significant twist. Judging from the title of the book, Osgood, by the intimate and diminutive usage of her nickname, appears as an appendage to Poe, the famous American writer. And the inclusion of only the Poe family tree at the outset of the book suggests the same. May's novel seems to affirm Bird's thesis. Yet on closer analysis, it qualifies as a double historical biofiction or a double *Künstlerroman*. *Poe & Fanny* fictionalizes a crucial period in both authors' lives. May's novel aims to reclaim for Osgood her due as an important poet in American literary history. The scandal of the supposed love affair serves as the trigger to resuscitate the memory of and renew interest in Osgood and her work. The novel thus becomes a medium of cultural memory (Erll, *Memory* 144–71). The epigraph to May's novel, a quotation from Osgood's poetry, suggests that *Poe & Fanny* aims at a rediscovery of the poet and her contribution to literature:

> Ah, *if* the clarion tones of fame
> Shall ever ring for me,
> They shall not drown – my *heart* shall hear
> The praise I won from thee! (May)

Like Glancy, May creatively fills blank spaces in the life story of historical characters. Yet different from Glancy, May's aim is not revision, but recovery. His novel salvages an almost-forgotten poet and her work from historical oblivion and revisits a literary relationship between two nineteenth-century poets. But by attempting to prove a consummated love affair, May's slightly sentimental novel also turns out to be somewhat voyeuristic and sensationalist. Readers may ask themselves "how much of May's plot might be factual, how much fabrication and how much a terrific guess" ("Reviews"), but the reading of the novel may also be wrapped up in rhetorical questions: "Did any of this happen? Does it matter?" ("Reviews"). And with this, this chapter comes full circle to its initial reflections on the scandal surrounding James Frey's book.

The driving forces behind the craze for historical biofiction in the twenty-first century are revisionism and recovery. *City of Light*, *Stone Heart*, and *Poe & Fanny* display strong topicality when it comes to marginalized voices and social conflicts. Historical biofiction also tends toward nostalgia, sentimentalism, and escapism. The genre participates in what Jameson calls postmodernism's "nostalgia mode" (*Postmodernism* 20), creating the past through the re-creation of its surfaces. Often, the filling of blank spaces in the lives of historical personages serves readerly voyeurism and sensationalism or perpetuates myths and legends (Bergmann, "Historical").

5 Reanimated Classics

5.1 Theoretical Framework

In Charlotte Brontë's *Jane Eyre* (1847) – the classic nineteenth-century British female coming-of-age novel – when the housekeeper Mrs. Fairfax shows the new governess around Thornfield Hall, they eventually make it up to the attic. There, the first of a series of gothic scenes takes place:

> While I paced softly on, the last sound I expected to hear in so still a region, a laugh, struck my ear. It was a curious laugh; distinct, formal, mirthless. I stopped: the sound ceased, only for an instant; it began again, louder: for at first, though distinct, it was very low. It passed off in a clamorous peal that seemed to wake an echo in every lonely chamber; though it originated but in one, and I could have pointed out the door whence the accents issued.
> "Mrs. Fairfax!" I called out: for I now heard her descending the great stairs. "Did you hear that loud laugh? Who is it?"
> "Some of the servants, very likely," she answered: "perhaps Grace Poole."
> "Did you hear it?" I again inquired.
> "Yes, plainly: I often hear her: she sews in one of these rooms. Sometimes Leah is with her; they are frequently noisy together."
> The laugh was repeated in its low, syllabic tone, and terminated in an odd murmur.
> "Grace!" exclaimed Mrs. Fairfax.
> I really did not expect any Grace to answer; for the laugh was as tragic, as preternatural a laugh as any I ever heard; and, but that it was high noon, and that no circumstance of ghostliness accompanied the curious cachinnation; but that neither scene nor season favoured fear, I should have been superstitiously afraid.
>
> (Brontë 110)

Much later, Jane, at that point in love with her employer Edward Rochester, finds out that the laugh must be ascribed to Bertha Mason, his first wife from the West Indies, whom he keeps locked up in the attic of his manor because of her insanity.

In the twentieth century, the image of the madwoman confined to and haunting the upper story of an English manor has fallen on fertile ground with both writers and literary scholars. In 1979, Sandra M. Gilbert and Susan Gubar published a groundbreaking work of feminist literary criticism, *The Madwoman in the Attic: The Woman Writer and the Nineteenth-Century Literary Imagination*. The madwoman locked up in the attic of Thornfield Hall provides the two scholars with a symptomatic image of Victorian writing (xii). They undertake a feminist reexamination of Victorian literature, especially works by Jane Austen, Mary Shelley, Emily and Charlotte Brontë, George Eliot, and Emily Dickinson, which outlines the female writers' struggle to free themselves and their characters from social and literary imprisonment. Over a decade earlier, in 1966, Jean Rhys published a classic of postcolonial writing, the novel *Wide Sargasso Sea*. She too makes use of Brontë's haunting image of the Creole madwoman in the attic. She gives this minor character a background story, a past, drawing on her own childhood in the Caribbean. When Antoinette, reading a history of the lives of the saints, remarks about St. Innocenzia that "[w]e do not know her story, she is not in the book" (Rhys 45), this phrase might serve as an epigraph to the whole novel (Sanders 100). First, Rhys reclaims Bertha's voice, literally and metaphorically, because in Brontë's novel it is reduced to just screams and grunts: "She seemed such a poor ghost, I thought I'd like to write her a life" (Rhys, qtd. in Thieme 72). Furthermore, she writes back at the bias expressed against people from the Caribbean, which identifies Brontë's novel as a text that writes from the colonial center. The result of this attempt is a prequel to as well as a revision of *Jane Eyre*. *Wide Sargasso Sea* tells an alternative story, since, as Antoinette/Bertha in the novel remarks so aptly, "[t]here is always the other side, always" (Rhys 82). Despite its derivative outset, the novel manages to maintain artistic independence and originality, mainly by an unobtrusive handling of the indebtedness to Brontë and the choice of a distinctively twentieth-century style and tone (Ganner-Rauth 141). The novel is a feminist and postcolonial comment on its precursor. While *The Madwoman in the Attic* is secondary literature, *Wide Sargasso Sea* can be regarded as both: secondary primary literature or primary secondary literature (Breuer, "Ende" 673, 676).

Today's classics were first published in installments in magazines and newspapers, rendering serialization a dominant feature of English and American literature in the nineteenth century. Doyle, Dickens, and Wilkie Collins are among the many nineteenth-century writers who published their works in serial form (Allen/Berg). This form of publication today mostly characterizes visual media, but the trend toward serialization is being revived in literature as well (Kirchknopf 72–73; Barndollar/Schorn; Butter/

Christ; Allen/Berg). Sequels that consist not of single chapters but of whole novels are also not a new phenomenon (Parey, "Introduction" 1). Daniel Defoe's Crusoe trilogy (1719–20) is as much a case in point as are J. K. Rowling's Harry Potter novels (1997–2007). However, I am here concerned with another variety of literary serialization. The literary market is inundated by sequels, coquels, and prequels to, or parodies, rewritings, revisions, and variations of, well-known and canonical American and English novels, mainly of the nineteenth century. Such adaptation and appropriation, to allude to Julie Sanders's study, has become a key concept of contemporary cultural production (4; see also Kirchknopf 71–72). An inventive variety of adaptation is the transfer of elements of one text into another (con)text.

Rewriting has always been a feature of literature since antiquity (Garber; Breuer, "Re-writes" 96; Hutcheon, *Theory* 2), and "intertextuality, and its specific manifestation in the forms of adaptation and appropriation, is ... fundamental to the practice, and, indeed, to the enjoyment, of literature" (Sanders 1). There have always been authors who based their works on preexisting texts (Kakutani, "Within"), as "art is derived from other art; stories are born of other stories" (Hutcheon, *Theory* 2). That is why contemporary writers like Michael Chabon refute Harold Bloom's concept of the 'anxiety of influence': "[A]ll literature, highbrow and low, ... is fan fiction.... All novels are sequels; influence is bliss" (Chabon 45). Essentially, "[i]n the workings of the human imagination, adaptation is the norm, not the exception" (Hutcheon, *Theory* 177). Nonetheless, "in our postmodern collage-and-sampling-mad era, this sort of artistic recycling has become more prevalent than ever" (Kakutani, "Within").

The inventive varieties of serialization have variously been labeled "literary extensions" (Lesher 371–88), "reconfigurations" (Entzminger 1), "response texts" (Kirwan 127), "spinoff fiction" (Garber) or "literary spinoffs" (Spengler), "literary re-imaginings" (Johnson, *Historical* 720–21), "intertextual adaptations" (Nünning/Nünning 169–70), "companion novels" (Klein), "professional fan fiction" (Clerc), and "narrative or novel expansions" (Parey, "Introduction" 1), among other terms. I am concerned here with the serial as historical fiction, not with updates of classic texts that transfer the topics of the original into the present time, such as Jane Smiley's *A Thousand Acres* (1992), which successfully transfers William Shakespeare's *King Lear* (1606) to 1970s/80s Iowa. The characters, settings, or plotlines of this variety of historical fiction are familiar from classic texts. In the simplest case, the stories are continued by narrating new events in the future lives of the literary personae. In other variations, driven by a revisionist impetus, the plot of the original is retold from a different perspective, introducing a new character or giving a formerly marginalized character a voice (Johnson, *Historical* 720). Other forms present the origins of a famous character, or imagine possible answers to a void in the text. Though the form and technique of these novels may be innovative, the settings and topics remain recognizable. Always, the texts are set in the past, in the story time of the original, and frequently the language used anachronistically mimics the original's style and tone.

I suggest the term 'reanimated classics' as a fitting label for this group of texts. I am inspired by the title of Julia M. Klein's article "Giving New Life to Classic Characters" (2007), and by Sanders's remarks about James Wilson's *The Dark Clue* (2001), a sequel to Wilkie Collins's *The Woman in White* (1860): "Wilson's novel ... *reanimates* ... two of the protagonists from *The Woman in White*" (126; my emphasis). The term appropriately highlights that these novels breathe new life into popular characters of well-known texts, and thereby, more often than not, also revitalize languishing classics of world literature (Bergmann, "Reanimated").

It is impossible to cover all existing theories and terminology for this kind of fiction here (Ganner-Rauth 130). In order to establish a basic vocabulary and provide an elementary theoretical groundwork for the discussion of these texts as new historical fiction, I will give an overview of the most persistent terms and theories within the broader field of intertextual adaptations and appropriations. A "required feature" of the original novels that are adapted and appropriated by the new historical novels is "canonicity" (Sanders 120). Linda Hutcheon labels such texts "adapted text[s]" rather than "'source[s]' or 'original[s],'" aiming at a "purely descriptive" term (*Theory* xiii) that carries no value judgment. Cora Kaplan's notion of the "mnemic symbol" or "popular icon," defined as "a memorial or narrative that embodies and elicits a buried psychic conflict which cannot be resolved in the present" (7), also relates to all texts that evoke reanimated classics. Aleida Assmann's concept of cultural texts applies equally to the classics that the new historical fiction reanimates. Only texts that mediate concepts of cultural, national, or religious identity as well as collective values and norms, and whose reception is marked by enshrinement, repeated study, and rapture, can serve as models and templates for reanimated classics ("Was").

Texts by one author which draw on cultural texts by another author are "allographic sequels." The terms "autographic sequel" and "sequence novel" are used to define "a succession of novels by the same author" (Wolfgang G. Müller 317; Breuer "Essay"; see also Parey, "Introduction" 7-8; Budra/Schellenberg). Across the centuries, the writer of the cultural text and the author of the reanimated classic form some kind of "interauctoriality" or "interauthoriality" (Schabert, *Quest* 5; see also Schabert, "Interauktorialität"; Middeke 25), thus entering a discourse. The concept of intertextuality, a term coined by Julia Kristeva to describe the relations between texts (taking up Mikhail Bakhtin's idea of the dialogue between texts), can be made fruitful regarding reanimated classics, especially in its rendering by Genette. His overall term for all

forms of intertextuality is "transtextuality," and he differentiates between "hypotext," referring to the source, and "hypertext," the reworking of it (*Palimpsests* 1, 5). Wolfgang G. Müller criticizes Gérard
Genette's typology as "terminologically somewhat hypertrophic" (312)
and proposes the term "derivative literature, i.e. literature which is defined by the inseparable bond between a given text as a whole and an
anterior text as a whole" (314). Rolf Breuer, who also disapproves of
Genette's classification ("Re-writes" 100) but similarly "remains un-
convinced" by Müller's term, coins the terms "post-texts" (Breuer,
"Completions") and post-textual meta-literature ("*posttextuelle Meta-
Literatur*"; "Re-writes" 99). Christian Gutleben and Susana Onega reject Kristeva's notion of "intertextuality, which usually concentrate[s] on
the result of the interaction between a text and its hypotext(s)" (7), and
Genette's "reductive typology consisting of establishing the links between a given hypertext and its hypotext(s)" (9). Instead, they favor the
expression "refraction," which

> involves the assumption of a dialectic relation between the canonical
> and postmodernist texts, affecting the result as well as the source, the
> new text as well as the old one, the modern product as well as the
> original prototype.... [R]efraction obliterates any hierarchical or
> evaluative distinction between two related texts – however canonical
> one of the two might be. (7–9)

With its claim of eradicating hierarchies between the texts, the term is a
very fitting one when it comes to the new historical fiction with its
revisionist trajectory.

Breuer differentiates five main subcategories of post-textual meta-
literature: "Sequels, continuations," "completions," "precursors, ...
prequels," "adaptations," and "re-writes" ("Re-writes" 99). His definition of an adaptation as a transfer of a work into another genre or
medium ("Re-writes" 99) excludes novel-to-novel transformations.
Wolfgang G. Müller similarly defines adaptation as "the changing of a
text so as to make it suitable for the need of another genre or medium"
(314). Others, for example Sanders, allow for novel-to-novel conversions
under the label of adaptation, as it includes "reinterpretations of established texts in new generic contexts or perhaps with relocations of an
'original' or sourcetext's cultural and/or temporal setting, which may or
may not involve a generic shift" (Sanders 19). Hutcheon, although she is
mainly concerned with adaptations that involve a "remediation" (Bolter/
Grusin), allows for the more specific form of transfer involved in reanimated classics when she asserts that "adaptation is ... a transcoding
into a different set of conventions. Sometimes but not always, this
transcoding entails a change of medium" (Hutcheon, *Theory* 33–34). An
adaptation can be an "extended, deliberate, announced revisitation of a

particular work of art" (170). Ansgar and Vera Nünning label the kind of novel discussed here "intertextual adaptation," but they cover only one area of the field when they solely consider "rewriting[s] of ... famous novel[s] from English literature from a postcolonial perspective" (169). Additionally, they do not differentiate between novels that remain within the time frame of the original and therefore are historical novels and adaptations that modernize the story and transfer it into the present day. *Wide Sargasso Sea* and Peter Carey's *Jack Maggs* (1997) are re-animated classics, writing back against *Jane Eyre* and Dickens's *Great Expectations* (1861), while Sam Selvon's *Moses Ascending* (1975) modernizes Defoe's *Robinson Crusoe* (1719). Wolfgang G. Müller labels the transformation of a novel into another novel a "rewrite," which "is oriented towards a previous text as a structural and thematic entity which it never loses sight of," while "the model text is significantly changed, substantially made anew, so that the rewrite gains an identity of its own" (314–15). Examples are *Mary Reilly* and Emma Tennant's *Two Women of London: The Strange Case of Ms. Jekyll and Mrs. Hyde* (1989), which both rewrite Stevenson's classic; but while Martin's text changes the narrative perspective to that of a female maid and creates a historical fiction, Tennant's text not only feminizes but also modernizes the story by transferring it into the twentieth century (Nowak 347–62; Ganner). Breuer's last category, the "re-write" ("Re-Writes" 99) – here spelled with a hyphen – does include historical fiction: Alison Fell's *The Mistress of Lilliput, or The Pursuit* (1999) rewrites Jonathan Swift's *Gulliver's Travels* (1726) from the wife's perspective. In addition, Breuer's category encompasses texts that do not remain in the story time and genre of the original after the transformation, such as Helen Fielding's *Bridget Jones's Diary* (1996), which modernizes Jane Austen's *Pride and Prejudice* (1813) and transforms it into a parody of the self-examining Protestant journal tradition.

Many of the reanimated classics fall into three categories, which Wolfgang G. Müller labels by the umbrella term "derivative extension" and differentiates into "front extension, middle (intermediate) extension and end (back) extension" (317). He introduces these terms against Genette's similar terminology of "*continuation proleptique, continuation elleptique and continuation analeptique*" (317). This group of texts equals reanimated classics in many respects, as they hinge mainly on the characters of the cultural text: "There are extensions which deal with a phase of a character's life anterior to that presented in the pre-text, or such which close a gap in the period of the character's life described in the pre-text, or such which deal with a posterior period in the character's life" (317). The first variety of reanimated classics present the origins of a famous character in a "prequel" (Breuer, "Re-Writes" 99) or "front extension" (Wolfgang G. Müller 317). A second form is concerned with filling "a gap within the pre-text or, to be more precise, within the story of the pre-text" (Wolfgang G. Müller 317). Leaving such a gap in the text is, at least in the majority of cases, a willful literary device by the author (Ondaatje 36). The intention of reanimated classics to fill these voids in texts therefore, more often than not, runs counter to the intention of the author of the cultural text (James). But it plays into the hands of readers who nowadays unabashedly question the ontological status of literature (Breuer, "Ende" 676). A text that imagines (more or less) plausible fillings for the voids is a "middle or, rather, intermediate extension" (Wolfgang G. Müller 317). In the third case, the stories familiar from the cultural text are continued by narrating new events in the future lives of the literary personae. Those texts are "end or back extension[s] (i.e. ... sequel[s] in the strict sense of the term)" (317). Sue Clerc labels the first and third types introduced here "expansion of timeline," which most often appears as "a sequel or prequel focusing on the main characters of the original work." The second type she calls "recontextualization," a book that "fills gaps in the timeline of the original narrative or goes behind the scenes of the original text in order to clarify actions, motivations, or emotions." Armelle Parey proposes the term "coquel" ("Introduction" 4). Breuer subsumes such texts under the label "sequel," but extends the meaning of the term considerably: "A sequel is the continuation of a literary work in the same genre.... A sequel uses the same or some of the same characters of the original and continues the action of the original into the future; *sometimes it views the same action from a different perspective*" (Breuer, "Completions," my emphasis; see also Breuer, "Ende" 673).

The last aspect of Breuer's definition somewhat confuses the term 'sequel' and instead constitutes another, fourth variant of reanimated classics. In these variations, the plot of the original is retold from a different perspective by introducing a new character or giving a formerly marginalized character a voice. Parey describes this group of texts as

> a smaller category that re-works a single text. Going over a canonical narrative, they often throw light on a neglected character and/or give an alternative version of the story by filling in the blanks of the hypotext. The end-result is that those rewritings challenge the authority of the primary text. ("True")

Sarah L. Johnson singles these texts out as a separate variety, although she still calls them sequels: "Other authors of sequels retell classic stories based on the point of view of minor characters, either in a straightforward manner or in the form of parody" (*Historical* 720). Clerc's category of "refocalization" defines books that shift "the focus of the story from the main characters to a supporting character of the original or a new character created by the continuing author." She goes on to call such texts "rewrites," seeking "to confront the depredations of slavery and/or colonialism by viewing the original text through the eyes of the characters denied agency in the originals." Wolfgang G. Müller also subsumes such texts under his "rewrite" label (314). Grace Moore views the "recovery and reclamation of marginalized voices" as a "revisionist process [that] often marks the first stage for writers attempting to move away from subordination to the ... canon by revising or distorting 'classic' texts" (136). Marjorie Garber asserts that texts in which "a character with a minor or even absent role in the original novel ... takes center stage and speaks" are giving "a voice to those whom history has silenced." To her, such texts are examples of "literary ventriloquism, or what might be called ventriloquacity." She observes that today this "move has become almost second nature for novelists as well as playwrights and filmmakers" (Garber; see also Kakutani "Within").

Some adaptations seem to falsify Judith Fetterley's statement that "women obviously cannot rewrite literary works so that they become ours by virtue of reflecting our reality" (*Resisting* xxiii). There is "widespread revisioning of canonical male-authored texts" (King 5), especially undertaken by women: "While some may display the playful intertextuality of postmodernist fiction, each of them also challenges the images of women constructed by the literature of the past, the values inscribed in those images, and their enduring power" (King 6). And though the line of attack underlying the reworkings of cultural texts is similar to the feminist impetus Adrienne Rich diagnoses in "When We Dead Awaken: Writing as Re-Vision" (1972) – where she defines 're-vision' as an "act of looking back, of seeing with fresh eyes" and "an act of survival" (90) – it is here also more generally revisionist. Jeannette King's feminist claim can be extended to ethnic and racial minorities. J. M. Coetzee has programmatically stated for this kind of fiction that "[i]n every story there is a silence, some sight concealed, some words unspoken, I believe. Till we have spoken the unspoken we have not come to the heart of the story" (141). Postcolonial reanimated classics "destabilize both formal and cultural identity and thereby shift power relations" (Hutcheon, *Theory* 174). "[W]riting back" (Ashcroft/ Griffiths/Tiffin, *Empire*), "counter-discourse" (Tiffin), and "oppositional literature" are "terms that have been used to identify a body of postcolonial works that take a classic English text as a departure point, supposedly as a strategy for contesting the authority of the canon of English literature" (Thieme 1). The term "con-text" is used to "indicate postcolonial texts that engage in direct, if ambivalent, dialogue with the canon by virtue of responding to a classic English text," while "pretext" refers to "the canonical texts to which they respond" (Thieme 4). Reanimated classics such as *Wide Sargasso Sea*, Coetzee's *Foe* (1986), and *Jack Maggs* are among these novels. In these texts, "a political or ethical commitment shapes the writer's ... decision to re-interpret a source text" (Sanders 2). While these reanimated classics, both feminist as well as postcolonial, on the one hand, embody challenges to the canon, on the other hand,

> [a]daptation both appears to require and to perpetuate the existence of a canon, although it may in turn contribute to its ongoing reformulation and expansion.... Many of the texts ... are produced as much by the tenets of feminism, poststructuralism, postcolonialism, queer theory, and postmodernism as by the literary canon *per se*.
>
> (Sanders 8–13)

Always, "the appropriation of a canonical novel relies upon the reader's foreknowledge of the precursor text for a full appreciation of its questions and potential for critique, its revisionary achievement" (Sanders 143). A revision of a novel is rendered futile if the source is not a cultural text.

Reanimated classics often anachronistically mimic the original's style and tone, a device which turns the epigonal text into a pastiche. Pastiche can be defined as "an imitation of the style of an author" (Breuer, "Essay"; see also Sanders 106). In a more multifaceted way, pastiche can be understood as "a mixture of themes, stylistic elements or subjects borrowed from the works of an artist or of artists of a particular school, usually for the purposes of parody or imitation" (Ganner-Rauth 140). A pastiche may glorify the hypotext as a homage, but it may also be a "caricature, [which] is intended to ridicule the original" (Breuer, "Essay" 2000). Parody is "an ironic subset of adaptation" (Hutcheon, *Theory* 170). Pastiche and parody are acts of imitation, "carried out in a mode of celebration or critique" (Sanders 106).

Further classifications and terminology may be added, but there is a "profusion rather than fixity of terms offered" (Sanders 3) to describe this field. And eventually, the manifold classifications all have their shortcomings. Most reanimated classics are hybrid forms, and seldom will one particular text fit only one category. The classification is not a discerning insight in itself, but serves the analysis of single works (Breuer, "Re-writes" 100). Hutcheon's continuum model of adaptation offers "a way to think about various responses to a prior story" and "positions adaptations specifically as (re-)interpretations and (re-)creations" (*Theory* 172). It provides helpful guidance for a tentative classification of reanimated classics:

> At one end, we find those forms in which fidelity to the prior work is a theoretical ideal, even if a practical impossibility.... [N]ext come forms like condensations and bowdlerizations or censorings in which the changes are obvious, deliberate, and in some way restrictive. Next along the continuum we find ... "retellings" of

familiar tales and "revisions" of popular ones.... [H]ere stories are
both reinterpreted and rerelated. At the other end of the continuum,
but still part of this system of relations among works and thus part
of a system of diffusion, are a whole series of spin-offs – and not only
in the commercial sense of the term.... [O]vert and critical commentary ... finds a place here, but so too do academic criticism and
reviews of a work. This is also the space of sequels and prequels, ...
"expansions," and of fan zines and slash fiction.

(Hutcheon, Theory 171)

As a result of this broad stocktaking, I suggest the following permeable
terminology to classify reanimated classics: 'revision,' 'prequel,' 'intermediate extension,' and 'sequel.' The terms 'pastiche' and 'parody'
will be used to further define the author's trajectory (Bergmann,
"Reanimated").

Julie Sanders diagnoses an "ongoing interest in recreating and critiquing
the Victorian era in various acts of reworking and pastiche, not least in the
field of prose fiction" (13) for the British and former Commonwealth
realm. Again, the dominant number of American appropriations of classic
texts also falls back on the literary production of the nineteenth century.
If the copyright of the cultural text has already expired, which is the case
with classics published during the nineteenth century, the epigonal writer
does not have to face obstacles in publishing her or his work (Breuer,
"Essay"; Klein). Novels that fit the category of reanimated American
classics of the nineteenth century include Christopher Bigsby's *Pearl*
(1995), a sequel to Nathaniel Hawthorne's *The Scarlet Letter* (1850); Paul
Block's *Song of the Mohicans* (1995), a sequel to James Fenimore
Cooper's *The Last of the Mohicans* (1826); Sena Jeter Naslund's *Ahab's
Wife: or, The Star-Gazer* (1999) and Louise M. Gouge's *Ahab's Bride*
(2004), *Hannah Rose* (2004), and *Son of Perdition* (2006), respectively an
intermediate extension, a prequel, and two sequels to Herman Melville's
Moby-Dick (1851); and Nancy Rawles's *My Jim* (2005) and Jon Clinch's
Finn (2007), revisions and intermediate extensions to Mark Twain's *The
Adventures of Huckleberry Finn* (1885). Some of these texts are analyzed
in Betina Entzminger's *Contemporary Reconfigurations of American
Literary Classics: The Origin and Evolution of American Stories* (2013)
and Birgit Spengler's *Literary Spinoffs: Rewriting the Classics – Re-
Imagining the Community* (2015), but Kate Kirwan's "Contemporary
Responses to the Traditional American Historical Novel" (2012) is the
only publication which approaches these texts as historical fiction.

My own discussion focuses on a selection which includes reworkings
of twentieth-century American historical novels depicting the nineteenth
century, reanimations of nineteenth-century historical novels portraying
another time, and variations on nineteenth-century novels that are not
historical novels. The three novels that will be discussed in more detail

are Christopher Bigsby's *Hester* (1994), Alice Randall's *The Wind Done Gone* (2001), and Geraldine Brooks's *March* (2005).

5.2 Christopher Bigsby's *Hester* (1994)

Nathaniel Hawthorne's *The Scarlet Letter* (1850) tells the story of Hester Prynne and her life after she has committed the sin of adultery in Puritan New England. A host of literary spinoffs on this classic exist, ranging from John Updike's *S.* (1988) to Bharati Mukherjee's *The Holder of the World* (1993) (Entzminger). Updike updates and modernizes Hawthorne's story; Mukherjee only partly stays within the original's time frame, but creates an alternative story with similar, though not identical characters (Barlowe 17). Christopher Bigsby's debut novel *Hester* (1994) is a typical re-animated classic, a creative addition to *The Scarlet Letter*. It invents the hypotext's protagonist's past in England. Bigsby, a British American-studies scholar, is "[e]xtrapolating remarks made by the original Hester about her youth in England" (Kakutani, "How") and thus satisfies the curiosity of readers who wondered about the causes of and the motivations for various deeds and events that remain obscure in the classic (Durczak 109-10). The novel is likewise reevaluating events narrated in the hypotext and "overlaps with Hawthorne's original tale, ... re-embroider[ing] familiar developments" (Kakutani, "How"). Bigsby calls his novel a prequel (qtd. in Harper 422), but it is also a revision of Hawthorne's classic. His second novel, *Pearl* (1995), also a reanimated classic, is a sequel to *The Scarlet Letter*, tracing the life of Hester Prynne's daughter Pearl after she returns to England (Birch).

    Hester, like so many other historical novels, starts out with a paratext, in this case consisting of two epigraphs:

> Nathaniel Hawthorne laid aside
> his pen, one January day, and
> went skating on the frozen lake
> below his home. The ice bore the
> marks for three days, a signature
> which glowed crimson at sunset.
> The ice melted. The signature
> remained. What once is written
> can never be erased.
>
>   (Bigsby)

This first epigraph hints at the enduring status of *The Scarlet Letter* as world literature and at the persistent topicality of its issues – sin, guilt, repentance, redemption, and salvation – for American culture. The second epigraph turns from the author and his cultural product to his creation, the fictional character Hester:

Those who walk towards the sun
are followed by a shadow. The
future is the sun. The past is the
shadow. Hester walked towards
the sun.

(Bigsby)

The continuity of time – or rather, the contemporaneity of past, present, and future – is expressed, and the last sentence stresses Hester's progressiveness.

This specific kind of achronicity is continued by the first stanza of the song "Lord of the Dance," which precedes the beginning of the novel:

I danced in the morning
When the world was begun,
And I danced in the moon
And the stars and the sun,
And I came down from heaven
And I danced on the earth,
At Bethlehem I had my birth.
Dance, then, wherever you may be,
I am the Lord of the dance, said he,
And I'll lead you all wherever you may be,
And I'll lead you all in the dance, said he.

(Bigsby 1)

Stanzas two through four of "Lord of the Dance" are also quoted at significant stages in the novel; the fifth and last stanza ends the book (Bigsby 37, 149, 169, 187). The five stanzas of the song structure the text and divide it into four parts of differing lengths. The first part of the novel (1–36) traces Hester and Roger Chillingworth's relationship from their first meeting to their wedding night and the subsequent coldness between them. Part two (37–148) gives an account of Hester's escape. It mainly focuses on the sea journey from England to America and on the developing relationship between Hester and Arthur Dimmesdale, who are fellow passengers on the ship, fall in love, and have sexual intercourse the night before their landing. This part ends two years after their arrival in the New World, when they have met once more for a second sexual encounter during which their daughter Pearl is conceived. The third part (149–168) tells the story of Hester's pregnancy and how she is found out. When Hester persistently refuses to name the father of her illegitimate child, she is taken to prison, where she gives birth. Dimmesdale visits and confesses his weakness to speaking the truth. The first three parts are interspersed with seven diary entries by Hester. The fourth and last part (169-86) of *Hester* retells and revises the plot of

The Scarlet Letter, including a literal excerpt of the beginning of Hawthorne's novel. The book ends with an afterword entitled "A Note on Nathaniel Hawthorne," which reintroduces the reader to the author of the hypotext, his life and times.

The song "Lord of the Dance" is not simply a structuring device, it also hints at the novel's content. The lyrics tell the story of Jesus's life and deeds, his passion, his death on the cross, and his resurrection, though the way in which this is tied to the image of dancing seems to be pagan in origin. It is an unorthodox interpretation that might even be understood as heretical. Obviously, in this last aspect the link to Hester's story of sin within the confines of Puritan society and her salvation outside it is to be detected. The song's additional function as a temporal marker is significant. The lyrics of the song were written in 1963 by English Quaker songwriter Sydney Carter. The music of the song had mistakenly been thought to be an original Celtic tune throughout much of the twentieth century, but actually the tune was adapted from an American Shaker song titled "Simple Gifts" (1848) by Joseph Brackett, Jr. Hester and her contemporaries in the seventeenth century could not have known the song. With its origins in the nineteenth century, it points to the publication time of the hypotext. The twentieth-century English lyrics to the American song point to *Hester*'s author. The song invokes the ongoing transatlantic cultural cross-fertilization between the New World and the Old. Bigsby implicitly brings into play the three time levels of his historical novel, involving the seventeenth century on the story level, the nineteenth century with its reference to Hawthorne's classic, and the twentieth-century presence of the narrator (Bigsby 188). The past, the present, and the future, as well as temporality in general, are important issues of the text.

At the outset of the novel, the narrator introduces Chillingworth. He lives as a hermit at Colney Hall, in Norwich, Norfolk, and is stylized as a Faustian figure. Implicitly, the mad scientists of Hawthorne's short stories "The Birth-Mark" (1843), "Rappaccini's Daughter" (1844), and "Ethan Brand" (1851) are invoked (Bigsby 193; Kakutani "How"). Furthermore, Chillingworth is a member of a secret Masonic lodge and a Jew, aspects which further exaggerate his profile as an outsider to society. But the narrator delegitimizes this initial drawing of the character as a gothic or Victorian villain: "I have, perhaps, presented this man as a combination of Mr Rochester and Heathcliff, as a product of the mind of Mrs Radcliffe or Mr Poe. He was none of these.... He had no secret in an upstairs room and had never been troubled by passion" (Bigsby 10–11). This marked intertextuality, pointing toward classic gothic novels such as Ann Radcliffe's *The Mysteries of Udolpho* (1794), Charlotte Brontë's *Jane Eyre* (1847), Emily Brontë's *Wuthering Heights* (1847), and Edgar Allan Poe's gothic fictions, reveals Hawthorne's dependence on the literary conventions of his time and deconstructs it. The use of well-known genres such as the gothic novel, which constitute the genre memory of the nineteenth century, meets the expectations of readers who, on the one hand, look for the continuation of a nineteenth-century classic and, on the other, are well aware that a postmodern, twentieth-century text will eclectically play with all of the literary conventions available and thereby unveil its own epigonism.

When the narrator introduces Hester, he draws this seventeenth-century character as the nineteenth-century image of the independent new woman. She is "a nineteen-year-old girl," "no country yokel," "[n]either plain nor pretty, but with a kind of beauty nonetheless," and "a sense of composure and grace" (Bigsby 16, 8, 13). She is "proud, independent," and "her mind [is] her own" (35, 8). Hester's being out of her time is hinted at directly when she is described as "someone whose strengths and weaknesses owe so little to their setting or their time" (13–14). Bigsby draws on a common reading of Hawthorne's Hester as modeled after the author's neighbor and fellow writer Margaret Fuller, author of *Woman in the Nineteenth Century* (1845), the first American feminist treatise (Bigsby 198).

The first meeting between future husband and wife takes place when Chillingworth, exhausted and half dead after a riding accident that ended in the river, faints on a country road in front of the young Hester. She takes him in and helps him recover. A relationship between the young woman and the hunchbacked loner, who is "twenty years and more" (Bigsby 16) her senior, commences. From the beginning, it is marked on her side by a mix of pity and admiration for his learnedness and cosmopolitanism. On his side, it is characterized by curiosity. For him, who sees himself as "a student of men," the young girl is "another mystery to be solved" (15, 168). Both mistake their feelings for love and soon find themselves trapped in an unconsummated marriage. After a year of coldhearted cohabitation, Hester flees to America, "a New World whose name alone was token of the desire to be born again" (16, see also 48). Aboard the ship, aptly named *Hope*, she meets Dimmesdale, a would-be minister, who similarly longs for a new beginning in the New World. He is echoing Winthrop's famous adage of the "city upon a hill" (41) when he declares that he wants to build "a new Jerusalem" (Bigsby 98).

The journey makes up the major part of the text; "the sea voyage becomes a metaphor for the sea change in Hester's life" (Kakutani, "How"). A whole range of incidents gain symbolic importance for Hester's identity crisis and foreshadow her fate in America (Hughes). The three most important of these incidents revolve around the topic of death. At the beginning of the journey, a young sailor falls from his lookout atop the mainmast, where he has frozen to death. The color symbolism of his blood on the deck gives a foreshadowing of Hester's stigmatization as an adulteress with the scarlet letter A. Three days after the young man's burial at sea, the crew discovers his corpse, covered by a canvas shroud, entangled with the rudder of the ship: "And did we but know it we, too, carry with us what we thought to have left to time and memory. It lives with us and will, whenever we imagine ourselves free, present itself anew" (Bigsby 103-04). Hester's future will be determined by her past, by her status as a married woman (Durczak 112). Another foreshadowing occurs when Hester describes, in one of her diary entries, how a butterfly, which has just transformed from a caterpillar, flutters around in her ship cabin, only to die moments later because of the cold. Hester suspects that "there is a moral here for me" (Bigsby 104). The diary, the typical form of Puritan self-inspection, gives a forecast of Hester's future. The butterfly, a symbol of metamorphosis, hints at the transformation and development of the protagonist. And finally, the first glimpse of the New World evokes death as a metaphor for a third time. When the ship first comes in sight of land, Hester observes hunters and their brutal killing of seals (118). She contemplates the significance of this for her future life in her diary: "Was this, then, the world I was entering, a world far harsher than I had supposed? Was I, perhaps, travelling back in time to man's beginnings, a world before civility, compassion and belief?" (119).

The most far-reaching incident aboard the ship is the sexual encounter between Hester and Dimmesdale. Before this final apex of the sea voyage, the *Hope* significantly has one more storm to weather (Bigsby 113–15). The natural force is meant to signify on the one hand the two lovers' mental turmoil, and on the other hand it presents love as yet another natural force. Hester believes her sexual intercourse with Dimmesdale was inevitable and good, not evil or sinful (123). Dimmesdale plunges into a stage of literal and metaphorical darkness and turmoil after their intercourse (124). Coinciding with the end of the sea journey, Dimmesdale becomes the restless and driven character that he will remain for most of *The Scarlet Letter*. Hester has gone through a different, no less significant change: "As for Hester, she was not what she had been but there was a quiet contentment in her, nonetheless" (123).

The whole novel can be read as a novel of development, a bildungs-roman, or herstorical biofiction. Bigsby, drawing on the genuinely American genre of the story of initiation (Freese, *American*), styles Hester as a female initiate (Bergmann, *And*, "Stories"): "There comes a time when a young woman decides that the moment is ripe for change, that she must move on, metamorphose" (Bigsby 20). While stories of male initiation typically require an outward journey, including the character-istic stages of "exit, transition, and re-entrance" (Freese, *American* 52), stories of female initiation usually focus on an inward, psychological passage, at least in the nineteenth century, when women were confined to the domestic sphere (Bergmann, *And* 58–64). But Hester, again out of – or rather ahead of – her time, performs a physical exit. She flees confinement and leaves home in order to start a new life in a foreign country, on another continent. The sea journey can be read as the transitory phase, with its sexual connotations and strong nature symbolism: "[S]he knew that Hester – child, daughter, bride – was dead, while another Hester was struggling to be born" (Bigsby 53). During a second sexual encounter with Dimmesdale in Boston, she conceives his child, and when her pregnancy becomes obvious, she is shunned as a sinner and becomes an outsider to Boston Puritan society. In Hester's case, no entrance into a society commences. She remains a pariah, although her experiences lead her to full maturity and self-discovery. Hers is a "denitiation," indicating an initiation away from society (Lewis 115). In her seventh diary entry, Hester speaks directly to the reader for the last time: "I feel a freedom, here; yet I sit in a prison cell.... I came on a journey of escape but to find that it were one of discovery" (Bigsby 168). The birth of Pearl coincides with Hester's rebirth. Where at the outset of her journey she was "like a child in the womb with nothing but a distant heartbeat for comfort" (58), Hester's journey toward herself has now come full circle: "For I am become myself and myself is what I shall be" (168). It is on this note that Bigsby's prequel concludes.

But the novel *Hester* does not end here. Another almost twenty pages give a summary of the hypotext. The beginning of the retelling of *The Scarlet Letter* is marked by an extensive literal quote from Hawthorne's text. Two passages – one from the second chapter, "The Market-Place," and one from the third chapter, "The Recognition" (Hawthorne, *Scarlet* 38–39, 42–44) – are cited verbatim (Bigsby 170–71) and accentuated by the use of a different font. The remaining last part of the novel is not just a retelling of Hawthorne's text; Bigsby sketchily recapitulates the main events of *The Scarlet Letter* and slightly revises the novel.

Three new scenes are invented within the frame of the original, which cast a fresh light on the classic and evoke a reinterpretation. The first new scene is a meeting between Dimmesdale and Hester on the occasion of the funeral of a neighbor's boy. Dimmesdale's eulogy seems directly addressed to Hester: "He spoke of dust and ashes, of a life ended, and what could he mean but the end of a story which had once held them fast in its truth" (Bigsby 174). The interment of the child turns into a symbolic burial of their mutual love for each other. A second scene invents a conversation between Hester and her daughter Pearl, where a piece of needlework triggers a revelatory conversation and the feminist reinterpretation of the hypotext is affirmed: "'Why do girls stitch and boys do not?' 'Because we be the ones who must hold this life together. They be the ones who do tear it apart'" (177). Pearl's stitching is her own rendering of a dictum: "The days that are past are gone for ever. Those that are to come may not come to us. The present time is only ours. Let us therefore take the moment for our own" (178). Hester remarks that the last line should rightfully read "Let us improve it as much as possible" (178), but is persuaded by her daughter that her rendering makes a much better maxim: "It is a good saying, and I think on it, for in making [the present] our own we do improve it as I believe" (178). It is the motto of a woman who left a mark on her society: "She had stood alone. She had written her life. She was the author of more than her fate. In this new found land she had inscribed her name and in doing so turned the first page of a book whose narrative has yet to reach its end" (186). The conversation between mother and daughter again evokes the contemporaneity of past, present, and future: "'And is the past truly gone for ever as it says?' 'The past is never dead. Look at thyself. Though art the past for thou art what the past has made of thee. Yet thou art here. Thou art the future, too'" (179). The third, and probably most significant, newly invented scene in this revision of *The Scarlet Letter* is Hester and Dimmesdale's third and final sexual encounter at night in the forest, seven years after their first meeting (Durczak 123–25). Hawthorne's classic also features a meeting of the two lovers in the forest, covering the chapters "A Forest Walk," "The Pastor and His Parishioner," "A Flood of Sunshine," and "The Child at the Brook-Side" (Hawthorne, *Scarlet* 124–45, especially 129–35). In his rendering of the forest scene, Bigsby links, for the last time, the forest to the sea metaphor, when the narrator remarks that "[s]he was at sea again" (Bigsby 180). Dimmesdale, without his black minister's tunic and in white shirtsleeves, and Hester, in her white nightgown, walk into the forest like sleepwalkers, and are followed by Pearl, also clad in white: "It was as though nature had restored what man and nature had taken from her: innocence" (181). Father, mother, and child turn into the epitome of purity, a version of the Holy Family. The scene is sexually overcharged and romantically plotted (Durczak 118), yet it is "probably the novel's most important scene," since "Arthur eventually overcomes his sense of guilt – as he never does in the original story – to embrace his relationship with Hester as sinless and holy" (Durczak 112–13).

Apart from these three scenes, Bigsby significantly bestows additional meaning on the scarlet letter A, a polyvalent symbol in Hawthorne's text whose meanings range from adulteress to angel. In *Hester*, the sign is astutely identified as a symbol of Hester's love for Dimmesdale:

> I have sewed my scarlet cloth with a golden thread because the letter that they bid me write may stand for him I love. He who is the beginning of my alphabet, who is the author of my fate, the one earthly authority to whom I long to bow my knee, is thus pronounced aloud for those with eyes to see and ears to hear, shining at my breast where he should be. Bear his mark as he, I know, bears mine. I ride to battle with his favour thus emblazoned and will not remove it though they bid me to. So, I fancy, with the world. What one will see is not what others see.
> (Bigsby 168)

Likewise, Dimmesdale interprets the sign in his own way:

> [F]or him, too, the "A" which he traced with his finger in the air meant not adulteress but first and only, the alpha of his being, the angel whose wings had brushed his soul and bruised it in the passing. To him it would be no more than the merest birthmark, the imperfection by which perfection may be known and rendered thereby more complete.
>
> (Bigsby 158)

In Hester's and Dimmesdale's understandings of the letter, it "becomes almost a mockery of Puritan justice, and of the Puritans themselves" (Durczak 120).

Hester, already indicated by its title, is a text that puts its female protagonist at the center of the narration. Especially the seven excerpts from Hester's diary give her a voice. In the aforementioned afterword, Bigsby interprets Hawthorne's Hester as "a young woman of independent mind inserted back into the very beginnings of a republic dedicated to male endeavour: first true heroine of American fiction, first true confession of a nation's error" (Bigsby 192). Michiko Kakutani sees the concentration on Hester as a diminishing of "Hawthorne's vision, reducing a capacious tale of guilt, shame and redemption into a far smaller tale of a woman's coming of age" ("How"). But Hester can also be read as "the quintessential American pioneer, a relative to a legion of characters to be found in American fiction" (Durczak 122). Like Hawthorne's, Bigsby's narrator persona repeatedly comments on the overall issue of America's self-conception as the land of the elect:

> The land might not be more than grass and soil, an untimbered slope, but they would make it heaven's mirrored self and themselves its angels, winnowed by sin but burnished by faith. The land was without sin; not those who ventured there, though they did so in redemption's name. They thought to leave a dream of perfection but the dream itself was perfection's flaw. For they thought to be what no man or woman ever was: the inheritors of heaven's grace with the right to judge and the destiny to prosper as though deeds alone must speak of their entitlement.
>
> (Bigsby 126)

Hester is pointing toward America's precarious belief in its manifest destiny and its hubris of exceptionalism, which is explicated by this story of intolerance. These myths, never fallen into oblivion, have gained renewed topicality in the late twentieth century: "What they did lives on in us so that this story is in part our own" (Bigsby 126). *Hester* is a new historical novel which must be understood as a historical lesson. It is not an escapist return to a well-known literary realm: "Story is our grasp upon the past" (108).

5.3 Alice Randall's *The Wind Done Gone* (2001)

Historical fiction which centers on the African American experience has flourished since the latter decades of the twentieth century, with novels such as William Styron's *The Confessions of Nat Turner* (1967), Alex Haley's *Roots* (1976), Ishmael Reed's *Flight to Canada* (1976), Charles Johnson's *Middle Passage* (1990), and Edward P. Jones's *The Known World* (2003). The field has been quite thoroughly researched (Rushdy; Spaulding; Keizer; Byerman; Ryan; Jordan; Derburg; McDowell/ Rampersad; Benesch; Stone; Holton; Reichardt, *Alterität*). Nineteenth-century African American women and their experiences are the focus of another group of historical novels. Examples are Octavia Butler's *Kindred* (1979), Toni Morrison's *Beloved* (1987), Gloria Naylor's *Mama Day* (1988), Valerie Martin's *Property* (2003), and Jacqueline Sheehan's *Truth* (2003). By giving these women a voice, the texts write black herstory. The novels have been discussed in a number of scholarly studies (Beaulieu; Patton; Rody; Angelyn Mitchell; Dandridge; Nunes). Many of these texts use the form of the nineteenth-century slave narrative, for which Frederick Douglass's *Narrative of the Life of Frederick Douglass, An American Slave* (1845) is the archetypal model. Alice Randall's debut novel *The Wind Done Gone* (2001) is such a "neo-slave narrative," a "residually oral, modern narrative[] of escape from bondage to freedom" (Bernard W. Bell, qtd. in Newman 28).

The Wind Done Gone gained notoriety because it was the subject of one of the major lawsuits in American literary history (Kirkpatrick, "Asked," "Halts"; Haddox 120–22; Jarrett; Roh; Schur). Randall's novel, as the title already indicates, is a companion novel to Margaret Mitchell's Pulitzer Prize-winning *Gone With the Wind* (1936). In 2001, the Mitchell Trust petitioned a court in Atlanta to prevent publication of *The Wind Done Gone* because of copyright infringement. The court case highlighted the "blurry boundary between unlawful plagiarism and legitimate critical reinterpretation" (Kirkpatrick, "Halts"). Famously, Nobel laureate Toni Morrison, in her "Declaration to the Court" (2001), asked, "Who controls how history is imagined?" The case was settled when Randall's publisher accepted that the book could only be published bearing the addendum "The Unauthorized Parody" on the cover (Reid). Probably because of the media attention the lawsuit received, the novel became a best seller (Maryles; Teachout). Interestingly, the Mitchell Trust has commissioned various authorized sequels (Higgins 42; Gómez-Galisteo).

Randall's "novelistic response" (Garber) is a "revisionist view of *Gone With the Wind*" (Maryles). It was inspired not only by the historical novel but additionally by Victor Fleming and David O. Selznick's Academy Award-winning film (1939), starring Vivien Leigh and Clark Gable (Randall v). Mitchell's novel and Fleming/Selznick's movie are the hypotexts that Randall writes back to. She positions her book in the tradition of postcolonial writing when she declares: "I like to think that my parody creates a con-text, an opposition text, which illuminates the text to which it responds" (qtd. in Teachout). *The Wind Done Gone*, though a fictional story, claims veracity as a true image of the past. This is hinted at in the "Notes on the Text," which are part of the "authenticating apparatus" (Haddox 125). Randall uses a well-known topos of both nineteenth-century historical novels and slave narratives: "This document was discovered in the early 1990s. It was among the effects of an elderly colored lady who had been in an assisted-living center just outside Atlanta" (Randall v). The paratext mirrors classic prefaces of American historical novels, most notably Hawthorne's *The Scarlet Letter*: "Pressed into the diary was a photo-postcard of the Washington Monument under construction, a fragment of green silk, and a poem by Ernest Dowson, 'Non sum qualis eram bonae sub regno Cynarae'" (Randall v). The claim that not only the document but also material proof – a piece of Scarlett's famous green draperies dress – are authentic positions the preface in the tradition of "The Custom House," in which not only a manuscript, but also a "most curious relic" (Hawthorne, *Scarlet* 26), the scarlet letter A, is found.

Gone With the Wind is more than just a novel (Laura Miller) or a movie; it holds a unique status as an American iconic 'text' (Kirkpatrick, "Halts"). As "a prime source of knowledge about plantation life for much of mainstream America" (Bagdikian/Berendt/Brown), it has become "a kind of history, in accord with the deeply mythologized sense the South has of itself" (Laura Miller). Randall suggests that *Gone With the Wind* "is more powerful than history because it is better known than history" (qtd. in "Reader's"). Consequently, "Mitchell's characters long ago burst through the restraint of their form and, like folk- or fairy-tale figures, passed directly into mainstream consciousness" (Pierpont 100). The characters "live in the imaginations of millions of readers" ("Hoarding"). As Umberto Eco observes: "When fictional characters begin migrating from text to text, they have acquired citizenship in the real world and have freed themselves from the story that created them" (126). As has been pointed out, "[w]riting back to a text always implies the acknowledgement of its cultural import" (Baschirotto 60). During the court hearing, Randall argued that the aim of her novel was "to explode the romantic myth of the Old South which ... falsified and concealed the brutal realities of a slave society and depicted slaves and former slaves in a blatantly racist manner" (Zimmerman). She therefore chose to retell the story from the marginalized perspective of the slaves of Tara, and in order "to reach the same audience as the original – ordinary readers of historical novels" (Zimmerman) – she chose this genre (Baschirotto 61). *The Wind Done Gone* is a "counter-hegemonic fiction" (Kunow, "Beginning" 85), writing against history as it is traditionally conceived. It is writing against the racism of *Gone With the Wind*, which can most obviously be pinpointed in phrases like "the faint niggery smell from a slave cabin," "emancipation has just ruined the darkies," and "the negroes were far better off under slavery," as well as the description of African Americans as "black apes," "creatures of small intelligence," and "like monkeys or small children" (Mitchell, qtd. in Zimmerman). As a "[r]econstructive narrative," the novel aims "to confront stereotypes, representations of Otherness *in* the dominant discourse" (Reichardt, "New" 72). Randall gives the black characters who are misrepresented in Mitchell's novel a voice. In the hypotext, they are mainly flat characters, never "active agents in the story" (Williamson 105), and often the target of ridicule:

> *The Wind Done Gone* is a commentary and a critique of *Gone With the Wind*. It is also a commentary on the mythology of the South.... My father once told me, "I want you to speak for those who can't speak for themselves." That's what I'm doing here. We cannot give up *our stories*. We cannot deny *our history*. (Randall, qtd. in Bass; my emphasis)

By filling in "narrative spaces and silences never once touched upon nor conceived of in Mrs. Mitchell's novel" (Morrison), Randall gives the other, marginalized members of Tara plantation a voice. Randall's novel "seeks to present an alternative world to that of *Gone With the Wind*, a world in which African Americans are fully human creatures who act on the world with intelligence and feeling, and whose lives and travails are not by themselves the subject of ridicule and obloquy, but are sympathetic and authentic" (Zimmerman). She not only puts the slaves at the center of her story, she also presents them as the real agents behind the scenes, as "savvy slaves who knew how to manipulate their white masters" (Kakutani, "Within"; see also Laura Miller). The well-known character of Mammy, for example, is presented as "the real mistress of the house" (Randall 52). The result of this technique is that Randall's novel becomes a "topsy-turvy treatment of Mitchell's work, one in which the slaves are wise and the White folks are foolish" ("Ebony"). *The Wind Done Gone* depicts the white characters as flat and ridicules them. Most of them are caricatures, "cowardly, ineffectual or deluded. The Rhett figure emerges ... as a lovelorn, befuddled fellow.... Ashley is pictured as a wimpy closeted homosexual" (Kakutani, "Within"). It is Randall's point that her "in-depth treatment of black characters, and superficial treatment of white ones, is the reverse of Mitchell's, and that her work is therefore a parody" (Laura Miller).

The Wind Done Gone is presented as the diary of a newly invented character. Cynara, the daughter of Mammy and Gerald O'Hara, is a mixed-race half-sister to Scarlett O'Hara. She is the result of miscegenation, common in the nineteenth-century South but a silence in Mitchell's classic (Ryan 61). Cynara is the narrator and protagonist of *The Wind Done Gone*. Her name derives from Dowson's poem "Non sum qualis eram bonae sub regno Cynarae" (1896), which is quoted in full in the book. The poem, inspired by Horace's *Odes* (23-13 BC), links Cynara to the semantic field of darkness, a fitting hint at Scarlett's darker sister and the overall issue of color. Also, the poem bemoans the past that is long gone – apt, too, for a historical novel that builds upon a historical novel. Furthermore, the poem inspired Mitchell's title for *Gone With the Wind*, which she adopted from the first line of its third stanza. The title of Randall's novel, *The Wind Done Gone*, is a rendering of the title of Mitchell's book in a phrase that is supposed to imitate African American vernacular. In Standard American it means something like 'the wind has gone.'

The first-person narrative of the fictive diary places *The Wind Done Gone* significantly in the tradition of the autobiographical style of slave narratives. As a neo-slave narrative, it echoes these tales as it narrates Cynara's life story from slavery to freedom (Baschirotto 62; see also Haddox). Cynara deliberately evokes the tradition of the slave narrative when she declares: "This is my book.... I'm going to write down everything. Something like Mr. Frederick Douglass" (Randall 7). She openly opposes white writings about slavery: "I read *Uncle Tom's Cabin*. I didn't see me in it.... I don't want to write no novel. I'm just afraid of forgetting" (7). Cynara's diary is written to put the record of the past straight, to remember the hardships of slavery correctly, from the point of view of those who suffered from them. The fictive diary is told in 114 short sections. Cynara starts her diary on May 25, 1873, when she is twenty-eight years old. Alternatingly, memories of the antebellum era are juxtaposed with present events of the Reconstruction era (Wodianka 195). Cynara's diary features both retrospective and contemporaneous narration. The insistence on the importance of reading and writing also echoes other black narratives. Literacy among slaves was generally forbidden, because it was thought to provide them with a means to escape: "[T]hus, the quest for freedom in slave narratives often runs parallel to the quest for literacy" (Baschirotto 67). To Cynara, her ability to read and write makes her specifically aware of her status as a slave: "It's a pissed bed on a cold night to read words on paper saying your name and a price, to read the letters that say you are owned.... It be better never to read than to read that page with your name on it" (Randall 35).

Her ability to write about her life allows her to gradually ascertain an identity of her own making. As a child, Cynara is a slave on her father's plantation. When she is older, he sells her, and after an interlude as a maid at Beauty's (alias Belle Watling's) brothel, R. (alias Rhett) eventually buys and then marries her. But she leaves him for a black congressman, who has high ambitions for himself and his race (Haddox 125). When she bears his child, she urges him and his wife to keep the baby as theirs. Finally, she manages to live according to her own rules, free of anyone's agency over her life (Kakutani, "Within"; Baschirotto 67).

The whole text can be read as a bildungsroman (Kakutani, "Within"), a novel of development, or herstorical biofiction. Cynara's struggle for independence is paralleled by the evolution of her names. First, when she is a child on Cotton Farm, she is called "Cinnamon" (Randall 2–3). This is her father's name for her, and he is the one who not only created her but also owns her. Later, when she is grown up, he sells her and she finds herself in a form of sexual enslavement and then marriage with R., who calls her "Cindy" (36). When she finally has found herself in Washington, during and after her affair with the black congressman, she starts using her birth name. She is "[e]ager to let the old Cinnamon die and let the new Cynara be born all the nights to come" (187). No longer can others define her identity by giving her a name. In the end, Cynara has become an independent and self-reliant black woman, who shook off the chains of slavery and freed herself of her marriage vow. *The Wind Done Gone* uncovers the sexual exploitation of female slaves and unravels the oppressive mechanisms of slavery.

A diary is a subjective and private form of articulation. The homodiegetic form of narration adds to a representation of the story as an individual memory. Cynara's significant mix of the public and the private resonates with the feminist adage that "[t]he public is the private, just as the personal is political" (Hoffman/Graham 337). Her diary is a paralleling of her own emancipation with that of black people in general: "[B]efore the country was at war ... I went to war, and I was a battlefield" (Randall 174). The novel is not only the story of an individual's search for identity, it is also a "collective history" (Baschirotto 65). One significant example of this can be found in Cynara's trip to London, which "both represents and reverses the Middle Passage" (Baschirotto 69). On the one hand, Cynara is "one of these new people who sail for pleasure" (Randall 156), and on the other hand, she bears the collective memory of all slaves: "We are sailed people. We sailed to America. We taste the path of our abduction in our tears" (156). Cynara's journal fulfills its aim as "a vehicle for cultural memory" and "a document of important political events" (Gorp/Musarra-Schroeder vii). It is the (re) claiming of an African American history, a black past, not as an/other voice, but as a truly American one: "What I want now is what I always wanted and never knew – I want not to be exotic. I want to be the rule itself, not the exception that proves it" (Randall 161).

Scarlett, the heroine of Mitchell's novel, becomes "Other" (Randall 1) in *The Wind Done Gone*. Randall uses the concept of otherness (Bhabha, *Location* 68) and meaningfully reverses it. Also, she draws upon W. E. B. Du Bois's concept of the "double consciousness," "this sense of always looking at one's self through the eyes of others" (qtd. in Talley 323). Other is identified as Cynara's counterpart, her antagonist, as well as her double. Cynara and Other are competitors for the love of their mothers, Mammy and Lady; for the attention of their father, Planter; and for the love of R. The interdependence between the two characters and the central role that Other plays in Cynara's life is an appropriate rendering of the young slave's situation. Other is naturally a towering presence in absence in Cynara's life. She can be interpreted as a signifier of the master narrative. The version of history represented by *Gone With the Wind* is here a "for-granted presence of background knowledge" (Middleton/Woods 31; see also Kunow, "Return" 258). For a long time, Cynara lets her masters define her and longs to be like Other. After Other's death, she realizes that she pursued Other's dreams only because she thought they were hers. With the acceptance of her blackness, her past as well as that of her race, she gains her own identity, no longer dependent on Other's and others'. She can formulate and realize her own dreams. Most importantly, it is revealed that Other has black ancestors, as Lady's great-grandmother was "a Negresse" (Randall 124). This makes Other a mixed-race person too, an even more perfect double of Cynara. Cynara's entitlement to freedom and happiness is as good as Other's: "I will not play in the shadow of Other" (Randall 74).

Randall's book revolves around the topic of hybridity. Many other characters, whose white origins are never questioned in *Gone With the Wind*, are also revealed to have mixed ancestry (Baschirotto 65). One main aspect of the parody, then, is that literally none of the characters belong to a non-marginalized group. Randall's ruling concept of hybridity is over the edge and therefore mirrors Mitchell's concept of racial purity. In Randall's universe, one is either white and gay, black and straight, or black and gay, but rarely white and straight.

The Wind Done Gone is a parody. In common understanding, a parody is "1: a literary or musical work in which the style of an author or work is closely imitated for comic effect or in ridicule; 2: a feeble or ridiculous imitation" (*Merriam-Webster*). In literary studies, the definition of parody is more complex and controversial:

> The word parody, deriving from the Ancient Greek παρωδία, has acquired a range of different meanings in its long history. If in Greek and then Latin parody signified a specific form of mock poetry or ode, adopting elevated diction and applying it to trivial topics, parodia was also used to denote a more neutral practice of quotation and allusion. Nowadays, parody is predominantly

defined as any type of mocking imitation, although this usage is contested by critics.

(Baschirotto 61)

In *The Signifying Monkey: A Theory of African-American Literary Criticism* (1988), Henry Louis Gates, Jr., describes the important role of parody in the African American tradition:

> Parody is at the heart of African American expression, because it is a creative mechanism for the exercise of political speech, sentiment, and commentary on the part of people who feel themselves oppressed or maligned and wish to protest that condition of oppression and misrepresentation. (qtd. in Talley 323–24)

The renaming of the well-known characters of Mitchell's novel in Randall's hypertext openly mocks the original figures: Gerald O'Hara is Planter, Elle O'Hara is Lady, Rhett Butler is R., Ashley Wilkes is Dreamy Gentleman, his wife Melanie is Mealy Mouth, Scarlett and Rhett's daughter Bonnie is Gorgeous, Belle Watling is Beauty, Pork is Garlic, Prissy is Miss Priss, and so forth. Place names are also transformed: Tara becomes Tata or Cotton Farm, and Twelve Oaks is turned into Twelve Slaves Strong as Trees. The parodic impetus of Randall's novel is apparent. But "[t]he act of writing a parody of another novel can [also] be understood as an act of literary vengeance" ("Reader's"). In this respect, the image of the cakewalk is central. Cynara dances at a ball in Washington, first with the black congressman, then with R. The two men symbolize her past and her future, slavery and freedom: "This is our cake walk" (Randall 144). The reference to the cakewalk offers an interpretive key to the whole novel as parody:

> The cakewalk was originally a plantation dance. But it's more than a dance: it's a sly parody of European quadrilles created by enslaved African Americans.... Blacks observed whites and created a commentary, with dance, based on their observations.... [W]hite folks living on great plantations misunderstood the dance to be an imitation of European dance. Many Southern aristocrats perceived the cakewalk to be a gross or vulgar mimicry, which ultimately they found amusing, as an illustration of black inferiority. In truth, the cakewalk was a subtle and critical commentary on the differences between the aesthetics of black and white dance styles. In time, plantation owners began to encourage cakewalk contests or competitions between black dancers. The winning dancer or dance pair were rewarded with a cake, so to win the contest was to "take the cake." ... In performing this dance, a parody of plantation masters' aristocratic manners that incorporated loose leg movements and

abdominal and hip action as well as rigidity, face-to-face elements, and side-by-side elements, early black dancers asserted that "I can do what you do and do it better, maintaining pattern and rigidity"; "I can do something you can't do — achieve a level of looseness"; and (by far the most complex statement embedded in the dance) "I can acknowledge that I both understand and have mastered your aesthetics while baffling you with a coded expression of my own. I can make a fool of you and get you to pay me with pastry. Now don't that take the cake?"

("Reader's")

The cakewalk is a subversive practice, although white plantation owners understood it as mere imitation. This is where the image ties in with Randall's novel. First perceived as "a mere imitation of the hypotext," *The Wind Done Gone* must be understood as a "critical commentary and a parody" of *Gone With the Wind*, "borrowing its themes, characters, and plot, but bending them to its own ends" (Baschirotto 67). The cakewalk is "a metaphor of the book, which is at once a rewriting and a rebuttal of the hypotext" (Baschirotto 69). This positions *The Wind Done Gone* "in the tradition of African-American parody" ("Ebony").

In *Calls and Responses* (2008), Tim A. Ryan concludes that Randall's novel is not "an innovative challenge to a once-hegemonic discourse about slavery and race in American culture" (20). The literary quality of the novel itself, with its "soap opera hooks" (Bates 127), might not have been able to create a stir alone, but the public controversies the lawsuit ignited about the book created its subsequent best-selling status. The commotion the controversy produced accomplished what had been Randall's aim (Baschirotto 58): it questioned the status of *Gone With the Wind* as a truthful rendering of the past and chipped away bits of its myth-like status. The reanimated classic *The Wind Done Gone* fulfills its revisionist function (Gros 140), despite its literary flaws.

5.4 Geraldine Brooks's *March* (2005)

Geraldine Brooks's *March* (2005), which received the Pulitzer Prize for Fiction in 2006, reanimates Louisa May Alcott's *Little Women* (1868). Brooks is not the first author to fill the gaps of Alcott's original. Joyce Carol Oates, for example, created her own version of *Little Women*, titled *A Bloodsmoor Romance* (1982), out of her discomfort with the character Jo(sephine) March's seeming abandonment of her desire to become a writer, which is today read as a "horrific annihilation of individuality and human potential" (Walters 157). For contemporary readers, among them writer Cynthia Ozick, this results in "unease and dissatisfaction" with Jo's fate and triggers the identification with "some Jo of the future" (qtd. in Showalter, "Introduction" xxviii). In Oates's novel, "one talented sister becomes an actress, another an inventor, a third a spiritualist medium, and the fourth, magically, a man" (Showalter, "Introduction" xxviii).

March is the second historical novel by Australian author Brooks and the first to use an American *sujet*. In *Year of Wonders* (2001), she tells the history of the village of Eyam in Derbyshire that, when beset by the plague in 1666, issued a quarantine to prevent the disease from spreading. In *March*, Brooks uses the void of the absent father gone to war in Alcott's American classic as her incentive (Tucker et al. 3; Geraldine Brooks 275). At the beginning of *Little Women*, March has already left to serve as a chaplain in the American Civil War. The women of the March family – Marmee and the four daughters, Meg, Jo, Beth, and Amy – only occasionally hear from him through his letters. The father always remains a background figure. Although it is often called a "Civil War story" (Abate 60; see also Fetterley, "Little"; Young 170; Kreyling 10), *Little Women* is not one, at least not literally. Brooks's text, contrary to Alcott's, is a Civil War novel proper. It is an intermediate extension which fills the void concerning the father in Alcott's original. Brooks's starting point is March's letters home and the meager facts she can extrapolate from them. But she also draws on real historical events from the pre–Civil War and Civil War era, such as the life of radical abolitionist John Brown or the historical Battle of Ball's Bluff.

Additionally, Brooks is appropriating for her reanimated classic the most common reading of *Little Women* as an autobiographical novel (Crisler 27; Geraldine Brooks 275–76). *March* builds on an "analogy [which] compares the absent, penniless scholar-father of *Little Women* to Louisa May Alcott's father, Amos Bronson Alcott, one of Concord's transcendentalists whose unworldly improvidence was legendary" (Englund 204). Brooks's protagonist is a barely disguised, fictive version of the elder Alcott (Tucker et al. 10; see also Porter 6; Bassil 188; Saxton 162), which is acknowledged in the "Afterword" (Geraldine Brooks 275–80). Emblematically, the first description of March in the novel shows him sitting "under the shelter of a great tree" (3), drawing on the best-known photograph of the philosopher of Concord. Alcott does not explicitly allude to Concord, the Transcendentalists, or other circumstances of her real life (Crisler 32–33). Brooks evokes this background deliberately and welcomes the opportunity to bring in as many Alcottiana and historical figures as possible. She is thereby satisfying the curiosity of readers as well as expanding the historical dimension (Spengler 253–59). In *March*, Ralph Waldo Emerson, his wife Lidian, Henry David Thoreau, and John Brown appear as characters.

March is a bricolage of Brooks's narration, historical facts of the period, events in the life of the Concord philosopher and his neighbors (Geraldine Brooks 275), and her own experiences as a war correspondent. Brooks also incorporates original excerpts from additional intertexts, for example, from Bronson Alcott's, Emerson's, and Thoreau's writings, and, of course, from *Little Women* (Geraldine Brooks 276; see also Padmore 66, 75). Brooks's novel consists mainly of two disproportionate I-narrations. The longer first part, chapters 1 through 13, is told by March. In the form of a journal, he recounts his experiences in the war, while the interspersed letters to his family starkly contrast with his narration. The briefer second part of the novel, chapters 14 through 17, is told by Marmee, March's wife and the mother of their four daughters, who hastens to him when he is lying wounded in a military hospital in Washington. The two last chapters of the novel, 18 and 19, are again told by the almost convalescent March. They retell, partly even in Alcott's actual wording, his homecoming to his family as it is known from *Little Women*, but from his perspective (Tucker et al. 4). Writing, self-inspection, and self-monitoring are an important aspect of the March family's life, and Brooks has adapted this from a habit of the Alcotts (Abate 80). The novel is an epistolary novel, a fictional diary, and a historical biofiction.

The action of *March* encompasses, in analogy with *Little Women*, the space of a year during the Civil War (1861/62), but also includes flashbacks which reach far into the past of the characters. While Brooks gives the date of "October 21, 1861" (3) on her first page, Alcott's novel starts out shortly before Christmas, some time in December 1861 (Showalter, "Introduction" 497; Geraldine Brooks 277). The initial date of Brooks's book marks the event of March's first letter home, and it is also the date of the Battle of Ball's Bluff (Geraldine Brooks 277). The Battle of Ball's Bluff offers itself as the perfect starting point for a novel which aims at unraveling the absurdity as well as the cruelty of war. The battle was the result of a mistake to begin with. Trying to raid a Confederate camp falsely reported at Ball's Bluff, Union troops caught the attention of the Confederates. Soon enough a battle commenced, during which the Unionists found themselves trapped with their backs to the bluff. As the coming defeat of the Union troops became obvious after their failed attempts to break out, panic spread among the men. The peculiarity of the battle is then that most of them were not killed in the actual fight. Many were shot while trying to climb or jump down the cliff or trying to swim the Potomac to Harrison's Island. Numerous soldiers simply drowned. Although a comparatively small battle, this pointless bloodshed reveals the futility of the war ("Ball's").

In Brooks's novel, the significance of the circumstances of the infliction of wounds is as important as the symbolism of the kind of the injury. The injury that March bears away from this battle is not caused by the encounter with the enemy, but by his young comrade Silas Stone, who is trying to save himself from drowning (Geraldine Brooks 6–7). In order to save his own life, March has to sacrifice this young man of only twenty. The scene is reminiscent of the classic nineteenth-century Civil War novel, Stephen Crane's *The Red Badge of Courage* (1895). Similar to the young volunteer of Crane's classic, March proves himself a coward. The wound itself, his "aching" or "weeping eye" (Geraldine Brooks 3, 4), is symbolic of the psychological wounds of war, not to be expressed in real tears. Moreover, it is symbolic of March's blurred vision, in not a literal but a metaphorical sense. March is a volunteer, like Crane's protagonist. He enthusiastically joined the forces against the approval of his family and without knowing what awaited him.

Some scenes are significantly told twice, in both parts of the novel, in March's and Marmee's narration. For example, the twofold depiction of March's decision to volunteer for the war unmistakably illustrates the discrepancy between male and female perception, and reveals, through its double perspective, that individual memories do not create a common collective memory. The convergent accounts of husband and wife reveal instead that (at least) two opposing, though equally valid versions of the past exist. March's retelling of this scene reads as follows:

> I paused to wipe the sweat from my forehead, and I looked over the bent heads, and saw Marmee, her head held high, looking straight at me with tears in her eyes. She had heard a truth in my words and recognized my intention even before I knew it myself. We held each other's gaze for a long moment. I read the question in her face as clearly as if she shouted it aloud, and I nodded.
> I had said "we will go." She knew, even before I did, that I meant it. She lifted her palms in a gesture of assent, as if to put wind beneath my wings. And so I cried out: "I say 'we,' my friends, because if the army will have me, I propose to go with you." The youths raised their heads then, and made me a great Huzzah. I hushed them, and went on. "We will go forth together. And together we will return, God willing, on that great and shining day, when all children of Israel have come into their inheritance: and that inheritance will be one nation, and that one nation will be forever free!"
> I stepped down from the stump, and made my way through the press to Marmee. She was so proud of me that she could not speak, but only took my hand and clasped it, the pressure of her grip hard as a man's.
>
> (Geraldine Brooks 183)

When Marmee relates her version of the scene, it is revealed that her husband has gravely misinterpreted her reaction:

> When I saw him stand on that tree stump in the cattle ground, surrounded by the avid faces of the young, I knew that as he spoke to them, he was thinking that it was unfair to lay the burden so fully on that innocent generation. I could see the look of love for those boys

in his eyes, and I saw also that the moment was carrying him away. I raised my arms to him, imploring him not to say the words that I knew were forming in his mind. He looked me full in the face, he saw my tears, and he ignored them and did as he pleased. And then I in my turn had to pretend to be pleased by my hero of a husband. When he stepped down, and came to me, I could not speak. I took his hand and dug my nails into the flesh of it, wanting to hurt him for the hurt he was inflicting upon me.

(Geraldine Brooks 210–11)

March, inebriated by his own words, interprets Marmee's gesture of resistance as approval and believes that her tears are a sign of rapture rather than fury. This unmasking of the ostensibly ideal world of *Little Women* is further supported by the account of a romantic relationship with the slave Grace, reaching back to March's young adult years. The romantic involvement flares up again during his absence from his family.

Brooks's replacement of Alcott's purely female perspective on the Civil War with a war novel, told predominantly from a male point of view, may appear misogynist. It recalls Virginia Woolf's ironic statement: "This is an important book, the critic assumes, because it deals with war. This is an insignificant book because it deals with the feelings of women in a drawing-room. A scene in a battlefield is more important than a scene in a shop." (*Room* 74; see also Dobson 67). But on closer inspection, *March* is a feminist text, which further develops the proto-feminist trajectory of its precursor (Schäfer 68). The events revolving around the two female protagonists, Marmee and Grace, distinctly deploy one issue, the oppression of women in the nineteenth century. Marmee and Grace are both emotionally involved with March and function virtually as two sides of a coin, because for Brooks, the oppression of white women in society and marriage corresponds to the exploitation of black women in slavery. The black slave Grace and Marmee, the white member of the New England intelligentsia, are oppressed, the first in slavery because of her race and the other in her marriage because of her gender. Both women are strong, proud, and dutiful. They endure great pains to follow their convictions. As a young woman, Grace arranges for a little slave girl to be taught reading and writing by young March (Shelden 212–13), behind the back of her master/father. This obvious rebellion is punished severely, and she is brutally whipped when she is found out. Marmee is similarly rebelling against her position. In a significant scene, she is outraged about Emerson's passivity apropos the abolition of slavery and his reservations toward radical abolitionist Brown. She tells him so, in the presence of many other Concord worthies. Marmee's outburst is met by general incomprehension and indignation. Both Grace and Marmee are intelligent and opinionated, and this is mainly what draws March to them.

March is sexually attracted to both women, and this tension may be rooted in a male impulse to overpower strong-willed women and become their master in every sense. Besides the costs of rebellion, the novel moreover presents the inner dilemma of self-reliant and independent women in the nineteenth century. Despite their natural impulse to rebel, these women also desperately try to fit in and adopt the accepted role of women in society. Grace, notwithstanding her status at that point as a freed slave, cares for her aged father/master as a dutiful daughter. Marmee never openly objects to March's resolution to go to war, knowing her place as his wife. The novel showcases women in the nineteenth century, who, against their natural impulse toward rebellion, try to accept and adopt the ideal predetermined by society. The central topic in *March*, as in *Little Women*, is the inner civil war of the female characters (Fetterley, "Little"; see also Spengler 270).

Brooks is not only using *Little Women* as a thematical and structural "scaffolding" (275) for her novel. In analogy with Alcott's classic, which follows the growing up of the March sisters in the course of one year, she depicts how March and Marmee go through crisis and development. While Alcott repeatedly uses direct and indirect intertextual devices – most prominently John Bunyan's work of religious edification, *The Pilgrim's Progress* (1678/84) – this intertextuality remains conspicuously unmarked in Brooks's novel. This is remarkable because other, also unmarked intertextual devices, as well as secondary sources, are listed in her "Afterword" (Geraldine Brooks 279). Yet the title of the novel gains some significance with regard to Bunyan's classic. *March* refers first of all to the title character, Mr. March, and to the last name of the whole family. But it is also the month that marks the beginning of springtime and thus suggests the beginning of a progress. Furthermore, a march can be a journey and involve a quest. It might also be read as a hint at the war itself (Auerbach 24).

This is especially significant in a comparison of the final scenes of Part I of *Little Women* and of *March*. In Alcott's novel, the father returns at Christmas, bringing the year 1861 full circle. The chapter is titled "Pleasant Meadows." For the first time in the novel, the father is present as a person. *Little Women*'s Mr. March does not relate how he fared while away at war. As in his letters, he spares his family the harsh realities. Instead, he praises his girls: "Rather a rough road for you to travel, my little pilgrims, especially the latter part of it. But you have got on bravely" (Alcott, *Little* 222). He looks on the girls with "fatherly satisfaction" (222) and finds that their pilgrimages have been successful.

Brooks reinvents a Bunyanesque pilgrimage for March (David E. Smith 98). The novel is a novel of development or a bildungsroman, in which March's midlife crisis substitutes for the typical coming of age (Schäfer 65). His development can also be read as a reenactment of the evolution of the nation (Haase/Schäfer 93). One lesson March has learned has to do with his covert racism. Although he was in love with the enslaved Grace in his youth, he still has not freed himself of some of the remnants of his upbringing until he lives on a plantation with contrabands during the war, teaches their children, and starts to regard some of them as family. Brooks, again, seems to draw on Bronson Alcott here as a model for March (Abate 70-71), whose attitude echoes "the racist associations of whiteness with civility, decorum, and self-control, and blackness with rudeness, wildness, and even excess" (Abate 71). Using this background, Brooks creates black children for March and a black stand-in for his wife. The black characters of the novel – Grace, Jimse, Zannah, and Cilla – become as dear to him as his own family, but he loses them all. It is not surprising that he thinks of them when he finally meets his own children again (Geraldine Brooks 272-73). March has learned that his association of dark skin with evil is not right. But none of his family "thought to ask their father how a year at war had changed *him*" (273).

When Brooks includes the final scene from Alcott's text almost verbatim and leaves the father speechless, we see the ending of the nineteenth-century classic in an entirely new, revised light. March's programmatic diary entry – "I never promised I would write the truth" (Brooks 4) – resonates with the notion that "trauma epitomizes the final impossibility of objective history" (Meinig 350). At the end of the novel March is a veteran, traumatized by his wartime experience, who cannot easily readapt to his family life and who is not able to relive the ordeals he had to face by recounting them: "So this was how it was to be, now: I would do my best to live in the quick world, but the ghosts of the dead would ever be at hand" (Geraldine Brooks 273). On the plot level, this scene hints at March's development or awakening. With regard to the reanimation, these revelations encourage readers to reassess the hypotext (Padmore 69). Brooks's reconfiguration of *Little Women* comments on the race and gender politics of the original (Entzminger 98). The disclosure of March's thoughts exposes the impossibility of narrating past events. And on yet another level, *March* is a "narrative of nation" (Kreyling 11), in which the protagonist symbolically embodies the evolution of the South and the USA.

Brooks herself puts a lot of emphasis on the fact that her journalistic work, especially her first book, has prepared her for the writing of fiction. *Nine Parts of Desire* (1994) depicts the lives of women in the Middle East, where Brooks herself lived for six years. Taking into account her intimate knowledge of this region, some episodes of *March* appear in a new light. Flashbacks presenting the March family as a station of the Underground Railroad, scenes depicting the controversies around the support of the radical abolitionist Brown, and the differing attitudes of the March couple toward the Civil War can be read as a commentary on twenty-first-century terrorism and the war in Iraq

(Tucker et al. 7). The diction of some of March's statements strikingly resembles both President George W. Bush's remarks about the axis of evil and the justifications of radical Islamists for the holy war, the jihad (Geraldine Brooks 182). Marmee's disillusioned conclusion about the war is indistinguishable from statements that reached the world public from Iraq and the USA (210). Brooks is demonstrating that historical fiction is not per se, simply by the choice of a setting in the past, a form of escapism from the urgent problems afflicting the present. She is generally writing about war, violence, and inequality as universal topics (Tucker et al. 13). *March* may therefore be labeled a 9/11 novel. By introducing the figure of Brown, Brooks is also hinting at terrorism. The radical abolitionist can be perceived as a martyr who died for his beliefs, or as a fanatical terrorist who used violence in order to make his message heard (Reynolds). This topicality of *March*, besides its more universal statements concerning the cruelties of war, won it the Pulitzer Prize. The message of the novel mainly lies in a depiction of the "moral dilemma of war" (Tucker et al. 5).

The Wind Done Gone and *March* are new historical novels which aim at a revision of the historical record. They write back against the race and gender politics of the nineteenth century. *Hester* similarly is a feminist revision of Hawthorne's classic. All three texts provide historical lessons about intolerance on the grounds of gender, race, and religion. The texts reconstruct an already fictional past, thereby drawing attention toward the epistemological problem of the ultimate unknowability and unnarratability of historical truth. And they (re-)create American cultural memory and national identity.

6 Revis(it)ing History and Fiction

In conclusion, a tentative resume of the renaissance of historical fiction and the emergence of the new American historical novel in the USA shall be undertaken here. Naturally, this can be neither exhaustive nor definitive. This study has raised a number of questions and tried to answer them. The most prominent of those shall be given recapitulatory consideration here.

First of all, the question why the nineteenth century especially fuels the imagination of writers and stimulates the imagination of readers remains highly intriguing. An answer might be that this dominance of the preoccupation with the nineteenth century is only a mirror of the specific position this key phase of the formation of a national identity holds within the American cultural memory. At the beginning of the nineteenth century, the conflict with the British had finally found its terminus with the War of 1812, and subsequently Americans were striving to actively create a distinctive cultural identity. The nineteenth century was a time of change in many respects, with feminist concerns and racial issues coming to the fore and the transformation of everyday life accelerated by the Industrial Revolution and technological progress. Despite its far-reaching historical changes, such as the Civil War, the era forged an American national identity, and the then-emerging genre of the historical romance furthered the creation of a cultural memory.

The American literary fascination with the era more generally ties in with a view of the nineteenth century as "a harbinger of our own culture" (Kohlke 7). And the assumption that historical fiction is a critique of the present, transferred into a past setting (Feuchtwanger 130), holds true for the new historical fiction. More often than not, these texts are not simply a simulacrum of the past but may just as well be read as a simulacrum of the present or even the future. The new historical fiction, although tending toward nostalgia, nevertheless displays strong topicality. Therefore, it must mostly be understood as aiming at a historical lesson rather than at providing an escape from late-twentieth- and early-twenty-first-century reality. The new American historical novels, in their historiographic revisionism, create a new cultural memory for the United States, which is linked to the present time. The new historical fiction creates a revised version of the national history of the United States, "exploring and exploding national ... identities" (Heilmann/Llewellyn 6).

In literary history, specific genres emerge within a historical period as attempts to answer social and cultural problems. Sometimes, in later periods, those genres reappear or are revived when similar problems surface (Gorp/Musarra-Schroeder ii). Then specific genre norms of various subgenres of the novel (and of fiction in general) are mixed to create a new genre hybrid. The new historical novel is "the composite novel of its epoch" (Gutleben 223). This function of the new historical fiction turns it into multi- or poly-genre memory.

This echoes Jane Tompkins's theory of cultural work apropos American nineteenth-century literature. In the early decades of the nineteenth century, the invention of the historical romance served the purpose of creating a cultural identity for the new nation. Now, the new historical fiction is fulfilling a similar purpose. Especially since the millennial hysteria gained momentum and the traumatic events of 9/11 unsettled not only the United States but the whole world, the American nation is again in search of a cultural identity (Krueger xi). As John Dos Passos remarked almost eighty years ago, "[e]very generation rewrites the past. In easy times history is more or less of an ornamental art, but in times of danger we are driven to the written record by a pressing need to find answers to the riddles of today" (3). The turn of the millennium and the first decades of the twenty-first century must be viewed as such a period of extreme national crisis (Elliott 230).

The new historical fiction and especially the novels discussed in this study fulfill the demand of a national cultural memory, without drowning out the ambiguities or concealing the diversity of the American nation. The entirety of the new historical novels depicting the nineteenth century creates a "landscape of memory" (Kirmayer), the cultural memory of a crucial period in the becoming of the American nation. Readers revisit and thus experience America in the nineteenth century in the fictional texts: "As the metaphor of landscape suggests, the narrative reconstructions of memory are ... lived in – offering vistas that reveal and conceal" (Kirmayer 182).

In the new historical fiction, revisionism and the search for truth are juxtaposed by fictionalization and pseudo-authenticity. The renaissance of the historical novel at the turn of the twenty-first century seems to be owed to a general trend of a renewed wish for handholds and fixed value systems. The turn to history signals a desire to rediscover meaning and make sense of the void (Elias, *Sublime* 47–48). Human beings have a basic desire for a "meaningful order upon reality" (Berger 22), and the new historical novels "*de*construct and, at the same time, *re*construct historical knowledge" (Middeke 4). The enthusiasm for the new historical fiction is hardly curbed by an awareness that what is presented is "truthiness" (Grossman) or at best a "truth of the human heart" (Hawthorne, *House* 1), but not by any stretch the absolute truth. What readers encounter is a "mediated image" that comes with "inevitable distortion" (Joyce 4). Though the reading public obviously finds fault with fictionalization in the classic genres of life writing, it accepts the typical mix of fact and fiction inherent to the genre when it comes to historical fiction and its subgenres. As long as the authors of the new historical fiction aim with Aristoteles at relating what may have happened, readers willingly consume the novels as if they were entertaining substitutes for uninspiring history textbooks.

Accordingly, the rules for romance writing which Hawthorne collected in his preface to *The House of the Seven Gables* (1851) are still observed by writers of the new historical fiction today:

> When a writer calls his work a Romance, it need hardly be observed that he wishes to claim a certain latitude, both as to its fashion and material, which he would not have felt himself entitled to assume had he professed to be writing a Novel. The latter form of composition is presumed to aim at a very minute fidelity, not merely to the possible, but to the probable and ordinary course of man's experience. The former – while, as a work of art, it must rigidly subject itself to laws, and while it sins unpardonably so far as it may swerve aside from the truth of the human heart – has fairly a right to present that truth under circumstances, to a great extent, of the writer's own choosing or creation. If he think fit, also, he may so manage his atmospherical medium as to bring out or mellow the lights and deepen and enrich the shadows of the picture. He will be wise, no doubt, to make a very moderate use of the privileges here stated, and, especially, to mingle the Marvelous rather as a slight, delicate, and evanescent flavor, than as any portion of the actual substance of the dish offered to the public. He can hardly be said, however, to commit a literary crime even if he disregard this caution. (1)

It is not helpful to view historical romance, historiographic metafiction, and the new historical novel as distinct genres. Rather, they should be examined as developmental stages of historical fiction, as a literary continuum.

The current literary trend of the new historical novel in the United States has finally bridged the gap between popular and serious literature. This claim was filed as early as the 1970s by Leslie A. Fiedler with his catchphrase "cross the border – close the gap." It was Van Wyck Brooks who, in *America's Coming-of-Age* (1915), first defined the bifurcation of American culture and coined the terms 'lowbrow' and 'highbrow' (Levine). While Fiedler's aim was not fully realized by (early) postmodernism, it has emerged at the turn of the twenty-first century, with the new historical fiction's broad success with both readers and critics. In this respect, our age seems to mirror the Victorian era, in which "interaction and cross-fertilization between the high and low arts" (Sanders 121) was evident. The genre which most obviously "bridged the threshold between high and low, élite and popular, in the nineteenth century was the novel" (122).

Another significant aspect of the new historical fiction is the fluid mix of realist and postmodernist features. The texts offer their readers both postmodern experiments in form and narrative "[c]oherence and closure" (Byatt, *Possession* 422). They are working on "the double-edged project of simultaneously de- and reconstructing history" (Kunow, "Beginning" 91). Not only do the novels bridge the chronological gap between the nineteenth and the late twentieth and early twenty-first centuries in terms of content, they are also a combination of the typical art forms of the two eras, "moderately rather than radically" experimenting "with or within the realist tradition" (Burgass 30). Andrea Kirchknopf's claim that post-Victorian fiction invites redefinitions of postmodernism, is a compromise between modernist and postmodernist features, and may facilitate a terminological correction to postmodernism holds true for the new historical novel in the United States (73; see also Hornung 108). Winfried Fluck likewise observes that realism and experiment merge in new ways ("Surface" 82). He introduces the term "new realism" (65) and describes it as a response to cultural and aesthetic developments without a recourse to traditional patterns (79). What results is "a hybrid – a mixture of modes," in which relations between several narrative strategies are negotiated (79). The new realism can be linked to two different literary traditions, namely experimental postmodern literature and the realistic novel of the nineteenth century (67). The new realism

> retains a realistic mode of writing in order to remain connected with the world of a reader who is not a professional academic; at the same time it also uses such realistic forms of representation in ways that undermine their self-evident reliance on the authority of experience and the claim for representativeness linked with it. One of the results is the almost paradoxical phenomenon of a realism that no longer wants to offer a representative version of reality but is content to explore and represent a decontextualized surface. It is a realism that does not claim to know the real, but wants to come to terms with the fact that it is nevertheless there in an amorphous, ever changing shape. In the final analysis, this realism refers us to a cultural situation whose complexity and variety can no longer be represented by any single text or mode of writing, only by a set of relations within a growing plurality of cultural styles and modes of writing. (84–85)

Moreover, "[r]ealism is the medium of new voices" (Shechner 32; Bradbury, *American* 264). In the new historical fiction one finds "a new awareness of voice and of language as the echo chamber of history and tradition, a consciousness of region and place, a revived ethnic and regional sensitivity, a new awareness of traditional folk narrative, a distinct political animus" (Shechner 31). The new historical fiction revisits history and thereby revises the historical record, bringing on a shift from master narrative to micro narrative. Especially in texts by female authors, the issue of identity construction becomes an equally important theme along with historical representation (Rothaug 16). The narration of individual memory gains universal validity, providing a collective or cultural memory and creating a cultural or national identity. There is a return to traditional storytelling and problems of subjectivity "which had seemed passé during the heyday of metafiction, language games, and self-reflexive experiments in the sixties" (Jay Clayton, *Pleasures* 91). The terms 'revisit' and 'revise,' which I bring into play in the title of this study, were chosen to stress that the new historical novels generally "evoke, transmit, enhance or destroy (a) cultural memory" (Gorp/ Musarra-Schroeder iii). Cora Kaplan's diagnosis of the neo-Victorian novel in Britain can be adopted for similar cultural products in the American sphere: "At once philosophical, political and generic, the new historical fiction positions itself as both a complement and rival to academic writing on the period" (9).

The new historical fiction is a synthesis of tradition and innovation, of realism and experiment – terms applied by various scholars to the contemporary British novel (Nünning, *Roman* 140; Zerweck 2), a fact that only underlines the transatlantic scope of the phenomenon. The double character of contemporary historical fiction undermines the programmatic opposition of mimesis versus crisis of representation or tradition versus form experiment, in favor of a combination of all the various elements (Rothaug 55). The new historical novel is an astounding amalgamation of a continuation of the long-standing tradition and an attempt at a radical innovation of the genre.

Whether ready-made labels, such as 'post-postmodernism' (Hassan, "Beyond"), "postmodern" (Ickstadt 205), "new" (Fluck, "Surface" 65), or 'neo-realism' (Versluys; Claviez/Moss; Bradbury, "Neorealist") can aptly classify the contemporary development remains to be seen (Ribbat 8). Refusing to add any new labels, I have favored a descriptive approach here. It must suffice, for the moment, to agree with author Russell Banks that we are experiencing "a very interesting and fruitful period in American fiction" which is "making realism viable again" (qtd. in Wylie 740).

All the same, "[t]here is no doubt ... that the obsession with history, combined with an increased sense of its elusiveness, ... has ... become one of the most prominent signatures of contemporary American fiction"

(Kurt Müller 51). The new historical fiction is "a genre at the cutting edge of postmodern conceptualizations of the past" (Heilmann/Llewellyn 6). All signs seem to point to the fact that the renaissance of the American historical novel at the turn of the twenty-first century is the avant-garde of American literature itself – a change of paradigm, away from postmodernism, and yet not a straightforward return to realism. The new historical fiction is the genre in which literary experiment, critical acknowledgment, and best-selling success preeminently coalesce in an almost unprecedented way.

7 Works Cited

Abate, Michelle Ann. "Topsy and Topsy-Turvy Jo: Harriet Beecher Stowe's *Uncle Tom's Cabin* and/in Louisa May Alcott's *Little Women*." *Children's Literature* 34 (2006): 59–82. Print.

Abrams, M. H. *A Glossary of Literary Terms*. Boston: Thomson Wadsworth, 2005. Print.

Achilles, Jochen. "Chasing the Devil's Tail/Tale – Teuflische amerikanische Literatur: Überlegungen zur Territorialisierung des Bösen." 28 June 2006. Unpub. MS of a guest lecture at Freie Universität Berlin.

Ackermann, Zeno. *Messing with Romance: American Poetics and Antebellum Southern Fiction*. Frankfurt a. M.: Lang, 2012. Print. Regensburger Arbeiten zur Anglistik und Amerikanistik 51.

Adams, Mary E. "Diane Glancy. Stone Heart: A Novel of Sacajawea." *World Literature Today* 78.2 (2004): 93–94. Print.

Adamson, Lynda G. *American Historical Fiction: An Annotated Guide to Novels for Adults and Young Adults*. Phoenix: Oryx, 1999. Print.

———. *Recreating the Past: A Guide to American and World Historical Fiction for Children and Young Adults*. Westport: Greenwood, 1994. Print.

Agatucci, Cora. "Seminar #1 Summary: What is Historical Fiction? – 9 April 2003." *Central Oregon Community College*. Web. 4 July 2006.

Alberts, Crystal. "In the Talking Leaves: Diane Glancy's Reclamation of Voice and Archive." *The Salt Companion to Diane Glancy*. Ed. James Mackay. Cambridge: Salt, 2010. 114–34. Print.

Alcott, Louisa May. "*Behind a Mask, or a Woman's Power*." *Scribbling Women: Short Stories by 19th Century American Women*. Ed. Elaine Showalter. New Brunswick: Rutgers UP, 1997. 115–212. Print.

———. *Little Women*. Ed. and introd. Elaine Showalter. New York: Penguin, 1989. Print.

Alighieri, Dante. *Inferno*. Trans. Henry Wadsworth Longfellow. Ed. Matthew Pearl. New York: Modern Library, 2003. Print.

Allen, Rob, and Thijs van den Berg. *Serialization in Popular Culture*. New York: Routledge, 2014. Print. Routledge Research in Cultural and Media Studies.

Anderson, Benedict. *Imagined Communities: Reflections on the Origin and Spread of Nationalism*. London: Verso, 1983. Print.

Anderson, Linda. "The Re-Imagining of History in Contemporary Women's Fiction." *Plotting Change: Contemporary Women's Fiction.* Ed. Linda Anderson. London: Edward Arnold, 1990. 128–41. Print.

Arch, Stephen Carl. "Romancing the Puritans: American Historical Fiction in the 1820s." *ESQ* 39 (1993): 107–32. Print.

Ashcroft, Bill, Gareth Griffiths, and Helen Tiffin. "Introduction: Feminism and Postcolonialism." *The Post-Colonial Studies Reader.* Ed. Bill Ashcroft, Gareth Griffiths, and Helen Tiffin. London: Routledge, 1995. 249–50. Print.

———. *The Empire Writes Back: Theory and Practice in Post-Colonial Literatures.* London: Routledge, 1989. Print.

Ashley, Mike. *The Mammoth Encyclopedia of Modern Crime Fiction.* New York: Carroll, 2002. Print.

Assmann, Aleida. "Was sind kulturelle Texte?" *Literaturkanon – Medienereignis – kultureller Text: Formen interkultureller Kommunikation und Übersetzung.* Ed. Andreas Poltermann. Berlin: Erich Schmidt, 1995. 232–44. Print.

Assmann, Jan. *Das kulturelle Gedächtnis: Schrift, Erinnerung und politische Identität in frühen Hochkulturen.* München: Beck, 1997. Print.

———. "Kollektives Gedächtnis und kulturelle Identität." *Kultur und Gedächtnis.* Ed. Jan Assmann and Tonio Hölscher. Frankfurt: Suhrkamp, 1988. 9–19. Print.

Athanasourelis, John Paul. "Caleb Carr and the Historical Detective Novel." *McNeese Review* 45 (2007): 37–48. Web. 13 Feb. 2020.

Atwood, Margaret. *In Search of Alias Grace: On Writing Canadian Historical Fiction.* Charles R. Bronfman Lecture in Canadian Studies. Ottawa: U of Ottawa P, 1997. Print.

Auerbach, Nina. "Austen and Alcott on Matriarchy: New Women or New Wives?" *Novel* 10 (Fall 1976): 6–26. Print.

Bagdikian, Ben H., et al. "Letter of Support." *Houghton Mifflin Harcourt.* Web. 21 Mar. 2009.

Bakhtin, Mikhail. "Discourse in the Novel." *The Dialogic Imagination: Four Essays.* Trans. Caryl Emerson and Michael Holquist. Austin: U of Texas P, 1981. 259–422. Print.

———. "Forms of Time and of the Chronotope in the Novel: Notes toward a Historical Poetics." *The Dialogic Imagination: Four Essays.* Trans. Caryl Emerson and Michael Holquist. Austin: U of Texas P, 1981. 84–258. Print.

Baldick, Chris. *The Concise Oxford Dictionary of Literary Terms.* Oxford: OUP, 2001. Print.

Balestrini, Nassim Winnie, and Ina Bergmann. "Intermediality, Life Writing, and American Studies: A Brief Introduction." *Intermediality, Life Writing, and American Studies: Interdisciplinary Perspectives.* Ed. Nassim Winnie Balestrini and Ina Bergmann. Berlin: de Gruyter, 2018. 1–8. Print.

"Ball's Bluff Battlefield Regional Park." *Northern Virginia Regional Park Authority.* Web. 8 June 2009.

Banita, Georgiana. "Race, Risk, and Fiction in the War on Terror: Laila Halaby, Gayle Brandeis, and Michael Cunningham." *Lit: Literature Interpretation Theory* 21.4 (Oct. 2010): 242–68. Web. 10 Feb. 2020.

Barlowe, Jamie. *The Scarlet Mob of Scribblers.* Carbondale: Southern Illinois UP, 2000. Print.

Barndollar, David, and Susan Schorn. "Revisiting the Serial Format of Dickens's Novels." *Functions of Victorian Culture at the Present Time*. Ed. Christine L. Krueger. Athens: Ohio UP, 2002. 157–70. Print.

Barth, John. "Historical Fiction, Fictitious History, and Chesapeake Bay Blue Crabs, or, About Aboutness." *The Friday Book: Essays and Other Nonfiction*. New York: Putnam, 1984. 180–192. Print.

Barthes, Roland. *Roland Barthes by Roland Barthes*. Trans. Richard Howard. Berkeley: U of California P, 1994. Print.

Baschirotto, Corinna. "'I want to be the rule itself, not the exception that proves it': Rewriting *Gone With the Wind*." *Cultural Memory and Multiple Identities: Transnational and Transatlantic American Studies*. Vol. 5. Ed. Rüdiger Kunow and Wilfried Raussert. Berlin: LITVerlag, 2008. 57–75. Print.

Bass, Patrik Henry. "First Person Singular." *Essence* 31.9 (2001): 60. Print.

Basseler, Michael, and Dorothee Birke. "Mimesis des Erinnerns." *Gedächtniskonzepte der Literaturwissenschaft: Theoretische Grundlegung und Anwendungsperspektiven*. Ed. Astrid Erll and Ansgar Nünning. Berlin: de Gruyter, 2005. 123–47. Print.

Bassil, Veronica. "The Artist at Home: The Domestication of Louisa May Alcott." *Studies in American Fiction* 15.2 (1987): 187–97. Print.

Bates, Karen Grigsby. "A Through-the-Looking-Glass Version of *Gone with the Wind*." *The Journal of Blacks in Higher Education* 33 (Autumn 2001): 126–27. Web. 17 Feb. 2020.

Baudrillard, Jean. *Simulacra and Simulation*. Ann Arbor: Michigan UP, 2006. Print.

Beaulieu, Elizabeth Ann. *Black Women Writers and the American Neo-Slave Narrative: Femininity Unfettered*. Westport: Greenwood P, 1999. Print.

Belfer, Lauren. *City of Light*. New York: Delta, 2003. Print.

———. "On Writing *City of Light*." *Boldtype: A Monthly Review of Books: Looking Backwards* 3.2 (May 1999). Web. 26 May 2008.

Bell, Michael Davitt. *Hawthorne and the Historical Romance of New England*. Princeton: Princeton UP, 1971. Print.

Benesch, Klaus. *The Threat of History: Geschichte und Erzählung im afro-amerikanischen Roman der Gegenwart*. Essen: Die Blaue Eule, 1990. Print.

Benjamin, Walter. *Illuminations*. Ed. Hannah Arendt. Trans. Harry Zohn. New York: Shocken, 1968. Print.

Bennett, Andrew, and Nicholas Royle. *An Introduction to Literature, Criticism, and Theory*. London: Prentice Hall, 1995. Print.

Berger, Peter L. *The Sacred Canopy: Elements of a Sociological Theory of Religion*. Garden City: Doubleday, 1967. Print.

Bergmann, Ina. *And Then the Child Becomes a Woman: Weibliche Initiation in der amerikanischen Kurzgeschichte 1865–1970*. Heidelberg: Winter, 2003. Print. American Studies - A Monograph Series 110.

———. "'I Have Heard Many Stranger Stories Than This, in the Villages Along the Hudson': Magic Realism in Upstate New York." *Liminality and the Short Story: Boundary Crossings in American, Canadian, and British Writing*. Ed. Jochen Achilles and Ina Bergmann. New York: Routledge, 2015. 159–74. Print. Routledge Interdisciplinary Perspectives on Literature.

———. "'To You, Perceptive Reader, I Bequeath my History:' Die Renaissance des historischen Romans im 21. Jahrhundert." *Amerikanisches Erzählen nach 2000: Eine Bestandsaufnahme.* Ed. Sebastian Domsch. München: Text & Kritik, 2008. 56–77. Print.

———. "Eine *Divine Comedy* für das 21. Jahrhundert: Matthew Pearl's *The Dante Club.*" *Dante Intermedial: Die Divina Commedia in Literatur und Medien.* Ed. Irmgard Scharold. Würzburg: Königshausen & Neumann, forthcoming.

———. "*From Hell*: Dante, Tod und Teufel im amerikanischen Serienmörderroman." *Unterwelten: Modelle und Transformationen.* Ed. Joachim Hamm and Jörg Robert. Würzburg: Königshausen & Neumann, 2014. 247–270. Print. Ringvorlesungen der U Würzburg.

———. "Historical Biofiction: Writing Lives in Diane Glancy's *Stone Heart* (2003) and John May's *Poe & Fanny* (2004)." *The American Novel in the 21st Century: Cultural Contexts – Literary Developments – Critical Analyses.* Ed. Michael Basseler and Ansgar Nünning. Trier: WVT, 2019. 309–22. Print.

———. "In Poe's Shadow: Frances Sargent Osgood." *Herstory Re-Imagined: Women's Lives in Biographical Fiction.* Ed. Julia Lajta-Novak and Caitríona Ní Dhúill. Basingstoke: Palgrave, forthcoming. Palgrave Studies in Life-Writing.

———. "Jack the Ripper's American Cousins: Representations of Good and Evil in Historical Crime Fiction." *Representations of Evil in Fiction and Film.* Ed. Jochen Achilles and Ina Bergmann. Trier: WVT, 2009. 137–56. Print. Anglistik – Amerikanistik – Anglophonie 11.

———. "Reanimated Classics: Canon Appropriation and Serialization in Contemporary Fiction." *Proceedings: Anglistentag 2009 Klagenfurt.* Ed. Jörg Helbig and René Schallegger. Trier: WVT, 2010. 135–51. Print.

———. "Stories of Female Initiation: Flannery O'Connor's 'Good Country People' and Joyce Carol Oates' 'How I Contemplated the World from the Detroit House of Correction and Began My Life Over Again.'" *A History of the American Short Story: Genres – Classics – Model Interpretations.* Ed. Ansgar Nünning and Michael Basseler. Trier: WVT, 2011. 307–22. Print.

———. "The Liberty of Solitude: Einsamkeit und Freiheit im Leben und Werk von Emily Dickinson, Louisa May Alcott und Sarah Orne Jewett." *Rückzug: Produktivität des Solitären in Kunst, Religion und Geschlechtergeschichte.* Ed. Jenny Haase, Xenia von Tippelskirch, and Beatrix Trînca. Würzburg: Königshausen & Neumann, forthcoming.

———. "The New Historical Fiction – Between Tradition and Innovation." *Narrative is the Essence of History: Essays on the Historical Novel.* Ed. John Cameron. Newcastle upon Tyne: Cambridge Scholars Pub., 2012. 139–51. Print.

———. "Working Girls: The *New Woman* in Juvenile and Adult Fiction by Elizabeth Stuart Phelps, Sarah Orne Jewett, and Mary E. Wilkins Freeman." *LWU (Literatur in Wissenschaft und Unterricht)* XLII.4 (2009): 259–66. Print.

Bertens, Hans. *The Idea of the Postmodern: A History.* London: Routledge, 1995. Print.

Bertens, Hans, and Theo D'haen. *Contemporary American Crime Fiction*. New York: Palgrave, 2001. Print.

Bhabha, Homi K. "Cultural Diversity and Cultural Differences." *The Post-Colonial Studies Reader*. Ed. Bill Ashcroft, Gareth Griffiths, and Helen Tiffin. London: Routledge, 1995. 206–09. Print.

———. *The Location of Culture*. London: Routledge, 1994. Print.

The Bible. Authorized King James Version. Introd. Robert Caroll and Stephen Prickett. Oxford: OUP, 1998. Print.

"Big Love." *HBO*. Web. 4 May 2009.

Bigsby, Christopher. *Hester*. New York: Penguin, 1994. Print.

Birch, Carol. "A Strange and Elfish Child." *The Independent*. 15 July 1995. Print.

Bird, Stephanie. *Recasting Historical Women: Female Identity in German Biographical Fiction*. Oxford: Berg, 1998. Print.

Blake, Linnie. "Whoever Fights Monsters: Serial Killers, the FBI and America's Last Frontier." *The Devil Himself: Villainy in Detective Fiction and Film*. Ed. Stacy Gillis and Philippa Gates. Westport: Greenwood, 2002. 197–210. Print.

Böger, Astrid. "Envisioning Progress at Chicago's White City." *Space in America: Theory, History, Culture*. Ed. Klaus Benesch and Kerstin Schmidt. Amsterdam: Rodopi, 2005. 265–84. Print.

Bölling, Gordon. *History in the Making: Metafiktion im neueren anglokanadischen Roman*. Heidelberg: Winter, 2006. Print.

Bolter, Jay David, and Richard Grusin. *Remediation: Understanding New Media*. Cambridge: MIT P, 2000. Print.

"Books Briefly Noted: *The 19th Wife* by David Ebershoff." *The New Yorker*. Print. 8 Sept. 2008.

Borges, Marana. "A Misunderstanding: Trauma and Terrorism in the '9/11 Fiction.'" *Trans: Revue de Littérature Générale et Comparée* 15 (2013). Web. 10 Feb. 2020.

Borgmeier, Raimund, and Bernhard Reitz. "Einleitung." *Der historische Roman I: 19. Jahrhundert*. Ed. Raimund Borgmeier and Bernhard Reitz. Heidelberg: Winter, 1984. 7–37. Print. Anglistik & Englischunterricht 22.

Bormann, Daniel Candel. *The Articulation of Science in the Neo-Victorian Novel: A Poetics (and Two Case-Studies)*. Bern: Peter Lang, 2002. Print.

Boyle, T. C. *World's End*. New York: Penguin, 1988. Print.

Bradbury, Malcolm. "Neorealist Fiction." *Columbia Literary History of the United States*. Ed. Emory Elliott, Martha Banta, and Houston A. Baker. New York: Columbia UP, 1988. 1126–41. Print.

———. *The Modern American Novel*. Oxford: OUP, 1992. Print.

———. *The Modern British Novel*. Harmondsworth: Penguin, 1994. Print.

———. "Writing Fiction in the 90s." *Neo-Realism in Contemporary American Fiction*. Ed. Kristiaan Versluys. Amsterdam: Rodopi, 1992. 13–25. Print.

Brady, Erik. "Lighting Past's Current Events: Debut Novel Pours Through Intrigue in Buffalo Society." *USA Today*. 25 May 1999. Print.

Breinig, Helbrecht, and Susanne Opfermann. "Historischer Roman und Gesellschaftsroman." *Amerikanische Literaturgeschichte*. Ed. Hubert Zapf. Suttgart: Metzler, 1997. 77–84. Print.

Breuer, Rolf. "Jane Austen etc.: An Essay on the Poetics of the Sequel." *Jane Austen etc.: The Completions, Continuations and Adaptations of Her Novels.* Erfurt Electronic Studies in English (EESE). EESE Resources. 2000. Web. 30 Aug. 2008.

———. "Jane Austen etc.: The Completions, Continuations and Adaptations of Her Novels – Bibliography." *Jane Austen etc.: The Completions, Continuations and Adaptations of Her Novels.* Erfurt Electronic Studies in English (EESE). EESE Resources. 2000. Web. 30 Aug. 2008.

———. "Jane Austen und kein Ende: Zur Poetik des Folgeromans." *Sinn und Form* 51.4 (1999): 673–81. Print.

———. "Re-writes/Kontrafakturen/Wi(e)dererzählungen." *Germanisch-Romanische Monatsschrift* 53.1 (2003): 95–110. Print.

Brodhead, Richard H. *Cultures of Letters: Scenes of Reading and Writing in Nineteenth-Century America.* Chicago: U of Chicago P, 1993. Print.

Broich, Ulrich. "Intertextuality." *International Postmodernism: Theory and Literary Practice.* Ed. Johannes Willem Bertens, Hans Bertens, and Douwe Fokkema. Amsterdam: John Benjamins, 1997. 249–55. Print.

Brontë, Charlotte. *Jane Eyre.* New York: Signet, 1982. Print.

Brooks, Geraldine. *March.* London: Harper Perennial, 2006. Print.

Brooks, Van Wyck. "On Creating a Usable Past." *The Dial* (11 Apr. 1918): 337–41. Web. 12 June 2020.

Brown, Charles Brockden. "The Difference between History and Romance." *Monthly Magazine* II.4 (Apr. 1800): 251–53. Print.

Budra, Paul, and Betty A. Schellenberg, eds. *Part Two: Reflections on the Sequel.* Toronto: U of Toronto P, 1998. Print.

Buisine, Alain. "Biofictions." *Revue des Sciences Humaines* 224 (1991): 7–13. Print.

Burgass, Catherine. *Challenging Theory: Discipline After Deconstruction.* Aldershot: Ashgate, 1999. Print.

Burgess, Michael, and Jill H. Vassilakos. *Murder in Retrospect: A Selective Guide to Historical Mystery Fiction.* Westport: Libraries Unlimited, 2005. Print.

Burstein, Miriam Elizabeth. "Rules for Writing Neo-Victorian Novels." *The Little Professor.* Web. 17 Oct. 2007.

Burt, Daniel S. *What Historical Novel Do I Read Next?* Detroit: Gale, 1997. Print.

Butter, Michael. "Historiographic Metafiction." *The Encyclopedia of Twentieth-Century Fiction.* Vol. II. 2010. Web. 20 Feb. 2020.

———. *The Epitome of Evil: Hitler in American Fiction, 1939–2002.* New York: Palgrave Macmillan, 2009. Print.

Butter, Michael, and Birte Christ. "Teaching Reading in Installments: An Experiment." *Proceedings: Anglistentag 2011 Freiburg.* Ed. Monika Fludernik and Benjamin Kohlmann. Trier: WVT, 2012. 253–60. Print.

Byatt, A. S. *On Histories and Stories: Selected Essays.* Cambridge: Harvard UP, 2000. Print.

———. *Possession.* London: Vintage, 1991. Print.

Byerman, Keith. *Remembering the Past in Contemporary African American Fiction.* Chapel Hill: U of North Carolina P, 2005. Print.

Caputi, Jane. "The New Founding Fathers: The Lore and Lure of the Serial Killer in Contemporary Culture." *Journal of American Culture* 13.3 (1990): 1–12. Print.

Carnes, Marc C. "Introduction." *Novel History: Historians and Novelists Confront America's Past (and Each Other)*. Ed. Marc C. Carnes. New York: Simon & Schuster, 2001. 13–25. Print.

Carr, Caleb. *The Alienist*. New York: Bantam, 1998. Print.

Cayton, Andrew R. L. "Insufficient Woe: Sense and Sensibility in Writing Nineteenth-Century History." *Reviews in American History* 31.3 (2003): 331–41. Print.

Certeau, Michel de. *The Writing of History*. New York: Columbia UP, 1988. Print.

Chabon, Michael. *Maps & Legends: Reading and Writing Along the Borderlands*. London: Fourth Estate, 2010. Print.

Champagne, Roland A. "The Dante Club." *World Literature Today* 77.2 (July-Sept. 2003): 98. Print.

Channing, Walter. "Essay on American Language and Literature." *North American Review 1* (Sept. 1815): 307–14. Print.

Charles, Ron. *"Big Love."* *The Washington Post*. 10 Aug. 2008. Print.

Child, Lydia Maria. *Hobomok and Other Writings*. Ed. Carolyn L. Karcher. New Brunswick: Rutgers UP, 1986. Print.

Clarke, Lynn A., and Joyce A. Clarke. "Viewpoints: From Book to Screen: Here's an Opportunity." *The Buffalo News*. 22 Sept. 1999. Print.

Claviez, Thomas, and Maria Moss, eds. *Neorealism – Between Innovation and Continuation*. Heidelberg: Winter, 2004. Print.

Clayton, Jay. *Charles Dickens in Cyberspace: The Afterlife of the Nineteenth Century in Postmodern Culture*. Oxford: OUP, 2003. Print.

———. *The Pleasures of Babel*. New York: OUP, 1993. Print.

Clayton, Virginia Tuttle. "Picturing a 'Usable Past.'" *Drawing on America's Past: Folk Art, Modernism, and the Index of American Design*. Ed. Virginia Tuttle Clayton et al. Chapel Hill: U of North Carolina P, 2002. 1–43. Print.

Clerc, Sue. *Neverending Stories: Professional Fan Fiction*. Southern Connecticut State U. Web. 2 Apr. 2009.

Coetzee, J. M. *Foe*. Harmondsworth: Penguin, 1987. Print.

Colerdige, Samuel Taylor. "Work without Hope." *The Norton Anthology of English Literature*. Vol. II. Ed. M. H. Abrams et al. New York: Norton, 1986. 384. Print.

Collingwood, R. G. *The Idea of History*. Oxford: OUP, 1966. Print.

Connelly, Sheryl. "19th Wife tells Compelling Tales of Mormon Polygamy." *NY Daily News*. 22 Aug. 2008. Web. 23 Apr. 2009.

Conrath, Robert. "The Guys Who Shoot to Thrill: Serial Killers and the American Popular Culture." *Revue Française d'études Américaines* 60 (May 1994): 143–52. Print.

Cooley, Mason. *City Aphorisms: Fifth Selection*. New York: Pascal P, 1996. Print.

Cooper, James Fenimore. *Notions of the Americans: Picked Up by a Travelling Bachelor*. Vol. II. New York: Frederick Ungar, 1963. Print.

———. *The Pioneers*. New York: Viking Penguin, 1988. Print.

Cooper, Katherine, and Emma Short, eds. *The Female Figure in Contemporary Historical Fiction*. Basingstoke: Palgrave Macmillan, 2012. Print.

Cowart, David. *History and the Contemporary Novel*. Carbondale: Southern Illinois UP, 1989. Print.

Crèvecoeur, J. Hector St. John de. *Letters from an American Farmer*. 1782. New York: Dutton, 1957. Print.

Crisler, Jesse S. "Alcott's Reading in *Little Women*: Shaping the Autobiographical Self." *Resources for American Literary Study* 20.1 (1994): 27–36. Print.

"The Critics: Briefly Noted." *The New Yorker*. 31 Mar. 2003. Print.

Crittenden, Yvonne. "More Than Just Buffalo Wings." *The Toronto Sun*. 29 Aug. 1999. Print.

Croft, Barbara. "Power Politics." *Women's Review of Books* 16.10/11 (July 1999): 40. Print.

Cuddon, J. A. *Literary Terms and Literary Theory*. London: Penguin, 1999. Print.

Cullick, Jonathan S. *Making History: The Biographical Narratives of Robert Penn Warren*. Baton Rouge: Louisiana State UP, 2000. Print.

Cunningham, Michael. *Specimen Days*. New York: Farrar, Straus and Giroux, 2005. Print.

Dandridge, Rita B. *Black Women's Activism: Reading African American Women's Historical Romances*. New York: Peter Lang, 2004. Print.

Danforth, Samuel. "A Brief Recognition of New-Englands Errand into the Wilderness (1670)." *Libraries at U of Nebraska-Lincoln*. Web. 13 May 2009.

Dannenberg, Hilary. *Coincidence and Counterfactuality: Plotting Time and Space in Narrative Fiction*. Lincoln: U of Nebraska P, 2008. Print.

Däwes, Birgit. "'The Obliging Imagination Set Free': Repräsentation der Krise/Krise der Repräsentation in der U.S.-amerikanischen 9/11 novel." *Nine Eleven – Ästhetische Verarbeitungen des 11. September 2001*. Ed. Ingo Irsigler and Christoph Jürgensen. Heidelberg: Winter, 2008. 67–87. Print.

D'Cruz, Glenn. "Representing the Serial Killer: 'Postmodern' Pedagogy in Performance Studies." *Southern Review* 27.3 (Sept. 1994): 323–32. Print.

Debord, Guy. *Society of the Spectacle*. Trans. Ken Knabb. London: Rebel P, 2006. Print.

Decker, Mark. "Mormon Pulp with a Reading Group Guide." *Dialogue: A Journal of Mormon Thought* 43.2 (2010): 201–05. Web. 10 Feb. 2020.

DeJong, Mary. "Poe & Fanny: A Novel by John May." *The Edgar Allen Poe Review* 6.1 (2005): 60–63. Web. 12 Feb. 2020.

Dekker, George. *James Fenimore Cooper, the American Scott*. New York: Barnes and Noble, 1967. Print.

——. *The American Historical Romance*. New York: CUP, 1987. Print.

Dening, Penelope. "Dark Deeds in the City of Light." *The Irish Times*. 19 June 1999. Print.

Derburg, William Van. *Slavery and Race in American Popular Culture*. Madison: U of Wisconsin P, 1984. Print.

"Diane Glancy: Stone Heart." *Amazon.com*. Product Description. Web. 24 Nov. 2008.

Dimock, Wai Chee. *Through Other Continents: American Literature across Deep Time*. Princeton: Princeton UP, 2006. Print.

Dobson, Joanne. *The Raven and the Nightingale*. New York: Bantam, 1999. Print.

Doctorow, E. L. "False Documents." *E. L. Doctorow: Essays and Conversations*. Ed. Richard Trenner. Princeton: Ontario Review, 1983. 16–27. Print.

Domhnall, Mitchell. "Acts of Intercourse: 'Miscegenation' in Three 19th Century American Novels." *American Studies in Scandinavia* 27 (1995): 126–41. Print.

Donovan, Josephine. *New England Local Color Literature: A Women's Tradition*. New York: Frederick Ungar, 1983. Print.

———. "The Unpublished Love Poems of Sarah Orne Jewett." *Critical Essays on Sarah Orne Jewett*. Ed. Gwen L. Nagel. Boston: Hall, 1984. 107–17. Print.

Dos Passos, John. *The Ground We Stand On: Some Examples from the History of a Political Creed*. New York: Harcourt, Brace & Company, 1941. Print.

Downing, Sybil. "Speculating on Sacagawea's Thoughts." *The Denver Post*. 9 Mar. 2003. Print.

Duggan, Robert. "Ghosts of Gotham: 9/11 Mourning in Patrick McGrath's *Ghost Town* and Michael Cunningham's *Specimen Days*." *Journal of Postcolonial Writing* 46.3–4 (July 2010): 381–93. Web. 10 Feb. 2020.

Durczak, Joanna. "Two Tales of Two Hesters: Christopher Bigsby's *Hester* and Nathaniel Hawthorne's *The Scarlet Letter*." *American Studies: America's Cultural Crossroads*. Ed. Marta Wiszniowska. Torun: Wydawnictwo Uniwesytetu Mikolaja Kopernika, 1996. 109–25. Print.

Dyer, Richard. "Kill and Kill Again." *Sight and Sound* 9 (1997): 14–17. Print.

Eaton, Erna P. "A Day to Call Her Own." *The Buffalo News*. 26 Oct. 1999. Print.

Ebershoff, David. *The 19th Wife*. London: Doubleday, 2008. Print.

"Ebony Bookshelf." *Ebony*. Oct. 2001. Print.

Eco, Umberto. *Six Walks in the Fictional Woods*. Cambridge: Harvard UP, 1994. Print.

Elias, Amy J. "Metahistorical Romance, the Historical Sublime, and Dialogic History." *Rethinking History* 9.2/3 (2005): 159–72. Print.

———. *Sublime Desire: History and Post-1960s Fiction*. Baltimore: Johns Hopkins UP, 2001. Print.

Elliott, Emory. "Cultural Memory and the American Novel." *Literature, Literary History, and Cultural Memory*. Ed. Herbert Grabes. Tübingen: Gunter Narr, 2005. 225–37. Print. REAL: Yearbook of Research in English and American Literature 21.

Emerson, Ralph Waldo. *The Collected Works of Ralph Waldo Emerson*. Vol. I-IV. Ed. Alfred R. Ferguson, Jean Ferguson Carr, and Joseph Slater. Cambridge: Harvard UP, 1979. Print.

Engler, Bernd. "The Dismemberment of Clio: Fictionality, Narrativity, and the Construction of Historical Reality in Historiographic Metafiction." *Historiographic Metafiction in Modern American and Canadian Literature*. Ed. Bernd Engler and Kurt Müller. Paderborn: Schöningh, 1994. 13–33. Print.

Engler, Bernd, and Kurt Müller. "Preface." *Historiographic Metafiction in Modern American and Canadian Literature*. Ed. Bernd Engler and Kurt Müller. Paderborn: Schöningh, 1994. 9–12. Print.

Engler, Bernd, and Oliver Scheiding. "Re-Visioning the Past: The Historical Imagination in American Historiography and Short Fiction."

Re-Visioning the Past: Historical Self-Reflexivity in American Short Fiction. Ed. Bernd Engler and Oliver Scheiding. Trier: WVT, 1998. 11–37. Print. Mosaic – Studien und Texte zur amerikanischen Kultur und Geschichte 3.

Englund, Sheryl A. "Reading the Author in *Little Women*: A Biography of a Book." *American Transcendental Quarterly* 12.3 (1998): 199–219. Print.

Entzminger, Betina. *Contemporary Refigurations of American Literary Classics: The Origin and Evolution of American Stories.* London: Routledge, 2013. Print.

Erll, Astrid. "Gedächtniskonzepte in der Literaturwissenschaft." *Metzler Lexikon Literatur- und Kulturtheorie: Ansätze – Personen – Grundbegriffe.* Ed. Ansgar Nünning. Stuttgart: Metzler, 2004. 219–20. Print.

———. "Literatur als Medium des kollektiven Gedächtnisses." *Gedächtniskonzepte der Literaturwissenschaft: Theoretische Grundlegung und Anwendungsperspektiven.* Ed. Astrid Erll and Ansgar Nünning. Berlin: de Gruyter, 2005. 249–76. Print.

———. *Memory in Culture.* Trans. Sara B. Young. Basingstoke: Palgrave Macmillan, 2011. Print.

Erll, Astrid, and Ansgar Nünning. "Literaturwissenschaftliche Konzepte von Gedächtnis: ein einführender Überblick." *Gedächtniskonzepte der Literaturwissenschaft: Theoretische Grundlegung und Anwendungsperspektiven.* Ed. Astrid Erll and Ansgar Nünning. Berlin: de Gruyter, 2005. 1–9. Print.

Erll, Astrid, and Klaudia Seidel. "Gattungen, Formtraditionen und kulturelles Gedächtnis." *Erzähltextanalyse und Gender Studies.* Ed. Ansgar and Vera Nünning. Stuttgart: Metzler, 2004. 180–208. Print.

Evans, Alice. "Within the Legend of Sacajawea: Novel Finds a Genuine Heroine With Heart." *The Sunday Oregonian.* 23 Mar. 2003. Print.

Faderman, Lillian. "Boston Marriage." *Surpassing the Love of Men: Romantic Friendship and Love between Women from the Renaissance to the Present.* New York: William Morrow, 1981. 190–203. Print.

Fay, Brian. "Unconventional History." *History and Theory* 41.4 (Dec. 2002): 1–6. Print.

Fay, Jeanne. "A Scandal Riding on Niagara Falls." *The San Francisco Chronicle.* 18 July 1999. Print.

Feldman, Ellen. "Out of Darkness." *The New York Times.* 16 May 1999. Print.

Fetterley, Judith. "Little Women: Alcott's Civil War." *Feminist Studies* 5.2 (1979): 369–83. Print.

———. "Reading Deephaven as a Lesbian Text." *Sexual Practice, Textual Theory: Lesbian Cultural Criticism.* Ed. Susan J. Wolfe and Julia Penelope. Cambridge: Blackwell, 1993. 164–83. Print.

———. *The Resisting Reader: A Feminist Approach to American Fiction.* Bloomington: Indiana UP, 1978. Print.

Fetterley, Judith, and Marjorie Pryse. "Sarah Orne Jewett 1849–1909." *American Women Regionalists 1850–1910: A Norton Anthology.* Ed. Judith Fetterley and Marjorie Pryse. New York: Norton, 1992. 185–87. Print.

Feuchtwanger, Lion. *The House of Desdemona: or, The Laurels and Limitations of Historical Fiction.* Trans. Harold A. Basilius. Detroit: Wayne State UP, 1963. Print.

Fiedler, Leslie A. "Cross the Border – Close the Gap." *Cross the Border – Close the Gap*. New York: Stein and Day, 1972. 61–85. Print.

Fierman, Daniel. "Review: Larson's White City Dazzling." *Entertainment Weekly*. 24 Feb. 2003. Print.

Fish, Stanley. "One University Under God?" *The Chronicle of Higher Education*. Web. 6 Feb. 2008.

Fleishman, Avrom. *The English Historical Novel: Walter Scott to Virginia Woolf*. Baltimore: Johns Hopkins UP, 1971. Print.

Flis, Leonora. *Factual Fictions: Narrative Truth and the Contemporary American Documentary Novel*. Newcastle: Cambridge Scholars, 2010. Print.

Fluck, Winfried. *Das kulturelle Imaginäre: Eine Funktionsgeschichte des amerikanischen Romans 1790-1900*. Frankfurt: Suhrkamp, 1997. Print.

———. "Surface Knowledge and 'Deep' Knowledge: The New Realism in American Fiction." *Neo-Realism in Contemporary American Fiction*. Ed. Kristiaan Versluys. Amsterdam: Rodopi, 1992. 65–85. Print.

———. "The Activist and the Actor: The Re-Authorization of Historical Criticism in New Historicism." *Romance with America? Essays on Culture, Literature, and American Studies*. Ed. Laura Bieger and Johannes Voelz. Heidelberg: Winter, 2009. 39–48. Print.

———. "The American Romance and the Changing Functions of the Imaginary." *Romance with America? Essays on Culture, Literature, and American Studies*. Ed. Laura Bieger and Johannes Voelz. Heidelberg: Winter, 2009. 139–77. Print.

Föcking, Marc. "Serienmörder und Verschwörungstheorien: Warum Dante-Krimis so populär sind." *Italienisch: Zeitschrift für italiensiche Sprache und Literatur* 74.2 (2015): 13–30. Print.

Fokkema, Aleid. "The Author: Postmodernism's Stock Character." *The Author as Character: Representing Historical Writers in Western Literature*. Ed. Paul Franssen and Ton Hoenselaars. Madison: Fairleigh Dickinson UP, 1999. 39–51. Print.

"Forecasts: Fiction." *Publishers Weekly* 246.14 (5 Apr. 1999): 218. Print.

Foucault, Michel. *The Archaeology of Knowledge*. London: Routledge, 2002. Print.

Franken, Christien. "The Gender of Mourning: A. S. Byatt's 'The Conjugial Angel' and Alfred Lord Tennyson's 'In Memoriam.'" *The Author as Character: Representing Historical Writers in Western Literature*. Ed. Paul Franssen and A. J. Hoenselaars. Madison: Fairleigh Dickinson UP, 1999. 243–52. Print.

Franssen, Paul, and Ton Hoenselaars. "The Author as Character: Defining a Genre." *The Author as Character: Representing Historical Writers in Western Literature*. Ed. Paul Franssen and Ton Hoenselaars. Madison: Fairleigh Dickinson UP, 1999. 11–38. Print.

Free, Rosemary. "Buffalo Gal's History Lessons." *The Herald*. 15 July 1999. Print.

Freeman, Charles, and Lauren Bufferd. "Solving a Mormon Murder Mystery." *Book Page*. Web. 23 Apr. 2009.

Freeman, Judith. "Book Review: *The 19th Wife*. A Novel." *Los Angeles Times*. 10 Aug. 2008. Print.

Freese, Peter. "Doctorow's 'Criminals of Perception', or, What Has Happened to the Historical Novel." *Reconstructing American Literary and Historical Studies*. Ed. Günter H. Lenz, Hartmut Keil, and Sabine Bröck-Sallah. Frankfurt: Campus/New York: St. Martin's, 1990. 345–71. Print.

———. *The American Short Story I: Initiation*. Teacher's Book. Paderborn: Schönigh, 1986. Print.

Freud, Sigmund. *The Letters of Sigmund Freud to Arnold Zweig*. Ed. Ernest L. Freud. New York: Harcourt Brace World, 1970. Print.

Friedrich, Hans-Edwin. "Die Wiederkehr des historischen Romans seit den 1980er Jahren." *Der historische Roman: Erkundung einer populären Gattung*. Ed. Hans Edwin Friedrich. Frankfurt: Peter Lang, 2013. 1–13. Print.

Fryer, Judith. "What Goes on in the Ladies Room? Sarah Orne Jewett, Annie Fields, and Their Community of Women." *Massachusetts Review* 30 (1989): 610–28. Print.

Fuchs, Dieter, and Wojciech Klepuszewski, eds. *The Campus Novel: Regional or Global?* Boston: Brill Rodopi, 2019. Print.

Fukuyama, Francis. *The End of History and the Last Man*. New York: Free P, 1992. Print.

Gamble, Sarah. "Angela Carter's *American Ghosts and Old World Wonders*." *Metafiction and Metahistory in Contemporary Women's Writing*. Ed. Ann Heilmann and Mark Llewellyn. Basingstoke: Palgrave Macmillan, 2007. Print. 30–44.

Ganner, Heidi. "Intertextuality and Paradigm Shifts in Valerie Martin's *Mary Reilly*, Emma Tennant's *Two Women of London: The Strange Case of Ms. Jekyll and Mrs. Hyde*, and Robert Swindells' *Jacqueline Hyde*." *The Self at Risk in English Literatures and Other Landscapes: Honoring Brigitte Seer-Schäzler on the Occasion of the 60th Birthday*. Ed. Gudrun M. Grabher and Sonja Bahn-Coblans. Innsbruck: Inst. für Sprachwiss., 1999. 193–202. Print. Innsbrucker Beiträge zur Kulturwissenschaft 29.

Ganner-Rauth, Heidi. "To be Continued? Sequels and Continuations of Nineteenth-Century Novels and Novel Fragments." *English Studies: A Journal of English Language and Literature* 64.2 (1983): 129–43. Print.

Garber, Marjorie. "The Chapter After 'The End.'" *The New York Times*. 8 Apr. 2001. Print.

Garner, Dwight. "The Salon Interview, Caleb Carr." *Salon* (4 Oct. 1997): 2. Web. 12 Mar. 2020.

Gaudenzi, Cosetta. "Dante's Introduction to the United States as Investigated in Matthew Pearl's *The Dante Club*." *Italian Culture* 26 (2008): 85–103. Print.

Gelder, Ken. "Introduction to Part Three: Monstrosities." *The Horror Reader*. Ed. Ken Gelder. New York: Routledge, 2000. 81–83. Print.

Genette, Gérard. *Narrative Discourse: An Essay in Method*. Trans. J. F. Lewin. Ithaca: Cornell UP, 1980. Print.

———. *Palimpsests: Literature in the Second Degree*. Lincoln: U of Nebraska P, 1997. Print.

———. *Paratexts: Thresholds of Interpretation*. Cambridge: CUP, 1997. Print.

Georgi-Findlay, Brigitte. "Concepts of History in Contemporary Native American Fiction." *Minority Literatures in North America: Contemporary Perspectives*. Ed. Wolfgang Karrer and Hartmut Lutz. Frankfurt: Lang, 1990. 159–74. Print.

Gilbert, Sandra M., and Susan Gubar. *The Madwoman in the Attic: The Woman Writer and the Nineteenth-Century Literary Imagination.* New Haven: Yale UP, 1984. Print.

Giles, Paul. *Transatlantic Insurrections: British Culture and the Formation of American Literature, 1730–1860.* Philadelphia: U of Pennsylvania P, 2001. Print.

Gilmour, Robin. "Using the Victorians: the Victorian Age in Contemporary Fiction." *Rereading Victorian Fiction.* Ed. Juliet John and Alice Jenkins. Basingstoke: Palgrave, 2002. 189–200. Print.

Glancy, Diane. *Stone Heart: A Novel of Sacajawea.* Woodstock: Overlook, 2003. Print.

Glazener, Nancy. *Literature in the Making: A History of U.S. Literary Culture in the Long Nineteenth Century.* Oxford: OUP, 2016. Print. Oxford Studies in American Literary History.

Glover, David, and Cora Kaplan. *Genders.* London: Routledge, 2000. Print.

Gómez-Galisteo, M. Carmen. *The Wind Is Never Gone: Sequels, Parodies And Rewritings of* Gone With The Wind. Jefferson: McFarland, 2011. Print.

Gonshak, Henry. "The Child is Father to the Man: The Psychopathology of Serial Killing in Caleb Carr's *The Alienist.*" *Notes on Contemporary Literature* 15.1 (1995): 12–13. Print.

Goodman, Nelson. *Ways of Worldmaking.* Indianapolis: Hackett, 1978. Print.

Gordon, Linda. "What's New in Women's History?" *Feminist Studies/Critical Studies.* Ed. Teresa deLauretis. London: Macmillan, 1986. 20–30. Print.

Gorp, Hendrik van, and Ulla Musarra-Schroeder. "Introduction: Literary Genres and Cultural Memory." *Genres as Repositories of Cultural Memory.* Ed. Hendrik van Gorp and Ulla Musarra-Schroeder. Amsterdam: Rodopi, 2000. i–ix. Print.

Gould, Philip. *Covenant and Republic: Historical Romance and the Politics of Puritanism.* Cambridge: CUP, 1996. Print.

Grabbe, Hans-Jürgen. "Geschichtslosigkeit." *Lexikon der populären Amerikabilder.* Ed. Werner Kemp and Wolfgang Tönnesmann. Trier: WVT, 2008. 40–45. Print.

Grabes, Herbert. *Erfundene Biographien: Vladimir Nabokovs englische Romane.* Tübingen: Niemeyer, 1975. Print.

Grabes, Herbert, and Margit Sichert. "Literaturgeschichte, Kanon und nationale Identität." *Gedächtniskonzepte der Literaturwissenschaft: Theoretische Grundlegung und Anwendungsperspektiven.* Ed. Astrid Erll and Ansgar Nünning. Berlin: de Gruyter, 2005. 297–314. Print.

Gray, Stephanie. "Sacagawea: A Fascination with Story Gaps." *Heritage of the Great Plains* 41.2 (2009): 18–37. Web. 18 Feb. 2020.

Gray, William. "First Novel Generates Plenty of Electricity in Buffalo, NY." *Tampa Tribune.* 6 June 1999. Print.

Green, Michael. *Novel Histories: Past, Present, and Future in South African Fiction.* Johannesburg: Witwatersrand UP, 1997. Print.

Greenblatt, Stephen. *The Power of Forms in the English Renaissance.* Norman: Pilgrim Books, 1982. Print.

———. "The Touch of the Real." *Practicing New Historicism.* Ed. Catherine Gallagher and Stephen Greenblatt. Chicago: U of Chicago P, 2000. 20–48 Print.

Groot, Jerome de. *Consuming History: Historians and Heritage in Contemporary Popular Culture*. London: Routledge, 2009. Print.

———. *Remaking History: The Past in Contemporary Historical Fictions*. London: Routledge, 2016. Print.

———. *The Historical Novel*. London: Routledge, 2010. Print. The New Critical Idiom.

Gros, Emmeline. "*The Wind Done Gone* or Rewriting Gone Wrong: Retelling Southern Social, Racial, and Gender Norms through Parody." *South Atlantic Review* 80.3–4 (2015): 136–60. Web. 17 Feb. 2020.

Grossman, Lev. "The Trouble with Memoirs – An Author is Accused of Making up Key Parts of his Best-selling Life Story: Does Truth Really Matter?" *Time Magazine*. 23 Jan. 2006. Print.

Gutleben, Christian. *Nostalgic Postmodernism: The Victorian Tradition and the Contemporary British Novel*. Amsterdam: Rodopi, 2001. Print.

Gutleben, Christian, and Susana Onega. "Introduction." *Refracting the Canon in Contemporary British Literature and Film*. Ed. Christian Gutleben and Susana Onega. Amsterdam: Rodopi, 2004. 7–15. Print.

Haase, Felix, and Stefanie Schäfer. "Revisioning and Rewriting American History in Geraldine Brooks' *March* (2005), James McBride's *The Good Lord Bird* (2013), and E. L. Doctorow's *The March. A Novel* (2005)." *The American Novel in the 21st Century: Cultural Contexts – Literary Developments – Critical Analyses*. Ed. Michael Basseler and Ansgar Nünning. Trier: WVT, 2019. 87–100. Print.

Habich, John. "Talking Volumes: On the Trail of Sacajawea." *Star Tribune*. 16 Mar. 2003. Print.

Haddox, Thomas F. "Alice Randall's *The Wind Done Gone* and the Ludic in African American Historical Fiction." *MFS: Modern Fiction Studies* 53.1 (2007): 120–39. Web. 17 Feb. 2020.

Hanrahan, Phil. "*City of Light* is Aglow with History: Suspense." *Milwaukee Journal Sentinel*. 23 May 1999. Print.

Harlan, David. "Historical Fiction and the Future of Academic History." *Manifestos for History*. Ed. Keith Jenkins, Sue Morgan, and Alun Munslow. New York: Routledge, 2007. 108–30. Print.

Harper, Graeme. "Interview with Chris Bigsby." *New Writing: The International Journal for the Practice and Theory of Creative Writing* 9.3 (2012): 419–25. Web. 14 Feb. 2020.

Hassan, Ihab. "Beyond Postmodernism: Toward an Aesthetic of Trust." *Beyond Postmodernism: Reassessments in Literature, Theory, and Culture*. Ed. Klaus Stierstorfer. Berlin: de Gruyter, 2003. 199–212. Print.

———. *The Postmodernist Turn: Essays in Postmodern Theory and Culture*. Columbus: Ohio State UP, 1987. Print.

Haven, Tom de. "Book Review: *The Great Divorce*." *Entertainment Weekly*. 8 Apr. 1994. Print.

Hawthorne, Nathaniel. *The House of the Seven Gables*. New York: Penguin, 1986. Print.

———. *The Scarlet Letter*. A Norton Critical Edition. Ed. Seymour Gross et al. New York: W. W. Norton, 1988. Print.

Hebel, Udo J. "'A Proper Recollection of These Things': New England Forefathers' Day Orations 1769–1820 and the National Consecration of a

Colonial Past." *Remembering the Individual/Regional/National Past.* Ed. Waldemar Zacharasiewicz. Tübingen: Stauffenburg, 1999. 31–58. Print.

Heilmann, Ann, and Mark Llewellyn. "Introduction." *Metafiction and Metahistory in Contemporary Women's Writing.* Ed. Ann Heilmann and Mark Llewellyn. Basingstoke: Palgrave Macmillan, 2007. 1–12. Print.

Heise, Ursula K. *Chronoschisms: Time, Narrative, and Postmodernism.* Cambridge: CUP, 1997. Print.

Hellekson, Karen Lee. *Refiguring Historical Time: The Alternate History.* Kent: Kent State UP, 2001. Print.

Hewison, Robert. *The Heritage Industry: Britain in a Climate of Decline.* London: Methuen, 1987. Print.

Hewitt, Martin. "Why the Notion of Victorian Britain Does Make Sense." *Victorian Studies* 48.3 (Spring 2006): 395–438. Print.

Higgins, Geraldine. "Tara, the O'Haras, and the Irish Gone With the Wind." *Southern Cultures* 17.1 (Spring 2011): 30–49. Print.

Himmelfarb, Gertrude. *One Nation, Two Cultures.* New York: Knopf, 1999. Print.

"Hoarding the Wind." *The Boston Globe.* 13 Apr. 2001. Print.

Hoberman, Ruth. "Biography: General Survey." *Encyclopedia of Life Writing: Autobiographical and Biographical Forms.* Vol. 1. Ed. Margaretta Jolly. London: Fitzroy Dearborn, 2001. 109–12. Print.

Hobsbawm, Eric. "Introduction: Inventing Traditions." *The Invention of Tradition.* Ed. Eric Hobsbawm and Terence Ranger. Cambridge: CUP, 1983. 1–14. Print.

Hochbruck, Wolfgang. "Metafictional Biography: Michael Ondaatje's *Coming Through Slaughter* and *The Collected Works of Billy the Kid.*" *Historiographic Metafiction in Modern American and Canadian Literature.* Ed. Bernd Engler and Kurt Müller. Paderborn: Schöningh, 1994. 447–63. Print.

Hockensmith, Steven. "Evermore: The Enduring Influence of Edgar Allan Poe." *Mystery Scene* 99 (2007): 14–18. Print.

Hodgkin, Katharine. "The Witch, the Puritan and the Prophet: Historical Novels and Seventeenth-Century History." *Metafiction and Metahistory in Contemporary Women's Writing.* Ed. Ann Heilmann and Mark Llewellyn. Basingstoke: Palgrave Macmillan, 2007. 15–29. Print.

Hoffert, Barbara, and Ann Burns. "Writing That Counts: Spring Successes." *Library Journal* 124.16 (1 Oct. 1999): 49–52. Print.

Hoffman, John, and Paul Graham. *Introduction to Political Theory.* Harlow: Pearson Education, 2006. Print.

Hoffmann, Gerhard. "Historical Consciousness, Aesthetics, and the Experimental Southern Novel." *Rewriting the South: History and Fiction.* Ed. Lothar Hönnighausen and Valeria Gennaro Lerda. Tübingen: Francke, 1993. 397–424. Print.

Hohendahl, Peter Uwe. "Nach der Ideologiekritik: Überlegungen zu geschichtlicher Darstellung." *Geschichte als Literatur: Formen und Grenzen der Repräsentation von Vergangenheit.* Ed. Hartmut Eggert, Ulrich Profitlich, and Klaus R. Scherpe. Stuttgart: Metzler, 1990. 77–90. Print.

Hollenberg, Donna Krolik. "An Interview with Carol Shields." *Contemporary Literature* 39.3 (1998): 338–55. Print.

Holton, Robert. *Jarring Witnesses: Modern Fiction and the Representation of History*. New York: Harvester Wheatsheaf, 1994. Print.

Homans, John. "Fair and Foul." *New York Magazine*. 17 Feb. 2003. Print.

Hornung, Alfred. "Postmodern – post mortem: Death and the Death of the Novel." *Neo-Realism in Contemporary American Fiction*. Ed. Kristiaan Versluys. Amsterdam: Rodopi, 1992. 87–109. Print.

Horsley, Lee. *Twentieth-Century Crime Fiction*. Oxford: OUP, 2005. Print.

Houston, Robert. "Disintegrated Lives." *The New York Times*. 13 Mar. 1994. Web. 17 Feb. 2009.

Howe, Daniel Walker. "Victorian Culture in America." *Victorian America*. Ed. Daniel Walker Howe. Philadelphia: U of Pennsylvania P, 1976. 3–28. Print.

Howe, Irving. "The Idea of the Modern." *The Idea of the Modern in Literature and the Arts*. Ed. Irving Howe. New York: Horizon, 1967. 11–42. Print.

Hughes, Kathleen. "Review of Christopher Bigsby: *Hester*." *Booklist*, qtd. on *Amazon.com*. Web. 2 Apr. 2009.

Hulbert, Matthew Christopher, and John C. Inscoe, eds. *Writing History with Lightning: Cinematic Representations of Nineteenth-Century America*. Baton Rouge: Louisiana State UP, 2019. Print.

Humphrey, Richard. "Literarische Gattung und Gedächtnis." *Gedächtniskonzepte der Literaturwissenschaft: Theoretische Grundlegung und Anwendungsperspektiven*. Ed. Astrid Erll and Ansgar Nünning. Berlin: de Gruyter, 2005. 73–96. Print.

Hutcheon, Linda. *A Poetics in Postmodernism: History, Theory, Fiction*. New York: Routledge, 1988. Print.

———. *A Theory of Adaptation*. London: Routledge, 2006. Print.

———. *The Canadian Postmodern: A Study of Contemporary English-Canadian Fiction*. Toronto: OUP, 1988. Print.

———. *The Politics of Postmodernism*. London: Routledge, 1989. Print.

———. "'The Pastime of Past Time:' Fiction, History, Historiographic Metafiction." *Genre* 20.3–4 (1987): 285–305. Print.

Huyssen, Andreas. *Twilight Memories: Marking Time in a Culture of Amnesia*. New York: Routledge, 1995. Print.

Ickstadt, Heinz. *Der amerikanische Roman im 20. Jahrhundert: Transformation des Mimetischen*. Darmstadt: Wiss. Buchgesellschaft, 1998. Print.

Irving, Washington. "English Writers on America." *The Legend of Sleepy Hollow and Other Stories*. New York: Penguin, 1999. 43–49. Print.

Iser, Wolfgang. *Das Fiktive und das Imaginäre: Perspektiven literarischer Anthropologie*. Frankfurt: Suhrkamp, 1993. Print.

Jacobs, Naomi. "Michael Ondaatje and the New Fiction Biographies." *Studies in Canadian Literature* 11.2 (1986): 2–18. Print.

James, Caryn. "Now Starring, Killers for the Chiller 90's." *The New York Times*. 10 Mar. 1991. Print.

Jameson, Fredric. *Postmodernism, or, the Cultural Logic of Late Capitalism*. Durham: Duke UP, 1991. Print.

———. "The Historical Novel Today, or, Is It Still Possible?" *The Antinomies of Realism*. London: Verso, 2015. 259–313. Print.

Jarrett, Gene Andrew. "Law, Parody, and the Politics of African American Literary History." *Novel: A Forum on Fiction* 42.3 (2009): 437–42. Web. 17 Feb. 2020.

Jefferson, Margo. "Revisions: To the Barricades for an Idea: Then, Now, and Always." *The New York Times*. 3 Apr. 2000. Print.

Jenkins, Philip. *Using Murder: The Social Construction of Serial Homicide*. New York: de Gruyter, 1994. Print.

John, Juliet, and Alice Jenkins. "Introduction." *Rereading Victorian Fiction*. Ed. Juliet John and Alice Jenkins. Basingstoke: Palgrave, 2002. 1–12. Print.

Johnson, Sarah L. *Historical Fiction: A Guide to the Genre*. Westport: Libraries Unlimited, 2005. Print.

———. "What Are the Rules for Historical Fiction?". MS of a lecture given at the Associated Writing Programs Annual Conference 2002. *Historical Novel Society*. Web. 19 May 2009.

Johnston, Andrew J., and Kai Wiegandt. "Introduction." *The Return of the Historical Novel? Thinking About Fiction and History After Historiographic Metafiction*. Ed. Andrew J. Johnston and Kai Wiegandt. Heidelberg: Winter, 2017. 9–18. Print.

Jong, Mary G. de. "Lines from a Partly Published Drama: The Romance of Frances Sargent Osgood and Edgar Allan Poe." *Patrons and Protégées: Gender, Friendship, and Writing in Nineteenth-Century America*. Ed. Shirley Marchalonis. New Brunswick: Rutgers UP, 1988. 31–58. Print.

Jordan, Margaret I. *African American Servitude and Historical Imaginings: Retrospective Fiction and Representation*. New York: Palgrave Macmillan, 2004. Print.

Joyce, Simon. *The Victorians in the Rearview Mirror*. Athens: Ohio UP, 2007. Print.

Justice, Daniel Heath. *Our Fire Survives the Storm: A Cherokee Literary History*. Minneapolis: U of Minnesota P, 2006. Print.

Kakutani, Michiko. "A Captive Black Leopard from Three Perspectives." *The New York Times*. 18 Feb. 1994. Print.

———. "How Hester Prynne Got That Tell-Tale Letter." *The New York Times*. 21 Oct. 1994. Print.

———. "Within Its Genre: A Takeoff on Tara Gropes for a Place." *The New York Times*. 5 May 2001. Print.

Kaplan, Cora. *Victoriana: Histories, Fictions, Criticism*. Edinburgh: U of Edinburgh P, 2007. Print.

Karcher, Carolyn L. "Introduction." *Hobomok and Other Writings*. Lydia Maria Child. Ed. Carolyn L. Karcher. New Brunswick: Rutgers UP, 1986. ix–xiv. Print.

Katz, Tamar. "City Memory, City History: Urban Nostalgia, *The Colossus of New York*, and Late-Twentieth-Century Historical Fiction." *Contemporary Literature* 51.4 (2010): 810–51. Web. 13 Feb. 2020.

Katzenbach, John. "Ragtime Ripper." *The Washington Post*. 27 Mar. 1994. Print.

Keegan, Rebecca Winters. "O.K., Now He's in a Million Little Pieces." *Time Magazine*. 6 Feb. 2006. Print.

Keen, Suzanne. *Romances of the Archive in Contemporary British Fiction*. Toronto: U of Toronto P, 2001. Print.

Keener, John F. *Biography and the Postmodern Novel*. Lewiston: Edwin Mellem, 2001. Print.

Keizer, Arlene R. *Black Subjects: Identity Formation in the Contemporary Narrative of Slavery*. Ithaca: Cornell UP, 2004. Print.

Kich, Martin. "American Murder: The Cultural Meanings of Mayhem: Citation Lists of Books and Films on Outlaws, Mobsters, and Serial Killers." *Wright State U*. Web. 9 Nov. 2007.

King, Jeannette. *The Victorian Woman Question in Contemporary Feminist Fiction*. Houndmills: Palgrave Macmillan, 2005. Print.

Kirchknopf, Andrea. "(Re)Workings of Nineteenth-Century Fiction: Definitions, Terminology, Contexts." *Neo-Victorian Studies* 1.1 (Autumn 2008): 53–80. Web. 6 Nov. 2008.

Kirkpatrick, David D. "Court Asked to *Stop Gone With the Wind* Rewrite." *The New York Times*. 28 Mar. 2001. Print.

———. "Court Halts Book Based on *Gone With the Wind*." *The New York Times*. 21 Apr. 2001. Print.

Kirmayer, Laurence J. "Landscapes of Memory: Trauma, Narrative and Dissociation." *Tense Past: Cultural Essays on Memory and Trauma*. Ed. Paul Antze and Michael Lambek. London: Routledge, 1996. 173–98. Print.

Kirwan, Kate. "Contemporary Responses to the Traditional American Historical Novel." *Narrative is the Essence of History: Essays on the Historical Novel*. Ed. John Cameron. Newcastle upon Tyne: Cambridge Scholars Pub., 2012. 127–38. Print.

Klein, Julia M. "Giving New Life to Classic Characters." *Los Angeles Times*. 18 Mar. 2007. Print.

Köhler, Angelika. *Ambivalent Desires: The New Woman Between Social Modernization and Modern Writing*. Heidelberg: Winter, 2004. Print.

Kohlke, Marie-Luise. "Introduction: Speculations in and on the Neo-Victorian Encounter." *Neo-Victorian Studies* 1.1 (Autumn 2008): 1–18. Web. 6 Nov. 2008.

Kohlke, Marie-Luise, and Christian Gutleben. "Introduction: Bearing After-Witness to the Nineteenth Century." *Neo-Victorian Tropes of Trauma: The Politics of Bearing After-Witness to Nineteenth-Century Suffering*. Ed. Marie-Luise Kohlke and Christian Gutleben. Amsterdam: Rodopi, 2010. 1–34. Print.

Koselleck, Reinhart. "Geschichte, Historie." *Geschichtliche Grundbegriffe: Lexikon zur politisch-sozialen Sprache in Deutschland*. Vol. 2. Ed. Otto Brunner, Werner Conze, and Reinhart Koselleck. Stuttgart: Klett, 1975. 593–717. Print.

Kretschmann, Tabea. "Editorial: 'Dante-Boom' im Kriminalroman." *Italienisch: Zeitschrift für italienische Sprache und Literatur* 74.2 (2015): 1. Print.

Kreyling, Michael. "Mourning, Mockery, and the Post-South in Lars von Trier's *Manderlay* and Geraldine Brooks's *March*." *The Oxford Handbook of the Literature of the U. S. South*. Ed. Fred C. Hobson and Barbara Ladd. Oxford: OUP, 2016. Web. 16 Mar. 2020.

Kristeva, Julia. "The Bounded Text." *Desire in Language: A Semiotic Approach to Literature and Art*. Ed. Leon S. Roudiez, Trans. Thomas Gora, Alice Jardine, and Leon S. Roudiez. New York: Columbia UP, 1980. 36–63. Print.

———. "Word, Dialogue, and Novel." *The Kristeva Reader*. Ed. Toril Moi. New York: Columbia UP, 1986. 35–61. Print.

Krueger, Christine L. "Introduction." *Functions of Victorian Culture at the Present Time*. Ed. Christine L. Krueger. Athens: Ohio UP, 2002. xi–xx. Print.

Kucich, John, and Dianne F. Sadoff. "Introduction: Histories of the Present." *Victorian Afterlife: Postmodern Culture Rewrites the Nineteenth Century*. Ed.

John Kucich and Dianne F. Sadoff. Minneapolis: U of Minnesota P, 2000. ix-xxx. Print.

Kunow, Rüdiger. "Beginning/Ending/Rewriting History: Historiographical Scenarios in the Multiculturalism Debate." *American Studies in Germany: European Contexts and Intercultural Relations*. Ed. Günter H. Lenz and Klaus J. Milich. Frankfurt: Campus/New York: St. Martin's, 1995. 77–95. Print.

———. "Making Sense of History: The Sense of the Past in Postmodern Times." *Making Sense: The Role of the Reader in Contemporary American Fiction*. Ed. Gerhard Hoffmann. München: Wilhelm Fink, 1989. 167–97. Print.

———. "Manifest History and Its Blind Spots: Historical Fiction and National Memory in 19th-Century America." *Remembering the Individual/Regional/ National Past*. Ed. Waldemar Zacharasiewicz. Tübingen: Stauffenburg, 1999. 59–76. Print.

———. "Nineteenth-Century History for the Twentieth-Century Self: Hemingway's *For Whom the Bell Tolls*." *Democracy and the Arts in the United States*. Ed. Alfred Hornung, Reinhard R. Doerries, and Gerhard Hoffmann. München: Fink, 1996. 205–18. Print. American Studies – A Monograph Series 73.

———. "Simulacrum as Sub-Text: Fiction Writing in the Face of Media Representations of American History." *Simulacrum America: The USA and Popular Media*. Ed. Elisabeth Kraus and Carolin Auer. Rochester: Camden House, 1999. 23–36. Print.

———. "The Return of Historical Narratives in Contemporary American Culture." *Ethics and Aesthetics: The Moral Turn of Postmodernism*. Ed. Gerhard Hoffmann and Alfred Hornung. Heidelberg: Winter, 1996. 255–73. Print.

Kunow, Rüdiger, and Wilfried Raussert. "Cultural Memory and Multiple Identities: An Interdisciplinary Approach to 20th Century Identity Politics." *Cultural Memory and Multiple Identity: Transnational and Transatlantic American Studies*. Vol. 5. Ed. Rüdiger Kunow and Wilfried Raussert. Berlin: LITVerlag, 2008. 7–17. Print.

Kwiatowski, Jane. "*City of Light* Lends Buffalo a Novel Appeal." *The Buffalo News*. 22 June 1999. Print.

LaCapra, Dominick. *History and Criticism*. Ithaca: Cornell UP, 1985. Print.

———. "Representing the Holocaust: Reflections on the 'Historians' Debate.'" *Probing the Limits of Representation: Nazism and the "Final Solution."* Ed. Saul Friedlander. Cambridge: Harvard UP, 1992. 108–27. Print.

Lachmann, Renate. *Gedächtnis und Literatur: Intertextualität in der russischen Moderne*. Frankfurt: Suhrkamp, 1990. Print.

Lackey, Michael. "Locating and Defining the Bio in Biofiction." *a/b: Auto/biography Studies* 31.1 (2016): 3–10. Print.

Landon, Brooks. "Slipstream Then, Slipstream Now: The Curious Connections between William Douglas O'Connor's 'The Brazen Android' and Michael Cunningham's *Specimen Days*." *Science Fiction Studies* 38.1 (2011): 67–91. Print.

Lange, Alexandra. "*City of Light*." *New York Magazine*. 17 May 1999. Print.

La Piana, Angelina. *Dante's American Pilgrimage: A Historical Survey of Dante Studies in the United States 1800–1944*. New Haven: Yale UP, 1948. Print.

Larson, Erik. *The Devil in the White City: Murder, Magic, and Madness at the Fair That Changed America*. London: Bantam, 2003. Print.

Lauretis, Teresa de. "Feminist Studies/Critical Studies: Issues, Terms, and Contexts." *Feminist Studies/Critical Studies*. Ed. Teresa de Lauretis. London: Macmillan, 1986. 1–19. Print.

Leckie, Jr., William H. "'Our Squaw' Sacagawea? Indian Writer Portrays Her as Heroic." *St. Louis Post-Dispatch*. 16 Feb. 2003. Print.

Lee, Richard. "History is but a Fable Agreed Upon: The Problem of Truth in History and Fiction." MS of a Lecture at the Romantic Novelists' Association 2000. *Historical Novel Society*. Web. 4 July 2006.

Lehmann-Haupt, Christopher. "Illuminating Dark Secrets in Victorian Buffalo." *The New York Times*. 2 Aug. 1999. Print.

———. "Of an Erudite Sleuth Tracking a Madman." *The New York Times*. 29 Mar. 1994. Print.

Leisy, Ernest E. *The American Historical Novel*. Norman: U of Oklahoma P, 1950. Print.

Lerner, Gerda. *The Majority Finds Its Past: Placing Women in History*. New York: OUP, 1979. Print.

Lesher, Linda Parent. *The Best Novels of the Nineties*. Jefferson: MacFarland, 1999. Print.

Letissier, Georges. "Dickens and Post-Victorian Fiction." *Refracting the Canon in Contemporary British Literature and Film*. Ed. Christian Gutleben and Susana Onega. Amsterdam: Rodopi, 2004. 111–28. Print.

Lévi-Strauss, Claude. *Structural Anthropology*. New York: Basic, 1963. Print.

Levine, Lawrence W. *Highbrow/Lowbrow: The Emergence of Cultural Hierarchy in America*. Cambridge: Harvard UP, 1988. Print.

Lewis, R. W. B. *The American Adam: Innocence, Tragedy, and Tradition in the Nineteenth Century*. Chicago: U of Chicago P, 1955. Print.

Link, Alex. "City Limits: Fixing New York in Caleb Carr's *The Alienist*." *Clues: A Journal Of Detection* 23.3 (2005): 31–41. Print.

"Lionel Lincoln." *The Albion: A Journal of News, Politics and Literature* 4.6 (23 July 1825): 44. Print.

Lipsitz, George. *Time Passages: Collective Memory and American Popular Culture*. Minneapolis: U of Minnesota P, 1990. Print.

Löffler, Philipp. *Pluralist Desires: Contemporary Historical Fiction and the End of the Cold War*. Rochester/New York: Camden House, 2015. Print.

Lonsdale, Kate. "Rounding Up the Usual Suspect: Echoing Jack the Ripper." *Functions of Victorian Culture at the Present Time*. Ed. Christine L. Krueger. Athens: Ohio UP, 2002. 97–114. Print.

Löschnigg, Martin. "'The Prismatic Hues of Memory': Autobiographische Modellierung und die Rhetorik der Erinnerung in Dickens' *David Copperfield*." *Poetica* 31 (1999): 175–200. Print.

Lowenthal, David. *The Past is a Foreign Country*. Cambridge: CUP, 1985. Print.

———. *Possessed by the Past: The Heritage Crusade and the Spoils of History*. New York: Free P, 1996. Print.

Luckenbill, Rachel. "'Walk-in-2-Worlds': An Interview with Diane Glancy." *Studies in American Indian Literatures* 27.4 (2015): 106–23. Web. 18 Feb. 2020.

Lukács, Georg. *The Historical Novel.* Trans. Hannah and Stanley Mitchell. Lincoln: U of Nebraska P, 1983. Print.

Lyotard, Jean-François. *The Postmodern Condition: A Report on Knowledge.* Minneapolis: Minneapolis UP, 1984. Print.

Maack, Annegret. "Charakter als Echo: Zur Poetologie fiktiver Biographien." *Klassiker-Renaissance: Modelle der Gegenwartsliteratur.* Ed. Martin Brunkhorst, Gerd Rohmann, and Konrad Schoell. Tübingen: Stauffenburg, 1991. 247–58. Print.

———. "Das Leben der toten Dichter: Fiktive Biographien." *Radikalität und Mässigung: Der englische Roman seit 1960.* Ed. Annegret Maack and Rüdiger Imhof. Darmstadt: Wiss. Buchgesellschaft, 1993. 169–88. Print.

———. "'The Life We Imagine': Byron's and Polidori's Memoirs as Character Construction." *Biofictions: The Rewriting of Romantic Lives in Contemporary Fiction and Drama.* Ed. Martin Middeke and Werner Huber. Rochester: Camden House, 1999. 138–51. Print.

Macintyre, Ben. "Gaslight." *The New York Times.* 12 Oct. 1997. Print.

Mackay, James. "Ghosts in the Gaps: Diane Glancy's Paradoxes of Survivance." *Survivance: Narratives of Native Presence.* Ed. Gerald Vizenor. Lincoln: U of Nebraska P, 2008. 247–69. Print.

Macksey, Richard. "Foreword." *Paratexts: Thresholds of Interpretation.* Gérard Genette. Cambridge: CUP, 1997. xi–xxii. Print.

Makowsky, Veroncia. *The Fiction of Valerie Martin: An Introduction.* Louisiana State UP, 2016. Ebook.

Malamud, Randy. "The Problem with Zoos." *The Handbook of Animal Studies.* Ed. Linda Kalof. Oxford: OUP, 2017. 397–410. Print.

Mantell, Suzanne. "Debut Novelists – Spring Eternal: Lauren Belfer." *Publishers Weekly* 246.2 (11 Jan. 1999): 38–39. Print.

Manzoni, Alessandro. *On the Historical Novel.* Trans. Sandra Bermann. Lincoln: U of Nebraska P, 1996. Print.

Martin, Valerie. *The Great Divorce.* New York: Vintage, 1994. Print.

Maryles, Daisy. "This Wind Done Arrived." *Publishers Weekly.* 25 June 2001. Print.

Maslin, Janet. "Add a Serial Murderer to 1893 Chicago's Opulent Overkill." *The New York Times.* 10 Feb. 2003. Print.

———. "A Dead Polygamist Leaves Lots of Wives and One Big Mystery." *The New York Times.* 4 Aug. 2008. Print.

———. "All Literary Allusions Abandon, Ye Who Enter Here." *The New York Times.* 7 Feb. 2003. Print.

Masteller, Jean Carwile. "The Women Doctors of Howells, Phelps, and Jewett: The Conflict of Marriage and Career." *Critical Essays on Sarah Orne Jewett.* Ed. Gwen L. Nagel. Boston: Hall, 1984. 135–47. Print.

Mathews, J. Chesley. "A Historical Overview of American Writers' Interest in Dante (to about 1900)." *Dante's Influence on American Writers 1776–1976.* New York: Griffon House Pub., 1977. 12–21. Print.

Mathijsen, Marita. *De mythe terug: Negentiende-eeuwse literatuur als travestie van maatschappelijke conflicten.* Amsterdam: Vossiuspers AUP, 2000. Print.

Matthiessen, F. O. *Sarah Orne Jewett.* Gloucester: Peter Smith, 1965. Print.

Mauch, Christof. "23. Wie 'grün' sind die Indianer?" *Die 101 wichtigsten Fragen: Amerikanische Geschichte.* München: Beck, 2008. 41–42. Print.

May, John. *Poe & Fanny*. New York: Plume, 2004. Print.

McCullough, Kate. *Regions of Identity: The Construction of America in Women's Fiction, 1885–1914*. Stanford: Stanford UP, 1999. Print.

McDowell, Deborah E., and Arnold Rampersad, eds. *Slavery and the Literary Imagination*. Baltimore: Johns Hopkins UP, 1989. Print.

McDowell, Edwin. "All the Rage in Fiction: Serial Murder, Multiple Murder, Hideous Murder." *The New York Times*. 15 Apr. 1991. Print.

McElwee, Johanna. *The Nation Conceived: Learning, Education, and Nationhood in American Historical Novels of the 1820s*. Uppsala: Uppsala U Library, 2005. Print.

McGuire, Patrick. "A Hard Look at Blind Faith: 19th Wife Sheds Light on Polygamy." *Journal Interactive*. Web. 23 Apr. 2009.

McHale, Brian. *Postmodernist Fiction*. New York: Methuen, 1987. Print.

McKible, Adam. "'These Are the Facts of the Darky's History': Thinking History and Reading Names in Four African American Texts." *African American Review* 28.2 (Summer 1994): 223–35. Print.

Mehegan, David. *"The Dante Club." The Boston Globe*. 3 Mar. 2003. Print.

Meinig, Sigrun. *Witnessing the Past: History and Post-Colonialism in Australian Novels*. Tübingen: Gunter Narr, 2004. Print.

Melville, Herman. *Israel Potter: His Fifty Years of Exile*. Evanston: Northwestern UP, 2000. Print.

Mengel, Ewald. *Geschichtsbild und Romankonzeption: Drei Typen des Geschichtsverstehens im Reflex der Form des englischen historischen Romans*. Heidelberg: Winter, 1986. Print.

Merriam-Webster Online Dictionary. Web. May 23, 2009.

Middeke, Martin. "Introduction." *Biofictions: The Rewriting of Romantic Lives in Contemporary Fiction and Drama*. Ed. Martin Middeke and Werner Huber. Rochester: Camden House, 1999. 1–25. Print.

Middleton, Peter, and Tim Woods. *Literatures of Memory: History, Time, and Space in Postwar Writing*. Manchester: Manchester UP, 2000. Print.

Miller, J. Hillis. "Parody as Revisionary Critique: Charles Palliser's *The Quincunx*." *Refracting the Canon in Contemporary British Literature and Film*. Ed. Christian Gutleben and Susana Onega. Amsterdam: Rodopi, 2004. 129–48. Print.

Miller, Laura. "Mammy's Revenge." *Salon*. 2 May 2001. Print.

Miller, Quentin. "'A Tyrannically Democratic Force': The Symbolic and Cultural Function of Clothing in Catharine Maria Sedgwick's *Hope Leslie*." *Legacy* 19.2 (2002): 121–36. Print.

Miller, Ron. "Poe's the Tragic Center of this Romantic Novel." *Dark Corridors* 5.41. Web. 27 May 2008.

Miscall, Peter D. "Isaiah: New Heavens, New Earth, New Book." *Reading Between Texts: Intertextuality and the Hebrew Bible*. Ed. Danna Nolan Fewell. Louisville: Westminster, 1992. 41–56. Print.

Mitchell, Angelyn. *The Freedom to Remember: Narrative, Slavery, and Gender in Contemporary Black Women's Fiction*. New Brunswick: Rutgers UP, 2002. Print.

Mitchell, Kate, and Nicola Parsons. "Reading the Represented Past: History and Fiction from 1700 to the Present." *Reading Historical Fiction: The Revenant and Remembered Past*. Ed. Kate Mitchell and Nicola Parsons. Basingstoke: Palgrave Macmillan, 2013. 1–18. Print.

Miyashita, Masatoshi. "An Introduction to the American Plot of Self-(Re) Naming." *Language and Culture* 17 (1989): 177–94. Print.

Montaigne, Michael Eyquem de. "Of the Caniballes (1562)." *Key Concepts in American Cultural History: From the Colonial Period to the End of the 19th Century.* Ed. Bernd Engler and Oliver Scheiding. Trier: WVT, 2007. 38–40. Print.

Moore, Grace. "Twentieth-Century Re-Workings of the Victorian Novel." *Literature Compass* 5.1 (2008): 134–44. Print.

Morgan, Gwendolyn A. *The Invention of False Medieval Authorities as a Literary Device in Popular Fiction.* Lewiston: Edwin Mellen, 2006. Print.

Morone, James. *Hellfire Nation: The Politics of Sin in American History.* New Haven: Yale UP, 2003. Print.

Morrison, Toni. "Declaration to the Court." *Houghton Mifflin Books.* Web. 21 Mar. 2009.

Moseley, Merritt, ed. *The Academic Novel: New and Classic Essays.* Chester: Chester Academic P, 2007. Print.

Moulthrop, Stuart. "You Say You Want a Revolution? Hypertext and the Laws of Media." *The Norton Anthology of Theory and Criticism.* Ed. Vincent B. Leitch. New York: Norton, 2001. 2504–24. Print.

Mousoutzanis, Aris. "Uncanny Repetition, Trauma, and Displacement in Michael Cunningham's *Specimen Days.*" *Critical Survey* 21.2 (2009): 129–41. Web. 10 Feb. 2020.

Müller, Kurt. "The Development Toward Historiographic Metafiction in the American Novel." *Historiographic Metafiction in Modern American and Canadian Literature.* Ed. Bernd Engler and Kurt Müller. Paderborn: Schöningh, 1994. 35–51. Print.

Müller, Wolfgang G. "Derivative Literature: Notes on the Terminology of Intertextual Relationships and a British-American Case Study." *Transatlantic Encounters: Studies in European-American Relations.* Ed. Udo J. Hebel and Karl Ortseifen. Trier: WVT, 1995. 312–21. Print.

Munteán, László. "The Lure of Space: Psychasthenia as Mnemonic Device in Michael Cunningham's *Specimen Days.*" *A Poetics of Neurosis: Narratives of Normalcy and Disorder in Cultural and Literary Texts.* Ed. Elena Furlanetto and Dietmar Meinel. Bielefeld: transcript, 2018. 37–54. Print.

Myles, Anne G. "Writing the Go-Between." *The North American Review* 288.6 (2003): 53–56. Print.

Nadel, Ira B. "Narrative and the Popularity of Biography." *Mosaic* 20.4 (1987): 131–42. Print.

Nadj, Julijana. "Towards a Theory and Typology of Fictional Metabiographies: Forms and Functions of a New Genre." *Anglistentag 2005 Bamberg: Proceedings.* Ed. Christoph Houswitschka, Gabriele Knappe, and Anja Müller. Trier: WVT, 2006. 411–23. Print.

Neumann, Birgit. "Literatur, Erinnerung, Identität." *Gedächtniskonzepte der Literaturwissenschaft: Theoretische Grundlegung und Anwendungsperspektiven.* Ed. Astrid Erll and Ansgar Nünning. Berlin: de Gruyter, 2005. 149–77. Print.

Newitz, Annalee. "Serial Killer, True Crime, and Economic Performance Anxiety." *Cine-Action* 38 (Sept. 1995): 38–46. Print.

Newman, Judie. "Slave Narratives and Neo-Slave Narratives." *The Cambridge Companion to the Literature of the American South*. Ed. Sharon Monteith. Cambridge: CUP, 2013. 26–38. Print.

Nicholson, Linda, ed. *The Second Wave: A Reader in Feminist Theory*. New York: Routledge, 1997. Print.

Nora, Pierre. "From Lieux de Mémoire to Realms of Memory." *Realms of Memory: Rethinking the French Past. Vol. 1: Conflicts and Divisions*. Ed. Pierre Nora and Lawrence D. Kritzman. New York: Columbia UP, 1996. XV–XXIV. Print.

Novak, Julia. "Experiments in Life-Writing: Introduction." *Experiments in Life-Writing: Intersections of Auto/Biography and Fiction*. Ed. Lucia Boldrini and Julia Novak. Basingstoke: Palgrave Macmillan, 2017. 1–36. Print.

Nover, Peter. *The Great Good Place? A Collection of Essays on American and British College Mystery Novels*. Frankfurt: Lang, 1999. Print.

Nowak, Helge. *"Completeness is all": Fortsetzungen und andere Weiterführungen britischer Romane als Beispiel zeitübergreifender und interkultureller Rezeption*. Frankfurt: Peter Lang, 1994. Print.

Nünning, Ansgar. "An Intertextual Quest for Thomas Chatterton: The Deconstruction of the Romantic Cult of Originality and of the Paradoxes of 'Life-Writing' in Peter Ackroyd's Fictional Metabiography *Chatterton*." *Biofictions: The Rewriting of Romantic Lives in Contemporary Fiction and Drama*. Ed. Martin Middeke and Werner Huber. Rochester: Camden House, 1999. 27–49. Print.

———. *Der englische Roman des 20. Jahrhunderts*. Stuttgart: Klett, 1998. Print.

———. "Editorial: New Directions in the Study of Individual and Cultural Memory and Memorial Cultures." *Journal for the Study of British Cultures: Fictions of Memory* 10.1 (2003): 3–10. Print.

———. "Fictional Metabiographies and Metaautobiographies: Towards a Definition, Typology and Analysis of Self-Reflexive Hybrid Metagenres." *Self-Reflexivity in Literature*. Ed. Werner Huber, Martin Middeke, and Hubert Zapf. Würzburg: Königshausen und Neumann, 2005. 195–209. Print.

———. "'Moving back and forward in time': Zur Gleichzeitigkeit verschiedener Zeitstrukturen, Zeiterfahrungen und Zeitkonzeptionen im englischen Roman der Gegenwart." *Zeit und Roman: Zeiterfahrung im historischen Wandel und ästhetischer Paradigmenwechsel vom sechzehnten Jahrhundert bis zur Postmoderne*. Ed. Martin Middeke. Würzburg: Königshausen & Neumann, 2002. 395–419. Print.

———. *Von historischer Fiktion zu historiographischer Metafiktion. Vol. 1: Theorie, Typologie und Poetik des historischen Romans*. Trier: WVT, 1995. Print.

———. *Von historischer Fiktion zu historiographischer Metafiktion. Vol. 2: Erscheinungsformen und Entwicklungstendenzen des historischen Romans in England seit 1950*. Trier: WVT, 1995. Print.

Nünning, Ansgar, and Vera Nünning. *An Introduction to the Study of English and American Literature*. Stuttgart: Klett, 2007. Print.

Nunes, Ana. *African American Women Writers' Historical Fiction*. New York: Palgrave Macmillan, 2011. Print.

Ó Cuilleanáin, Cormac. "Dante in *The Zebra-Striped Hearse*." *Echi danteschi / Dantean Echoes*. Ed. Giuliana Adamo. Dublin: Trauben Edizioni, 2003. 107–24. Print.

O'Gorman, Rochelle. "Lauren Belfer is First-Time Author who Entwines." *The Sunday Oregonian.* 30 Jan. 2000. Print.

Öhlschläger, Claudia. "Gender/Körper, Gedächtnis und Literatur." *Gedächtniskonzepte der Literaturwissenschaft: Theoretische Grundlegung und Anwendungsperspektiven.* Ed. Astrid Erll and Ansgar Nünning. Berlin: de Gruyter, 2005. 227–48. Print.

Ondaatje, Michael. "The Silent Partner: Photography in Fiction." *Photo Communiqué* 9.3 (Fall 1987): 36–40. Print.

Onega, Susana. "Postmodern Re-Writings of the Puritan Commonwealth: Winterson, Ackroyd, Mukherjee." *Intercultural Encounters: Studies in English Literatures.* Ed. Heinz Antor and Kevin L. Cope. Heidelberg: Winter, 1999. 439–66. Print.

Opfermann, Susanne. "Lydia Maria Child, James Fenimore Cooper, and Catharine Maria Sedgwick: A Dialogue on Race, Culture, and Gender." *Soft Canons: American Women Writers and Masculine Tradition.* Ed. Karen L. Kilcup. Iowa City: U of Iowa P, 1999. 27–47. Print.

Orians, G. Harrison. "Romance Ferment After Waverley." *American Literature* 3 (1931/32): 408–31. Print.

Osterhammel, Jürgen. *Die Verwandlung der Welt: Eine Geschichte des 19. Jahrhunderts.* München: C. H. Beck, 2010. Print.

Padmore, Catherine. "A Coquel Set 'Far Away, Where the Fighting Was': On Geraldine Brooks' *March* and Louisa May Alcott's *Little Women*." *Prequels, Coquels and Sequels in Contemporary Anglophone Fiction.* Ed. Armelle Parey. New York: Routledge, 2018. 65–80. Print.

Palfrey, John Gorham. "Review of *Yamoyden*." *North American Review* 12 (Apr. 1821): 466–88. Print.

Parey, Armelle. "Introduction: Narrative Expansions – The Story So Far ...." *Prequels, Coquels and Sequels in Contemporary Anglophone Fiction.* Ed. Armelle Parey. New York: Routledge, 2019. 1–24. Print.

———. "The True History of the Convict in Peter Carey's *Jack Maggs*?" *U de Lyon Archives.* Web. 17 Oct. 2007.

Parish, Peter J. *Confidence and Anxiety in Victorian America: Plenary Lecture Delivered at the EAAS Conference London, April 9, 1990.* The Swedish Institute for North American Studies, Uppsala U Faculty of Arts. Uppsala: Reprocentralen HSC, 1991. Print.

Packer-Fletcher, Dorothy, and Kenneth E. Fletcher. "The Alienist." *Psychiatric Services* 47.3 (Mar. 196): 311–12. Print.

Parrish, Timothy. *From the Civil War to Apocalypse: Postmodern History and American Fiction.* Amherst: U of Massachusetts P, 2008. Print.

Pate, Nancy. "'Evermore': Poe lives on in his – and others' – tales." *Milwaukee Journal Sentinel.* 14 Mar. 2004. Print.

Patmore, Coventry. "The Angel in the House (1854)." *Project Gutenberg.* Web. 30 May 2008.

Patterson, Christina. "Books: First Novels: Bad Blood in Buffalo." *The Observer.* 25 July 1999. Print.

Patton, Venetria K. *Women in Chains: The Legacy of Slavery in Black Women's Fiction.* New York: U of New York P, 2000. Print.

Pearl, Matthew. "Preface." *Inferno.* Dante Alighieri. New York: Modern Library, 2003. xi–xvi. Print.

———. *The Dante Club*. London: Vintage, 2004. Print.

Penzler, Otto. "Introducing Bibliomysteries: Short Tales about Deadly Books!" *Mysterious Press*. Web. 12 Mar. 2020.

Perloff, Marjorie. "Introduction." *Postmodern Genres*. Ed. Marjorie Perloff. Norman: U of Oklahoma P, 1988. 3–10. Print.

Pertile, Lino. "Introduction." *Inferno*. Dante Alighieri. New York: Modern Library, 2003. xvii–xxiv. Print.

Peters, Catherine. "Secondary Lives: Biography in Context." *The Art of Literary Biography*. Ed. John Batchelor. Oxford: Clarendon, 1995. 43–56. Print.

Phillips, Philip Edward. "Adaptations of Dante's *Commedia* in Popular American Fiction and Film." *Medieval and Early Modern English Studies* 17.2 (2009): 197–212. Print.

Pierce, Kingston. "Power Plays." *January Magazine*. Web. 29 May 2008.

Pierpont, Claudia Roth. *Passionate Minds: Women Rewriting the World*. New York: Knopf, 2000. Print.

Pieters, Jürgen. *Speaking with the Dead: Explorations in Literature and History*. Edinburgh: Edinburgh UP, 2005. Print.

Polaski, Donald C. *Authorizing an End: The Isaiah Apocalypse and Intertextuality*. Boston: Brill, 2001. Print.

Pollin, Burton R. "Poe and Frances Osgood, as Linked through 'Lenore.'" *Mississippi Quarterly* 46.2 (Spring 1993): 185–97. Print.

Porter, Maria S. *Recollections of Louisa May Alcott, John Greenleaf Whittier, Robert Browning*. Boston: New England Magazine Corporation, 1893. Print.

Pound, Ezra. *Guide to Kulchur*. New York: New Directions, 1968. Print.

Prose, Francine. "Picks & Pans: *City of Light* by Lauren Belfer." *People* 52.5 (9 Aug. 1999): 45. Print.

Purdy, Matthew. "On the Lower East Side with Caleb Carr: Writing to Flee the Past." *The New York Times*. 19 May 1994. Print.

Randall, Alice. *The Wind Done Gone*. Boston: Houghton Mifflin, 2001. Print.

Ranke, Leopold von. *Geschichten der romanischen und germanischen Völker von 1494 bis 1535*. Vol. 1. Leipzig: G. Reimer, 1824. Print.

"Reader's Guide: *The Wind Done Gone* by Alice Randall." *Houghton Mifflin Harcourt*. Web. 23 Mar. 2009.

Redling, Erik. "Of Heroes and Mockingbirds: Transatlantic Translations and the Struggle between 'High' and 'Low' Cultures in Nineteenth-Century America." *Traveling Traditions: Nineteenth-Century Cultural Concepts and Transatlantic Intellectual Networks*. Ed. Erik Redling. Berlin: de Gruyter, 2016. 63–78. Print.

Reichardt, Ulfried. *Alterität und Geschichte: Funktionen der Sklavereidarstellung im amerikanischen Roman*. Heidelberg: Winter, 2001. Print. American Studies – A Monograph Series 86.

———. "The New Historicism: History as Process and Narratives of Emergence." *American Studies in Germany: European Contexts and Intercultural Relations*. Ed. Günter H. Lenz and Klaus J. Milich. Frankfurt: Campus/New York: St. Martin's, 1995. 68–76. Print.

Reid, Calvin. "HM, Mitchell Estate Settle *WDG* Suit." *Publishers Weekly*. 13 May 2002. Print.

Renders, Hans, Binne de Haan, and Jonne Harmsma. *The Biographical Turn: Lives in History*. New York: Routledge, 2017. Print.

Renk, Kathleen J. *Caribbean Shadows & Victorian Ghosts: Women's Writing and Decolonization*. Charlottesville: UP of Virginia, 1999. Print.

"Reviews." *Poe & Fanny: A Novel by John May*. Web. 27 May 2008.

Reynolds, David S. *John Brown, Abolitionist: The Man Who Killed Slavery, Sparked the Civil War, and Seeded Civil Rights*. New York: Knopf, 2005. Print.

Rhys, Jean. *Wide Sargasso Sea*. London: Penguin, 1997. Print.

Ribbat, Christoph. "The Windshield and the Rear-View Mirror: An Introduction to Twenty-First Century Writers, Books, and Readers." *Twenty-First Century Fiction: Readings, Essays, Conversations*. Ed. Christoph Ribbat. Heidelberg: Winter, 2005. 7–32. Print. Anglistik und Englischunterricht 66.

Rich, Adrienne. "When We Dead Awaken: Writing as Re-Vision." *Adrienne Rich's Poetry*. Ed. Barbara Charlesworth Gelpi and Albert Gelpi. New York: Norton, 1975. 90–98. Print.

Rickli, Christina. "Wegweiser aus dem Trauma? Amerikanische Romane nach dem 11. September." *Amerikanisches Erzählen nach 2000*. Ed. Sebastian Domsch. München: Text & Kritik, 2008. 126–45. Print.

Ricoeur, Paul. *Das Rätsel der Vergangenheit: Erinnern – Vergessen – Verzeihen*. Trans. Andris Breitling and Henrik Richard Lesaar. Göttingen: Wallstein, 1998. Print.

———. *Time and Narrative*. Vol. 1. Chicago: U of Chicago P, 1990. Print.

———. *Time and Narrative*. Vol. 2. Chicago: U of Chicago P, 1985. Print.

———. *Time and Narrative*. Vol. 3. Chicago: U of Chicago P, 1988. Print.

Robinson, Alan. *Narrating the Past: Historiography, Memory, and the Contemporary Novel*. Basingstoke: Palgrave Macmillan, 2011. Print.

Rody, Caroline. *The Daughter's Return: African-American and Caribbean Women's Fictions of History*. Oxford: OUP, 2001. Print.

Roh, David. "Two Copyright Case Studies from a Literary Perspective." *Law and Literature* 22.1 (2010): 110–41. Web. 16 Feb. 2020.

Rollason, Christopher. "The Detective Myth in Poe's Dupin Trilogy." *American Crime Fiction: Studies in the Genre*. Ed. Brian Docherty. New York: St. Martins, 1988. 4–22. Print.

Roman, Judith. "A Closer Look at the Jewett-Fields Relationship." *Critical Essays on Sarah Orne Jewett*. Ed. Gwen L. Nagel. Boston: Hall, 1984. 119–34. Print.

Rose, Phyllis. "Biography as Fiction." *Tri-Quarterly* 55 (1982): 111–24. Print.

Rosenfeld, Gavriel D. *The World Hitler Never Made: Alternate History and the Memory of Nazism*. Cambridge: CUP, 2005. Print.

Rosenzweig, Roy, and David Thelen. *The Presence of the Past: Popular Uses of History in American Life*. New York: Columbia UP, 1998. Print.

Rothaug, Susanne. *Autorinnen des amerikanischen Südens: Geschichte und Geschichtenerzählen*. Paderborn: Schöningh, 2006. Print.

Rousselot, Elodie. "Introduction: Exoticising the Past in Contemporary Neo-Historical Fiction." *Exoticizing [sic] the Past in Contemporary Neo-Historical Fiction*. Ed. Elodie Rousselot. London: Palgrave Macmillan, 2014. 1–16. Print.

Rowe, John Carlos. *The New American Studies*. Minneapolis: U of Minnesota P, 2002. Print.

Rozett, Martha Tuck. *Constructing a World: Shakespeare's England and the New Historical Fiction*. Albany: SUNY P, 2003. Print.

Rubenstein, Jill. "Auld Acquaintance: New Lives of Scott and Hogg." *Biofictions: The Rewriting of Romantic Lives in Contemporary Fiction and Drama*. Ed. Martin Middeke and Werner Huber. Rochester: Camden House, 1999. 64–76. Print.

Rüsen, Jörn. "Einleitung: Für eine interkulturelle Kommunikation in der Geschichte: Die Herausforderungen des Ethnozentrismus in der Moderne und die Antwort der Kulturwissenschaft." *Die Vielfalt der Kulturen: Erinnerung, Geschichte, Identität*. Vol. 4. Frankfurt: Suhrkamp, 1998. 12–36. Print.

———. *Grundzüge einer Historik. Vol. 1: Historische Vernunft: Die Grundlagen der Geschichtswissenschaft*. Göttingen: Vandenhoeck und Ruprecht, 1983. Print.

———. "Preface to the Series." *Western Historical Thinking: An Intercultural Debate*. Ed. Jörn Rüsen. New York: Berghahn Books, 2002. vii–xiii. Print.

Runia, Eelco. "Thirsting for Deeds: Schiller and the Historical Sublime." *Schiller und die Geschichte*. Ed. Michael Hofmann, Jörn Rüsen, and Mirjam Springer. München: Wilhelm Fink, 2006. 93–103. Print.

Rushdy, Ashraf H. A. *Neo-slave Narratives: Studies in the Social Logic of a Literary Form*. New York: OUP, 1999. Print.

Ryan, Tim A. *Calls and Responses: The American Novel of Slavery Since Gone With the Wind*. Baton Rouge: Louisiana State UP, 2008. Print.

Saldívar, Ramón. "Historical Fantasy, Speculative Realism, and Postrace Aesthetics in Contemporary American Fiction." *American Literary History* 23.2 (2011): 574–99. Web. 11 Feb. 2020.

Samuels, Shirley. *Romances of the Republic: Women, the Family, and Violence in the Literature of the Early American Nation*. Oxford: OUP, 1996. Print.

Sanders, Julie. *Adaptation and Appropriation*. London: Routledge, 2006. Print.

Sandweiss, Lee Ann. "City of Buffalo's Golden Era Drives Wonderful First Novel by Lauren Belfer." *St. Louis Post-Dispatch*. 23 May 1999. Print.

Santaulària, Isabel. "'The Great Good Place' No More? Integrating and Dismantling Oppositional Discourse in Some Recent Examples of Serial Killer Fiction." *Atlantis* 29.1 (June 2007): 55–67. Print.

Sauerberg, Lars Ole. *Fact into Fiction: Documentary Realism in the Contemporary Novel*. New York: St. Martin's, 1991. Print.

Saunders, Max. *Self Impression: Life-Writing, Autobiografiction, and the Forms of Modern Literature*. Oxford: OUP, 2010. Print.

Savu, Laura E. *Postmortem Postmodernists: The Afterlife of the Author in Recent Narrative*. Madison: Fairleigh Dickinson UP, 2009. Print.

Saxton, Martha. *Louisa May: A Biography of Louisa May Alcott*. London: Andre Deutsch, 1978. Print.

Scaggs, John. *Crime Fiction*. New York: Routledge, 2005. Print.

Schabert, Ina. *Der historische Roman in England und Amerika*. Darmstadt: Wiss. Buchgesellschaft, 1981. Print.

———. "Gender als Kategorie einer neuen Literaturgeschichtsschreibung." *Genus: Zur Geschlechterdifferenz in den Kulturwissenchaften*. Ed. Hadumod Bußmann and Renate Hof. Stuttgart: Kröner, 1995. 162–205. Print.

———. *In Quest of the Other Person: Fiction as Biography.* Tübingen: Francke, 1990. Print.

———. "Interauktorialität." *Deutsche Vierteljahrsschrift für Literaturwissenschaft und Geistesgeschichte* 57 (1983): 679–701. Print.

Schachinger, Carol. "Sarah Orne Jewett's Maine: A Journey Back." *Jewett and Her Contemporaries: Reshaping the Canon.* Ed. Karen L. Kilcup and Thomas S. Edwards. Gainesville: UP of Florida, 1999. 277–86. Print.

Schäfer, Stefanie. "Geraldine Brooks, *March.*" *Zweiundzwanzig amerikanische Romane aus dem neuen Jahrhundert: Literaturkritische Essays zur Einführung.* Ed. Dietmar Schloss and Heiko Jakubzik. Trier: WVT, 2009. 59–69. Print.

Scheiding, Oliver. *Geschichte und Funktion: Zum Funktionswandel des frühen amerikanischen Romans.* Paderborn: Schöningh, 2003. Print.

———. "Intertextualität." *Gedächtniskonzepte der Literaturwissenschaft: Theoretische Grundlegung und Anwendungsperspektiven.* Ed. Astrid Erll and Ansgar Nünning. Berlin: de Gruyter, 2005. 53–72. Print.

———. "Introduction: Reel Histories." *Zeitschrift für Anglistik und Amerikanistik* 53.3 (2005): 199–210. Print.

———. "James Fenimore Cooper and Sir Walter Scott: Entwürfe nationaler Leitfiguren im Spiegel der amerikanischen Literaturkritik des 19. Jahrhunderts." *Kulturelle Leitfiguren – Figurationen und Refigurationen.* Ed. Bernd Engler and Isabell Klaiber. Berlin: Duncker & Humblot, 2007. 185–205. Print. Schriften zur Literaturwissenschaft 30.

Scheidweiler, Alexander. "Matthew Pearl, *The Dante Club.*" *Zweiundzwanzig amerikanische Romane aus dem neuen Jahrhundert: Literaturkritische Essays zur Einführung.* Ed. Dietmar Schloss. Trier: WVT, 2009. 223–36. Print.

Schlereth, Thomas J. *Victorian America: Transformations in Everyday Life, 1876-1915.* New York: Harper Collins, 1991. Print.

Schmid, David. *Natural Born Celebrities: Serial Killers in American Culture.* Chicago: U of Chicago P, 2005. Print.

Schur, Richard. "*The Wind Done Gone* Controversy: American Studies, Copyright Law, and the Imaginary Domain." *American Studies* 44.1-2 (2003): 5–33. Print.

Scott, Joan Wallach. *Gender and the Politics of History.* New York: Columbia UP, 1988. Print.

Seltzer, Mark. *Serial Killers: Death and Life in America's Wound Culture.* New York: Routledge, 1998. Print.

Sesto, Christina del. "Maid of the Mist." *The Washington Post.* 27 June 1999. Print.

Shaw, George Bernard. "Blood Money to Whitechapel." *The Star.* 24 Sept. 1888. Web. 29 May 2020.

Shechner, Mark. "American Realisms, American Realities." *Neo-Realism in Contemporary American Fiction.* Ed. Kristiaan Versluys. Amsterdam: Rodopi, 1992. 27–50. Print.

Shelden, Mary Lamb. "A Coming-of-Age for *Little Women* and Alcott Scholarship." *Children's Literature* 34 (2006): 209–23. Print.

Sherman, Sarah Way. *Sarah Orne Jewett, an American Persephone.* Hanover: UP of New England, 1989. Print.

Shields, David. *Reality Hunger: A Manifesto*. New York: Vintage, 2011. Print.

Shiller, Dana. "The Redemptive Past in the Neo-Victorian Novel." *Studies in the Novel* 29.4 (Winter 1997): 538–60. Print.

Showalter, Elaine. *Faculty Towers: The Academic Novel and Its Discontents*. Oxford: OUP, 2005. Print.

———. "Introduction." *Little Women*. Louisa May Alcott. Ed. and introd. Elaine Showalter. New York: Penguin, 1989. vii–xxviii. Print.

Shuttleworth, Sally. "Natural History: The Retro-Victorian Novel." *The Third Culture: Literature and Science*. Ed. Elinor S. Shaffer. Berlin: de Gruyter, 1998. 253–68. Print.

Simon, Jeff. "*City of Light:* How a First-Time Novelist Reached Back to Buffalo's Glittering Past; and Came Up Big." *The Buffalo News*. 5 May 1999. Print.

Simpson, Anne. "Weird World of a Missionary Pioneer." *The Herald*. 6 Apr. 1998. Print.

Simpson, Philip L. *Psycho Paths: Tracking the Serial Killer Through Contemporary American Film and Fiction*. Carbondale: Southern Illinois UP, 2000. Print.

Singh, Amrijit, Joseph T. Skerrett, Jr., and Robert E. Hogan. "Introduction." *Memory and Cultural Politics*. Ed. Amrijit Singh, Joseph T. Skerrett, Jr., and Robert E. Hogan. Boston: Northwestern UP, 1996. 3–17. Print.

Slemon, Stephen. "Post-Colonial Allegory and the Transformation of History." *Journal of Commonwealth Literature* 23.1 (1988): 157–68. Print.

Smith, Christopher. *The Development of the Reimaginative and Reconstructive in Historiographic Metafiction: 1960–2007*. 2010. Web. 18 Feb. 2020.

Smith, David E. *John Bunyan in America*. Bloomington: Indiana UP, 1966. Print.

Smith-Rosenberg, Carroll. "The Female World of Love and Ritual: Relations between Women in Nineteenth-Century America." *Signs* 1.1 (Autumn 1975): 1–29. Print.

Sommer, Mark. "*City of Light* in Footlights." *The Buffalo News*. 19 Dec. 2000. Print.

———. "'Light' Speed." *The Buffalo News*. 20 July 2001. Print.

———. "Paperback Writer: Belfer Visits Buffalo as *City of Light* Celebrates New Edition." *The Buffalo News*. 29 Aug. 2003. Print.

Spaulding, A. Timothy. *Re-Forming the Past: History, the Fantastic, and the Postmodern Slave Narrative*. Columbus: Ohio State UP, 2005. Print.

Spengler, Birgit. *Literary Spinoffs: Rewriting the Classics – Re-Imagining the Community*. Frankfurt: Campus, 2015. Print.

Spiller, Robert E., ed. *The American Literary Revolution, 1783-1837*. Garden City: Anchor, 1967. Print.

Srebnick, Amy Gilman. "Does the Representation Fit the Crime? Some Thoughts on Writing Crime History as Cultural Text." *Crime and Culture: An Historical Perspective*. Ed. Amy Gilman Srebnick and René Lévy. Burlington: Ashgate, 2005. 3–19. Print.

Stableford, Brian. *Science Fact and Science Fiction: An Encyclopedia*. New York: Routledge, 2006. Print.

Staehelin-Wackernagel, Adelheid. *The Puritan Settler in the American Novel before the Civil War*. Solothurn: Gassmann, 1961. Print.

Stanzel, Franz K. "Historie, Historischer Roman, Historiographische Metafiktion." *Sprachkunst: Beiträge zur Literaturwissenschaft* 26 (1995): 113–23. Print.

Steele, Selina. "Light Read." *Sunday Mail*. 20 June 1999. Print.

Steelman, Ben. "Novel Explores Poe's Possible Life with Lover." *Wilmington Star-News*. 25 Apr. 2004. Print.

Stelzriede, Danelle Dyckhoff. "Representing Spectral Subjects in Historical Crime Fiction." *Arizona Quarterly: A Journal of American Literature, Culture, and Theory* 73.3 (2017): 77–100. Web. 13 Feb. 2020.

Steuber, Jr., William F. "Using History for Fiction." *Wisconsin Magazine of History* 41 (1960): 242–52. Print.

Stone, Albert E. *The Return of Nat Turner: History, Literature, and Cultural Politics in Sixties America*. Athens: U of Georgia P, 1992. Print.

Straub, Julia. "The Transatlantic Dante in the Nineteenth Century: Literary Authority and Reception Histories." *Traveling Traditions: Nineteenth-Century Cultural Concepts and Transatlantic Intellectual Networks*. Ed. Erik Redling. Berlin: de Gruyter, 2016. 78–93. Print.

Sturken, Marita. *Tangled Memories: The Vietnam War, the AIDS Epidemic, and the Politics of Remembering*. Berkeley: U of California P, 1997. Print.

Sweet, Matthew. *Inventing the Victorians*. London: Faber and Faber, 2001. Print.

Tallack, Douglas. "Caleb Carr: Running Away from the Darkness." *The Detective as Historian: History and Art in Historical Crime Fiction*. Ed. Ray B. Browne and Lawrence A. Kreiser, Jr. Bowling Green: Bowling Green State U Popular P, 2000. 251–64. Print.

Talley, Sharon. *Southern Women Novelists and the Civil War: Trauma and Collective Memory in the American Literary Tradition Since 1861*. Knoxville: U of Tennessee P, 2014. Print.

Teachout, Terry. "Entitlement Publishing." *National Review*. 20 Aug. 2001. Print.

Tey, Josephine. *The Daughter of Time*. London: Arrow, 2002. Print.

Thiem, Jon. "Cultural Memory in the Novel of Biographical Quest." *Genres as Repositories of Cultural Memory*. Ed. Hendrik van Gorp and Ulla Musarra-Schroeder. Amsterdam: Rodopi, 2000. 421–32. Print.

Thieme, John. *Postcolonial Con-Texts: Writing Back to the Canon*. London: Continuum, 2001. Print.

Thomas, Joan. "'The Golden Book': An Interview with Carol Shields.'" *Prairie Fire* 14.4 (Winter 1993/94): 56–62. Print.

Thomas, Louisa. "Plurality Tale." *The New York Times*. 31 Aug. 2008. Print.

Tiffin, Helen. "Post-Colonial Literatures and Counter-Discourse." *Kunapipi* 9.3 (1987): 17–34. Print.

Todorov, Tzvetan. *The Fantastic: A Structural Approach to a Literary Genre*. Trans. Robert Scholes. Ithaca: Cornell UP, 1985. Print.

Tofantšuk, Julia. "Time, Space and (Her)Story in the Fiction of Eva Figes." *Metafiction and Metahistory in Contemporary Women's Writing*. Ed. Ann Heilmann and Mark Llewellyn. Basingstoke: Palgrave Macmillan, 2007. 59–72. Print.

Tompkins, Jane. *Sensational Designs: The Cultural Work of American Fiction 1790-1860*. New York: OUP, 1985. Print.

Tönnies, Merle. "A New Self-Conscious Turn at the Turn of the Century? Postmodernist Metafiction in Recent Works by 'Established' British

Writers." *Twenty-First Century Fiction: Readings, Essays, Conversations*. Ed. Christoph Ribbat. Heidelberg: Winter, 2005. 57–82. Print. Anglistik und Englischunterricht 66.

Tucker, Louise, et al. "P.S.: Ideas, Interviews & Features." *March*. Geraldine Brooks. London: Harper Perennial, 2006. 1–18. Print.

Tüllmann, Mareike. *Writers, Readers, and True Crime: Negotiating Truth and Meaning in Contemporary American Nonfiction*. Essen: Die Blaue Eule, 2012. Print.

Turner, Frederick Jackson. *The Significance of the Frontier in American History*. Ed. Harold P. Simonson. New York: Continuum, 1990. Print.

VanMeter, Vandelia L. *America in Historical Fiction: A Bibliographic Guide*. Englewood: Libraries Unlimited, 1997. Print.

Verene, Donald Phillip. "Vico, Giambattista." *Hopkins Guide to Literary Theory*. The Johns Hopkins UP. Web. 4 Oct. 2005.

Versluys, Kristiaan, ed. *Neo-Realism in Contemporary American Fiction*. Amsterdam: Rodopi, 1992. Print.

Wägenbaur, Thomas. "Rezension: Ansgar Nünning: *Von historischer Fiktion zu historiographischer Metafiktion*, Band 1 und 2." *Zeitschrift für Anglistik und Amerikanistik* 4 (1997): 371–73. Print.

Wallace, Diana. *The Woman's Historical Novel: British Women Writers, 1900-2000*. Basingstoke: Palgrave Macmillan, 2005. Print.

Walsh, John Evangelist. *Plumes in the Dust: The Love Affair of Edgar Allan Poe and Fanny Osgood*. Chicago: Nelson-Hall, 1980. Print.

Walters, Karla. "Seeking Home: Secularizing the Quest for the Celestial City in *Little Women* and *The Wonderful Wizard of Oz*." *Reform and Counterreform: Dialectics of the Word in Western Christianity Since Luther*. Ed. John C. Hawley. Berlin: Mouton de Gruyter, 1994. 153–71. Print.

Waltje, Jörg. *Blood Obsession: Vampires, Serial Murder, and the Popular Imagination*. New York: Peter Lang, 2005. Print.

Ward, Susan. "The Career Woman Fiction of Elizabeth Stuart Phelps." *Nineteenth-Century Women Writers of the English-Speaking World*. Ed. Rhoda B. Nathan. New York: Greenwood, 1986. 209–19. Print.

Warhol, Robyn R., and Diane Price Herndl. "History." *Feminisms: An Anthology of Literary Theory and Criticism*. Ed. Robyn R. Warhol and Diane Price Herndl. New Brunswick: Rutgers UP, 1997. 853–59. Print.

Waugh, Patricia. *Metafiction: The Theory and Practice of Self-Conscious Fiction*. London: Routledge, 1984. Print.

Webster, Daniel. "First Settlement of New England: A Discourse Delivered at Plymouth, on the 22nd of December, 1820." *The Works of Daniel Webster*. Vol. I. Boston: Little and Brown, 1851. 1–54. Print.

Wells, Sean. "Poe and Fanny: A Novel, By John May." *Southern Scribe: Our Culture of Storytelling*. Web. 17 May 2008.

Welsh, Marcia. "Word of Mouth." *Library Journal* 124.14 (1 Sept. 1999): 264. Print.

Welter, Barbara. "The Cult of True Womanhood, 1820-1860." *American Quarterly* 18.2 (Summer 1966): 151–74. Print.

Wesseling, Elisabeth. *Writing History as a Prophet: Postmodernist Innovations of the Historical Novel*. Amsterdam: John Benjamins, 1991. Print.

Whitcomb, Claire. "Discovering a Once Shiny City of Light." *Victoria* 14.5 (May 2000): 29–30. Print.

White, Hayden. *Metahistory: The Historical Imagination in Nineteenth-Century Europe*. Baltimore: Johns Hopkins UP, 1973. Print.

———. *The Content of Form: Narrative Discourse and Historical Representation*. Baltimore: Johns Hopkins UP, 1987. Print.

———. *Tropics of Discourse: Essays in Cultural Criticism*. Baltimore: The Johns Hopkins UP, 1978. Print.

Widmann, Andreas Martin. *Kontrafaktische Geschichtsdarstellung: Untersuchungen an Romanen von Günter Grass, Thomas Pynchon, Thomas Brussig, Michael Kleeberg, Philip Roth und Christoph Ransmayr*. Heidelberg: Winter, 2009. Print.

Wilentz, Sean. "America Made Easy: McCulloch, Adams, and the Decline of Popular History." *The New Republic*. 2 July 2001. Print.

Williamson, Joel. "How Black Was Rhett Butler." *The Evolution of Southern Culture*. Ed. Numan Bartley. Athens: U of Georgia P, 1988. 87–107. Print.

Wilson, Susan. *Literary Trail of Greater Boston*. Boston: Houghton Mifflin, 2000. Print.

Winthrop, John. "A Model of Christian Charity." *The Norton Anthology of American Literature*. Ed. Nina Baym. New York: Norton, 2003. 31–49. Print.

Wittke, Gabriele. *Female Initiation in the American Novel*. Frankfurt: Peter Lang, 1991. Print.

Wodianka, Stephanie. "Zeit – Literatur – Gedächtnis." *Gedächtniskonzepte der Literaturwissenschaft: Theoretische Grundlegung und Anwendungsperspektiven*. Ed. Astrid Erll and Ansgar Nünning. Berlin: de Gruyter, 2005. 179–202. Print.

Wolfreys, Julian. "LIT 4930 Victoriographies: Inventing the Nineteenth Century." *University of Florida – Courses*. Web. 10 Nov. 2008.

Woodcock, Susan H. "Belfer, Lauren. *City of Light*." *School Library Journal*. Web. 19 May 2009.

Woodward, C. Vann. "The Uses of History in Fiction: Ralph Ellison, William Styron, Robert Penn Warren, C. Vann Woodward." *Conversations with Ralph Ellison*. Ed. Maryemma Graham and Amritjit Singh. Jackson: UP of Mississippi, 1995. 141–72. Print.

Woolf, Virginia. *A Room of One's Own*. San Diego: Harcourt Brace, 1989. Print.

———. "Professions for Women." *The Death of the Moth and Other Essays*. San Diego: Harcourt Brace, 1970. 235–42. Print.

Wylie, Herb, Jennifer Andrews, and Robert Viau. "Introduction: Past Matters/Choses du passé." *Past Matters: History and Canadian Fiction/Choses du passé: L'histoire et le roman historique au Canada*. Ed. Herb Wylie, Jennifer Andrews, and Robert Viau. *Studies in Canadian Literature/Études en Littérature Canadienne* 27.1 (2002). Web. 19 May 2009.

Wylie, J. J. "Reinventing Realism: An Interview with Russell Banks." *Michigan Quarterly Review* 39.4 (Fall 2000): 737–45. Print.

Young, Elizabeth. *Disarming the Nation: Women's Writing and the American Civil War*. Chicago: U of Chicago P, 1999. Print.

Zangwill, Israel. *The Melting Pot: Drama in Four Acts*. 1909. Whitefish: Kessinger, 2005. Print.

Zerweck, Bruno. *Die Synthese aus Realismus und Experiment: Der englische Roman der 1980er und 1990er Jahre aus erzähltheoretischer und kulturwissenschaftlicher Sicht.* Trier: WVT, 2001. Print. ELCH – Studies in English Literary and Cultural History 3.

Zimmerman, Mitchell. "Injunction Done Gone; First Amendment Still Here." *Intellectual Property Today.* 9 Aug. 2001. Print.

Index

For Product Safety Concerns and Information please contact our EU
representative GPSR@taylorandfrancis.com
Taylor & Francis Verlag GmbH, Kaufingerstraße 24, 80331 München, Germany